Praise for the novels of Michelle Major

"A dynamic start to a series
with a refreshingly original premise."
—*Kirkus Reviews* on *The Magnolia Sisters*

"A sweet start to a promising series,
perfect fans of Debbie Macomber."
—*Publishers Weekly* (starred review)
on *The Magnolia Sisters*

"*The Magnolia Sisters* is sheer delight,
filled with humor, warmth and heart....
I loved everything about it."
—*New York Times* bestselling author RaeAnne Thayne

Wildflower Season

MICHELLE MAJOR

HQN

ISBN-13: 978-1-335-54779-8

Recycling programs for this product may not exist in your area.

Wildflower Season
Copyright © 2021 by Michelle Major

A Carolina Promise
Copyright © 2021 by Michelle Major

This edition published by arrangement with Harlequin Books S.A.

For questions and comments about the quality of this book, please contact us at CustomerService@Harlequin.com.

HQN
22 Adelaide St. West, 40th Floor
Toronto, Ontario M5H 4E3, Canada
www.Harlequin.com

Printed in Spain

CONTENTS

WILDFLOWER SEASON   7

A CAROLINA PROMISE   305

WILDFLOWER SEASON

This one is dedicated to all the readers who believe in hope and happily-ever-afters. We need you and your faith in the world—thank you for your light.

CHAPTER ONE

"ANOTHER ROUND."

Emma Cantrell smacked her open palm onto the worn oak bar top, her gaze focused on the empty shot glass in front of her. "Please." She didn't meet the bartender's sympathetic glance. There were plenty of people who had it worse in the world than Emma.

Even if her life was one sloppy, soggy mess.

She traced a finger over the nails on her opposite hand. Pre-Magnolia, her hands had been soft and her nails regularly manicured. Now her polish was chipped to the point of being almost nonexistent. Her nails were uneven and ragged, her skin in sore need of moisturizing cream. She turned over her hand to study the blister that had emerged yesterday as she spent hours raking pine needles from the front yard of her new house.

The house that seemed bound and determined to pull her under.

"Do you want me to call your brother?" Al, the kindly gray-haired bartender, asked as he placed a short glass of amber liquid in front of her.

"Good Lord, no." The last thing Emma needed was for Ryan to come and rescue her. Again. "This is my last one for the night, and I'm walking home. It's all good."

"If you say so." Al arched a bushy brow but didn't argue, although it was clear nothing about Emma's current situation could accurately be described as good. She was sitting in a local bar in Magnolia, North Carolina, unshowered and sticky with dried sweat caked to her skin, her entire life spectacularly wrecked by five long days of pounding thunderstorms and devastatingly high winds.

Coming to Magnolia and buying the dilapidated house once owned by famed artist Niall Reed was supposed to be the start of a new chapter. A reclaiming of her life. A fresh start. Instead, it had quickly become a mess of epic proportions.

A hundred-year storm was what the insurance adjuster called it when he came to survey the damage to her property. One that hit well before hurricane season could be expected to start.

"I told you so," was what her mother had said when she called last week, censure and repudiation tightening her tone.

Someone climbed onto the bar stool next to her, and Emma kept her gaze straight ahead. She didn't want to talk to anyone tonight. Or ever.

Then the smell of freshly baked cookies wafted toward her. Not a typical scent for late-night at the local pub.

She glanced over to see a woman who might be near her own age. The woman turned and offered a watery smile. "I hope you don't mind company."

Emma did mind, but the delicate redhead's eyes were so miserable, puffy and bloodshot that Emma couldn't bring herself to say so. It would have been like kicking a puppy.

She glanced down the row of nearly empty bar stools. There was one other man who had bellied up to the bar, but he sat at the far end, stroking his beard and gazing into his empty pint glass like he could will a refill to appear.

"Do you come here often?" the woman next to her asked with a sniff.

"She's our newest regular," Al answered, flipping a towel over his shoulder as he winked at Emma.

She wasn't sure why the declaration comforted her. Maybe she was so desperate for a place to belong in the world that she'd grab on to any alliance to call her own.

"That's nice." The woman eyed Emma's shot glass. "I'll have what she's having."

"One glass of liquid forget-your-troubles coming right up." Al stepped away to pour the drink, and the woman breathed out a soft laugh.

"Does it really work like that?"

The woman sounded so hopeful Emma's teeth clenched in response. Hope was a pain in the butt.

"You'll forget for a bit tonight," Emma said, "and tomorrow you can focus on the ensuing headache instead of your problems." She glanced at the woman's elegant hand. The fingers tapping on the bar sported a brilliant diamond ring. Blindingly large and nearly flawless. "Let me guess, fiancé trouble?"

"His family hates me," the woman muttered, then swiped at her cheeks.

"You don't seem like the type of person anyone could dislike. Fairy-tale princesses are universally loved."

"I'm Holly, the opposite of a princess, which is part of the problem." The woman held out a hand just as Al brought her shot.

"Cheers, not-a-princess Holly." Emma lifted her glass in a toast instead of shaking. "I'm Emma."

Holly let out a hiss and a sputtering cough after sipping the whiskey. "It burns," she said on a gasp of air.

"That's the point," Emma told her, licking the last bit

of moisture off her lips. "The burn means you can feel something."

"I feel like I'm going to puke."

"Take a breath," Emma advised. "I'm not up for holding back a stranger's hair over the toilet tonight."

Holly giggled and pressed two fingers to her mouth. "I grew up in Magnolia, and I've never been to this bar. It always seemed so scary to me, but it's actually quite cozy."

Emma raised a brow as Al stepped forward with a wince. "First time this place has ever been called cozy. Another round, ladies?"

"Definitely." Holly grinned.

"Two waters," Emma told the bartender. She wasn't going to be responsible for getting sweet, naive Holly drunk.

"And a glass of white burgundy," Holly said. "Do you have Montrachet?"

Al looked toward Emma, confusion clear on his face.

"It's white wine," Emma translated. "But we'll stick with water. You order like a princess," she told Holly.

"The first time I went to a dinner with Brett, I ordered a brand that comes from a box. His mother laughed at me. I learned about wine after that."

Emma grimaced. "This is your future mother-in-law? I hope she lives on the other side of the country."

"She lives a couple of streets over from Brett's house outside of Boston, although we'll be in DC most of the time since..." Holly squeezed shut her eyes. "If he doesn't break up with me because I'm acting so crazy. His family has been pressuring him to ditch me since we met. I'm nowhere near a princess. I'm a girl from a small town who doesn't even have a college degree." She shrugged. "I'm a nail technician."

"You have nice nails," Emma said. "I noticed right away."

Holly laughed without humor. "Brett and I met when he came into the salon for a manicure."

"Your husband-to-be gets manicures?"

"He had an appearance."

"Is he an actual prince or a movie star or something?"

"Something," Holly whispered.

Al brought their waters. "Still good?"

"Yes, thank you." Emma gave the other woman an arch look when the bartender walked away. "I'm not above getting you drunk so you tell me your secrets." Talking to Holly was the best distraction she'd had from her own troubles in weeks.

"He's in politics," Holly said, almost apologetically.

"What kind of politics?"

"The US senator kind." Holly bit down on her lower lip.

"Your fiancé is a senator?"

"From Massachusetts."

"Wait." Emma felt her mouth drop open. "Are you engaged to Brett Carmichael?"

Holly nodded.

"How old are you?" Emma's shock over that simple nod made her forget her manners.

"Twenty-four. He's twelve years older than me. His mom hates that, too."

"You know his family is like the second coming of the Kennedys, right?"

"I don't care about his family." Holly's voice held an undertone of steel Emma wouldn't have expected. "I love him. I want to spend the rest of my life with him. No matter what his mom thinks about me—what anyone thinks about me—I'll be a good wife. I don't care about the politics and fame. I want to be with him."

Emma touched a hand to her throat, which clogged with unexpected emotion. She'd been married once and thought she'd found a man who felt that way about her. She'd believed Martin loved her for who she was and not because of her family's money or the perks that came with it.

One expensive, embarrassing, heartbreaking divorce later and she understood how wrong she'd been. Another mistake her mom loved to throw back in her face.

But she believed Holly when she professed her devotion. Somehow she knew the woman was incapable of lying. It might not be the smartest trait for a political wife, but Emma felt suddenly and inexplicably protective of her new friend.

"Why would Brett Carmichael break up with you? If you love him and he loves you, then—"

"I've ruined the wedding, and his mom is trying to convince him I did it on purpose. His family thinks I'm going to embarrass him and cost him his career and everything he's achieved so far. Mitsy Carmichael says I'm selfish and immature and I'll hold him back." She sniffed. "He has big goals. White House kind of goals."

"Is that the life you want?" Emma asked quietly. She knew all about trying to squeeze herself into a box that would never fit. Trying to push out of the mold was what had led her to Magnolia. The world had seemed full of possibility for a few weeks. Until a massive storm had torn apart all of her dreams.

"I want to be with him, no matter what." Once again, she heard the thread of conviction in Holly's tone, her gaze softening as she obviously thought about the man she loved.

Emma might not believe in love for herself, but that

didn't make her a total cynic. "Tell me about this wedding and why his troll of a mother thinks you ruined it." She tipped her water glass in Holly's direction. "For the record, your fiancé taking his mother's side over yours this early in the game is a red flag. A giant, cherry-red flag."

"He's not taking her side." Holly shook her head. "Brett has been great, but he's busy and I don't want to bother him with my problems. His mother pushed to handle all the details of the wedding. She had her heart set on a big society affair in Boston with her friends and I wanted..." She shrugged. "My family doesn't have a lot of money, but my parents love me. My sister died a few years ago in a car accident. Mom has struggled with depression ever since. I thought if I came here and we planned a small, intimate ceremony and reception, she'd have fun with it. It would give her something joyful to think about for a while."

"So what happened?"

"The storm happened," Holly said with a sniff. "Not just the one that blew through Magnolia, either. My wedding venue on the beach was destroyed, and the couple that owned the house left town with my money. They'd made me pay the entire amount up front and then they walked away. I sold my car and ran up thousands of dollars in credit card debt to rent the house for two months so I could prepare everything. I didn't have the money for a wedding planner or any help. Part of why they gave me the deal was I'd agreed to do some cosmetic updates on the house. They were going to sell it after the wedding. I promised they'd get tons of media coverage and I'd make the property look like a million bucks."

She swallowed and Emma noticed her hands were shaking. "Now it's gone. Everything was in that house—the invitations, my dress, all of the decorations I'd been working on putting together. It's all gone."

"Seriously? I thought I had it rough, but you've got me beat by a mile." Emma made a face. She could understand why Holly was so upset. The house Emma owned and was planning to turn into a bed-and-breakfast had been damaged by the storm, delaying her plan to open and leaving her in need of income in a bad way.

"What about insurance? That should cover—"

"The policy had lapsed," Holly said slowly. "In fact, the couple was behind on their mortgage payments and someone from the bank called me yesterday. I guess my wedding was their last-ditch effort to turn things around. Without a house, I can't have the wedding." She laughed without humor. "No house, no dress, no invitations. I have no hope."

"There's always hope," Emma said, reaching out to place her hand over Holly's with a gentle squeeze. If someone had asked her about hope an hour ago, she would have laughed in their face. But she couldn't let this woman give up. Emma had always been better at taking care of other people than herself.

"Do you think so?" Holly took a long drink of water, then eyed the empty shot glass with obvious longing. "Because I can't see how. I've nearly maxed out my credit cards and my parents don't have the money to help me. I can do nails from sunup to sundown every day and still won't scratch the surface of what it would cost to book another venue. Brett is helping, of course, and he'd happily take care of everything. From the start, my parents wanted to honor the tradition of the bride's family paying for most of the wedding expenses. It's why I was handling so much of it in the first place."

"The Carmichaels are political royalty in this country," Emma pointed out. "Surely they—"

"No." Holly looked horrified. "If I let Brett's mom take over, I'm giving up. Giving in. If she railroads me on something this big, then I lose before Brett and I even begin our lives together. What if she makes our lives such a living hell that Brett doesn't think I'm worth it? You don't understand how she is."

Emma thought of her mother, who had immediately cut Emma off when she quit her job at the family foundation to relocate to Magnolia. After talking to her mom almost every day of her twenty-eight years, Emma'd been pushed aside without a second thought. She pressed an open palm against her chest. It shouldn't hurt the way it did. She was a grown woman and could manage her own life. But to know she could be cast aside so easily for not filling the role assigned to her. Well, that part she couldn't quite get over.

"I have a venue," she blurted. "A house. I'm converting it to an inn. I closed on it at the beginning of the summer, and I've had a crew working around the clock."

"Are you serious?" Holly blinked. "Here in Magnolia?"

"It's Niall Reed's old house," Emma told the other woman. The painter had been Magnolia's most famous resident before his death the previous year. He'd enjoyed decades of commercial, if not critical, success and had held local leaders under his thumb because of the way he'd single-handedly put Magnolia on the map at the height of his fame.

The stories Emma heard told of legions of fans streaming into the area for a chance to meet him and to attend the events and workshops he hosted. At least they had until his art fell out of favor and he squandered away his fortune on bad investments.

He'd also revealed the identity of two previously unknown daughters in his will, one of whom was now in love with Emma's brother. His three daughters had come together to undo the financial mess he'd created in town, and it was clear Magnolia was better for it.

Avery Keller Atwell, Carrie Reed Scott and Meredith Ventner didn't have much in common from the outside, but even in her short time in Magnolia, Emma appreciated the trio's dedication to the town and each other.

She wanted that type of bond with someone—the kind she'd never had with her brother but was now trying to forge. She wanted friends, although she'd never been good at making them.

She wanted a life of her own.

Maybe she could start by helping Holly with hers.

"Niall Reed was creepy," Holly said with a wince. "I know he was a big deal back in the day, but I remember him as a nasty old man who was rude to anyone he didn't deem important. My mom was a waitress at the restaurant where he'd breakfasted a few times a week. He was a terrible tipper, which says a lot about a person."

"It does," Emma agreed. "But his house has great bones." She sighed. "There's some flooding and other damage from the storm."

Holly arched a brow. "Other damage?"

"Part of the roof came off." Emma tried and failed to keep her features neutral. "A few broken windows. Some damage to the exterior siding. Apparently, the contractor I hired cut some corners."

"This is your idea for the perfect wedding venue?"

"I can fix it. I just need a new contractor."

"The wedding is in six weeks." Holly shook her head. "I need to get invitations out now. I have no dress, very little budget. I don't even know how I'm going to pay for any of it." She let out a small groan. "This is a disaster, right? Even more than I'm admitting. I have to call Brett. He has to call his mom. How am I going to handle letting her take over my life?"

"You're not." Emma swiveled on her bar stool so she fully faced the other woman. "We can handle this. I can do this. I'm motivated and insanely organized."

"*Insane* is one word for it," Holly said with a laugh. "Why do you want to help me?"

"Because I need a fresh start as much as you." She wasn't sure why helping Holly felt so important to her, but it did. Just like this woman with her influential in-laws, Emma could cut her losses and call her mom to bail her out. Gillian would do it, but the price was far too high. She had to find a way to make this work on her own.

"We'll arrange the payment details as we go along, and I want to document everything for the inn's website. The progress on renovating the house once more might be picked up by a few regional or national press outlets. The publicity from an event like this could launch my inn as a premier destination location. It's like hosting a royal wedding."

"It could launch you or it could sink you." Holly scrunched up her nose. "It could sink us both. Even if you somehow pull off getting Niall's house ready to host, there's so much more that was destroyed in the storm." Her gaze turned wistful. "You won't believe it, but I found the most beautiful wedding dress in a secondhand store right here in town. It was a Belle Vie and perfect for me. Brett's mom was even mad about that because the designer caused some big scandal in New York City. But the dress was so beautiful I didn't care. Now I've got nothing."

"You've got me," Emma told her, excitement thrumming through her. It was madness to make this kind of deal with a total stranger, but it felt right, and Emma had few other options at this point. "We'll figure it out. At least give it a try. Come to the house tomorrow and we'll talk about a plan. Everything is more manageable with the right plan."

Holly traced a finger around the rim of her shot glass. "I showed up here tonight because I thought everything was more manageable with alcohol."

Emma laughed and then caught Al's attention, lifting her empty shot glass with one hand and two fingers on the other. "Then let's drink to our new partnership. The one that's going to save us both."

CHAPTER TWO

BY THE TIME the doorbell rang the following morning at ten, Emma was nursing a headache caused in tandem by the whiskey and facing the reality of her current situation.

She took a fortifying breath as she opened the door, ready to crush her new friend's dreams under the heel of her colorful clogs.

"This could actually work."

"This won't work."

Holly and Emma spoke at the same time, a frown line creasing the pale skin between Holly's brows. "It's a gorgeous property," Holly murmured. "This house was the biggest and the best in Magnolia for so many years."

They both turned to survey the front yard. Although it was still strewn with a few random branches that had fallen from the canopy of oak trees overhead, it didn't look nearly as bad as it had the morning after the storm.

The yard wasn't Emma's problem.

"I don't have anyone to do the repairs." She gestured Holly into the house. "Not in the time frame we need, anyway. When I talked to the guy who's been working on the house, he said my project is now taking a back seat to his longtime clients. That was before the insurance adjuster came out. Based on what he pointed out about the type of damage to the house, I'm almost positive my original contractor cut corners and overcharged me. Even if he was available, I'm not sure I want him here again."

"There has to be more than one contractor in Magnolia, right?" Holly drew in a sharp breath as they got to the rear of the house, where most of the damage had occurred. The window over the sink had been boarded up and the drywall was peeling where water had come in through the exterior siding. Emma watched as the other woman's gaze took in the warped floor as well as the sagging ceiling. She made a noise somewhere between a squeak and a groan. "It's not bad."

Emma snorted. "Neither was the *Titanic* by those standards. This is just one room. The others are nearly as bad. Remind me not to give you a violin. You might be playing until all hope is lost."

"No." Holly ran a hand over the printed maxidress she wore. She looked not quite as delicate today as she had in the bar. "No take-backs on hope. I hit rock bottom last night and you made me believe we could make this work. I believed in you."

"A mistake caused by impaired judgment. I blame whiskey." Emma grabbed a mug from the cabinet and poured Holly a cup of coffee. "I've called every construction company listed online within a fifty-mile radius. I even reached out to my brother's girlfriend, and she can't help me. I'm sorry, Holly. No one in Magnolia can start on my project before the end of summer, so unless you want to postpone—"

"I know a guy." Holly bit down on her lower lip.

"That sounds ominous."

"It's my brother-in-law." She made a face. "Or my former brother-in-law. I told you my sister died a few years ago. Her husband could do the job. He's a talented carpenter and can build or fix anything."

Emma shrugged. "I probably already talked to him or left a message. I swear I called everyone in this town."

"Not Cam." Holly gave a weak laugh. "I'm not even sure he has a phone. He definitely wouldn't be on anyone's list to call about work. The last I heard, he's running fishing charters about ten miles south of town on the coast."

"That doesn't sound like a licensed contractor."

"He's the best," Holly said, glancing around the room. "And he'll do it for me."

Emma wasn't sure what to make of Holly's faith in her former brother-in-law. Or the woman's faith in Emma, for that matter. But she wouldn't—couldn't—deny she wanted a chance to make this new dream a reality. To prove she could even when things got tough.

"So will you get in touch with him and let me know what he says?"

"You have to be the one to convince him."

"He doesn't know me. You said he'll help you. Why would I talk to him about a job?"

"I can't." Holly crossed her arms over her chest. "Cam had a falling-out with my parents after Dana's accident. They would freak out if they knew I asked him to help."

Emma blinked. "But it's okay if I ask him to help? Won't there still be some freaking out?"

"I'm not going to tell them until the wedding. If we pull this off—and Cam is the guy to do it—we can maybe move on from my sister's accident. Like I said, my mom hasn't been the same since Dana died. Now she's excited about the wedding. She's happy for me. She's happy."

The situation was becoming more complicated by the second. Far more complex than Emma was equipped to handle.

At least that's what her mother would tell her, which made Emma want to handle it all the more.

Despite the nerves fluttering through her as she debated whether she could pull off the miracle Holly needed, Emma nodded and grabbed a notebook from the counter. "Let's make a plan. I like a plan. If the plan is doable, you can tell me how to find this mysterious carpenter guru, and we'll get it done. The invitations, the repairs, the dress, all of it. I've never organized a wedding, but how hard can it be?"

She clamped her mouth shut as soon as she'd asked the questions, hoping she hadn't just jinxed herself and this endeavor.

Holly reached out and wrapped Emma in a tight hug. "You're the best." Her voice clogged with tears. "A total lifesaver, Emma. Thank you."

"PLEASE DON'T LET me die." Emma repeated the words to herself like a mantra as she walked down the overgrown driveway on Camden Arlinghaus's property.

At least she hoped she had the right place. She also hoped she didn't get attacked by the dog mentioned in the Beware of Dog sign affixed to the gate blocking the driveway's entrance. And that whoever lived here was friendly and not quick with a shotgun aimed at trespassers. And that no snakes or wild boars or giant spiders came rampaging out of the thick tangle of trees and vines surrounding her.

The air was heavy with the scent of the fecund earth. Birds chirping and insects buzzing were the only noises that broke the silence. At this point, she felt grateful for any sound that wasn't the nervous beating of her heart in her own ears.

She'd gone to the dock south of town as Holly instructed, only to be told Cam was at home today. The guys that gave her directions to his property appeared both curious and amused a woman was seeking him out. But they'd been nice enough to her face—polite in a down-home kind of way—even with the comments about Cam not having friends or entertaining ladies at his home.

Emma could see why as she approached the house. It wasn't run-down per se, and the front yard was relatively tidy compared to the chaos on the way in. But there was something unapproachable about the cabin. A weighty emptiness hung in the already thick, sultry air.

If only one of the contractors she'd contacted earlier had returned her call. Maybe she should turn around and try them again. Or insist Holly come with her to talk to Camden.

"Can you read?"

She stopped in her tracks at the question that carried to her from the cabin's front door, spoken in a deep, almost disbelieving tone.

"Yes, I can read." She plastered a smile on her face and took another step forward. "Are you—"

"Then you need to turn right around, ma'am. Because the signs posted are pretty clear to someone claiming to be literate."

"I'm not looking for trouble." She lifted her sunglasses to the top of her head, held a hand over her eyes and squinted up at the porch, but all she could make out was the silhouette of a man in the door.

He chuckled, a rusty sound that reverberated through her like the vibration of a tuning fork. "Somehow I don't believe you."

The screen door squeaked open. Emma heard a booming bark and caught a streak of tan fur and then she was on her backside in the dirt with at least a hundred pounds of damp dog circling her in glee.

Emma liked dogs, all animals, really. She'd never actually owned one, but when she ran her family's charitable foundation they'd funded various local shelters and animal rescue organizations.

The dog seemed overenthusiastic but not threatening. "Good boy," she said, peering under his belly to confirm he was indeed a boy. She got to her feet as he ran back to the house with her sunglasses in his mouth.

Sunglasses that had cost her over three hundred dollars and that she couldn't afford to replace on her current salary of less than nothing. She wasn't about to explain that to the man who stared down at her from the top step.

Her breath hissed out like she'd just taken a blow to the stomach. Holly had failed to mention that her former brother-in-law was hot as all get-out, in a Paul Bunyan sort of way. Rugged had never been Emma's type. Her ex-husband was handsome enough, polished and a little nerdy. But Cam Arlinghaus was every lumberjack fantasy Emma had never had come to life. He had dark, wavy hair and a shadow of stubble covering his angular jaw. It was nearly ninety degrees so there was no flannel to be seen, but he wore the low-slung cargo shorts and faded T-shirt like he was a cover model for a deep-sea fishing guide magazine.

"You ignored the No Trespassing and the Beware of Dog signs," he said, his voice flat. "Those signs are there for a reason."

She nodded, her flummoxed mind trying hard to put together a coherent thought in the face of all that strapping masculinity. It rolled off him in waves and felled Emma like a riptide. *Turn around*, her sense of self-preservation screamed. *Run as fast as you can.*

"I'm sorry," she managed, swallowing against the sudden dryness in her throat. "I needed to talk to you."

One thick brow lifted. "You were at the dock asking about me."

"How did you know?" she asked with a frown. "I thought you didn't have a cell phone."

"Ever heard of a landline?" His mouth curved at the corner. "Mine has a cord and everything." He moved down a step, and Emma resisted the urge to back up. "I can't imagine any good reason someone like you..." His dark eyes raked over her, leaving her skin hot in the wake of his gaze. "Would need to talk to me, but this is private property. I have a charter to run tomorrow morning. You can—"

"Holly Adams sent me," Emma blurted, then held her breath as a maelstrom of emotions played over his strong features. Pain, sorrow and confusion rioted in his dark eyes for a few brief moments until his face went blank again.

He reached out and grabbed the porch's iron railing like he might lose his balance. His full mouth took on a thin line. "Why?"

The word was spoken on a whisper of breath but carried to Emma like a challenge.

"She needs your help. *I* need your help."

"I don't know you."

"No." She did her best to flash an encouraging smile. "I'm Emma Cantrell, and I'm helping Holly plan her wedding."

"That has nothing to do with me."

"Her wedding venue was destroyed in the storm."

"Nothing to do with me," he repeated.

"She lost everything," Emma explained, her heart hammering in her chest. If she couldn't convince Cam to help with the repairs on her house, she didn't know what she'd do. As much as she'd toyed with the idea of walking away from Magnolia, that wasn't what she wanted. She had to make this work. "Even her dress and the decorations she was putting together. It's kind of a disaster for her."

"Nothing—"

"I got it." She held up a hand. "If you'd stop interrupting me, I can explain what this does have to do with you."

"I don't want to know."

"You're her last hope."

He massaged a hand over the back of his neck as he stared at her in disbelief. "Are you trying to remake *Star Wars*, small-town Southern-style?" He made a show of looking past her. "Hiding a droid behind you?"

"It's not funny."

"I know." He closed his eyes, and she watched as he blew out a long breath. When he met her gaze again, his stormy eyes offered no hint of emotion. "Tell me what Holly needs from me."

CAM WAITED FOR this Emma Cantrell to speak, hoping he'd be able to process her answer through the roaring in his head.

Holly needed him.

His late wife's little sister, who'd held tight to her sobbing mother at Dana's funeral despite her grief. Holly was six years younger than Dana, so Cam had met her when she was a gangly preteen in braces. She'd become as much a little sister to him as she was to Dana, and he hated that his selfishness had caused the accident that took Dana from her family.

His former in-laws blamed him, and rightfully so. He had no idea how Holly felt because he hadn't seen or talked to her since the funeral five years earlier. There was almost no one from his former life he'd stayed in contact with. Hell, Toby, the yellow Lab sprawled on the porch behind him, was his best friend. In some ways, the dog was his only friend.

The signs at the gate were meant to dissuade visitors, but in truth, the only thing people had to beware of from his dog was being slobbered on.

"Holly is engaged to Brett Carmichael. Have you heard of him?"

"Political family, right?" Cam didn't keep up on news or current events but the Carmichaels were a household name. One had made it to the White House as a vice president. And little Holly was marrying into that family? He rubbed a hand over his jaw. He really had lost track of her.

"Political dynasty is more like it," Emma clarified. "She hasn't exactly been welcomed with open arms by Brett's mom. He's a US senator with bigger aspirations. It doesn't sound like his family thinks Holly is the best choice for him."

Cam muttered a curse, then quickly apologized. His mom had taught him to watch his mouth in front of ladies. "The Holly I knew is sweet and caring. Any family would be lucky to have her. Hell, this country would be lucky to have her."

Emma's grin was so bright it almost blinded him. In an instant he went from being distracted by the thought of his past to a distraction of another sort.

The woman who'd barged into his world was beautiful in a girl-next-door or sexy-librarian sort of way. She had caramel-colored hair and delicate features. Her skin looked soft, and a smattering of freckles covered the bridge of her nose like she'd spent too much time in the sun recently.

She didn't strike him as the outdoorsy type, but what

did Cam know? He was so out of practice conversing with women—other than the wives or girlfriends of the guys who ran the boats near him—it was almost comical.

"I bought a house in town. I'm converting it to an inn," Emma said, and Cam forced himself to pay attention to her words. She looked nervous and unsure of herself, at complete odds with the woman who'd faced him moments earlier. Hell, even getting knocked on her back end by Toby hadn't rattled her. But talking about her property seemed to. "At least that was the plan until the storm damaged the roof and a good part of the house's south side."

He narrowed his eyes. "Where is this house exactly?"

"On Fig Tree Lane," she said, hitching her chin.

"Niall Reed's place?" He shrugged at her surprised expression. "There aren't a lot of properties in town that could work in the capacity you're talking about. I heard about the mess with his will and the long-lost daughters."

"They aren't lost anymore. I want to help Holly with her wedding, but there's no one to help me with the repairs the house needs."

"Why?"

She blinked, her big eyes going even wider.

"Because of the storm," she told him after several drawn-out moments. "People who work in construction around here are busy, and I'm new to town so I'm not a priority."

"Why do you want to help Holly?"

The play of conflicting emotions across her delicate features fascinated him. "She and I are helping each other. Even if she keeps the guest list small, her wedding is going to be a big deal. I can't pay for that sort of publicity."

The answer made sense, but he didn't believe that was the extent of Emma's motivation. He forced himself not to push her on it. The less he was involved in her life—in

Holly's life—the better. The smart thing would be to say no. To turn around and slam the door on Emma and her repairs and taking part in any of it.

But he stood his ground. The last words he'd said to Dana's little sister before he walked away from the gravesite were if Holly ever needed anything he would be there for her.

A part of him had hoped she'd reach out and give him a way to assuage his guilt over his part in Dana's accident. But she hadn't, and Cam had retreated farther into himself, putting more and more distance between his lonely shell of an existence and the life he used to have.

"Why did she send you?" he asked. Not that it mattered. He couldn't say no whether the request came via this beautiful messenger or from Holly herself.

"Holly didn't want you to feel pressure to agree," Emma said, almost reluctantly. "She thought it would be too difficult to say no to her face."

"What about her parents?" His chest ached at the memory of the accusations his mother-in-law had thrown at him. He deserved every one. "Do they know?"

"I don't think so," Emma admitted, looking uncomfortable. "Although Holly seems to believe her wedding is going to fix everything if it goes off without a hitch." She sniffed. "Weddings don't fix things."

Don't be curious about this woman, he reminded himself. *Not now, not ever.* He'd buried his ability to care along with his wife.

As much as he wouldn't allow himself to care, the promise he'd made to Holly wouldn't let him walk away.

"Maybe not." He drew in a deep breath and blew it out along with his good sense. "But I'll take care of whatever repairs you need done to give Holly the wedding she wants."

Emma took a step toward him. "Really?" She laughed, shaking her head. "I thought you were going to tell me no."

"I'd tell you no a hundred times over," he answered, because he needed her to understand the deal. To understand him and what this was about. "But for Holly, I'll always say yes."

Even though he knew it could be a huge mistake.

CHAPTER THREE

THE FOLLOWING MORNING, Emma walked down the sidewalk of Magnolia's bustling downtown business district silently lecturing herself about what a stupid wimp she was.

It didn't help her mood to realize her internal voice sounded a lot like her mother.

She had a meeting with Cam Arlinghaus and Holly at the house in an hour but had needed a distraction from the unwelcome anticipation she felt at the thought of seeing the gruff carpenter again. The excitement shimmering around her like early-morning mist was ten kinds of stupid. He'd made it extremely clear he was willing to handle the repair of her house and, in doing so, help her achieve her dream of opening the inn because it benefited Holly.

If not for his history with the bride-to-be, he would have literally slammed the door in Emma's face. That fact shouldn't hurt, but her stomach clenched just the same.

Unfortunately, his surliness hadn't dimmed her attraction to him in any way, something she had to get under control. She checked her watch. Preferably in the next fifty-five minutes.

As she glanced up, her gaze caught on a white dress in the window of the clothing shop a few buildings down from the cross street she was nearing. The sign above the door read A Second Chance, and Emma wondered if it was the store Holly had mentioned where she'd found her perfect—and now ruined—wedding gown.

Emma hadn't noticed the store before today, which she took as a sign to check out the dress on display. Anything to get her mind off her nerves about the impending meeting with Cam.

Sipping her latte, she turned the corner and headed for the store. Her breath caught as she got closer and noticed the intricate detail of lacework on the gown. It was magnificent.

The chimes above the entry jingled as she entered and a woman's voice greeted her with a friendly, "Be right with you."

Emma stepped toward the front window and reached out a hand to touch the dress but pulled away at the last minute. Something about the gown reminded her of her own wedding. She'd worn a silk sheath, nothing like the detailed lace and scalloped collar of this one. But the precision workmanship felt familiar. Her dress had been created by the famed designer out of New York City who Holly had mentioned. She couldn't imagine another Belle Vie dress would have found its way to a secondhand shop in Magnolia, but she peeled the dress away from the mannequin. The tag had been cut out of the back.

"May I help you?"

She whirled at the feminine voice directly behind her.

"It's you." Emma glanced at the dress, then at the slender blonde with the tortoiseshell glasses who was now looking at her with an expression that bordered on panic.

"I'm not."

"Mariella Jacob. I know you. We've met. You designed my wedding dress."

The bells over the door tinkled again as the customers Mariella had been helping exited the store. "Have a nice day," she called, then narrowed her gaze on Emma. "My name is Mari, and I own a secondhand clothing store in Magnolia, North Carolina. The woman you knew doesn't exist in this tiny town."

As Emma stared in shock, Mariella reached around her and yanked the dress from the window. She gathered the lacy fabric in her arms and stalked toward the back of the store.

Emma didn't understand what was happening. Why was one of the most famous wedding designers in the world hiding away in this tiny town, denying her identity?

The shop was cute, with racks of colorful clothes and displays of purses and scarves coordinated to match. There was a section of home decor, mostly boho in style, and a corner of kitchen gadgets. Emma still couldn't believe she'd overlooked the store before now. A floral-print jacket with overlarge brass buttons called to her from a nearby hanger, but she ignored the unique find along with Mariella's obvious reluctance to own up to who she was.

This had to be the place where Holly found her first dress. An actual Belle Vie gown. The typical retail price for one of Mariella's designs started at nearly five figures.

"I'm living in Magnolia, too," Emma said, following the other woman to the register. "It's a great place to start over."

Mariella glanced up sharply, her blue eyes both fierce and guarded. "I'm not the person I used to be."

"Me neither." Emma kept her tone light. Mariella's fingers gripped the delicate fabric like a lifeline, and Emma half suspected the other woman might bolt out of the store never to be seen again. "I'm trying to make myself into someone different, anyway. Someone better."

"I just want to forget," Mariella said quietly, looking away. "You can't tell anyone about me. I haven't been recognized here. No one from my old life comes to Magnolia. It's how I want it."

"But why?" Emma gestured at the dress. "You're so talented. I'd never felt more beautiful than when I wore your dress. *You* made me feel beautiful."

"You mentioned starting over. Is your husband here with you? Are you making yourself over at his side?"

Emma frowned. "No."

"That's the point." Mariella flashed a brittle smile. "The elegant beauty of your wedding day was an illusion. Smoke and mirrors. I helped create them. I'm done with all the lies." She laughed, and the sound was so hollow it made Emma's chest ache. "The fashion community is done with me, too. I made sure of it." She shoved the dress to one side. "I'm selling off my old stock to pay the bills, but after, no more silk and lace for me. Who needs it?"

"I do," Emma answered. "A bride I'm working with does."

"No. No more brides or bridezillas for me."

"Please. Just hear me out. I don't know what you went through—"

"Google me. Pretty sure the video is still on YouTube. Last I checked, I was at almost a half million views."

"I don't care about the internet or what you did to go viral."

"Then you're the only person from my old life who feels that way."

"I'm from your life now, here in Magnolia. Your store is called A Second Chance."

"It refers to the merchandise."

"It can be more," Emma insisted. Something that looked like hope sparked in Mariella's eyes—so fast Emma would have missed it if she hadn't been paying attention.

Another cluster of potential customers entered, bringing with them a blast of humid air that seemed to deflate Mariella like a flower drooping in the harsh heat of a summer day.

She called out a greeting, then shook her head at Emma. "I don't want more," she said simply, and walked away.

WAS HE BEING PUNKED?

After knocking for a third and final time, Cam turned and started down the porch steps of the old Reed house. The air smelled like flowers, although he couldn't pick out any particular variety. This part of Magnolia had never held much interest for him.

He'd grown up on the outskirts of town, along the coast. His dad had been a fisherman and his mom was a secretary for one of the higher-ups at the regional power company. They were simple folks but happy with their lot in life. Neither of them wanted more than what the good Lord gave them, a lesson Cam should have learned.

His ambition and the dreams he'd had of a bigger life than the one expected for him led to Dana's accident. He'd reached for something more and lost everything that mattered in the process.

If he had to guess, he'd say Emma Cantrell was reaching for far more than she could handle, at least on her own. Although he didn't personally know Niall Reed or his daughters, the man's reputation cut a wide swath across the area. Growing up, people had talked about him like he was some kind of benevolent king in town, but Cam wasn't interested in royalty.

He and Dana had had that in common, which was why it was strange to think of her sister marrying into the Carmichael family. Was that the kind of life Holly wanted?

He couldn't imagine it, just like he couldn't believe he was about to see her again after five long years.

If anyone showed up. He glanced at his watch and started for his truck, just as he heard a car coming toward the house along the quiet, tree-lined street.

A shiny silver BMW pulled up to the curb and Emma jumped out, waving as she hurried toward him.

Once again, Cam cursed his reaction to her. She wore simple black leggings and a fitted T-shirt, her long hair pulled back into a loose ponytail. Even dressed so casually, she looked every inch like a refined society matron in training. A woman well above his pay grade.

"I'm sorry I'm late. I got stuck in town longer than I'd planned." She pointed a finger at him. "You need a cell phone."

"Nope."

"I'm not even sure it's legal to not have a cell phone," she said as if he hadn't spoken. "Definitely a pain in the rear if people want to get ahold of you."

"What makes you think I want to be gotten ahold of?"

She stopped a few feet from him, and her light brown eyes went dark, like a tangy, bittersweet chip that would burst on his tongue if he bit down on it. He imagined she was thinking about what she'd want to do with him—to him—if she got ahold of him. Damn if he didn't want to know what was in her mind right now.

One white tooth caught on her lower lip, and Cam forced himself not to groan out loud. Apparently, he wasn't the only one affected by the current of attraction pulsing between them.

Unwanted, unwelcome and undeniable.

As if needing something to do with her hands, she yanked the rubber band from her hair, sending the honey waves cascading over her shoulders. Clearly oblivious to her effect on him, she gathered it in her hands again and secured a knot high on her head.

Too late for Cam, who couldn't manage to scrub the image of all that thick hair cascading over his pillow from his brain.

"What if I got you a phone just for this project?" She tugged her lip between her teeth once more. "Only I'll have the number."

The urge to agree if she promised to call him late at night was on the tip of his tongue. A joke, really, and also not at all.

"So this is your place?" He jerked a thumb behind him toward the house.

"The Wildflower Inn," she told him with a nod. "The yard is blanketed with them, and I figured that would be an easy name for guests to remember." She pointed to the smaller house next door. "I bought that property, as well. The plan is to turn it into a guest cottage that could be used for professional retreats or family reunions."

"Ambitious," he murmured. "You think there's a market for that in Magnolia?"

"Absolutely." She led him toward the front of the house. "Things are turning around in this town. New businesses and restaurants are opening. Even a sportswear company is in talks to move their headquarters here."

She glanced over her shoulder at him, and Cam pretended like he hadn't been checking out her butt in those leggings. He shouldn't be checking out anything about Emma.

"You run fishing charters, right?"

He nodded.

"Have you noticed things have picked up?"

"Now that you mention it, I guess so." He scratched a hand over his jaw. "All my business is word of mouth, but the other guys around the area seem busier than usual this season. Busy is normal for me."

"Not too busy to help, I hope?" she asked with a nervous laugh and led him into the house. He could smell furniture polish and soap, a comforting mix of scents that seemed to fit the venerable mansion. They passed a formal sitting room to one side and a dining room to the other. The furniture had been pushed against the far walls in both. Thick rugs were rolled up tight, as well. He could see the wide oak planks bowing in some places and found it ironic that water damage might be the least of his worries.

"What kind of experience do you have running an inn or hosting weddings?"

Her shoulders stiffened and she didn't look back at him as she answered. "Why does it matter to you?"

"Because you're involved with Holly, and you don't exactly strike me as the hospitality-industry type."

They'd come to the large kitchen now, and he could see the evidence of the storm and that earlier someone had updated much of the space. He'd place money on shoddy workmanship. That could have made the house more susceptible to being ravaged by the recent surge of storms.

It was hard to tell how bad it was. He'd certainly seen plenty of damage on his way through town. Blocks where blue tarps covered every roof, and windows were boarded up like a crowd of late-night marauders had struck out in all directions. There were piles of branches in front of a number of houses, and once again, Cam considered himself lucky that the heavy winds and rain hadn't done much to his property.

Luck was a luxury he no longer took for granted.

"I'm plenty hospitable." She turned to face him.

He frowned at the look of panic that flashed in her eyes. It wasn't his intention. "I just mean—"

"If I want someone to judge me, I'll give my mom a call." Emma crossed her arms over her chest and he could see her fingers digging into her palms. Hell, he'd hurt her feelings with his comment.

That was why he stayed away from people. He could do less damage.

"This property belongs to me, and I'm going to make it a success, with or without your help. Holly thinks the world of you." Her jaw tightened as she added, "Although I'm seriously questioning her assessment."

She grabbed a piece of paper from the nearby counter and thrust it in his direction. "Here's the list I've made of the repairs that are needed. You might find more, and I'm sure there are things Holly will want to make her event perfect. Take a look, tell me your price and we'll either work out a deal or not. Your opinion of my choices doesn't matter, so I'd appreciate it if you'd keep it to yourself."

The doorbell rang, and Emma made to move past him, but he grabbed her arm.

She immediately stilled, and he realized his mistake in an instant. As he'd guessed yesterday, her skin was impossibly soft. His thumb rested in the crook of her elbow, and he could feel her pulse thrumming under his touch. The urge to press his mouth to that soft skin was almost irresistible. But resist he did because he wasn't a leech and figured a woman like Emma would either haul off and deck him or have him arrested. Both options would be smart on her part.

Instead, she swayed toward him, ever so slightly. She had the self-preservation instinct of a baby giraffe. They both stared at the place where his hand wrapped around her arm. He liked the look of her pale skin under his rough hand far more than he should.

The doorbell rang again, effectively snapping her out of her trance. "It's Holly," she told him as she shrugged out of his grasp.

"Yeah. I'm sorry, Emma. For whatever I said." It was easy enough to apologize.

"Don't ever be sorry for the truth," she countered, surprising him. "Even if I don't want to hear it."

She left him standing in the kitchen, wondering again what kind of trouble he was getting himself into with this project. Cam didn't doubt his ability to fix the problems in this house and make it better than new. But could he keep his distance from Emma in the process? He didn't trust himself one iota in that respect.

His gaze strayed to the exterior door off the kitchen. Three long strides and he could escape from this situation. Climb into his truck and drive away without a backward glance.

Just as he started to move, a pair of arms wrapped around him from behind. "I knew you'd come," Holly said against his back, a flood of memories rushing through him at her sweet, familiar voice. "I can always count on my big brother."

Just like that, Cam knew he wouldn't walk away.

CHAPTER FOUR

AN HOUR LATER, Emma wasn't sure whether to be terrified or hopeful. She looked down to the five pages of notes gripped tightly in her hand and tried not to hyperventilate.

Neat lists of ideas for the wedding and even more notes on what she'd need to do to get the inn up and running. She reminded herself the property wasn't an inn yet. Right now, it was still an old house in need of a ton of work.

Work that would cost money.

Money Emma didn't have.

Holly seemed oblivious to the monumental size of the task in front of them, and Emma appreciated the bride-to be's faith in Emma's ability to pull off the event. She didn't stop to scrutinize whether that confidence came from a true belief in Emma or was simply born out of desperation.

Desperation was a heck of a motivator.

As Holly moved through the backyard, spouting off ideas for an arbor under which to say her vows and a flagstone patio with a firepit for guests to gather after the ceremony, Emma glanced up from her clipboard to find Camden staring at her, one heavy brow lifted. No question as to whether her reluctant carpenter thought she could pull off Holly's dream wedding.

That would be a definite no.

"Cam, are we giving you too much work?" Holly asked with a sweet smile as she turned to him. "I know you have your fishing business to run, as well, so I don't want to overwhelm you."

"I'll take care of whatever you need," he said solemnly, his gaze steady on Holly, who rolled her eyes.

"It's not really what I need," she corrected. "My wedding is one day. Emma is going to be hosting all kinds of guests and events at the inn. This is more about her vision for the property."

Emma did her best not to squirm under their attention. Buying this big house in Magnolia had been the first decision in her life that was spontaneous and made strictly on instinct, and she'd been sure it was the right move.

Now she doubted everything, not a great sign for the future. Emma wasn't used to doubt. She'd always operated on forward momentum, propelled by whatever goal she set for herself. In truth, her goals had been more about making her mom happy or checking off boxes on her list because they seemed appropriate.

Yes, she'd had a vision for her life in Magnolia. But it was an idealized version of reality—the kind where she effortlessly and easily transitioned to her new existence. She hadn't factored in a hundred-year storm or construction delays or doubting her ability to run a successful business on her own. Everything looked so easy when she flipped through the glossy pages of home decorating magazines or scrolled the internet for photos of cozy cottages.

The money pit behind her wasn't exactly Pinterest-worthy.

"I love your ideas," she said, because it was the truth. Holly's aesthetic meshed with her own, and the bride-to-be seemed to have a style that was both classic and unique. Emma had to admit she hadn't expected to receive so many clever design concepts. "We're going to make your wedding perfect."

Holly's beaming smile both inspired and alarmed her. The woman pulled out her cell phone when it rang from inside her purse. "That's Brett." She lifted the phone to her ear. "Hey, Boo-boo bear. I'm just finishing a meeting with the wedding planner. I'll call you back in a minute... Okay... Love you, too." She disconnected, then glanced at her watch. "I need to get to the salon, anyway. I took on a few shifts while I'm in town to make some extra money."

"Boo-boo bear?" Cam said, disbelief and gentle mockery clear in his tone. "That's embarrassing for a guy."

Emma hid her smile.

"It's an inside joke, so Brett doesn't mind. Don't be a cynic." Holly reached out and squeezed his arm. "It's good to see you. I've missed you, Cam. Mom and Dad—"

"I don't want them to know," he interrupted. "Not a word."

"They'll appreciate it," Holly argued, her smooth brow furrowing. "It's been too long. Don't you think it's time to let go of the past?"

"They lost their daughter because of me," he said, and Emma could hear the pain in his voice.

She wanted to excuse herself. The moment suddenly felt too personal, too charged. She'd never done well with displays of outright emotion.

"It was an accident," Holly insisted. Her phone rang again. "I've got to go. I won't say anything yet, but you're coming to the wedding, Cam. I want you to be there. Dana would want it, too." Holly shifted her gaze to Emma. "Let me know how else I can help as we move forward. I'm so excited. This is going to be even better than the house on the beach."

With another wide smile, Holly walked around the side of the house.

Cam stood looking out at the trees bordering the property like they held all the secrets of the universe. His jaw was tight and his posture rigid like he was holding himself in check.

"She has a lot of enthusiasm," Emma said quietly. She ran a fingertip along the edge of her clipboard.

"Dana was the same way and look where it got her." Cam's voice was rough with emotion.

Emma wasn't sure how to answer. She knew nothing about this man or his late wife, but obviously the past tortured him, and he blamed himself. She could relate to self-blame at least. She was a damn expert on that front.

Somehow the realization Cam Arlinghaus might be even more broken than Emma felt helped to pull her out of the pit of pity where she seemed to be swirling. She might do blame, but Emma didn't wallow.

And she wouldn't let anyone around her succumb to that, either.

Failure simply wasn't an option—at least for the short term.

"Are you going to be able to handle this?" she asked, keeping her tone neutral, a bit strident even. "Because if you're going to muck around in sorrow and wear your guilt like a hair shirt, I'm not going to hire you. This is my new life, and I want it full of happy people."

"Happy people," he repeated, sounding almost stunned. "Do you consider yourself a happy person?"

The question was a challenge, and they both knew it.

"As a clam," she lied.

One corner of his mouth tilted up, and she was relieved to see his shoulders relax slightly. Regular Cam was intimidating enough, but Cam on the brink of despair was truly terrifying.

"Let's talk about how many clams are in your bank account?" He inclined his head toward the roof. "I'm assuming insurance will pay for some of the damage from the storm, but you and Holly came up with quite a wish list. And time is ticking away. I can round up some guys to put together a crew, but that's going to take money. If I handle it on my own—"

"I'll be your crew," she said, telling herself not to react to his soft snort of disbelief.

"Do you know anything about construction?"

"Yes." She shook her head. "I mean, I'm a quick study and I work hard and I'm stronger than I look." She frowned. "Unless you think I look strong, in which case I'm as strong as I look."

He took a step closer. Was it her imagination or did the temperature just go up about a thousand degrees?

"I think you look like the type of woman who belongs in a fancy restaurant or a five-star hotel or holed up in some sort of insulated, air-conditioned office with sleek desks and ergonomic chairs that cost more than most people's monthly mortgage."

Okay, that described Emma's life before she'd arrived in Magnolia, and it chapped her hide that he seemed to have such a poor—if accurate—assessment of her.

"I work hard," she repeated. "This is my dream. I want to help get it to where it needs to be." She shrugged. "I should have trusted myself more in the first place. I have your email address. I'll send over the numbers from the insurance adjuster and make a plan to pay for anything the claim doesn't cover."

He studied her for a long moment. A warm breeze kicked

up, blowing her hair into her face, and the scent of him—all male and spice—wafted over her. *Do not turn to goo*, she commanded her already gooey insides. *He's just a man.*

A tall, broad, handsome-as-heck man.

The worst kind as far as her rational mind was concerned.

Her body still needed to pick up that memo.

"Why?" he asked suddenly.

"Why didn't I trust myself?" She drew in a sharp breath. *Way to go for the jugular, hottie carpenter.*

"Why is this your dream?" He gestured to the house.

She followed his gaze. Something shifted in her chest, just like it had the first time she'd driven up to the house. "Because this place is special. The town is special. I don't give a rip about five stars, but people should have a beautiful place to get away to. One that's affordable but still luxurious and makes them feel special. People like Holly should have that, and I want to give it to them. I want to showcase this property and the town. I'm not naive enough to believe it will be *Field of Dreams*—I build it and they'll come—but I'm willing to work as hard as I need to for Holly and for other guests who grace the door of the Wildflower Inn. But mostly for myself."

He studied her for several long minutes. "Okay," he said finally. "I'll put together a budget and you can prioritize some of the extras. I know a guy who's an excellent landscaper. He'll help with the backyard. The pergola and arbor for the wedding are easy enough. The rest will come together. I'll make sure of it."

"Thank you," Emma said, suddenly too choked up to manage anything else.

Cam nodded and then turned to go.

"She's going to insist you come to the wedding," Emma called after him, somehow unwilling to let him go.

"That's not going to happen," he said, and walked away nevertheless.

As CAM WALKED into the hardware store two days later, the familiar scents of sawdust and oily machine parts hit him, churning up a tumult of memories.

Once upon a time, he'd spent hours in the shop each week and had known everyone who worked there by name, and not just because of his work as a foreman for a local construction crew. Phil Wainright, who owned the store, had been the one to introduce Cam to the woodworking techniques he'd used for the furniture he built. Live-edge pieces of wood and reclaimed barn siding that Cam would craft into unique and functional furniture.

They'd spent hours talking about tree species and the advantages of specific tools. Each item had been one-of-a-kind, and he'd put his heart and soul into every precision cut. Until Dana's death had ripped the heart right out of him.

He approached the contractors' counter, which hadn't changed in the years he'd been away from town. Neat aisles of stock—from lengths of rope, plumbing and electrical items, a paint department and other home improvement supplies—as well as a colorful candy display near the front of the store and an old-time popcorn machine pushed up against one wall.

But instead of Phil's bushy gray head turning to greet him, a young woman smiled as he approached.

"Lily?" he asked, snapping his mouth shut.

Phil's youngest daughter, Lily, looked as shocked as Cam

felt. "Cam, it's you. I didn't realize you were still in Magnolia."

"I thought you'd moved to Hollywood to be a famous actress," he answered.

She shrugged and fiddled with the clip holding back her long hair. "I came back last year. Dad had hip surgery and needed help with the store, and I was tired of LA. When did you return?"

"I never left," he said.

She frowned. "I haven't seen you in here once. Don't tell me you've found another supplier. Dad will be heartbroken he missed you."

"I run fishing charters now." Cam's throat had gone dry as memories came flooding back. The weeks and months after Dana's death when he could barely bring himself to do anything but stare at the ceiling and cradle a bottle of Jack Daniel's. Phil had come to visit him several times during that dark season. The old man had even convinced Cam to venture out to his workshop again. He'd been so sure that work would pull Cam out of his depression.

Instead, the unfinished projects had mocked him. The scent of linseed oil reminded him of the night Dana died, the extra shifts she'd taken on at the bar to help make more money so Cam could buy a new router. It had been two weeks before Christmas, and he'd been working around the clock. Days were spent on his regular job and every night he retreated to his workshop to fill the orders he had for holiday gifts.

But after she was gone, there was no comfort in the work. No motivation. Looking at the wood just made him angry, and he'd taken a sledgehammer to the wood. He'd wanted everything around him to be as broken as he felt.

He wanted to feel nothing.

And that had worked. He'd pushed away everyone who gave a damn about him. He'd torpedoed his old life until there was nothing left but a shell of an existence. His dad had brought by keys to an old boat a few months later, and Cam had spent long days on the water and then started taking out charters. It brought in enough money to pay the bills. The rhythm of the tides and the scent of the ocean soothed him enough that he'd eventually given up the booze and eased into his current way of living.

It had been five years since Dana's death. He would have continued with his nothing existence if it weren't for Holly.

If Emma Cantrell hadn't given his former sister-in-law hope. Still, he saw the same sadness in Emma's eyes he recognized in his own. Why wasn't it easier to move on as the years passed? The world tried to feed people that line of bull.

Time healed all wounds.

No. Nope. Not in the least.

Because Lily's simple question ripped the skin off him as sure as if she'd taken a knife to his flesh.

He realized how he must look because Lily studied him like he'd turned into some sort of dangerous, feral creature. "We sell lures and bait on the other side of the store," she said slowly.

"I know." He drew in a steadying breath. "I've taken on some work at Niall Reed's old house."

"I thought Larry Sachs was handling that renovation."

Cam raised a brow, and Lily grimaced. "The woman who bought the place hired him before anyone could warn her."

Larry had been running his construction company in the area for decades. He was a hell of a salesman, but he had a reputation for cutting corners on the quality of his material and craftsmanship. Mainly he worked with businesses or families new to the region who didn't know any better.

"It's not as bad as it could be," Cam said, placing the printed supply list on the counter. "If it weren't for the storm, she could have opened on schedule."

"I'm happy to see that house being used for something new." Lily glanced at the list. "Niall let it fall into a sad state, but it always had good bones."

Those words made the vise around Cam's gut loosen slightly. "You sound like your dad, Lily. How's he doing? If you're here…"

"He's retired." Her gaze gentled even more. "Or semi-retired. He still comes into the store almost every day, but only because it makes him happy." She glanced up again. "My fiancé and I are getting ready to buy a place. We've been renting outside of town. I'm going to need furniture, and I want it to be special. If you—"

"I'm out of the furniture-making business," he told her, and tried not to wince at the disappointment that sparked in her eyes.

"You're an artist," she countered. "I don't think that's ever out of you."

"How long will it take to get the supplies?" he asked, fiddling with a scratch on the edge of the counter. He didn't want to talk about art or his craft or everything he'd lost. Not in the middle of the damn hardware store. Not ever.

"I can have the lumber here day after tomorrow," Lily told him. "We have a truck coming up from Wilmington. Plumbing and electrical materials should be a standard order. The roof shingles might take a bit longer. Most of the coast was hit by the storm, so stock is back-ordered."

He nodded. "I need to update my account information, but I'd like to get a line of credit, if that's possible."

"Of course. The town is growing, Cam. There's a lot of need for a carpenter with your skill."

"This is a one-off favor for a friend."

"You're friends with the new owner of Niall's house? What's she calling it?"

"The Wildflower Inn," he said, and couldn't help but smile. The name conjured up images of the whimsy and charm sorely lacking in the property. Although he still couldn't quite see Emma in the role of an innkeeper, her determination as she spoke about her vision impressed him. He thought about what it would mean to be her friend. His body immediately threw up a dozen red flags. He didn't want friendship, but he did want her. "Holly's getting married there."

Lily's mouth formed a perfect O and then her gaze softened. "You're doing this for Holly," she murmured.

For Dana. Those words hung silently in the air between them.

"A few weeks of work won't change the past or what I cost her family." He ran a hand through his hair and realized his fingers were trembling. Damn, he missed his solitary days on the water.

Lily had been close to Holly's age and he remembered her in her red apron sweeping the aisles of the hardware store when she was in high school. Cam had gone to school in a neighboring district, so he hadn't been friends with most of the people his age in Magnolia. But it was a small town, and everyone knew about Dana's accident. Her mother had made sure the fact he bore responsibility for it was common knowledge.

They'd had plans for their older daughter. The kind of plans middle-class families made involving college and a big wedding and a nice house on a tree-lined street.

Cam hadn't been able to give Dana any of that, but at the time it hadn't mattered. They'd met in September their senior year of high school and fallen in love the way teenagers did—head over heels with no thought to the future beyond being together.

Together they could do anything.

On his own, Cam was worthless.

"I can put a rush on the order," Lily told him, and he was grateful she didn't push him on anything else. He was already wired so tightly he might snap if they delved any deeper into the past.

"Thanks. I'll check back in a couple of days."

"If you give me your cell number—"

"No cell phone."

She looked as horrified as Emma had been at that revelation. "Even my dad has a cell phone, Cam. For emergencies."

"You're not the first person to give me grief about a phone." He shook his head. "I have a landline. Not much use for anything else when I'm on the water every day."

"All right, then. Check back at your convenience. It's good to see you working again."

"I'm not." Cam shook his head. "I'm doing a favor for Holly. Nothing more. No doubt Magnolia has plenty of carpenters to fill the void."

"None with your talent," she said simply.

"You give me too much credit, Lily."

"You don't give yourself enough." She leaned forward. "Dad has several of your pieces, and they're as amazing now as the day you delivered them. The way people are so into interior decorating now, folks with money would go wild for your aesthetic, Cam. You were ahead of your time. If you started building again—"

"I'm a fishing guide," he said through clenched teeth. "Nothing more."

She eyed him like she wanted to argue but thankfully only nodded. "If you change your mind, there's a barn being torn down in Tyler County next week. Dad's friends with the farm manager so he has an inside track on the wood."

"Not my scene anymore," Cam said. He used to love spending weekends driving through the country to source antique tools or reclaimed wood from estate sales. That was his past, his happiness, which had been tied to the woman he'd loved.

Now he only cared about getting the job done at the inn before he made the mistake of wanting more.

CHAPTER FIVE

EMMA WAS ON her hands and knees early the next week, covered in sweat and dirt as she pulled weeds from the garden bed at the edge of the yard, when the familiar scent of Chanel No. 5 wafted over her.

She immediately sat back on her heels and looked over her shoulder, shocked to find her mother staring at her from a few feet away. Gillian Sorensen wore a pair of tailored slacks in a muted peach color along with a white buttondown and a printed scarf tied around her neck.

Despite the early hour, the heat was already oppressive, although her mother didn't show any indication of being affected by it. Not one bead of perspiration or even the faintest hint of a glisten. Her hair remained in its sleek bob, as if immune to the sticky humidity of the summer morning.

Emma scrambled to her feet and automatically smoothed a hand over her hair, which she'd fastened in a high bun when she'd washed her face after waking. She tucked a loose tendril behind one ear and tried not to think about the fact that without styling aids the little hairs around her face would be standing straight up like she'd stuck her finger in a light socket. Or that she wore cutoff denim shorts and a tank top with pink bra straps peeking out.

An outfit she would have never considered, even for the weekend, before moving to Magnolia. Based on the distasteful purse of her mother's matte lips, Gillian didn't approve.

Oh, how Emma wished she'd gotten over craving her mother's approval.

"This is a surprise," she said, offering a smile that wasn't returned.

"Your brother told me this..." Gillian waved a hand at the house. "This place was damaged in the recent storm. I thought you were supposed to be opening soon."

"Things got pushed back because of the damage." Emma glanced around. "It's fine because now I have a bit more time to get everything just the way I want it."

Her mother raised a brow as she looked past Emma toward the bedraggled garden. "That's how you want it?"

"That's what I'm working on," Emma clarified. "Did you come to check on progress, Mom? You could have called." It was a nearly three-hour drive from the Virginia town where her mother lived.

"We're ready to make an offer for your replacement at the foundation," Gillian said simply.

"Oh." Emma's stomach dropped, and she quickly schooled her features before her mother could tell how that news affected her. "Anyone I know?"

"Patricia Marquis."

Emma choked back a yelp of shock. "Patricia? Seriously?" She and Emma had been classmates at Yale, and the other woman was a smug and sanctimonious snob. "Are you certain she's the best candidate?"

"She has some forward-thinking ideas about selecting grant recipients."

"I'm sure she does," Emma mumbled. Her maternal grandfather, Duffy Howard, had established the Howard Family Foundation after hitting it big in the tech industry.

Emma's mother ran the foundation and Emma had been groomed to take the reins when Gillian retired. Emma never questioned her path in life until she'd come to Magnolia this past spring to visit her brother, Ryan, who was staying in town while he recovered from an injury.

She and Ryan hadn't exactly been close growing up. Although only a couple of years apart in age, they'd had very different outlooks on life. Ryan had taken after their father, who'd wanted nothing to do with the privileged life his wife favored.

Peter Sorensen insisted his kids be raised without the trappings of money and had done his best to make them understand how it felt to be a normal kid. Emma wished the lesson had taken earlier for her, especially since her dad had died a few years ago. The cancer had been quick and brutal, and she regretted the time she'd wasted thinking she had all the answers and not listening to his advice.

Her mother arched a brow. "I didn't raise you for this. You have an Ivy League education, Emma. You had an amazing future. I still don't understand why you'd walk away from that."

"I wasn't happy."

"Don't be ridiculous. Listen to a self-help book or write in a journal and work out whatever problems you have. Daddy issues, no doubt."

"Mom, that's mean."

"But true. Your father did you no favors with his negative attitude about your grandfather's money."

"He wanted us to make our own way in the world. Ryan is doing that, and you have no problem with it."

Gillian sniffed. "You aren't Ryan."

Emma felt the hair on the back of her neck bristle. "What's that supposed to mean?"

Her mother waved a hand in Emma's direction. "You don't belong on your hands and knees. It isn't what I want for you or the future we agreed on."

"I didn't agree on anything. Do you remember my first semester of college? I was miserable in New Haven and wanted to transfer to Middlebury to study history."

"If I'd known you were going to throw away your education to clean toilets, maybe I would have allowed it."

"I'm not throwing away anything." Emma crossed her arms over her chest as irritation bubbled to the surface. "I thought maybe you came here to see what I'd accomplished so far."

"I have Patricia's offer letter drafted. This is your last chance to return to the foundation and to the life you were meant to live, Emma. If you come back now, I'll pay off the mortgage and you can sell the house and keep the profits. Otherwise, no money and no inheritance. You'll be truly on your own, and I'm telling you that is no way to live." Her mother stepped closer. "Trust me, I tried being regular. It's not all it's cracked up to be."

The thread of emotion in her mother's voice made Emma's throat ache. She never thought about what it cost her mother to distance herself from her family in the early years of her marriage or why she was so motivated for Emma to live her life a certain way. But even if Gillian's intentions were pure, that didn't account for her high-handedness or the disrespect she showed toward Emma's choices.

Emma yearned to live her own life. It might not be perfect or pretty, but she was finally choosing. She couldn't guarantee it was the right choice, but it belonged to her.

"I'm not coming back."

"You'll get nothing from me."

"Not even a birthday phone call?" Emma asked with a sniffly laugh.

"This isn't a joke."

"Do you think the money matters so much to me?"

Gillian glanced over her shoulder at the old house, which would need constant upkeep and regular updating. "It should."

"I've booked my first wedding," Emma said defiantly. "Brett Carmichael will be married in this backyard."

Her mother's eyes widened and then narrowed. "And did your last name…" She paused, wrinkled her nose and then amended, "Did *my* last name help you secure that client? You and your brother might want to thumb your noses at where you came from, like being wealthy is some kind of curse. But those connections—"

"The bride hired me," Emma said, taking a deep breath. "She didn't know until we'd already started working together."

Her mother humphed. "I gave you everything, Emma. This is how you repay me?"

"I'm not trying to hurt you, Mom. I just want something different for my life than you wanted for me." She swiped a hand across her cheek, hating the tears that spilled from her eyes but unable to stop them. "Is that so wrong?"

Gillian closed her eyes for a moment, and Emma thought she might have finally gotten through. But her mother's gaze was frosty when she opened them; she squared her shoulders and took a step back. "Yes, it is." Then she turned and made her way to the front of the house.

Emma watched her go, unsure how to feel. Angry. Sad. Bitter. Hollow inside. Her mother had first threatened to disown her when Emma tendered her resignation at the foundation. But she hadn't thought her mom would truly go through with it. In Emma's mind, their estrangement was temporary. Once she got the inn up and running, she planned to invite her mother for a weekend so she could show off. Now she understood her mother had meant every nasty word she'd said.

The sound of a heavy piece of furniture being dragged across the patio broke the silence. She whirled toward the noise to see Cam Arlinghaus lowering himself into one of the wrought-iron deck chairs.

"She could give Joan Crawford a run for her money," he said, grimacing. "I bet you didn't have wire hangers in your closet growing up."

"How long have you been there?" Emma shoved her hands into her back pockets as she walked toward him. He wore another battered T-shirt along with faded jeans and a dark baseball cap pulled low on his head. This kind of man should not appeal to her…and yet…

"Long enough that I have more questions than answers." He pointed a long finger in her direction. "Are you some kind of American heiress?"

"Not anymore, and it's rude to eavesdrop."

"I didn't exactly sneak back here. I could have detonated a bomb and I doubt either of you would have noticed. It explains a lot."

She narrowed her eyes as she took the seat next to him. She kept her motions casual and hoped he didn't notice she was shaking like a leaf. As annoying as she found him, Cam was the perfect distraction after that miserable conversation.

"I'm going to regret my curiosity, but what does it explain?"

"Why you smell like money for one," he answered without hesitation.

She lifted an arm to her nose. "I smell like sweat."

He shifted to the edge of the chair and wrapped a big hand around her wrist, then leaned in and made a show of sniffing her. "Under the sweat is the unmistakable aroma of expensive lotion, the kind rich women slather themselves in like a calling card."

Emma bit down on her lower lip to capture the sob that tried to escape her throat. Just last week she'd cut in half her last tube of the emollient bath cream she thought of as her signature scent. It had been a hack she'd found on the internet for getting the last bit of goodness from expensive skin-care products. In the past, she would have thrown out the old tube when the lotion didn't come out easily. But spending a mint on lotion was no longer an option. So, yeah, she smelled wealthy. Not for long.

She didn't like what it said about her that she both cared she was losing the luxury she'd become accustomed to and was embarrassed at how she'd taken her lot in life for granted.

Butterflies flitted through her middle when she realized Cam hadn't released his grip on her arm.

He turned it over to expose the skin on the underside of her wrist and traced his thumb against the blue vein under her skin.

His touch did funny things to her insides. For the moment it wiped out all her sadness and anger toward her mother like a broom sweeping a dusty corner clean.

"Why did you give it all up?" he asked softly.

"I didn't give anything up. I chose something different for myself. It's about time, too."

"What if you regret it?"

His focus was on her arm, so she couldn't see his eyes,

but he asked the question as if there were more to it than wondering about Emma's possible regrets.

"At least I can own my mistakes now. I think that's more important than being boxed in by my mother's expectations."

"Until it's not," he whispered, and abruptly released her. He sat back, and when his whiskey-colored gaze crashed into hers, she almost lost her breath at the intensity of banked emotion in their depths.

Definitely something more.

She made a mental note to ask her brother's fiancée about Cam and his late wife. Meredith had grown up in Magnolia and might remember when a car accident killed a young woman. Of course, Emma could ask Holly but felt like it would cross some kind of invisible client line. She could ask Cam. But he seemed far too unsteady to discuss something so personal with her.

"Until then, I've got a lot of work to do."

"That's why I'm here." He reached down and plucked a thick manila file folder off the ground. She hadn't noticed it before because she'd been ridiculously distracted by the way his muscles bunched in his arms when he moved. The deep timbre of his voice and his general air of rugged manliness. It was bad enough Emma needed him for this project. She wasn't about to admit she felt anything other than professional courtesy for her surly contractor. Surely not smack-her-down lust.

Lust was fleeting. A well-built roof was her future.

"I put the numbers together for the project and factored in your insurance money."

"You could have emailed me." She pulled a sheet of paper from the folder.

"I wanted to discuss it in person. I've already ordered

most of the materials from the hardware store. If this isn't going to work, I need to call Lily and cancel. She put a rush on it."

"A rush," Emma repeated as she scanned the figures he'd given her. "How did you manage that?"

He shrugged. "It was a favor."

A woman named Lily did him a favor. Emma rolled her shoulders as jealousy spiked along her spine. *Down, girl*, she silently commanded. Cam Arlinghaus could receive favors from every female in town, and it was none of Emma's business.

"These numbers aren't right," she told him with a frown.

"They're right."

"I know insurance isn't going to cover this much."

"You're saving money on labor." He inclined his head. "Since you volunteered to be my slave."

Oh, she'd be his slave, all right. Emma had never been much into role-playing but...

She shook her head. "I can't let you do this."

"I was joking about the slave part," he said.

"I want to pay."

"Leave the money on the nightstand kind of pay?"

One side of his mouth quirked, and she suppressed a smile. It was difficult enough to stay focused when Cam was being grumpy. This teasing Cam with his rough charm was like a full assault on her senses. "Don't be ridiculous and stop trying to distract me."

"You seem like a woman who needs a distraction."

"Not from you," she blurted before she could stop herself. She meant the words from a pure self-preservation standpoint. Emma had a goal and getting involved with any man would mess with her concentration. It had nothing to do with the residual bitterness from an ex-husband who'd effectively blown apart her world and then taken most of her money on the way out the door.

And it had nothing to do with who Cam was as a person.

But just as clearly, that's how he'd interpreted the comment. "Duly noted," he told her with a tight smile. The teasing light in his eyes dimmed, and he was back to all business. "I'm sure that's one thing you and your mother could agree on. I'm not exactly the type of guy parents like their daughters to bring home for Sunday dinner."

"My mom doesn't cook," Emma answered, even though that wasn't the point.

At least it made his shoulders relax slightly. "What about you?"

"I make breakfast. I've been perfecting a French toast casserole."

"I do a mean Denver omelet."

She wanted to suggest they share a meal, but where would that lead? No place smart for either of them.

"I can afford to pay you without a discount," she lied.

"Really?" He studied her so long her palms got clammy with nerves. "Because when we met with Holly, you got a little green in the gills discussing the budget. I figured cash might be tight. Based on what your mom said, I'd guess that's a new way of being for you."

"I don't have the money," she amended, because there was no point in telling a lie when he'd find out the truth soon enough. "But I'll get it. Once Holly's wedding is featured in magazines, I expect bookings to take off. I didn't envision myself specializing in weddings, but it's perfect. I'm organized and great with details."

"Can I assume you also believe in true love?"

She snorted. "Oh, heck, no. Not at the moment, anyway."

As soon as the words were out of her mouth, Emma realized her mistake. But how could she truly regret blurting her true feelings when they earned a small, sexy-as-hell grin from Cam? Still, as a wannabe wedding planner...

"I believe in love for other people," she amended. "People like Holly."

"How is Holly different than you?"

"Well, I hope she's marrying a man who will cherish her forever."

"You have a husband?"

"An ex-husband."

"And did you have a fairy-tale wedding?"

Emma's stomach tightened at the memory of that day, walking down the aisle in the crowded church, the beautiful dress, exquisite flowers and months of preparation. "I did."

"But not the happily-ever-after marriage?"

She shook her head. "I got caught up in the illusion of the perfect life but forgot to be certain of one important factor." She held up a finger. "I didn't slow down to make sure my husband was a decent human being. My bad."

"You don't know Brett Carmichael," Cam pointed out.

"He's Holly's choice," she countered.

"No guarantee she's making a good one."

"I want to believe in love," she said, suddenly aware of the truth in those words. She might have been deeply hurt and left nearly broke by her ex's conniving duplicity, but she didn't want to give up on the dream of finding the right person to share a life with. Maybe love wasn't on Emma's priority list now, but that didn't mean she'd sworn off it for good. "In fact..." She leaned forward as a realization hit her. "I'm a great choice for a wedding planner. I've had my heart shattered, but I'm not giving up on love. Who better to work with brides getting ready to take the plunge? Thank you, Cam." She reached out and took his hands in hers, squeezing gently. "This is exactly the reassurance I needed to know I'm going in the right direction."

He blinked and looked down at their joined hands. "I didn't do anything."

She followed his gaze and noticed how small and pale her hands looked against his golden skin, although hers were smudged with dirt from working in the garden. There was a smattering of dark hair on the backs of his hands, and one of his knuckles was newly scraped. Would it be odd to offer him a Band-Aid?

"You reminded me I have more to offer than my mother believes."

"Not on purpose," he mumbled. "I'm taking on this project because it's what Holly wants, but this marriage is doomed for failure."

Emma sat back, released her grasp on Cam. He rubbed his palms across the soft denim covering his thighs like he was wiping away her touch. She couldn't explain why that hurt her feelings. "Why?"

"She's a sweet girl, but she comes from a different world than the Carmichaels. Those kinds of worlds don't mix."

"They could."

"Not without her giving up who she is. Trust me, she'd do better to fall for some local guy who's looking for the same things as her."

"That's not how love works." She shook her head. "If I could figure out a way to make sure people end up with just the right partner, that's the business I'd create. Until then, I'm going to make sure I give them the perfect day and the right start to their lives together."

"You're a dreamer."

"I'm not the only one," she shot back with an arched brow.

He huffed out a small laugh. "I'm going to start on the

roof tomorrow morning. The materials should be in so I can get the shingles replaced once I have the old ones ripped off. Some of the damaged drywall needs to come down, too. You have any leftover anger toward your ex?"

She blinked. "Buckets full."

"Then you can take it out on a wall. I'll bring an extra sledgehammer."

"I like the sound of that," she said. In truth, she liked way more than she should when it came to Camden Arlinghaus. And they'd only just begun their tentative partnership.

CHAPTER SIX

EMMA APPROACHED THE Reed Gallery, the art gallery that had long been the anchor to downtown Magnolia's business district when it was owned by Niall Reed. Of course she was familiar with his sappy paintings and prints, but she hadn't realized his impact on the town until she'd moved there.

Carrie, the only one of the sisters who'd been recognized as legitimate by her father during his life, had taken over the gallery. She was an immensely talented painter in her own right and also showcased several local and regional artists in the gallery, from painters to sculptures to printmakers.

Ryan's fiancée, Meredith, had introduced Emma to Carrie and been the one to make the suggestion Emma consign some of Carrie's pieces to hang in the inn.

It made Emma nervous because Carrie had grown up in the house, and Emma had no idea if the other woman approved of her plans to convert it to an inn. And what would she think about the wedding angle? Did the house hold good or bad memories for her?

As she entered the gallery, a brown dog of indiscriminate breeding got up from the polished wood floor and trotted over to greet her.

"You must be one of Meredith's animals," she said as she leaned down to scratch behind the dog's floppy ears. Emma had first met the love of her brother's life when the Howard Family Foundation funded Meredith's animal rescue while Emma still served as its program director. It had led her to Magnolia in the first place, and she'd been captivated by Meredith's dedication to and gift for working with the animals she took in.

"Has she gotten to you yet?" a gentle voice asked, and a tall, serene-looking woman approached from the next room. "That's Daisy, and yes, she was one of Meredith's rescues. My sister doesn't believe in boundaries when it comes to matching her fur babies with potential adopters."

Emma straightened and brushed a tuft of dog hair from her pant leg. She'd dressed in her business clothes for this meeting, and it had been the first time she'd put on a pair of silk trousers since moving to town. In contrast, Carrie wore a long, flowing skirt and peasant blouse, her caramel-colored hair cascading over her shoulders. Her delicate features were free from makeup as far as Emma could tell, and she pretty much embodied the image of a gorgeous bohemian artist. "I'm not a good candidate to be a dog or cat mom right now."

"I bet Meredith can find you the perfect partner. She managed to convince my husband, Dylan, when he was dead set against having a pet. Now this sweet girl gives me a run for my money on the love-of-his-life category." The dog stretched out on one of the thick rugs and rolled onto her back like she was some sort of canine centerfold.

Emma chuckled but uncertainty prodded a small part of her. She'd been in Magnolia for a while, and Meredith hadn't tried to match her with an animal yet. Was Emma a bad candidate?

"I'd like to be a bit more settled first," she said, keeping her voice neutral. "Thanks to the storm, I have a ways to go before the Wildflower Inn opens officially so—"

"Is that what you're calling the house now?" Carrie's expression took on a wistful tone.

"I hope this isn't too weird," Emma said. "I know you grew up there and now I've had it rezoned to be a commercial property."

Carrie shook her head. "Not at all. My memories there are complicated, so it's nice to think of it getting a whole new life. There have been a lot of fresh starts around here lately. I'm glad you're part of it." She crooked a finger and led Emma farther into the gallery. "It's a fun coincidence, though, because my mom was the one who first sprinkled the wildflower seeds around the property. For a few years she became obsessed with transforming the yard into a colorful oasis from early spring to late summer. It was one of the few projects that brought her and my dad together. Even after they divorced, the flowers continued to bloom. They're one of my favorite things about the property."

Emma breathed a sigh of relief. Cam had made great progress in the past week on demo in the areas that had been impacted by the storm, and she didn't want anything to intrude on the gossamer web of hope beginning to spin through her. "I came up with the name about a week after I moved in. I looked out the kitchen window one morning and the backyard, all the way to the woods, was awash with color, like it happened overnight. It felt like a sign, and I wanted the name to reflect it."

"Did the yard look something like that?" Carrie gestured to a large canvas that hung on the far wall. As Emma took in the painting, her heart began to hammer in her chest.

"Exactly." She drew closer to the painting like she was being pulled by an invisible string. The acrylic painting depicted a bright meadow surrounded by towering trees, much like the view from the back of the inn. The color palette Carrie had chosen was vivid but not overwhelming, almost surreal in its intensity.

"The start of summer always makes me think of the wildflowers," Carrie told her. "They don't grow as well on our side of town. There's something about the shade and moisture from the woods behind the houses on that side of the street. It's kind of magical."

Tears pricked the backs of Emma's eyes. "That's how I felt the first time I saw the house," she confided. "It was the day you and your sisters held the estate sale. I'd come to town for a site visit with Meredith and really to check out the woman who was having such a huge influence on my brother. But the house seemed to call to me."

She flattened her palm against her chest. "This is so embarrassing, but I went back to the hotel that night and cried my eyes out because I was so sad for your father's house. It just seemed unfair that such an amazing home had fallen into disrepair. I fell in love with it." She glanced up to find Carrie staring at her with a look of shock on her delicate features. "That sounds ridiculous, right? I have no real connection to it."

"You belong there," Carrie told her with a nod, then turned to look at the canvas. "This painting belongs there. I hope I don't sound presumptuous, but I can see it hanging in the foyer. Potentially, anyway. Depending on what you choose to do with the space."

"I love that idea." It felt weirdly reassuring to have Carrie suggest placing the painting in the exact spot where Emma would want it. A tacit approval of her plans to open the inn from a former resident of the house. Maybe she shouldn't expect one from a woman who was practically a stranger, but it gave her an infusion of confidence she desperately needed.

"Look around and let me know if there are other paintings or pieces of art that would work. I have so much stock coming in that it would be a huge help to consign some of it out to you. I'm more than willing to help with placement if you'd like another set of eyes."

"Yes, thank you. It will be a few weeks until I can take anything. The house had some significant damage from the storm. The guy helping me with the restoration and repairs starts tomorrow."

"You're lucky you found someone so quickly. Dylan has a few commercial developments and renovations in the works, and he had a couple of trees come down and damage one of the new buildings. Even his normal contractor has a backlog."

"Yeah, I'm lucky," Emma agreed, thinking about Cam. He might be surly and disagreeable, but she also had no doubt he'd make her inn shine, if only because of his dedication to Holly.

The door to the gallery opened, and Meredith came in with two adolescent-age puppies on matching leashes. The two sisters didn't resemble each other. Meredith was a tiny sprite of a woman with darker hair and a palpable energy surrounding her. Emma had met the third of Niall's daughters, Avery, and the sophisticated blonde rounded out the unlikely trio in a way that shouldn't work but somehow did. Like many things in Magnolia.

Daisy went over to greet them, and Carrie grinned. "That dog is the consummate gallery ambassador. These are new recruits, yes?" she asked as the puppies thumped their tails in unison.

"A family with young kids bought them from a pet store without understanding puppies need time and training. They're labradoodles and were left tied up in the backyard. The mom and dad didn't understand why the dogs became destructive. I'm sending them through puppy boot camp, and then I'll find better homes."

"They're so cute," Emma murmured as she squatted down, and one of the curly-haired dogs licked her hand.

"I'm calling them Lucy and Ethel because they're like a comedy duo."

"I could use some more laughter in my life," Emma offered, wondering if the other woman would pick up on the subtle hint.

Meredith only laughed. "Your bride wouldn't appreciate having dog paw prints on her white gown when these two greet her."

Emma forced a smile and tried not to be offended that she was brushed off so summarily as a potential adopter. She had tons of potential. Okay, she knew deep down that Meredith was right. Two rambunctious young dogs weren't a good fit for her. But she wanted a show of faith. Maybe it was greedy after Carrie's words of encouragement. Emma's mom would have thought so.

"What bride?" Carrie asked, also on her knees with the playful pups despite the flowing skirt she wore. Daisy kept nudging the dogs back toward Meredith when they wandered to the edge of their leash lines.

"I'm helping a local bride with her wedding. It's going to be the first event I host at the inn." She cleared her throat. "At your dad's house."

"It's the Wildflower Inn now," Carrie corrected. "And a perfect venue for a wedding." She glanced out the window, her brows furrowing. "Are you handling the food, as well?"

Emma cringed and then attempted to look in control. She and Holly had talked about a dress and flowers and the cake, but she'd forgotten she'd have to feed the guests. So much for her claim to Cam about being so detail-oriented. "Not personally," she said brightly. "But I'll hire a caterer. I'm sure there's someone great in town."

"As a matter of fact…" Carrie pointed out the front window. "You should talk to Angi Guilardi."

"Angi's a waitress," Meredith said. "I'll get you the number of Janie from Classic Catering. She's been handling events in Magnolia for decades."

"And using the same recipes every time," Carrie said with a dismissive sniff. "Angi works at her family's restaurant, but she wants to branch out on her own. Her dad died at the beginning of the year, so now she's struggling with the pressure to emotionally support her mom. I think she needs a push to try something new. She's an amazing cook and has innovative ideas for recipes."

"The Guilardis haven't changed their menu since the '80s," Meredith said. "Not that I'm complaining. Bianca's chicken parmesan is the best around, but it's not exactly cutting edge."

"That's the point," Carrie insisted. "Angi can't get her mom to consider anything new. She's frustrated." Her thin shoulders lifted and lowered. "I know about frustrated."

"Me, too," Emma said quietly.

"If you need a taste-tester, I'm available," Meredith said with a grin. "I can't cook worth a crap, but I'm a great eater."

"That's true." Carrie winked at Emma. "If you need any help around the inn, Sam, who is my unofficial stepson, just got his license. He's looking for part-time work after school to earn gas money."

"I might give him a call," Emma said, wondering if it could really be this easy to make event planning part of her innkeeper repertoire. "Although until I book more events, money is a little tight."

Carrie and Meredith stared at her with twin looks of disbelief as the dogs wrestled at their feet.

"I thought you had a trust fund," Meredith said after an awkward pause. "Or family money or whatever you want to call it."

"Um…" Emma realized her mistake. She hadn't told her brother she'd been cut off because she didn't want to become his charity case. She wanted to make it on her own, even if that meant she lived on a shoestring budget. What purpose would it serve to go from her mother's money to her brother's? "My mom wasn't thrilled with me choosing a new path for my life."

"What does that mean?" Carrie asked, although Emma had a feeling the other woman knew exactly what it meant.

"I've been officially disowned," she said, and did her best to make it sound like the fact didn't bother her. "Like I'm living my part in some Victorian melodrama." She made a show of gesticulating wildly. "You have brought shame on the family name," she said in a deep voice. "You are dead to me, daughter."

Neither Carrie nor Meredith seemed to find the situation funny, based on their stunned expressions.

Meredith tugged on the leashes and the puppies both dropped their butts to the floor like they understood the person on the other end wasn't playing anymore. "Your brother doesn't know this."

Emma shook her head. "It's not a big deal."

"But you must have your own money?" Carrie frowned. "Not trying to pry, but you must have made a decent salary at the foundation."

"I went through a rough divorce last year," Emma admitted. "I paid a lot…almost all of my money…to my now ex-husband."

Twin jaw drops greeted her revelation. "Why?"

"It was the easiest way to get rid of him," Emma said, which was the truth but not the whole truth. She hadn't shared the whole truth with anyone. She forced a bright smile. "So I'm well and truly starting over. On my own. Making my way in the world. I have to make it work because there is no backup plan."

"But there's more to the story with the ex-husband." Meredith said the words like an accusation. "What did he do?"

"Maybe she wants to keep some things private," Carrie suggested, moving closer to Emma almost protectively.

"We're nearly family," Meredith argued. "There's no private."

Those words made Emma smile for real. Family. She had such a convoluted sense of that word. Growing up, family had meant tension and disagreements. Long, pregnant silences between her parents and watching her brother keep moving, keep busy, keep occupied, so he didn't have to deal with it. She'd been the one to smooth things over. The mediator. Her mother's best girl, a chip off the polished block.

Which was another reason why she'd left her marriage with nothing. Less than nothing. Not even her pride intact.

"He blackmailed me." Her chest constricted with crushing humiliation. "With a sex tape."

One of the puppies let out a low whine.

"You made a sex tape?" Carrie swallowed audibly. "Oh, my."

"I…it wasn't… I didn't know." Humiliation flooded Emma and nausea rolled through her the same way it did every time she thought about what her ex-husband had done.

"So your husband taped the two of you knockin' boots." Meredith shrugged. "Doesn't seem like a reason to fork over your money."

"It wasn't him." Emma wished the ground would swallow her whole. "We were separated at the time because I suspected he'd been cheating on me, but I had no proof. Still, I was heartbroken. He made me feel like the whole thing was my fault because I worked too much and was too rigid. He's a history professor at a prestigious liberal arts college in eastern Virginia, but I was the main breadwinner. It was a rough patch we'd get over, or at least that's what I told myself."

She kept her gaze on the puppies as she spoke. "I went to a conference in Chicago, and I met the most charming man in the hotel bar." She closed her eyes and drew in a shaky breath at the memory of what a fool she'd been. "I was so low. My self-esteem was in the toilet. In my heart, I knew my marriage was over. It was more than a rough patch. I couldn't go back to him. So I had a weekend fling with a stranger."

"I hope he was a smoking-hot stranger," Meredith told her.

"Yeah." Emma sighed. "He'd also been hired by my husband to seduce me. No one knew we were separated, not even my family or close friends. Martin made it clear that if I didn't give him everything he wanted in the divorce settlement, he'd drag my name through the tabloids."

"What a jerk," Carrie said with a snort of outrage.

"I still don't understand why you agreed." Meredith bent to pet one of the pups but her gaze held on Emma. "Lots of people have survived the scandal of a sex tape. Hell, some of them built a career off it."

"I'm not a reality star," Emma countered. "I was an executive at one of the most well-known family foundations in the country. A sex tape leaking wasn't an option. My mother would have disowned me." She let out an almost hysterical belly laugh at the irony. "Turns out, I only bought myself a year before that happened, anyway." She looked out the front window toward the restaurant across the street. "But that's why I don't have any savings to speak of and why Ryan can't know. He'd go after Martin."

"As he should," Meredith said. "*You* should. That guy is a scumbag, and he needs to pay."

"My mom didn't want me to marry him in the first place. Told me he was a gold digger. But I believed I was in love, and I trusted him. It's a mistake I won't make again."

"You have to let us help you," Meredith insisted. "Your brother will want to help you."

"No." Emma shook her head. "I'm doing this on my own, even if ninety-nine percent of the work comes in the form of sweat equity."

"Do you need help?" Carrie asked. "Dylan has a lot of connections. If you need—"

"Cam can handle it." Emma nodded, surprised at how sure she was about that. "He's doing it as a favor to my first bride. He was married to her late sister."

"All in the family," Meredith said with a shrug.

Emma thought about asking these two women what they knew of Cam's story and his dead wife but couldn't bring herself to mention it. She owed him nothing but felt a sense of loyalty nonetheless. Despite how crusty and detached he acted, his vulnerability was raw and untethered. It was as if he'd become half a person when his wife died. Emma understood. She'd only lost a cheating ex but it had hurt her heart deeply to be betrayed by someone she thought she loved.

"I'm going to talk to Angi." She nodded at Carrie. "If she wants to get started with a catering company, maybe she'll be more likely to cut a deal on her rate at this point. I can use all the good deals I can get."

"Talk to Gabe at In Bloom, the floral shop down the street," Carrie suggested.

Meredith barked out a laugh. "Are you joking? Gabe Carlyle is the surliest, rudest florist the world has ever seen. If it wasn't for everyone's loyalty to his grandmother, he'd already be out of business. There's an upscale place the next town over on the way to Raleigh. They'll be much easier to work with."

"But you'll pay upscale prices," Carrie argued. "Plus, you'll get the most basic arrangements ever." She crooked a finger and Emma and Meredith followed her to the next room, the puppies scrambling along in their wake. Daisy watched from her dog bed in the corner, clearly done with the younger, energetic pups. "Gabe delivered it almost a week ago."

"The blooms still look fresh," Emma said as she approached the striking arrangement. It showcased a mix of wildflowers along with oversize lilies and a few sweetheart roses. She'd never seen such an eclectic selection of blooms arranged together, but somehow it worked.

"He moved to town to help his grandma with the shop when she had a stroke. I don't think being a local florist was part of his plan, but he's making the best of it."

"Other than the fact that he's outright rude to people around town, including people who come into the shop."

"He has some work to do on his customer service skills," Carrie admitted. "But he's trying to do the right thing. Working with Emma would be a huge opportunity for him. Besides…" She pointed a finger at Meredith. "I'd think you could understand someone who wasn't much of a people person."

Meredith scoffed. "I work with animals. I don't need to be a people person. And this isn't about me. Emma doesn't strike me as the type to put together the Bad News Bears team of wedding planners."

"What kind of person do I strike you as?" Emma asked, almost dreading the answer.

Meredith opened and closed her mouth several times before darting a beseeching look to Carrie.

"You seem organized and particular. Like you expect things to go your way without issue and could be extremely peeved if things don't work out in the manner in which you think they should."

"Anal, entitled and demanding," Emma interpreted.

"Basically," Meredith agreed, earning a swat on the arm from her sister. "That's not a bad thing," she amended quickly. "I thought your brother was arrogant and entitled. It runs in the family."

Emma felt her mouth drop open and quickly snapped it shut. "Do you have any filter?"

"She doesn't," Carrie said, and wrapped an arm around Meredith's shoulders, squeezing with more force than was probably necessary. "But she means well. Most people in town do. I think talking to Angi is a great idea. Pick whatever florist you want. Mary Ellen at Sunnyside Bakery makes the most amazing and beautiful cakes. You can do this. If there's one thing my sisters taught me..." Another squeeze for Meredith. "It's that taking big chances can produce big rewards."

"Or you can fall on your ass in a big way," Meredith added with a wink.

After choosing two additional paintings for the inn and

coordinating a time for Carrie to deliver them, Emma said goodbye to the sisters and headed out of the gallery. As she crossed the street, her phone rang, the number of the hardware store a couple of doors down displaying on the screen.

As she answered, she automatically turned toward Wainright's Hardware to see a crowd of people gathering around the front door.

"Hello?"

"Emma, it's Lily Wainright. Any chance you're near downtown?"

"As a matter of fact," Emma said as she changed direction, "I'm heading that way right now."

"Good, because we're having a bit of a Wild West contractor showdown in the middle of the store, and you're at the center of it."

CHAPTER SEVEN

WALK AWAY, CAM told himself as he continued to face down Larry Sachs in front of the pro desk at Wainright's Hardware. There was absolutely no reason to take a stand on Emma's project. He had nothing at stake and someone else could easily take over the job at this point.

He'd stopped at the store to finalize another order. As soon as he'd started demoing some of the damaged parts of the house, Cam had realized the repairs would be more extensive than he'd first thought. Just as he'd been about to sign for the supplies, a heavy hand had landed on his shoulder.

He'd turned to find Larry, who he'd recognized from years ago when Cam had worked on the crew of a rival local contractor, glaring at him. The other man had gotten wind of Cam's involvement in the repairs at the inn and didn't like the idea of someone poaching one of his clients.

They'd exchanged words about the basics of customer service and professional respect. In some respects, Larry's lifting of the proverbial leg to stake out his territory was the out Cam should have been looking for. He was no longer a master carpenter. He was a fishing guide and a loner, and he liked his life just fine.

Okay, *like* might be pushing it. He'd accepted the parameters he'd set on himself and how much he was willing to give. But he'd seen enough of the work Larry had done for

Emma to know the man had cut corners even more than Cam would have expected. Part of why her house had been so damaged in the storm was the shoddy workmanship on the recent renovation by Larry's crew.

Cam might not have much, but he hadn't abandoned his principles of a job well done for a client. He wouldn't let Emma be taken advantage of again.

"I'm sure this is just an easy-to-solve misunderstanding," Lily said as she came to stand behind the counter, like she needed a barrier between herself and the two men. She leaned forward, the front of her Carhartt overalls pressing into the edge of the counter. "Maybe it's one you want to talk about later and someplace else."

"There's nothing to talk about," Larry said, loud enough that his voice carried for the audience that had gathered. "After years of running a fishing boat, all that sun might have damaged Cam's brain. He knows an unbreakable rule of local business is not to steal other people's customers. The inn is mine."

The back of Cam's neck burned knowing he was the center of attention with the customers gawking at them, many of whom he'd known or at least met back in the day. He hated having eyes on him, especially when it meant they'd be thinking about his former life.

"Emma hired me because you wouldn't return her calls." Cam hitched his chin. "Probably because you knew you'd have to redo the crappy job you did for her in the first place."

"Are you suggesting my guys did subpar work? That's a hell of an accusation."

Cam lifted a brow. "I know you're not the sharpest knife in the drawer, Larry. But do I need to define *crappy* for you?"

"Not as much as I need to kick your meddling ass," Larry growled, and took a step forward.

"Not here," Lily commanded, slapping a hand on the counter.

"What's going on?" a familiar voice demanded. Cam shifted his gaze as Emma hurried around the corner and stepped between him and Larry.

"Just working out a bit of business," Larry said with an oily smile. "It's good timing that I ran into Camden here today. You were on my list to call about getting one of my crews out to the house for your storm repairs. We keep missing each other."

It was amazing how easily the man could lie, and Cam could have hugged Emma when she only snorted in response. "I left seven messages for you," she told Larry.

"You know how busy things have been around here," he said smoothly. "But I was getting to you."

"Not good enough," she said, straightening her shoulders. "I don't want my inn to be someone's afterthought."

Larry's smile dimmed and his eyes hardened. "I'd guess you also don't want your inn associated with a guy who is known to be mentally unstable." He jerked a thumb toward Cam. "That's not going to be a selling point for customers. What if he loses his temper and goes off on someone?"

Cam felt his throat go dry. "Shut up, Sachs."

"Everyone knows it." Larry waved a hand at the crowd. "Why do you think there's such an audience? People are waiting for Cam to break something or start flipping out." He shifted closer to Emma and said in a stage whisper, "He's been unhinged ever since the accident. Hell, before even. He was a moody, angry brute of a man from the get-go. Trust me, no one wants to be near him."

Spots swam in front of Cam's eyes. In many ways, Larry

spoke the truth. Cam felt more than unhinged when Dana died. It had been simple to wrap himself in a bubble of grief and sorrow, to not let anyone reach him. Not his parents or friends. Certainly not Holly or any of Dana's close circle. He also tended to be a surly jerk before her death. Dana had been like living with a ball of sunshine and cotton candy swirled into one. Bright and sweet, smoothing out his rough edges. Now all he had was rough, and it was more than just edges.

The hardware store had grown quiet in the wake of Larry's claims. Cam should have figured this was what people still thought of him. Hell, he didn't blame them. He'd agreed to help with repairs to the inn for Holly, and Emma had taken him on because she was desperate and because she didn't understand the full extent of his reputation. The darkness that had almost swallowed him whole and continued to inhabit the shadowy parts of his chest where his heart used to be.

"Just be patient," Larry continued, his tone at once patronizing and ingratiating. Cam had never learned the art of schmoozing people. He could only be what he was. Nothing more. "I'll get to your job, but you don't have to deal with this guy. It's not worth it." He flicked a glance toward Lily. "Cancel his order. I'll put in my own. I don't trust that he—"

"No."

Cam's breath caught at the steel in Emma's tone as she spoke that one word.

"Come on, darlin'," Larry crooned, Southern charm and that down-home accent on full display. "It's going to be all right. Let me take care of things."

"I don't need you to take care of me," Emma said, managing to look down her nose even though the man was almost six inches taller than her. "You made it clear where I landed on your list of priorities, Mr. Sachs." She did a little hair toss Cam imagined upper-class women were taught when they were still in pigtails. The message was as clear as if she'd flipped Larry the bird. "I hired Camden Arlinghaus to help me with repairs to the inn, and he's done a great job so far. I trust him."

Her tone went as cold as a desolate tundra in the dead of winter. "It's beneath you or anyone to speak so cavalierly about mental health issues. Your behavior reflects poorly on you, not Cam. He's been nothing but helpful and professional. I'm looking forward to opening the Wildflower Inn with his assistance." She leveled a sharp stare at the onlookers. "I'm new to town, but I moved to Magnolia because it felt like a community that gives people a second chance. I'm making a fresh start with the inn, and it's going to be a success. I hope other business owners around here show more professionalism in how they manage themselves than Mr. Sachs has done today." She returned her glare to Larry. "You should be ashamed of yourself."

Cam felt one side of his mouth tug upward. Larry gaped as if he couldn't believe she had the audacity to speak to him in that tone, like he was being scolded by a rigid schoolteacher for being the class bully.

"I think we're done here." Lily offered Emma a nod of approval. "Cam will be handling the Wildflower Inn, and like Emma, I have no doubt he'll do an amazing job."

"He has my vote, as well."

Cam's heart stuttered at the gravelly voice, and he turned to find Phil Wainright, Lily's father, walking toward him. Cam hadn't seen Phil since a month or so after Dana's death. The older man had been one of Cam's biggest supporters when he'd been working to get his custom furniture business off the ground. But Cam had turned his back on everyone who cared about him in the midst of his grief.

Phil had always been an imposing figure, but he seemed smaller now, thinner and moving slow. His salt-and-pepper hair had gone completely white, and regret washed through Cam at everything he'd missed when he let grief turn his life inside out.

"Dad's is the only vote that counts around here." Lily waved a hand at the small crowd of people still gathered. "Time to disperse, people. Grab a cup of coffee and some popcorn on your way out."

Larry looked like he wanted to argue with Lily before his angry gaze found Emma's again. "You're going to regret hitching your wagon to that head case. Don't come crawling to me to bail you out when you need it."

"No chance of that," Emma promised, then turned her back to him.

The other man stalked off as Phil held out a hand to Emma. "My daughter tells me you have big plans for the old Reed house."

"Yes, sir," she murmured, suddenly looking shy and unsure. Cam found this side of her just as appealing as when she'd been in full warrior mode on his behalf.

"I live a couple of blocks over," Phil told her. "That place needs some extra TLC, like a lot of houses in the neighborhood after the storm." He shifted to include Cam in the conversation. "I'm glad to know you're handling things now. If you need an extra pair of hands, these are available." He held up his gnarled hands, calloused palms facing Cam. "It's good to see you, son."

The moniker was like an emotional knife to the heart, but Cam forced a smile. "You, too."

"You're retired, Dad," Lily reminded him. She smiled at Emma. "Thanks for coming to mediate."

"I'm not sure I'd call what I did a mediation." Emma looked decidedly less warrior princess and more worrywart at the moment. "More like burning a bridge."

"You didn't have to step in," Cam felt the need to point out.

"Oh, yeah." She sniffed. "Because you were handling things so well on your own."

"I was handling it just fine. Larry's a blowhard and always has been."

"You don't have to concern yourself with anyone else," Phil said in his gentle tone. The man had been so good to Cam back in the day, and Cam couldn't help wondering what Phil saw now. A grief-stricken, unstable loner the way everyone else did or something else. Someone different.

Cam hoped it was different.

"Thanks again for the call, Lily," Emma said before narrowing her eyes at Cam. "Next time I'll let you take care of things on your own so you can live down to people's expectations. That's always fun. It was nice to meet you, Phil. Please stop by the house anytime. I'd love to show you around."

Without another glance toward Cam, she turned and walked away.

"She really did go out on a limb for you," Lily said quietly. "I haven't ever seen anyone receive the set-down she gave Larry."

"All I want is to make the repairs as a favor to Holly and go back to my regular life."

Phil frowned. "You're more than a part-time fishing guide."

"Actually, that's about the sum total of me," Cam countered. "I'll start tomorrow morning. The roof first and then making sure the HVAC system works. It's just me and Emma on the job, so if you want to while away your retirement hours with a pneumatic nail gun in your hand, I won't say no."

"Consider me hired," Phil said with a wide grin.

"Dad, no." Lily shook her head. "It's too much in the heat. Besides, I thought you wanted to help with inventory here."

Something flashed in the older man's eyes, but they were clear before he turned to his daughter. Cam appreciated Phil's devotion to Lily. "This place is yours, darlin'. I know I get in the way."

"You don't," she protested.

Phil shook his head. "I'm going to bother Cam for a few days. He needs more help than you, anyway. Give me your cell number," he told Cam. "And I'll text to confirm a time."

"Don't have one," Cam said, wondering if he was as much of a technology dinosaur as everyone around him seemed to think. "Stop by whenever. I'll be there by seven-thirty. I have something I need to talk to Emma about. I'll catch you both later."

The weight of what she'd done had finally punctuated his thick head, and he realized he owed her both a thank-you and an apology. And he knew just the way to go about it.

EMMA WAS JUST opening her car door when she heard heavy footfalls jogging up next to her. She'd stopped in at Il Rigatone on her way from the hardware store, but was told by the owner, Bianca Guilardi, that her daughter had gone to Raleigh to pick up new linens for the restaurant.

Bianca had asked Emma why she needed to talk to Angi, and Emma had told the truth about needing to hire someone to handle the catering for events at the inn. Based on the reaction she received, Emma would have thought she was trying to recruit the other woman for some nefarious gang.

Two people she'd tried to help today only to have her efforts thrown back in her face in both cases. She figured it was time to head home and regroup.

She turned to Cam, who offered a sheepish smile. "I forgot to say thank you."

"Larry was out of line," she said, ignoring what his smile did to her insides. "But you don't need me to tell you that. Apparently, you don't need me to defend you, either. Next time I'll remember to leave you alone to handle a potential fistfight in the middle of the hardware store. I'm sure someone watching had their phone ready to go for the video. You would have looked sharp tagged on social media." She tapped a finger to her chin. "Also great publicity for the inn. Totally the vibe I'm going for."

"I wasn't going to fight him," Cam said, although he realized he couldn't say that for sure. In the blurry months after Dana's accident, he'd come home late at night from a bar with a black eye or bloody knuckles more often than not. He'd even been banned for a time from one local pub, a low point in a season of low moments.

He'd gotten his drinking and his temper under control. Mostly because he stayed away from both booze and people.

"I'm opening an inn that will cater to out-of-town visitors and destination weddings." Emma spoke slowly, and Cam couldn't tell if she was trying to keep hold of her emotions or she thought he was truly too dense to understand. "I can't have bad publicity."

"You said you trusted me," Cam answered. Was that

disappointment in his dark gaze? Could her words really mean that much to him?

"I trust you to do the work." She nodded. "You have yet to prove you can keep your head in the game when challenges arise. I hope you can, Cam. This is important to me. I'm putting everything I have into the inn."

He went from vulnerable to defensive with one quick blink. "You shouldn't trust me, Emma. I'm not going to earn it. I don't want to earn it. Today was a good reminder for both of us." His chest rose and fell like he was struggling for air. "I'll get the renovation done, better than Larry Sachs ever could. Don't count on me for anything else." He turned and stalked away.

She watched him go, wondering what in the world she'd taken on. Her mother had always warned Emma about her penchant for rescuing wounded creatures. It's why the foundation had expanded its reach to both animal rescue organizations and a host of other community agencies once Emma came on board. Caring for people was her passion and she believed it would translate to the work as an innkeeper.

She'd also learned a hard lesson about trusting people other than herself, both thanks to her ex-husband and because of her mother turning her away. Cam hadn't agreed to work on the inn for her benefit. They weren't a team. He was a man who'd be a part of her life for a short season and then he could crawl back to the solitary existence he seemed to be so attached to.

She got in the car just as the first tear fell. Oh, just what she needed. A round of crying to cap off an already horrible day. She glanced at her watch and realized it was nearly five o'clock. She'd be returning home to an empty house and a freezer stocked with frozen dinners and very little else. What in the world did she truly know about creating something from nothing? She'd had everything in life handed to her. She wanted to be tough and independent, but what if she wasn't built for it?

As she drove out of town, she suddenly braked and turned her car into an angled parking space in front of the local bar. The feeling of being alone at the moment was just too much to handle.

Her entire life was too much.

Emma swiped a hand across her cheek as she walked through the heavy oak door. Despite the bright sunlight still hovering overhead and the thick humidity of the summer afternoon, the bar was cool and dark with its paneled walls and neon beer signs hanging above every booth.

She could forget herself here. Forget everything for a few minutes. The only problem was those problems would still be waiting when she finished. There was no getting rid of them.

The whole truth was she didn't want to get rid of them. At least the problems she faced now were her own, unlike the expectations from her mom and the betrayal of an ex-husband.

Those twin thoughts made her pause. Maybe she wasn't doing too bad, after all. She had a start and a plan and a whole heap of determination. What did it matter if some grumpy man didn't appreciate her? Emma hadn't come to Magnolia to worry about a man.

"What can I get you?" the bartender asked. He wasn't the same older man she'd come to know and eyed her with one brow raised as he dried a pint glass.

She opened her mouth to order, then quickly shut it and shook her head. "I don't belong here," she said, more to herself than him.

"You need directions?" he asked with a frown.

"No," she told him with a renewed sense of purpose. "I know the way home."

CHAPTER EIGHT

DESPITE THEIR ARGUMENT, Cam had shown up the following morning with the tool belt Emma was coming to appreciate more every day slung low on his hips and a truck bed full of roofing materials and lumber. He'd worked all day with barely a break and had given her a list of tasks to handle, which she couldn't help but notice kept her far away from him on the property.

Phil Wainright had stopped by, as well, and Cam was kind and deferential to the older man, obviously taking care to make him feel useful while being respectful to Phil's age and what he could handle.

Cam seemed surprised when Emma offered him coffee and a muffin, but she just shrugged and offered a smile. It was true she'd given him a wide berth when he first started the job. In a way, she owed him now more than ever. Their moment-of-truth conversation had forced her to take a long look at her current situation and given her a new resolve to make the plan she had for reinventing her life a success.

Holly came by several times to review wedding plans, and Emma promised the bride-to-be that everything was on schedule for the food and flowers as well as the rooms where Brett's family would stay during the festivities. Those assurances weren't lies. Not exactly. She had yet to track down Angi Guilardi, but after a disappointing conversation with the caterer Meredith had mentioned, Emma was determined to convince Angi to help.

Tiny pangs of guilt plagued her for agreeing to work with a florist in the next town over instead of the local flower shop, but the woman had been so kind, unlike the gruff man she'd spoken to when she called In Bloom, the florist located in downtown Magnolia. Maybe down the road she'd give him a try, but at the moment she had all the grumpy masculine energy she could handle in her life.

She took a break from the list of tasks Cam had left for her to help Holly address and mail the invitations, complete with an insert highlighting the Wildflower Inn's amenities that Emma planned to offer. Nothing like a bit of advanced advertising to motivate her to keep moving forward.

Emma's spine buzzed with nerves as they dropped the last of the invitations into the mailbox outside the local post office.

"When are we going to meet with the caterer?" Holly asked, rubbing her hands together. "Brett's mom is such a food snob. I don't want her to be disappointed." Her smile, which seemed to be permanently affixed to her face, wavered slightly. "Of course she'll be disappointed because it's me, but the fewer reasons I can give her to complain, the better."

"I'm working on that," Emma promised, keeping her tone bright.

"That doesn't sound good."

"It's all good, and trust me, I know how to impress hoity-toity society mavens. My mother is practically the president of that particular club."

Holly gave a shaky nod. "Brett's coming to visit next weekend, so it would be great if we could do a tasting and introduce him to the florist and go over the details and timeline for the ceremony and reception."

"Wait, what?" Emma blinked. "You didn't mention a trial run. I'm not sure we're ready for all of those sit-downs."

"Can we get ready?" Holly clasped her hands together as her tone took on a hysterical edge. "His mom has been trying to convince him to change the venue. She put a de-posit on a five-star resort outside of the capital. She sent me all the particulars last night."

"A deposit?" Emma glanced from Holly to the mailbox, then back again. "We just mailed over a hundred invitations for a wedding here in Magnolia. Don't you think you and Brett and his mom should be on the same page?"

Holly swallowed. "As a matter of fact, she's coming, too."

"Next weekend?" Emma sucked in a breath. "Mitsy Car-michael is coming to Magnolia?"

"I might have told her she could stay in one of the rooms in the inn."

"What inn?"

"The Wildflower, of course."

Emma felt stunned by that piece of news. "Holly, you were there this morning. The kitchen is torn apart, and most of the furniture I have left is pushed up against a wall and covered in tarps. How am I supposed to host guests, let alone one with Mitsy Carmichael's reputation? That would be like inviting my mother to stay."

"I like that idea." Holly gave an enthusiastic nod. "I men-tioned to Mrs. Carmichael that my wedding planner was the granddaughter of Duffy Howard. She seemed slightly mollified."

"But she put a deposit on a different venue."

"It's refundable," Holly said with a smile. "I'm sure once she's here and sees everything and tastes the food…"

"The food," Emma repeated numbly. Right. She'd told Holly that she'd already booked the caterer as well as convincing Mariella Jacob to design the gown. None of those were true, but Emma figured she had time. Not a lot, of course, and even less with the prospect of actual guests arriving at the inn in a week.

"Speaking of food, I need to grab some lunch. I'll mention the plan for your future mother-in-law's visit to Angi. I'm sure it will be fine with her."

"Do you want company?"

"No," Emma blurted. "I mean, if you want to come…"

Holly glanced at her watch. "I need to get back to the salon. Julie Martindale is coming in for French tips at noon. I might invite her to the bridal shower. Did you know she sells adult toys as her side hustle?"

Emma hid her smile. She'd met the older woman at her first town business owners' meeting. "I had no idea," she admitted. "Commercial banker by day, erotic salesperson by night. That's a heck of a résumé. But I'd keep her away from Mitsy. I'm not sure Brett's mom wants that much information about your plans for her son."

"Good point." Holly leaned in for a quick hug. "See, this is why you're so good at being a planner. You think about every detail."

Emma pasted on a smile that dimmed as soon as Holly walked away. Now was the time for her to get it together. She needed to live up to Holly's belief in her.

She drove downtown and walked into Il Rigatone, careful to check which section Angi was waiting tables in before taking a seat.

There was a decent crowd for lunch and the scent of tomato sauce and garlic wafted from the kitchen. The hostess placed a one-page lunch menu in front of Emma, which consisted mainly of classic Italian fare, simple pasta dishes and a variety of calzones and sandwiches. Tasty but not exactly food that she would expect to serve at an upscale wedding reception.

Carrie had seemed sure Angi would be the perfect person to cater her events and help with food at the inn, so Emma kept that in mind. In addition to stopping by and being sent away by Angi's mother, Emma had left several messages in the restaurant's voice mail, all of which had been ignored.

She should probably take a hint. There were several other catering companies that had popped up during a late-night internet search. But she had a gut feeling about Angi.

She just hoped her gut wasn't steering her wrong.

"Can I start you with something to drink?"

Emma looked up to find Angi staring down at her. She must have approached the table while Emma was lost in thought.

"Iced tea, please," Emma said with a smile.

"Got it. Do you need a minute or are you ready to order?"

Angi was efficient and smiled, but it didn't reach her eyes.

"Everything looks delicious," Emma answered. "What's your favorite?"

"The chicken parm panini is a crowd pleaser."

"This is your family's restaurant, right?" Emma asked casually, still studying the menu.

"Yes." She heard Angi's deep sigh. "The recipes have been passed down from previous generations of the Guilardi family in northern Italy."

"But you want to try something new?" Emma glanced

up to find the other woman's eyes wide with shock, like she couldn't believe Emma recognized that in her.

"You're the one."

"That sounds ominous. Unless you mean the one like a fairy godmother or something like that."

Angi's dark eyes narrowed. "The one who upset my mother by making her think I was going to leave the restaurant and go out on my own."

"I didn't realize it was a secret," Emma answered. "Carrie mentioned that you—"

"Carrie's wrong," Angi interrupted. "I'm happy here. My parents have been good to me. They gave my son and me a home when we needed one. My father passed away at the beginning of the year. I can't break my mother's heart all over again. You don't understand how it is."

Emma felt a sudden thread of allegiance with Angi. "I understand exactly how it is. I'm not certain my mother will ever speak to me again because of the choices I've made in my life. But it's *my* life." She placed her menu on the red-and-white-checked tablecloth and leaned forward. "It's your life, Angi. At least have a conversation with me to know whether what I'm thinking matches what you might want."

She saw the other woman's breath hitch as hope flared in her gaze, but Angi gave a small shake of her head. "I'll get that panini going, and we'll have your drink to the table right away."

Without waiting for an answer, Angi turned and hurried toward the kitchen. A minute later, another waitress brought Emma's iced tea over, and a few minutes after, the hostess delivered the panini. Angi continued to wait on the tables around Emma and managed to do it without making eye contact with Emma even one time.

She ate her lunch, which was amazing, and forced herself to come up with an alternative plan. Her gut had led her down a dead-end path. She'd allowed herself to indulge in the fantasy of building a business with like-minded women who shared her desire to create something for herself.

She should have learned to stick to the practical plan. Keep it simple. Not bite off more than she could chew.

Pushing away the plate with the half-eaten sandwich, she tried to stem the tide of platitudes circling through her mind.

There was no reason to be so disappointed that Angi Guilardi had no interest in working with her, let alone having a conversation. The stand-in waitress took her credit card, and Emma left a hefty tip along with her phone number and a note on the receipt for Angi to call if she changed her mind.

If there was one thing Emma didn't like to do, it was admitting failure.

A heavy breeze gusted through downtown, like having hot-oven air blown at her, as she unlocked her car. She'd go home and start calling other potential caterers, although she hated the thought of telling Holly her plan hadn't worked.

"Why do you want me?"

She turned to see that Angi had followed her out of the restaurant. She stood on the sidewalk in her uniform of a black shirt and pants and a green apron with Il Rigatone printed on the front, hands on her hips and posture rigid like she was readying herself for a fight.

"I'm not sure exactly," Emma admitted. "Carrie mentioned you to me, and I got a feeling. A gut instinct that said we'd make a good team. It's stupid. I don't even know that you can cook."

"I can cook." Angi spoke the words like a challenge.

"Well, I hope you convince your mom to give you a

chance to show it. I know I had to sacrifice a lot to get the chance I wanted."

Angi reached into the pocket on the front of her apron and pulled out her order pad. She scribbled something on it, then ripped off the top piece of paper and handed it to Emma. "This is my address. Be there at six tomorrow night for dinner. My kid will be joining us after soccer practice. Plan for casual, but you'll get an idea of what I can do. And then we can talk in detail about what you want from me."

Emma took the slip of paper and fought down the urge for a fist bump. It was ridiculous. She knew next to nothing about Angi or her culinary skills, but somehow just being invited to dinner felt like a win.

Which spoke volumes about Emma's lack of a social life, if nothing else.

"I'll be there at six," she promised, but before the words were even out of her mouth, Angi was walking back into the restaurant.

Emma tucked the address into her purse and headed for home, hope blooming in her chest like a bright sunrise.

THE FOLLOWING AFTERNOON, Cam paused in the act of soldering a copper pipe and listened for a few seconds to the sound of pounding coming from the floor below. He blew out a breath and straightened, dreading the conversation he was about to have with Phil Wainright.

As much as Cam appreciated that the older man wanted to feel useful and relevant, Cam was scared to death Phil might end up doing more harm than good—especially to himself. He'd insisted on getting up on a ladder yesterday. Minutes later, Cam had heard a crash. Phil had missed a step coming down, but luckily caught himself and it was just the drill he carried that had clattered to the hard concrete.

Cam knew from Lily it had been about a year since Phil's hip replacement. The last thing he wanted was to have the older man hurt on this job.

He rushed down the steps and realized the noise was coming from the powder room situated off a small sitting area. Yes, one wall still needed to be ripped out due to the water damage that side of the house sustained, but Cam was supposed to handle the messy jobs.

An ornery, stubborn old man was just one more headache in Cam's long list of reasons why being a solitary fishing guide was a much easier career path at this point.

He stopped in his tracks as he came around the corner of the hallway to see a shapely pair of denim-clad legs bending over just inside the bathroom doorway. His heart pounded and unwanted desire coursed through his veins at the sight of those curves.

Emma straightened, and his attention was riveted on a lock of hair that escaped her high ponytail and rested against her elegant neck. He felt rooted to the spot as she swung the sledgehammer overhead and then slammed it into the wall with a guttural shout.

The yell and the spray of drywall snapped Cam out of his strange trance. "What the hell are you doing?" he demanded as he moved forward.

Emma either didn't hear him or chose to ignore him, because she lifted the sledgehammer again. He grabbed it, but she didn't let go. Instead, she turned and shoved at his chest.

He stumbled over the pieces of broken drywall littering the tile floor but kept hold of the wooden handle. Emma followed him and ended up plastered against the front of him. The scent of her citrus shampoo mixed with a bit of drywall dust was a strangely heady combination, and he wished he didn't notice how good her body felt against his.

"What in the world..."

He released the sledgehammer to try to regain his balance by grabbing onto the sink, but Emma let go at the same time as him and then let out a yelp of pain and crumpled more fully against him.

Cam muttered a curse as he lifted her up and out of the bathroom. The heavy tool had fallen onto her foot, and much to his bafflement and irritation, she was wearing flip-flops.

"Who wears sandals while doing demolition?" he asked against her ear, but realized she had earbuds tucked in them. He plucked one out and started to repeat the question.

"I heard you," she said quietly, her voice tight with pain. "Put me down. I'm fine."

He hated that she was in pain, even if it was her own fault.

Carefully he deposited her on the sofa in the sitting room that had been covered with an old sheet to protect it during the repairs. He dropped to his knees in front of her and took her foot in his hands.

She tried to yank it away but he held tight. "Do you think you broke it?"

"No, but it hurts. Let go. I need to grab ice."

He rose. "Stay," he commanded, holding out his hand, palm forward.

"I'm not your pet," she countered.

"I'm well aware. Toby has more sense than you."

She shifted like she wanted to get up and stalk away. As soon as she tried to put weight on her foot, she winced.

"Just please stay here," he said, making his voice gentler.

"Maybe I will," she grumbled and looked away.

He got a plastic bag and filled it with ice. When he returned, Emma was leaning back on the sofa cushions, her creamy throat exposed. He could see the pulse at the base of her throat and his mouth went dry.

"Here's the ice," he said, so loud that she startled.

"No need to shout," she said, blinking. She reached out a hand. "Thank you."

"You're welcome." Instead of handing it to her, he crouched down and placed the bag of ice on the top of her foot.

She hissed out a breath and her leg jerked. "Easy, there." He placed a hand on the back of her ankle. "For the record, you need closed-toe shoes and safety goggles the next time you think about knocking down walls."

"I'll remember that," she said through clenched teeth.

"Why were you in that bathroom, anyway?"

"I was happy."

He frowned. "Not many people express their happiness with a sledgehammer. I more often find it helpful to take out frustration or anger on an innocent wall."

"I wanted to feel productive," she said with a shrug. "I have a great dinner date tonight, and I'm excited. I thought if I got something done around the inn that would help my nerves and make me even happier."

"A dinner date," Cam repeated, sitting back on his haunches and doing his best to keep from scowling. "That is exciting."

"You have no idea." She shifted and placed her foot on the floor. She leaned forward, so close her hair tickled his arm.

He couldn't resist reaching out and tucking it behind one ear, brushing a thumb over her cheek, which was covered by an adorable layer of dust.

No. Dust wasn't adorable.

This woman had just told him she had a date later. He needed to get up and walk away.

"I think it's better already," she said, her voice slightly breathless. "Thanks for helping. I'll get shoes and safety glasses before tomorrow."

"I'll supply them. You're part of my crew."

One corner of her mouth tipped up. "I'm on a crew. I'm used to being part of a team, but I thought I'd left that behind when I resigned from the foundation."

"Now you're a wolf pack of one."

"So it would seem. I have to admit, I miss it. It's kind of lonely to be on my own all the time."

"Yeah," he said, lifting his gaze until he was looking deep into her honey-colored eyes. She had a smattering of freckles across the bridge of her nose and a tiny birthmark on one earlobe. "I get that. I understand how it feels—like hell."

Her white teeth tugged on her bottom lip. His gut tightened. "But neither of us is alone anymore," she told him.

"We're not," he said, and without waiting for an answer, he leaned in and pressed his mouth to hers. She was as soft as he imagined, and the moan that escaped her drove him absolutely wild with need.

Desire pummeled him from all sides, washing through him fast and hard like a flash flood. He could lose himself in this moment, in this woman.

It should be impossible because he was already lost. He'd been rudderless for so long that he'd stopped bothering to look for a harbor. He'd given up feeling anchored and leaned into the dismal weight of his sorrow.

Emma Cantrell could be his anchor.

The thought of that, and what it would mean, had him

pulling back. He straightened and took a step away from her like she was an electric wire that would shock him if he touched her.

In many ways, she already had.

"Keep the ice on your foot and take a couple of ibuprofen to help with the swelling," he told her.

She blinked up at him, her gaze heavy-lidded with the same desire he felt, her mouth pink and nearly irresistible. So for good measure, because this moment was a mistake, he added, "What I'm doing here isn't a lark. I've got enough to deal with babysitting Phil most days—I can't worry about you, too."

Her gaze cleared and he could have kicked himself for being a jerk. Still, he continued. "If you can't take it seriously, stay out of the way."

"I take it seriously," she said, her voice low.

"Good. Have fun on your date." He hurled the words like they could hurt her as much as they did him and then stalked away.

CHAPTER NINE

EMMA KNOCKED ON the door of Angi's apartment at exactly six. After the unsettling moment with Cam, she'd thought about canceling tonight's plans, not sure if she was emotionally equipped to handle another potentially strange encounter.

The universe seemed to be giving her constant messages as far as taking chances and trying new things. The overriding lesson slapped her down like a reminder it wasn't worth the effort.

At this point, she was fueled by stark grit and little else. She'd always thought of herself as even-keeled, keeping her cool no matter what life threw at her. Turned out that was because for most of her life she hadn't faced much real hardship.

How pathetic for the poor little rich girl to whine about Mommy's expectations and a few months of struggle.

She'd just started to turn away, assuming Angi had changed her mind, when the door opened.

"Not one for patience?" Angi wore a pair of khaki shorts and a sleeveless shirt in a muted pattern. She was tall, beautiful and looked like she would just as soon kick Emma in the shin as feed her a meal.

"I shouldn't have forced you into this," Emma said with a shake of her head. "If you're content working at your family's restaurant—"

"I'm not," Angi answered tightly. "*Content* isn't a word I'd use to describe myself for a long time. You didn't force me to do anything. You're a sign."

"A sign?" Emma stepped into the living room of the homey apartment when Angi gestured her forward.

"A reminder that playing it safe isn't getting me anywhere but frustrated and bitter." She smoothed a hand through her dark hair. "I'm too young to be a bitter old woman."

Emma sighed. "I don't know. I might be more a harbinger of disappointment. After your invitation today I felt like I was on the right track and then it all went to…" She pointed to her foot, which was still swollen, although less painful than it had been. "I dropped a sledgehammer on myself, so if you want to talk about signs…"

Angi let out a low whistle. "We should talk over a glass of wine."

"That I can handle," Emma said with a chuckle.

"Mom, I'm going to ride bikes with Margo."

Emma glanced over to the sofa to see a young boy facing the television, clearly engrossed in whatever video game he was playing.

He was small in stature with thick, dark hair that curled at the ends. His eyes were almost too big for his face, and the smile he gave his mom was adorably impish. Emma liked him immediately.

"I thought you had a stomachache. That's why you couldn't go to soccer practice." Angi frowned as if just realizing she'd been played.

"I feel better now. A lot better."

"Well, it's almost dinnertime. I made my famous stuffed chicken."

"I'll eat when I get home." He flipped off the TV and

stood. "Please, Mom. Margo is leaving tomorrow for two weeks at her grandma's house in Florida. We have to plan what we're each going to do in the Minecraft world while she's gone."

"I guess it's okay," Angi said with a tight smile. "But don't stay out too long. Margo is welcome to eat here if she wants. Before you leave, I'd like to introduce you to our dinner guest. Emma, this is my son, Andrew. Drew, this is Emma..." Angi snorted. "I don't actually know your last name."

"Cantrell." Despite the boy's determination to skip out on dinner, he approached Emma with his hand extended, making eye contact and giving her a firm shake. "It's nice to meet you, Emma." He winked at his mom. "Can I go now?"

"Yes, you little devil." Angi ruffled his hair as he hurried past her. "Make good choices and wear a helmet."

"I always do," he called over his shoulder.

"Nine going on thirty-five," Angi murmured as she led Emma into the small kitchen. She pulled out a chair at the compact oak table. "Do you prefer red or white?"

"White," Emma answered, and lowered herself into the seat. "Your son is cute, and he has good manners. That's a credit to you."

"Only on occasion. He's a great kid. I'm lucky."

"He's lucky to live in a town like Magnolia. I grew up in a small town, as well, but I spent a couple of years in DC for graduate school. There aren't a lot of kids these days who can just head out on their bikes and feel safe."

"I was working in New York City the summer I found out I was pregnant." Angi took a bottle of wine from the refrigerator and poured two glasses. "Andrew is the reason I moved back to Magnolia."

"What about his dad?" Emma asked, then grimaced.

"Sorry, we should probably drink first and move to the awkward personal questions later."

"I can handle that one sober." Angi placed a glass in front of Emma, then slid into the chair across from her. "He owned the restaurant where I worked. I made the mistake of thinking our relationship meant more to him than it did. He wanted me to end the pregnancy, and when I refused he ended things."

"That's rough."

"He wasn't worth it."

"Does he have a relationship with Andrew now?"

Angi took a long sip of wine. "No, but he's well on his way to becoming a restaurant and real estate mogul. His career is thriving, and for all I know, he doesn't even remember he has a son. Andrew has my last name. We're a team. I'm not interested in letting any other man into my life."

"I hear you." Emma tried not to think about the gentle kiss Cam had given her earlier. She needed him to do a job, not to do her. She clinked her glass against Angi's and then took a drink. The wine was crisp and refreshing, but she could feel her cheeks heating.

"Oh, you have a story," Angi said as she grinned. "I'd bet money it involves a man."

"No man," Emma said, hoping she sounded convincing. "I'm divorced."

"A rebound, then?"

"Definitely not." Emma thought about the weekend with an innocent fling that had been the beginning of the end of the life she knew. "My only focus is opening the Wildflower Inn and hosting a wedding worthy of a US senator."

The timer on the stove dinged, and Angi held up one elegant finger. "Now I'm intrigued, so hold that thought."

As she opened the oven door the scent of roasting garlic and spices filled the small space. "What did you make?"

"Something wonderful," Angi murmured as she ground fresh pepper over the roasting pan. "It's chicken stuffed with garlic and a goat cheese sauce, which I consider my signature dish. Mac and cheese from a box is my signature dish if you ask my son, but this is a wee bit more impressive."

"I'm good at cinnamon rolls and breakfast quiches," Emma said. "But I can't serve those to wedding guests. Can I help with anything?"

"Drink more so you feel like spilling the dirt on whatever had you blushing earlier. Other than talking with moms at school functions or customers at the restaurant, I don't get out much."

Emma watched as Angi plated the food. She handled the pieces of chicken like each serving was precious to her. After adding a sprinkling of shaved parmesan and fresh parsley, Angi carried two plates to the small table.

"This beats mac and cheese." Emma's stomach growled. The food looked as delicious up close as it smelled.

"Unless you're a nine-year-old boy." Angi rolled her eyes. "I shouldn't give him grief when he's not here to give it back to me. He enjoys it when I make special meals. It just doesn't happen often."

"You must be incredibly busy as a single mom."

Angi sighed. "Yes, but that's not the reason I don't cook. I would never change the decision I made to leave the city and have my son, but when I'm in the kitchen it's a reminder of everything I left behind. Things I used to love."

"But you work in a restaurant." Emma paused with a forkful of food halfway to her mouth. The yearning in Angi's voice spoke to her on a soul-deep level.

"Waitressing at Il Rigatone has nothing to do with my abandoned dreams. Maybe when I first got back here I thought my parents might let me make some changes, but they made it clear that the restaurant worked fine the way it had for years. When Dad died, my mom became more committed to holding on to every tradition and recipe that invoked his memory."

"I understand parental expectations and family legacies," Emma said. She took a bite, the tastes exploding on her tongue. The chicken was tender, with a bit of tang from the lemon and a complementary saltiness thanks to the capers. "Your food is magic," she said when she'd swallowed. "People would line up around the block for this. Not that the panini wasn't great, but you have a gift."

"Flattery isn't going to make me agree to whatever you want." Angi wiggled her eyebrows. "Although I appreciate you trying."

"What's your dream?" Emma asked, taking another bite of the scrumptious meal.

"I'm a mom. All of my dreams involve Andrew's dreams coming true."

"I don't believe that." Emma shook her head. "I used to think my dreams had to include the things my husband wanted, too. He was my whole world. Marrying him was the first choice I ever made without my mom's approval."

"Some sort of white-collar rebel?" Angi guessed. "You have the scent of old money all over you."

Emma scrunched up her nose, thinking about the fact that Cam had made a similar assessment of her. "Why do people think that? I'm normal."

"So is every other high-class heiress," Angi countered. "When she's in the Hamptons or at some sort of society luncheon. Not in a place like Magnolia."

"I need to fit in. I *want* to fit in."

"Not really. People might get a kick out of a fallen princess scrubbing the toilets. Very fairy-tale kind of stuff."

"I don't want to be part of a fairy tale."

"Tell me about the prince who turned out to be a frog."

"He's a history professor," Emma said quietly. "Leather patches on the elbows of his tweed sweater and everything. Not the rebel you imagine, but also not the man my mom wanted me to marry. He didn't exactly fit into how she pictured my future. Turns out, I should have listened to her."

"It's the worst when moms are right."

Emma placed her fork on the table, her appetite suddenly vanished. "You don't know the half of it. I had a bit of a breakdown during my divorce. Mostly alone at night, but it ended up seeping into the rest of my life. Eventually, after I visited Magnolia and fell in love with Niall Reed's old house, I quit my job working for my family's foundation. I walked away from everything I knew."

"It's an impressive property. The guy was a character, that's for sure. He loved my mom's fried eggplant. One time he got a craving for it on Christmas Day. She left in the middle of our dinner to open up the restaurant for him because he insisted on it. I never liked him after that."

"I don't blame you."

"So how does your mom feel about this new chapter in your life?"

"I'm pretty sure I'm dead to her," Emma said, trying to sound like she was making a joke. Too bad her voice caught on the last word. She drained her wineglass and got up from the table to refill it.

"My mom helped me when I had no one else," Angi murmured. "I'm not sure how I would have managed to raise Andrew on my own without the support of my family. I owe her my loyalty."

"You owe your son the role model of a happy mom," Emma said as she turned from the counter. "You owe it to yourself to be happy." She took another slug of wine. "To be honest, I'm talking as much to myself as to you. And to be even more honest…" She held up her wineglass. "I didn't think this would be so hard. Lorelai Gilmore always made it look fun, even when she was going through the difficult times. She'd crack a joke or do some late-night pizza eating and all would be right with the world."

"What made you think real life was like a television show?" Angi asked with a snort.

"Hope and desperation in equal measure." Emma carried her wineglass, along with the bottle, back to the table.

"Relatable. I've got an excess of both of those."

"I can give you a chance for something new," Emma said quietly. "If you'll take a chance on me."

Angi fisted her hands on top of the table. "What guarantee do I have that this will work? I have to take care of my kid. I don't have the money to devote to some pipe dream."

"The inn will be a success because it's my only option," Emma said, letting every ounce of conviction she felt infuse her tone. "Trust me, I didn't exactly plan for my mom to cut me off when I told her I was moving to this town. I certainly didn't expect a hundred-year storm to destroy most of the repairs I made on the house and push back the opening of the inn. I can guarantee the bride I'm working with didn't think the owners of the venue she'd initially rented would take off with her money when things went south."

She leaned forward, palms flat on the tablecloth. "This is going to work because I don't have a choice but to make it work. Everyone around here might think I look like some

kind of high-society pampered princess, but that's not me."
She shook her head. "Not anymore."

"That's a regular *Steel Magnolias* speech," Angi murmured, sitting back in her chair. "Although I'm not sure what it has to do with me."

"I know I'm asking you to take a chance. Heck, I don't even know exactly what a partnership should look like. But we can make this work together. I have a good feeling about you and me."

"I'd control every part of the catering side of the business," Angi said with a speculative gleam in her eye. "From menu options to how we source ingredients to pricing."

"Done." Emma felt her heartbeat start to speed up. She hated giving up control over anything, but at this point she needed people she could trust running the catering and reception details while she concentrated on the inn and advertising for events. The ceremony piece might be all about true love and the vows and the dress, but guests wanted good food and great music at a reception.

"Seriously?" Angi gave her a disbelieving stare. "I've made one meal for you. I might be a total loose cannon. You don't even know if you can trust me."

Right. "But I do trust you," Emma said definitively. "I trust my instinct about you. I have to start trusting myself again."

"Then we've got a deal." Angi held out a hand and it felt right to shake it.

The front door opened with a bang, and Andrew came flying in. "I'm ready for dinner," he shouted.

Emma glanced toward the window, surprised to see that shadows fell across the trees outside. The time spent with Angi had flown by and gave Emma a renewed sense of hope. One that was only dashed slightly when she straightened from the table and put weight on her foot. Yes, she'd made a silly mistake earlier wielding a heavy tool in her sandals. But enthusiasm wasn't the worst trait in the world.

"Come by the inn tomorrow and you can meet Holly and tell me what you'll need in the kitchen." She met Angi's gaze and appreciated the hope she saw there. "This is going to be good."

SATURDAY AFTERNOON, CAM pulled his boat into the dock near the edge of the marina and helped the family who'd chartered him as a guide for the day out onto dry land.

It had been a great day on the water. The older couple and their teenage son were curious, kind and respectful of Cam's time and effort. The man clearly had experience with deep-sea fishing, something that was rare but made Cam's job far easier.

They'd reeled in over a dozen fish, and he'd listened to the kid's plans for college in the fall. The boy's mother had teared up on several occasions when discussing the prospect of being an empty nester. It made Cam think about his parents, and for the first time in ages he had the urge to reach out to them.

He knew he'd broken his mom's heart with how he'd distanced himself after Dana's death. It had just been too difficult to let himself be loved by anyone at that point. He had no doubt his parents, like everyone else in his life, understood Dana married down when she chose Cam as a life partner. Then she'd died on her way to the second job she'd taken to support him. No justice in the world could explain the unfairness of that.

"We'll plan another trip to the area once Justin leaves for school," Kevin, the husband, told his wife, wrapping an arm around her shoulders. "It will be like a second honeymoon. Rose petals and champagne and whatever you want."

"Gross," the teenager said with a good-natured eye roll. "You are making me want to leave right now."

"Not yet," his mother said with a sniff.

"Don't worry, Mom." Justin grinned. "I'll still make the three-hour drive to bring home my laundry." The kid's phone buzzed and he wandered down the dock as he returned the message.

"I can't offer much in the way of rose petals, but call me if you want to book another fishing trip." Cam really would be happy to have the couple on his boat again. He didn't usually talk so much with clients, but this family made it easier. Or perhaps Cam's small steps back into the real world were already changing him. "I'll supply the champagne."

"We'll take you up on that," Kevin told him.

"I do love this area," the woman, Connie, murmured, glancing around. Cam saw the area through her eyes—the charming marina surrounded by lush trees and a wide expanse of grass where a few younger kids played a game of pickup soccer. "I'd love to explore the town a bit, as well. Are there any cute hotels you'd recommend? I'm going to need all the distraction I can get once Justin is gone."

"There's a new place opening in town in a few weeks. It's called the Wildflower Inn, and I'm helping out with some last-minute renovations. They have a website if you want to see photos," he added even though he didn't know if Emma *had* a website. He assumed she would. "It's a great bet for a romantic weekend away. They also host weddings, so you can keep that in mind down the road when Justin finds that special someone."

His heart hammered in his chest. Kevin and Connie

didn't seem to notice, but Cam felt like a fool spewing out endorsements about Emma's place like he was some sort of human billboard.

"We'll check it out. Thank you." Connie smiled at him. "I hope we have some time with Justin, but my niece just got engaged and I know they were hoping for a destination wedding on the coast. This might be a great fit."

"Yeah," he agreed, amazed at how easily this stranger accepted his suggestions, like he was some kind of expert.

He'd been thinking about the inn and Emma all day. She'd been avoiding him since the kiss they'd shared, which might have more to do with him acting like a jerk. Not that he blamed her, but he didn't like it. He'd finished the drywall repairs and redoing some of the electrical and plumbing details that hadn't been taken care of in the first place. He had an electrician scheduled to come out next week to go over everything, but he'd had fishing trips booked the past two days so hadn't made it there. He still figured he was ahead of schedule, and he reminded himself that the project at the inn was just a temporary blip on the radar. The fishing charters were his life now.

Yet even after a couple days away, he missed the scent of sawdust and the weight of the tool belt around his hips.

The couple spoke to him for a few more minutes, then headed out with a recommendation for a lunch spot in downtown Magnolia. Cam stayed on the boat to clean things up.

"Aren't you turning into a regular Team Magnolia player?"

Cam glanced up from securing the trolling rods to see the town's mayor, Malcolm Grimes, staring down at him. Despite the heat and humidity, Mal wore his normal summer uniform of a seersucker suit, bow tie and straw hat. The pale blue of his button-down shirt only deepened the burnished brown hue of his mahogany-colored skin.

Mal had been a fixture in Magnolia for as long as Cam could remember. In fact, the older man was good friends with Cam's father.

"Il Rigatone has the best sandwiches in town," Cam said with a shrug. "It's not exactly a secret."

"You also recommended the Wildflower Inn and even pitched it as a wedding venue. Does Emma have you on retainer?"

"Very funny," Cam said without laughing. He didn't like being called out on trying to help, even by Magnolia's well-meaning mayor. "What can I do for you, Mal? Interested in a fishing trip?"

The mayor's deep laugh reverberated across the water. "Not until my grandkids are old enough to join me. I wanted to check in with you, Camden. A lot of people were hit hard by the storm. There are unscrupulous business owners around here that will take advantage of unsuspecting residents to bilk them out of insurance money or make an out-of-proportion profit to get repairs done in a timely manner."

"Do you think I'm taking advantage of Emma?" Cam asked, stepping from the boat onto the dock and straightening to his full height. As a kid, he remembered Malcolm as an imposing, larger-than-life figure, but now Cam towered over him.

"Don't get your boxer briefs in a bunch." Mal held out his hands. "It's good that you're the one helping her. I try not to stick my nose in where it doesn't belong, but Emma traded up with the quality of her contractor. The town needs more places like the Wildflower Inn and what she's trying to build with her business. So I'm glad to see you involved." The older man took off his hat and lowered it to his side. "I'm glad to see you making an effort."

Cam felt his jaw tighten. "Do you know why I'm doing it?"

"I saw Dave Adams the other day. He told me about the issues Holly had with the beach property she booked for her wedding. Explained that she'd switched her venue to Niall's old house."

"He and Karen don't know I'm involved."

"They aren't going to hear it from me," Mal promised. "Although it's past time you put the tragedy of the past behind you."

"Dave and Karen have every reason to hate me. I'm not doing this to try to mend fences. Holly needed help, and I'm helping."

"Your parents' house was hit pretty hard, as well."

Cam sucked in a breath. "How hard?"

Mal shrugged. "A tree came down onto the garage and they lost a couple of windows in the house. Luckily they were in the basement. Ash tried to set them up with a construction crew, but your dad is proud so he wants to handle things on his own."

"I should be there helping them," Cam muttered. "You forgot to add that part."

"I wasn't going to say that. It's your choice." Mal reached out a hand, but Cam flinched away. "I thought you'd want an update on them just like they appreciated hearing an update on you."

Cam shook his head even as he tried to push away the ache in his heart. "You shouldn't have mentioned me to them." He thought about Connie on the boat that morning and her misty eyes at the thought of her kid going to college. He wanted to punish himself by believing that his parents didn't think of him anymore, but they were good people. Loving parents. After Dana was gone, Cam couldn't stand to accept love or affection from anyone. Not when he regretted the pain he'd caused them.

"I'm doing the work so Holly gets the wedding she wants. That's the only reason." He spoke the words so definitively he almost believed them himself. "I don't know what you expected coming out here, Mal, but I'm sorry you wasted your time."

"You're never a waste of time, Camden." Mal placed the hat on his head once again and took a step back. "I hope someday you'll see that."

CHAPTER TEN

EMMA WAS HALFWAY through entering receipts into her monthly budget spreadsheet later that night when the hammering started. She removed her glasses, which she wore instead of her contacts during long sessions in front of the computer, and inclined her head. She couldn't figure out who would be making that kind of noise so late on a Saturday night.

It was practically dark, and she knew Cam was working as a fishing guide. At least that's what the note he'd left her said.

Taking out clients on Saturday so you won't have to spend time avoiding me.

The snarky tone had made her smile, although she didn't appreciate being called out on her cowardice. That's how she felt, but after the kiss she didn't trust herself to be around him. What if she threw herself at him or something equally embarrassing?

Emma didn't consider herself the type for impulsive gestures—the fact that she'd bought an entire house in an unfamiliar town notwithstanding. But her physical reaction to Cam Arlinghaus was something she'd never experienced and definitely couldn't explain.

As much as her body went onto high alert when he was

around, his presence in the house calmed her tension like nothing else. He was like the human equivalent of a worry stone. She knew that he would never rest until things were on track for the wedding. He was doing it all for Holly, but Emma couldn't help wondering what it would be like to be on the receiving end of that sort of devotion.

When the unmistakable grinding of a power saw split the quiet air, she got up and went to the window. Pulling aside the curtain, she saw Cam in the middle of the backyard, bathed in the glow from an industrial spotlight.

She glanced at her watch. It was nearly nine. There was no way she could let him make that kind of noise in this neighborhood. The houses all had huge, private lots but she wasn't ready to take the risk of aggravating her neighbors before she'd even hosted her first event. There had been no objections to the commercial variance she'd been approved for when she bought the property, but she still wanted to be respectful.

It only took a minute to make her way to the backyard. She padded across the grass, calling his name. When he didn't respond, she looked closer to see orange earplugs stuffed into each of his ears.

Night was quickly closing in around them, the sky turning deeper shades of pink and purple. This was her favorite time of day in Magnolia, when the oppressive heat of summer loosened its hold on the world. If it weren't for the whir of the saw, she'd be able to hear the insects chirping from the woods behind the house. Something about the stillness gave her hope and continually renewed her desire to believe in the path she'd chosen.

Cam clearly didn't share her appreciation for the peace that evening brought. His face, bathed in the glow of the spotlight, was drawn in taught lines, almost as if he were in pain.

Well, he was a pain in her butt.

Emma nearly tripped over the extension cord he'd run from his makeshift workspace to the house, which was the last thing she needed since her foot now felt completely healed. She picked it up and yanked it from the socket. The yard went dark and silent in an instant.

"What the hell…" Cam glanced up from the piece of lumber he was planing. "I'm trying to work here," he shouted, yanking the earplugs from his ears. "Do you mind?"

"I do," Emma said, frowning. She could almost see the tension radiating from him. He looked like a caged animal, and she wasn't sure whether to approach or retreat. "It's nine o'clock on a Saturday," she told him in case he didn't realize.

"You worried about the regular crowd stumbling in?" he shot back.

She nearly grinned as she realized that even with his strange mood, he had the wherewithal to reference the old Billy Joel song. "They shuffle not stumble, but you look like you could use a tonic and gin," she told him.

His lips twitched and he let out a long breath, then shook his head. Those few moments of bantering back and forth had at least taken the edge off whatever he was dealing with, and Emma felt a ridiculous sense of pride she'd done that.

"You're funny," he murmured, and it sounded like a compliment. She took it that way. The fact that her outwardly serious professor ex-husband had accused her of having no sense of humor wasn't lost on Emma. She'd never been the type of person to laugh easily. But that didn't mean she couldn't make a joke.

"What are you doing out here, Cam?" She gestured to his tools and the sawhorses he'd set up.

"I'm building a pergola," he answered, crossing his arms over his broad chest. He wore faded jeans, a gray T-shirt and a baseball cap turned backward on his head.

"How about you save the power tools for daylight hours? I don't want to hack off the neighbors already."

"It's not even loud." He took a pencil from behind his ear, oddly endearing, and marked another piece of lumber. "I would think you'd appreciate my dedication. The sooner I finish the repairs and new projects you and Holly have for me, the sooner you can be rid of me."

"Who said I wanted to be rid of you?" she asked, feeling a blush rise to her cheeks when the words came out on a husky breath.

"If you don't, you should." He gripped the pencil so tightly it suddenly snapped in two. "It's not smart to have me around."

"Did you have somebody get sick on the boat? I don't understand what's put you in this mood."

"Everyone on the boat today was fine. The couple is planning to return to Magnolia for a second honeymoon after their son leaves for college in the fall. I recommended the Wildflower Inn as a place to stay. They might even need a venue for their niece's wedding. And probably a wedding planner."

"You recommended the inn?" Emma's heart squeezed. "And me? Thank you, Cam. I got the impression you thought I wasn't equipped to run an inn or host the kind of events I'm hoping to attract."

"I don't think you fit here," he clarified, and her heart

pinched for another reason. Emma just wanted to find a place where she *would* fit, and she truly believed Magnolia would become her home. It shouldn't matter if this man didn't, but somehow the words still hurt. "But I have no doubt you'll find a way to make the inn work. You'll be a success, Emma. The determination is part of you."

"Why doesn't that sound like a good thing when you say it?"

"It's good. Better than I could be. You take risks to create a life you want for yourself, and I'm still ignoring everything I can and hurting the people I care about in the process."

Her mind whirled as she tried to follow his train of thought. "Who do you think you hurt?" She ran a hand through her hair, wanting to reach out to him but knowing it wasn't her place. "You defended me in the hardware store and you're working your tail off to help Holly with her wedding. Lily called me this morning to say how happy her dad has been coming over here to help. You've given him a purpose again. None of us has been hurt by you."

He shook his head. "I'm to blame for Holly losing her sister, and I know Phil was hurt when I pushed him away after Dana's death. But I don't even need to go that far back to find examples of the way I make a mess of things." His voice was so grim Emma clenched her teeth in response. "I found out today my parents' house was damaged in the storm. A tree fell on it. I didn't even know."

"Was someone injured?"

"No, but the house needs repairs. My dad is like Phil, proud but not as able as he once was. He's insisting on doing the work himself, and he's just not up for it. My brother, the patron saint of good sons everywhere, will step up, but Ash has a lot on his plate. I'm sure he doesn't have time..."

He jabbed two fingers against his chest. "I'm the one who should be there."

"So go to their house." Emma held up her hands. "Cam, we'll work around whatever else you need to do."

"I can't," he whispered, and he sounded so damn miserable that she couldn't help but reach out for him.

His eyes drifted closed as she traced her hand along his face, cupping his strong jaw. Dusk softened the hard lines of his face. He leaned into her with a sigh, like her touch was a cool oasis in some kind of personal hell tormenting him.

"Why?"

His body stiffened, but she moved toward him when he would have moved away. She lowered her hand to his, linking their fingers together. "Tell me, Cam."

"I haven't seen my parents since Dana's funeral. There was a scene. I made a scene."

"It's been five years."

He gave a tight nod. "They tried to reach out because they're good parents. Ash was the only one smart enough to let me go without a fight. I gave Mom and Dad a hell of a fight. I can't go back now."

"You can't go back," she agreed, and he startled at her words. She squeezed his hand. "You can only move forward. I'm sure your parents would want to see you, to hear from you."

"Slaughter the fatted cow and all that." Cam sniffed. "I don't make a good prodigal son."

"Maybe they should be the ones to decide that. Maybe all of you need a chance."

His eyes bored into hers. "I have the life I deserve."

"I think you have a right to more."

His gaze softened, and he swayed closer, like he wanted to believe her but just couldn't allow himself to do it. She understood the need to believe himself not worthy. Less chance of being hurt.

He lifted his gaze, and a small smile played on his lips. "Did you order this little display to distract me on purpose?"

She turned and her breath caught at the shadows that seemed to enfold them as darkness had fallen in earnest. All around them, the air lit up with the flashing glow of fireflies, evoking a sense of wonder and delight. Emma drew in a deep breath.

She realized he'd shifted so he was standing directly behind her. In the stillness of the night, with only the hum of the woods to break the silence, it felt as though they were wrapped in their own private cocoon. It was natural to lean back against him, and she almost sighed in pleasure as he wrapped his arms around her. She craved the closeness and the physical touch.

"The backyard has always been my break. The house got too quiet at night, and just reminded me that I was all alone."

"I'm sure Meredith and your brother would have made adequate companions."

"Ryan and I weren't exactly close growing up. I love him, but we're different people and now he's got this awesome new life and this amazing love story." She wrinkled her nose. "I have a big house that needs work."

"It's going to be just as amazing," he told her, and somehow she believed him. She wanted to believe. She wanted far more than she should from this man. Because of that and because she was so near to being caught up in the moment, she stepped away from his hold. Even though the night remained warm, a chill ran along her skin.

"Right after I bought the house, the backyard bloomed

with what seemed like a million wildflowers. It was beautiful. I came out here every night to sleep." She pointed to the hammock strung up between two oak trees near the corner of the yard. "When I woke up, it was like something out of a dream. There were so many lightning bugs in the yard, all pulsing with different light patterns. As the sun rose, the light caught on the morning dew covering the flowers. It seemed to embody the magic this place represented for me, and I knew I'd call it the Wildflower Inn."

"If you build it…" He waved a hand at the blanket of flowers that surrounded the patio. "They will come."

"The flowers and the fireflies were here first. We used to get lightning bugs in the yard when I was a kid, but never this many."

"Did you trap them in jars and put them on your dresser at night?"

"Only one time," she told him. "I was so sad when I woke up the next morning and the bottom of the mason jar was like a firefly cemetery. I couldn't stand to capture them after that. It seemed like torture."

Cam let out a choked cough, and Emma turned to find him massaging the back of his neck and studying the ground. "Let me guess," she said, holding back a smile. "You smeared their light all over your forehead."

"It wasn't just me." Cam held up his hands. "Everyone in the neighborhood did it. We weren't thinking about torture, just having fun."

"My brother and his friends did the same thing. Now you know better."

"Than to smear insects on my body?" Cam nodded. "Um, yeah."

"You still haven't told me exactly what put you on tonight's overzealous productivity spree."

"A friend of my parents came to see me today," he said quietly. "Have you met Malcolm Grimes?"

"The mayor?" Emma nodded. "He brought me an apple pie his wife made shortly after I moved in."

"She makes the best. Mal and my dad grew up together. Magnolia natives. They've been friends my whole life, and he was just another person I cut off when Dana died. He thought the fact that I'm doing work for you meant something had changed."

"He thought you were changing," Emma murmured, suddenly understanding.

"He was wrong."

"Maybe you don't have to change," she said, stepping toward him again. It was as if she was pulled to him like a magnet. "But give yourself a break, Cam. Everyone makes mistakes."

"Not like mine." He inclined his head. "I bet you never hurt the people you loved the way I have."

"I never loved anyone as much as you seem to have loved your wife." She looked away, thinking about the end of her marriage and all the ugly things she and Martin had said to each other. "And for darn sure no one ever felt that way about me. Everything I know about love is conditional at best. Once I stopped behaving the way people wanted, it was done."

She felt the soft touch of Cam's fingertip under her chin, gently lifting her head until she met his gaze. "You deserve more, too."

Emotions clogged her throat. "I'm fine with fireflies," she lied. "They keep me busy."

"Oh, Emma. The ways I've thought about keeping you busy."

She squeaked out a response. Then his mouth was on

hers, tempting and exploring. He cupped her cheeks between his rough hands, and it was the most erotic thing she'd ever experienced.

Standing in her backyard fully clothed, she couldn't remember ever wanting someone as much as she did Cam.

He deepened the kiss, or maybe that was her and soon it was difficult to tell where she left off and he began.

He lifted her into his arms, and she immediately wrapped her legs around his lean hips. It only took a few long strides before he was lowering her to the outdoor sofa. The fresh scent of the night air combined with Cam's spicy, male scent to make her senses reel and sway.

And all Emma could think about was how right it felt to be sharing this moment with him.

CAM'S BEFUDDLED BRAIN shot up a few valiant warning signals that his body immediately snuffed out. He knew at some deep, rational level that it was wrong to be with Emma in this way, but the rational part of him wanted nothing to do with this moment.

He hadn't come looking for this, of course. He'd only wanted a respite from the loneliness and thoughts of the past that plagued him after Malcolm's visit. Somehow Cam had managed to spend five years safe behind the walls he'd built around his life. He hadn't let anyone in since losing Dana. But now his involvement in Emma's inn had made a tiny crack in his defenses, and it was like his heart had sprung a leak. Need and tenderness pushed their way through, choking him with their power.

How could he believe his parents still wanted to see him after all the pain he'd caused? What could he have to offer? He'd already hurt them in so many ways, been a disappointment in almost every way that counted.

He'd come here tonight to distract himself, but power tools were a lot safer than having Emma in his arms. She made him feel vulnerable in a way he'd forgotten he was able.

She made him want things he'd shoved aside years ago.

But now he was here with her gazing up at him, her eyes cloudy with desire and her lips swollen from his kisses. Even in the dim glow from the porch light, he could see the flush that covered her neck and the bit of her chest exposed from the V-neck cotton shirt she wore.

Damn if he didn't want to make her whole body flush that way.

Unable to stop himself, he lowered his mouth to the base of her throat. Her thrumming pulse made an answering buzz hum through him and he trailed his mouth across her skin. She was so soft and delicate, but he'd seen the foundation of steel that she couldn't quite hide.

She was a study in contrasts, and it fascinated him. She captivated his attention, challenged him with her stubbornness and drove him to distraction. Someone had hurt her, and not just her overbearing, arrogant mother.

Cam didn't know her brother, Ryan, the doctor. He'd asked around, and the guy seemed to be well liked by the locals. He'd taken a job at the community hospital after moving to Magnolia to be with Meredith and also volunteered for the mobile medical unit that worked with underserved pockets of the community. Ryan Sorensen seemed to be a genuinely good person, just like his sister.

Cam would place bets that Emma's ex-husband had been the one to do the real damage. He would have liked to work out some of his frustration on that low-life loser.

Emma should be with someone who made her feel special every day. Cam might not be that man for the long haul, but he could sure as hell make her feel good in the moment.

He'd become a bit of an expert at no-strings-attached pleasure.

She ran her fingers along the muscles of his shoulders and then down his back, her touch trailing fire in its wake. When she tugged at the hem of his T-shirt, he gladly tossed it over his head and onto the flagstone patio. The night air had cooled several degrees, but he continued to feel like he was lit by a fire from the inside out. He kissed her again and the sweetest noises escaped her mouth, somewhere between a sigh and a moan. The sounds stoked the fire inside him even more. He ran his hand up the curve of her hip.

In the distance, the wail of a siren split the evening quiet. Memories came flooding into Cam's mind—a late-night call from his brother on duty at the sheriff's office, the flashing lights on the patrol car, the sound of the ambulance siren as it sped to the hospital. The lights of the emergency room waiting area, the smell of antiseptic, the calm, apologetic words of the doctor.

Cam wrenched away from Emma, up and off the sofa.

He took two steps away and ran a hand through his hair, trying to calm down. Doing his best not to have a complete panic attack in front of her.

"What happened?" Her voice was gentle and he let it soothe him even though he found it difficult to accept that kind of concern from her or anyone.

"I don't want to hurt you," he said, because that was at least part of the truth.

She stood, as well, smoothed a hand down the front of her shirt. "That was the opposite of hurting me," she said with a small smile.

He breathed out a laugh. "I'm only good for now, Emma. I can't be a long-term bet."

"Give me a little credit." She arched a brow. "I'm a big girl, Cam. I understand the difference between physical pleasure and real intimacy. I don't want something serious in my life any more than you do." She gestured to the house. "I already have my hands full, if you know what I mean."

"Yeah," he agreed, then looked past her to the darkness of the yard. But they weren't the same. She was light and possibility and he was just a black pit of emptiness. "I'm going to put the tools away in the shed, then I'll get out of your way."

"Fine." She sounded disappointed in his response, which shouldn't have bothered him, but it did. "Enjoy the rest of your weekend. I'll see you on Monday."

Right. Monday. He had an entire day to get through tomorrow and still wasn't sure he trusted himself.

"Have you ever been fishing?" he asked just as she turned away.

"Not since I was a kid at the pond on my grandpa's farm."

"I'm taking my boat out tomorrow to check out some new spots around the coast. Want to join me?"

Confusion and doubt played across her delicate features. It would be better for both of them if she said no, yet he couldn't stop the rush of relief when she nodded.

"It's an early morning. Be at the marina off the coastal highway at seven."

"Okay," she said. "I'll see you tomorrow."

Hope, Cam understood as Emma walked toward the house, was a blessed and blasted thing.

CHAPTER ELEVEN

EMMA COULDN'T EXPLAIN why she was so excited at the thought of a day spent fishing. She wasn't even sure she'd enjoy catching something wiggly and slimy on a sharp hook. She couldn't quite imagine a world where that was something she'd want to do on purpose.

Okay, who was she kidding? The anticipation fluttering across her belly was solely there because Cam had been the one to invite her. He might be moody and broody, but she liked that she could be herself with him. There was no worry about making the right impression or being judged for some set of arbitrary standards that had nothing to do with her. Maybe the butterflies doing a quick two-step across her midsection were also because his kiss had rendered her senseless on two different occasions.

In the wake of her ex's revelation about the sex tape, Emma's body had seemed to shut down when it came to desire or the need for physical intimacy. The idea that she'd been recorded without her knowledge and understanding she'd been used had cut her to the quick. She'd wanted nothing to do with men after that.

Plus, she'd been so busy walking away from one life and starting on her new path she hadn't had time to consider a dalliance, let alone the possibility of a relationship.

She understood Cam's resistance to the physical spark between them. He was working for her temporarily and the smart thing for both of them would be to keep their distance. But Emma didn't want distance. She wanted to feel, to overcome her hang-ups about sex so she'd be able to truly start over in every aspect of her life.

Not love or long-term commitment. She'd learned too many hard lessons in those areas. Physical pleasure, that was another story.

One she wanted to explore with Cam.

She liked the way he made her feel. Safe, despite all of his warnings about hurting her.

Been there, done that in the hurt department. Emma had no plans to travel that road again.

The sun was bright overhead, and the air smelled like freshly cut grass and salt water as she got out of her car and walked toward the docks. There was a white clapboard house tucked into one side of the cove with a sign advertising coffee and live bait. A small crowd of people congregated out front, most of them obvious locals.

She'd worn a floral-print sundress over her bathing suit and a floppy straw hat but suddenly realized she'd misjudged what boating meant in this part of the Atlantic coast.

There were a number of other women around, almost everyone wearing cutoffs with either tanks or bikini tops and baseball caps.

A few of them darted curious looks her way, and she had the urge to turn around and retreat before Cam saw her and told her she looked—

"You look beautiful."

She whirled to find him standing directly behind her, a fishing rod slung over one shoulder and carrying a large cooler with his free hand. Toby trotted along at his side, and the dog nudged her leg in greeting.

"I don't fit in here." She hated that she'd misjudged the situation so thoroughly.

"Sure you do," he said, one big shoulder lifting and lowering. "You class the place up quite a bit. Let's go."

He moved past her, then looked over his shoulder when she didn't follow. "Take a risk. Be yourself. Stop caring what other people think. I'm not much with the personal development mumbo jumbo, so pick your favorite and hit the repeat button in your brain."

She tried to bite back a snort of laughter. "You need to watch more *Dr. Phil*," she told him as she walked forward.

"I doubt it." He nodded toward the picnic basket she cradled in one arm. "Tell me you brought a better lunch than the day-old sandwiches I was going to buy at the bait shop."

"Way better," she promised.

Her heart seemed to skip a beat when he flashed a full smile. He didn't offer that expansive grin often, which was a good thing because being on the receiving end of it on a regular basis might make her totally smitten.

And she was not going to go all smitten over Cam.

"I have a new set of lures to pick up from Darryl at the front counter." Cam shifted the cooler strap onto his shoulder and reached for her picnic basket. "Would you mind grabbing them? I'll take everything to the boat and get it ready to go."

"Sure." She gave him the basket and headed toward the shop. A woman with mile-long legs and a messy bun of pale blond hair intercepted her as she approached the counter after wading through a few clusters of people.

"I saw you talking to Cam," the woman said, smacking her gum as she gave Emma a long once-over. "You gave him a froofy picnic basket."

"It's lunch," Emma said, wondering why the woman's

words felt like an accusation. She smiled as an older man lifted a brow in her direction.

He wore a faded button-down and a khaki-colored bucket hat with wisps of gray hair curling out from the bottom. "Can I help you, miss?"

"I'm picking up an order for Cam Arlinghaus."

"The poppers and walkers." Darryl nodded. Emma didn't understand what he was saying, but she smiled. "Got them right here. Camden's bound to slay some fish with these bad boys." He pulled a brown paper bag from a shelf behind the counter and handed it to Emma.

"Why are you picking up Cam's order?" the blonde demanded, coming to stand at Emma's side. "You work for him?"

"Not exactly," Emma said, glancing at the woman out of the corner of her eye.

"Give her a break," Darryl told the woman. "I don't need you interrogating my customers, and I'm sure Cam wouldn't appreciate you harassing his new woman."

Emma felt her eyes widen. "I'm not his woman," she said quickly, feeling heat rise to her cheeks. "We're work friends," she said, realizing how strange that must sound to the people who knew him from his job as a fishing guide. "I'm new to town and he's taking me fishing."

The woman gasped, clearly shocked. "No bananas on the boat," she said with a sniff. "Women are like bananas for Cam."

"I have no idea what you're talking about."

"Brandie, go make someone a coffee," Darryl said with a laugh before focusing on Emma. "I'm sure you're not a banana."

"Me, too," Emma said, unnerved by the encounter. Ignoring Brandie, who continued to glare at her, she thanked

Darryl and made her way to the end of the dock where Cam was fiddling with something in one of the compartments.

"Am I a banana?" she asked, staring down at him.

He fastened the latch and met her gaze, confusion muddying his dark gaze. "Did you hit your head between the shop and here?"

"Some leggy blonde in Daisy Dukes called me a banana. She said you don't take bananas on the boat."

He gave a small shake of his head and held out a hand. "You're not a banana."

She still didn't understand what that meant, but his hand grasping hers distracted her enough to forget her nerves. With Cam steadying her, she stepped onto the boat's carpeted hull. Her knees felt weak but she couldn't tell whether it was the gentle roll of the water or his touch causing the sensation.

He lifted the wide brim of her straw hat and bent so they were at eye level. "You are not a banana," he repeated solemnly, and then they both burst out laughing.

"What in the world does that mean?" she asked as she took the seat he indicated. Cam gripped the steering wheel and put the boat into gear, slowly maneuvering away from the dock and out of the cove toward open water.

"It's a superstition," he explained over the hum of the motor. "A banana on the boat brings bad luck for fishing."

"That's silly," she said, thinking about Brandie's words that women on the boat were like bananas for Cam. Surely he'd taken out female clients before. Hadn't he just told her about the couple that was planning their second honeymoon in Magnolia?

"No self-respecting fisherman would knowingly allow a banana on the boat." He glanced at her, then back at the water. "Tell me you didn't pack banana pudding."

"Oatmeal scotchies," she answered. "No bananas. Do you equate women to bananas on your boat, Cam?"

He eased up on the throttle for a moment and the water slapped against the craft as it slowed. "Not exactly. I've taken out plenty of paying clients who were women. Just not anyone on a personal level."

"No girlfriends on the boat?" Emma clarified.

"No girlfriends, period."

"Let me guess." She adjusted her hat when a breeze kicked up along the water. "Brandie wanted to go out on your boat. That sounds like a weird metaphor for something dirty."

"Probably what she had in mind," Cam said. He shifted toward Emma and lifted his mirrored sunglasses to the top of his head. "Are we friends?"

The question caught her off guard, and she couldn't help but notice the flash of disappointment in his bourbon-colored eyes when she didn't answer immediately. "Yes," she said finally. "I'm good at being work friends. They're pretty much the only kind I have."

"Work friends," he said, dropping the sunglasses to cover his eyes once more. "Okay, then."

She bit down on her lower lip but didn't say anything more, even though she wanted to. There was no reason why they should be anything other than casual friends who had a common goal in Holly's wedding. To pretend like it was more would just be…well…she was lying to herself either way.

"You might want to hold on to your hat," Cam told her as he surveyed the open water in front of them. The nearest boat was a couple hundred yards away. Toby stood at the front of the boat like he was in charge, making Emma smile. "We're going on a bit of a fast ride."

She gave him a thumbs-up and hoped he didn't notice that her smile was fake. The boat motor roared and Emma yelped as the front of the craft lifted out of the water and skimmed across the water.

He maneuvered the boat toward the horizon, and she grabbed her hat when a gust of wind blew it off her head.

"I warned you," he shouted with a devilish grin. "You good with the speed?"

She nodded. The speed. The man. All of it. Forget about putting what she felt for him into the safe column of work friends. Forget labels. It wasn't easy for Emma to just let go. She'd spent years honing her self-control until it was knife-blade sharp. Until it was second nature.

But with the boat ripping across the calm sea, she grinned and let the energy of the moment carry her away. This was going to be a good day. Definitely one with no bananas.

"I'M A BANANA."

Cam worked to keep his features neutral as he glanced over at Emma. Her wide mouth was pulled into an adorable pout, and he could practically feel the frustration radiating from her.

His uptight innkeeper with her type-A personality made him want to smile. The way the thin sundress she wore molded against her perfect curves in the ocean breeze made him want to pull her close and kiss her until she forgot the whole purpose of their outing.

"You're not a banana," he said, and handed her the rod he'd just rerigged after the lure had snagged on a giant wad of seaweed. "Sometimes the fish just aren't biting."

She rolled her eyes. "When was the last time you went fishing and didn't catch anything?"

They'd tried a half dozen spots along the coast, motoring in and out of coves and throwing line after line without even a bite.

"I'm not giving up, and neither are you." He reached out and tucked a loose strand of caramel-colored hair behind her ear, then took the rod from her and cast out a line. "If there's one thing I'm sure of, you aren't a quitter, Emma."

She froze for an instant, then let out a harsh laugh. "Oh, but I am," she argued. "I quit a great job. I quit my family and my marriage. I've been tempted more than once to quit my folly in Magnolia. Who am I to open an inn or help people plan weddings? I've failed with just about every person in my life I've ever loved." She let out a sigh so pitiful his chest tightened in response. "Why should today be any different?"

He saw a single tear track down her cheek. Oh, hell, no. This was not the plan for the day. Okay, maybe he hadn't exactly had a plan. The invitation to accompany him on the boat had been impulsive. He never took women other than clients out on the water with him, and it had nothing to do with bananas or superstitions.

Dana had preferred to stay home. His late wife hadn't enjoyed fishing in the least, but she was always happy to lay in the sun and read a book, and Cam was always happy when she was happy.

He'd wanted to distract both Emma and himself. Fishing seemed like an easy way to do it. He should have known Emma would take seriously her success at it. She took everything seriously.

He was about to pull her into his arms and do his damnedest to distract her when the rod jerked and the reel buzzed with the sound of the spinning line.

"I've got a fish," she said after an elated gasp. Toby let out an excited bark.

"A whopper," Cam confirmed as he made sure her hands were in the right place on the rod. "Are you ready for a fight, Emma?"

"I'm ready not to be so easily thrown into an emotional tailspin," she said, tightening her hold. "If that means reeling in this monster, then bring it on."

He gave her instructions on what to do, and no surprise she followed his words to the letter. "I wish all the people I took out could take direction as well as you."

She laughed at that, her eyes never leaving the water. "Trust me, Camden. This is the only place I'm going to let you boss me around."

He pulled the rod belt from the storage bin under a nearby seat and wrapped it around her waist. "You're going to need some leverage to land this guy."

Every few seconds, the fish crested, flailing about in the waves. Other than the splashing from the fish and the sound of the seagulls overhead, the water was peaceful and quiet. The ocean had been a refuge for him in his dark days of grief, but now he was glad to share it with Emma.

"I'm sorry I got emotional just before," she said after a moment. "I bet you don't get a lot of existential crises in the middle of a day of fishing."

"You'd be surprised," he answered with a laugh. "Getting tired?"

"Yes, but I'm not a quitter."

He returned the smile she gave him. "I know it, darlin'. I've known it all along."

She continued to work the line, and ten minutes later, he lifted a gorgeous tuna into the boat that he'd guess to be nearly fifty pounds.

"It's huge." Emma sounded shocked.

"That's what she said," he told her with a wink.

She made a gagging sound before laughing. "Will you take my picture with it? Ryan is never going to believe I caught something so massive."

"Seriously with the innuendos," Cam muttered as he took her phone and snapped a couple of photos of a beaming Emma with her catch.

"You need to get your mind out of the gutter." She trailed one finger along the tuna's spine as Cam held him still. "He's so pretty. The colors are magnificent."

"Are you thinking about sushi dinner?"

She looked from him to the fish and then back again. "I want to throw him back. Or her. She'll be okay, right?"

"She'll be fine." Cam took the fish and eased it into the water. It remained lifeless on the surface for several seconds, and Emma gripped his arm, squeezing tight.

"Why isn't it moving?"

"It's in shock," Cam said quietly, placing an arm around her shoulder. "Just watch."

After another few seconds, the fish flailed, then disappeared under the surface. Emma turned, then reached up and wrapped her arms around Cam's shoulders, her soft body pressing into his.

"That was amazing."

He chuckled and pulled back to look into her eyes. "You caught a fish."

"My first fish," she agreed, nodding. "I'm not the banana."

Cam threw back his head and laughed at her enthusiasm. The sound felt rusty in his throat, but he liked it. It had been too long since he'd felt the sense of lightness he did with Emma. The delight he took in her. Emotions he figured he'd never experience again after losing Dana. He was quickly coming to realize he'd orchestrated his existence to prevent himself from feeling them.

He'd held himself apart to make up for his mistakes. But in trying to prevent himself from feeling anything, he'd ended up hurting people, and that was no good. Maybe it was time for a change.

"Let's find a lunch spot, Ms. Not-the-banana."

"And then can we swim?" Her grin did funny things to his insides. "Then catch more fish?"

"We can do anything you want," he promised.

He stepped away from her and moved to take a seat behind the steering wheel.

"Can I drive the boat?" she asked, almost tentatively.

He tugged her close and brushed a soft kiss against her mouth. "Anything," he repeated, and then stepped back while she sat in the captain's chair.

Her enthusiasm was contagious, and he remembered the easy joy he'd once taken from boating. The first time his father let him drive the old fishing boat. Long summer Sundays spent on the water with Ash and his dad, laughing and eating candy and cheese puffs until his stomach ached from them.

They hadn't been a well-off family, but at times like that it didn't matter. Cam had had everything he needed and more.

Other memories tugged at him. The ones where he'd changed and rebelled and the anger at knowing he'd never compete with his perfect brother had pushed him to go in the opposite direction. To gain attention from his negative behavior because that was better than no attention at all.

He refused to be pulled under by the past and let darkness ruin this day. He sat next to Emma and smiled as she talked herself through steering the boat.

"Hit the gas," he said, leaning in to nip at her neck. "I'm hungry."

She gave him a playful push. "I'm concentrating. The last thing I need is you distracting me with your sexual voodoo."

"Sexual voodoo isn't a thing."

"What if I lose control and we crash and sink? You've heard of the *Titanic*, right?"

"I won't let anything happen to you." He shifted so he was behind her, and covered her hands with his. "We're in this together, Em."

He heard her breath hitch, but she kept her gaze forward. "Let's eat," she said, and hit the throttle.

They docked in a private cove. She unpacked lunch from the basket while he anchored the boat and put up the Bimini top that would shade them from the noonday sun. As promised, the sandwiches were amazing and she'd brought homemade cookies and pasta salad to go with them.

He handed her an iced tea from the cooler and tried not to moan out loud when a drop of condensation fell from the bottom of the bottle and dripped down her chest.

"I need to try more activities like this in town. Guests always appreciate personal recommendations when planning their visits."

"Would you recommend me?" he asked, not bothering to keep the teasing out of his tone.

"Oh, yes," she said, but he immediately realized she hadn't caught on to his rusty flirtation skills. "I went to Hawaii a few years back and the animal shelter on the island loaned out dogs to tourists to take around on day excursions. I bet Meredith would work with me on that."

"Toby would be highly offended if I let a strange dog onto the boat."

"How did you adopt him?" She scratched the dog behind the ears, and he looked up at her with adoring eyes.

"He found *me*," Cam said. "I couldn't stand to be in the house after Dana died, so I'd fish in a stream near our property on the inland waterway. Toby showed up one day."

"Had he been abandoned?"

Cam shrugged. "Probably. He had matted fur and burrs stuck between the pads of his paws. He wouldn't let me anywhere near him for almost a week, but I kept coming back to the same spot and he kept showing up. After the second day, I bought a bag of kibble and left some for him."

"You had to know what would happen when you fed him."

"I wasn't going to let him starve." Cam blew out a breath. He'd been all ready to go to sexy town and instead was sharing one of the more vulnerable times of his life. What was it about Emma that made it too damn easy to open up?

"You saved him."

"Don't give me too much credit. Honestly, Toby was the one who did most of the saving. I'd hit rock bottom, and things were swirling through my mind I couldn't control. Thoughts I'd never had before."

Emma frowned, and he had a feeling she knew what he was talking about. "What kind of thoughts?" she prompted.

He should have realized she wouldn't let him off the hook in facing the past. Hell, this was part of the reason he kept himself away from getting close to anyone. But he somehow didn't mind sharing his lowest point with her. "I didn't want to live," he said simply. "Not without Dana. Not when she'd died supporting me, and I'd done nothing to deserve it. A dog doesn't care about human mistakes, no matter how awful they are. He just wanted to be fed, and I was the one to do it."

Cam placed a hand on the dog's neck, the feel of the soft fur calming him the way it had from the start. "Then one day he hopped up in the back of my truck. It was as if he was telling me he was ready to go home."

"So you took him home."

"It didn't feel quite so lonely with him there." Cam stood and yanked his shirt over his head. "Enough deep thoughts with broken Cam. Let's swim."

To his immense relief, she didn't argue or press him for more. She placed her iced tea bottle on the dash and stood. Then she reached down to the hem of her sundress and shrugged out of it. Cam did his best not to gape, but he doubted he was successful.

She wore a navy blue bikini and her body was smooth and shapely. With an almost shy grin, she climbed up next to him on the side of the boat and took his hand. "Let's do this," she told him with a wink.

Emma made everything easy for Cam, even the thought of releasing some of his guilt. He was ready to release it. So on the count of three, they jumped into the water together.

CHAPTER TWELVE

THE DOORBELL RANG the next Wednesday morning, shortly after Angi had arrived at the Wildflower Inn to work on menu options for Holly's wedding.

"Were you expecting someone?" Angi asked, her voice filled with panic as she grabbed Emma's arm to prevent her from heading toward the front of the house.

"Not specifically, but maybe Cam had materials delivered. He's in back so I'll answer it."

"Don't." Angi's eyes were wide.

Holly looked up from the bridal magazine she was paging through. "Are we in a horror movie now? Normally the creepy stuff doesn't happen in broad daylight, right?"

"It could be my mother."

Emma blinked. "Why would your mother be here?"

"Because she's suspicious."

"Of what?" Holly asked, moving around the side of the counter. "Does she think Brett is too good for me or I'm some sort of gold digger the way his mom does? Because—"

"It has nothing to do with you." Angi shook her head as Emma put an arm around Holly's thin shoulders. She wished she could take away the bride-to-be's anxiety. Was this typical of planning weddings? As much moral support as arranging seating charts. It was comical to think that she might be equipped to offer life advice, but she was determined to try.

The doorbell sounded again.

First, she had to deal with a potentially irate parent. "So your mom doesn't know you're partnering with me?"

"I was going to tell her." Angi followed Emma down the hall. "But it would hurt her feelings so much. We almost lost the restaurant last year when Dylan Scott came back to town and threatened to redevelop our side of downtown. It was a blow to my parents that the business they'd devoted most of their lives to could be taken away so easily. Then my father died suddenly, and my mom has been fragile ever since. I understand it, and I'm trying to make it better. My brothers don't help by trying to force her to retire and give the restaurant to me."

Emma stopped in her tracks, then stumbled forward when Angi plowed into the back of her. "You forgot to mention the potential of taking over your family's restaurant."

"It's why I haven't told my mom yet. I'll break her heart."

"Do you think she tracked you here?"

"Maybe." Angi cringed. "I parked a few streets over so she couldn't have followed my car. I'm going to hide behind the door so I can listen in. Just don't give me away."

"I thought *I* had a complicated relationship with my mother."

"I'm Italian." Angi threw up her hands like those two words explained everything. "We've made an art of complicated maternal relationships."

Angi pressed herself against the wall next to the door, and Emma opened it, mentally preparing herself to face Bianca Guilardi.

Instead, Mariella Jacob stood on the other side, one

ballerina-flat-toed shoe tapping impatiently on the wood porch.

"What are you doing right now?" she demanded before her steely blue gaze flicked to the space between the door and the hinges. She wore slim pants that fit her perfectly and a crisp white button-down. "And why is that waitress from the pizza place hiding in the corner?"

"We're planning Holly's reception," Emma said, trying to sound in charge of the situation, which felt like it was quickly spiraling out of control. "As far as Angi..." She tugged the other woman forward. "It's a long story."

"As much as I'd love to hear the details of this Real Housewives of Magnolia moment..." Mariella gave a small shake of her head. "We don't have time."

"I'm not a housewife," Angi protested, straightening her back.

Mariella ignored her. "I need you to come with me," she told Emma. Her icy blue gaze snapped to Carrie's painting, which hung on the main wall of the foyer. "That's perfect there. I can't wait to see the others she consigned to you. I found some great furniture and decor for the place, but they're going to let the general public in at noon, so we don't have long."

Emma gaped at the slim designer, her mind reeling. "What are you talking about?"

Mariella gave her a strange look. "You said you needed furniture for the bedrooms and general bits and bobs for the rest of the house. An estate auction house called me to do a walkthrough on their inventory prior to opening the sale to regular people. Let's go."

"I didn't realize you were going to help me," Emma said, feeling dumbfounded.

"You need help," Mariella said, folding her hands across

her body. "You can't put Mitsy Carmichael on just any old bed that you put together from IKEA."

"I wasn't going to buy furniture for the guest rooms at IKEA."

"I love IKEA," Holly said as she approached from the kitchen. "On one of our first dates, Brett helped me put together a dresser and desk."

Angi snorted. "He must have really been into you to endure that sort of torture."

Holly beamed. "We're into each other."

"Wasting time." Mariella tapped on the face of her chunky watch.

"I'm up for a field trip," Angi said. "I'll grab my purse from the kitchen."

"Why are you even here?" Mariella said as she gave Angi a sharp once-over. "Are you the new Grubhub person for the restaurant?"

"I'm the new chef at the Wildflower Inn," Angi countered. "Emma and I are partners."

Mariella's mouth dropped open as she turned toward Emma. "You can't just serve Italian."

"I cook with a dizzying variety of flavors," Angi said, stepping between them and leaning toward Mariella. "I'm not just a one-trick pony, like, say, a wedding dress designer."

Mariella shifted to glare at Emma. "I told you I didn't want people to know that about me."

"I told her." Holly stepped forward. "Or she guessed after I showed her pics of the dress you're designing for me."

"Signature style," Mariella told Angi with a glare. "That's not one-trick anything."

Angi humphed but Meredith squeezed her arm before

she could say anything more. "We'll all go to this estate sale." She glanced at Holly. "Does that work for your timing?"

"Yep," the redhead answered. "I'm off until tomorrow."

Mariella pointed at Angi. "Holly is fine, but I don't know why *she* needs to come."

"What's your damage with me?" Angi demanded.

"I don't like you."

"I'm extremely likable."

"We should take two cars," Emma said before things could get even more heated. "Holly, you ride with Angi and I'll go with Mariella."

Angi opened her mouth to argue, but Emma shook her head and flashed a quelling glance. The one she'd learned from her mother. No surprise, it worked. She grabbed her purse from the hook near the entry and stepped onto the porch.

"What's the address?" she asked Mariella, who narrowed her eyes. "Give Angi the address."

With an exaggerated eye roll, Mariella explained the location of the estate sale. Angi knew the area, so Emma gave the snippy blonde a little push toward the porch steps and told Angi and Holly they'd meet them at the warehouse.

They were silent for several minutes as Mariella drove the Audi SUV like it was a getaway car in a high-speed chase. "Is the furniture that amazing?" Emma gripped the door handle as they took a turn onto the highway.

"Why make her your partner?" Mariella asked the question through clenched teeth.

"She cooked for me, and she's amazing. I need someone with skills who—"

"A cook is different than a partner," Mariella interrupted. "I thought I was going to be your partner."

Emma turned, adjusting the seat belt's chest strap. "No one is going to be my partner if you kill us in a car accident."

That earned a dismissive sniff. "I'm a fabulous driver."

"Right. Something New Yorkers are known for far and wide."

"Very conscientious," Mariella agreed with a nod, but she eased up on the gas enough that Emma felt free to take a full breath.

"For the record, I didn't think you wanted anything to do with the inn or designing dresses for my brides. Until Holly mentioned working with you today, I had no idea. You kind of shot me down when I came by the shop."

"I was playing hard to get," Mariella said, like it was the most obvious thing in the world.

"I don't have time for games," Emma said simply.

"And that long-legged waitress with mommy issues is a real straightforward gem."

"Seriously, what's your problem with Angi?"

"She looks like the former friend who bonked my fiancé."

"Don't say bonk." Emma grimaced. "That's gross."

"It's gross and awful and humiliating. Every time I see Angi, I want to smack her."

"But she's not that woman."

"She looks like the type who men would fall over themselves if it meant her noticing them. All that perfect skin and the thick mane of luscious locks."

"You need to get a grip," Emma advised. "Even more than I do. And take some damn personal responsibility. Yes, your so-called friend and your boyfriend betrayed you, but I watched the video from the wedding."

Mariella sucked in a sharp breath. "Is that why you don't want me to partner with you?"

"I didn't say that, but you were unhinged. No one can deny your talent, and I could use all the help I can get with both decorating and creative social media. You're good at both. But if you can't rein in your temper, all the talent in the world isn't worth it to me."

"Anger is my superpower," Mariella muttered.

"You design wedding gowns. Silk and lace and tears at the first sight of a bride. How is that possible?"

"I'm not exactly sure, but anger has always fueled me. Other than when I'm working on the dresses. It was balance, my place of peace, but the anger took over and I ruined everything. I moved to Magnolia because it felt like this would be a place where I could keep calm. Remember how the big green guy from the comics took off for a tiny hut in the mountains when his smashing got out of hand?"

Emma nodded. "But he came back when it was time to save the world."

"Hence, me showing up at the inn today."

"The inn," Emma murmured. "Why does it sometimes still feel like Niall Reed's house to me? I'm not sure if it will ever truly be mine."

"From what I gather, now that he's gone people around here feel fairly free to let their 'hate on Niall' flags fly. You'll be fine." She punched Emma gently on the arm. "Especially if you have the right partner."

"You have to be nice to Angi," she told Mariella. "She's a partner in the deal."

"She's a waitress with a chip on her shoulder."

"She's a gifted chef, and I need her." Emma placed her hand on Mariella's arm. "*We* need her. I'm working on confidence. She's going to learn to give up her guilt, and you're going to let go of the anger."

"The anger is my security blanket. It keeps me safe."

"How safe did you feel when you found out about your fiancé? How well did your anger serve you then?"

"You're mean," Mariella muttered with a pout.

"I know what it feels like to have everything you thought you wanted in life turn out to be a lie. And not to handle it well. No judgment but we're transforming ourselves here. The Wildflower Inn is going to be our new start, and you'll have to get on board if you want to be a part of it."

"So you're open to a partnership?" Mariella turned off the two-lane highway onto a narrow lane.

"I'm open to anything that will make the inn a success." Emma let out a hum of approval as they parked in front of a large barn with the doors wide open. Even from this distance she could see the deep polish of expensive wood. "Where did this furniture come from?" she asked as she got out of the SUV and joined Mariella walking toward the space.

"A historic estate about fifty miles south of here. They're tearing it down to build a new housing development, and the couple's grandkids contracted with this auction house to sell everything." She leaned closer. "I get a 'friends and family' discount because I designed the oldest granddaughter's wedding dress a few years ago."

Mariella waved to a silver-haired woman behind a cash register before leading Emma forward. "I have some ideas based on what you told me about your vision for the inn. I was at the estate sale, as well, and Carrie gave me a brief tour of the house."

"Did you consider buying it?" Emma asked. She knew

there'd been another interested party, which is what had led her to making an offer just over the asking price.

"Not one bit," Mariella said with a laugh. "I didn't have the vision for it, but I'm happy you did."

There were an assortment of occasional tables, a dining room set with Queen Anne legs and several impressive hutches that had pie-crust edges. Tears pricked the backs of Emma's eyes at the thought of a home that would have held these kinds of beautiful items being torn down to build a new development. It was the same way she'd felt when she first laid eyes on the Wildflower. A deep sorrow at something once so beautiful being left to disrepair.

"I can't afford most of this," Emma whispered, more to herself than to Mariella.

"That's where your new partner comes in." Mariella pulled one of the drawers out and nodded when it moved smoothly. "I have money."

"You can't spend it on furniture," Emma insisted.

"Why?" Mariella shrugged. "What else am I going to do with it? I've lived the high life already, and it got me nowhere. A fancy apartment on the Upper West Side, dinners out every night, expensive vacations. Through it all, I was at best complacent and more often than not dissatisfied."

"I know how that feels," Emma said. Her lifestyle hadn't been lavish, but she'd never struggled. And she'd taken that ease for granted.

Holly hurried up to them, her face awash with wonder. "It's like walking into a furniture museum. Even Mrs. Carmichael would be impressed."

"You shouldn't have to impress your future mother-in-law with a Chippendale armoire."

"I don't even know what that means." Holly's expression fell. "She's going to know I don't belong in her world. In

Brett's world. She already suspects it. I've watched every episode of *Downton Abbey* twice to learn table manners."

Angi snorted. "You're a good person, Holly. That's all that should matter."

"You don't know the social elite," Mariella said with a derisive sniff. "That's the last thing that matters."

"Which is why I have no use for the social elite." Angi narrowed her eyes. "Or people who suck up to them."

"It's called making a living," Mariella corrected. "And if you think you won't get your share of difficult guests at the inn—"

"Sweetheart, I've worked in the restaurant industry for half my life. So bless your heart for thinking I can't deal with jerks, but you're wrong."

"She blessed her heart." Holly leaned closer to Emma like she was sharing a state secret. "That's serious."

"I'm going to put the two of you in time-out." Emma blew out a frustrated breath. "If we're all going to work together "

"We're not," Mariella and Angi said in unison.

"Something they agree on," Holly muttered with a nervous giggle.

"Lovely," Emma agreed. "Let's focus on shopping now and we'll discuss the particulars of who does what at the inn later. We have six bedrooms to furnish. I lost the furniture in one due to water damage from the storm, so that will be covered." She gazed around the barn. "It will take some creativity to handle the rest. Hope you ladies are feeling creative."

THREE HOURS LATER, Emma lifted her margarita glass to toast the other women on a job well done.

"It's amazing how buying a few headboards can give

me so much hope for the future," she told Mariella, who sipped on a glass of water across the table from her. Angi and Holly were both day-drinking with Emma—just one round—but Mariella had easily said no to any alcohol.

Emma had assumed the former designer's booze-driven scene was a result of one incident of overindulging, but now she had a feeling it was something more.

Magnolia truly was a place for reinventing a life.

"Everything will be delivered tomorrow at ten," Mariella said, glancing down at her phone. "When does the royal family arrive?"

Holly took a deep gulp of her frozen margarita. "Brett is leaving Washington around lunch on Friday because he wants to get here before his mom and best man. They'll be down around dinnertime."

"And a couple of his friends are coming, too?" Emma asked, mentally making to-do lists that would hopefully stem the anxiety bubbling up inside her.

"Yes. They're going fishing as part of the bachelor party."

"That's boring as hell," Mariella muttered.

"Brett wants to keep things low-key." Holly nodded. "All the guys can hang out and it gives him a break from…"

"His mom?" Angi winked. "So he's leaving you to entertain her. Lucky girl."

Emma placed her glass on the table. "I forgot to ask about your bridal shower. I assume it's this weekend, as well? Do you need any help with last-minute detail?"

The smile Holly flashed was so patently fake it made Emma want to cringe in response. "I've decided not to have a bridal shower," she said. "With everything else going on, it just felt like too much hassle."

"What are you talking about?" Mariella asked as she

scooped up salsa onto a tortilla chip. "You're a first-time bride. Of course you'll have a shower."

"We'll host it at the inn," Emma offered. "While the guys are fishing. It's last-minute, but I bet Angi can pull off some great food."

"Oh, no," Angi whispered.

Emma glanced at the other woman in shock. How could anyone say no to helping Holly? But as she followed Angi's shocked gaze, Emma realized the words had nothing to do with anything being discussed at this table.

Bianca Guilardi was striding across the street toward their table with a look of fire in her gaze.

"Is this how I raised you?" The petite woman raised her hand in irritation as she got closer. "To ignore your responsibilities at work so you can go out carousing with your friends."

"Is lunch considered carousing?" Emma asked under her breath.

"We're not friends," Mariella added, not quite as quietly.

"Ma, please don't make a scene." Angi's tone was uncharacteristically placating. "I got Annie to cover my shift."

"You were supposed to put in the bread and cheese orders this morning," Bianca said, then flicked a glance at the rest of the women. "Shirking your duties for an afternoon of mindless pleasure."

Mariella chuckled. "That actually makes a simple lunch sound a lot more exciting than it is."

"Who are *you*?" Bianca demanded.

"Mom, stop." Angi put her napkin on the table and pushed back from the table. "I'll take care of the order now."

"I'm Mariella Jacob, owner of A Second Chance. We met at a downtown business owners' meeting last year. You weren't exactly welcoming."

Bianca's eyes sharpened. "I saw your video on the internet. You're lucky I kept my mouth shut. Maybe I won't the next time the association meets."

"Mrs. Guilardi, please don't be angry with Angi." Emma quickly stood. "I convinced her to partner with me on the inn, and she—"

"Partner?" Angi's mother said the word like it was poison on her tongue. "My daughter has a job and a future at Il Rigatone. She isn't partnering with you."

"We need to talk, Mom," Angi said quietly, then threw a beseeching glance toward Emma. "Nothing has been finalized yet."

Emma's heart started beating at a rapid pace. As a matter of fact, she was under the impression they *had* finalized their agreement. There was no contract, but Angi had agreed to cook for Mitsy Carmichael this coming weekend. Emma believed she could rely on the other woman, but right now Angi wouldn't even make eye contact with her.

"I can't believe this." Bianca shook her head as she faced her daughter. "Your father and I supported you when you needed us. This is how you repay me?"

"It's not like that," Angi insisted. The bravado and attitude she'd displayed when bantering with Mariella had been snuffed out in an instant. "Let's go, Ma. I'll do the order and then we can watch true-crime shows until the dinner rush."

Without saying goodbye, Angi tucked her hand into the crook of her mother's elbow and led Bianca out the door.

Emma, Mariella and Holly watched them go in stunned silence.

Every bit of forward progress Emma made seemed to be answered with several giant paces in the opposite direction.

"Do you want the good news or the bad news?" Mariella asked in a hushed tone.

"Good."

"My mother couldn't care less what I do with my time, so you won't lose me to an overbearing parent."

Emma huffed out a laugh but the sound held no humor. "And the bad news?"

"I can't cook," Mariella revealed. "So you might have just lost your best chance at impressing Mitsy Carmichael."

"That's horrible news," Holly said, her voice cracking on the last word. "I'm starting to feel like the universe is conspiring against me. Maybe this wedding was never meant to be."

"Don't say that," Emma warned, draining her glass. It was only one drink, but she'd take all the courage she could get—liquid or otherwise.

CHAPTER THIRTEEN

EMMA WAS IN the middle of painting the final guest bedroom when the doorbell rang. She flipped off the music she'd been listening to and headed downstairs, shocked but somehow not surprised to see Angi on the other side of the door despite the late hour.

"We need to talk," the statuesque brunette told her with no hint of a smile.

Emma kept her features neutral as she stepped back to allow Angi to enter. "Mind if we talk while I finish painting? I'm on the last wall."

"It's nearly ten o'clock," Angi pointed out. "I had to get a neighbor to stay at the apartment while Andrew slept."

"I know it's late, but I want everything to dry by the time the furniture is delivered tomorrow." She led the way up the stairs and down the hall.

"Nice color choice," Angi murmured, turning in a circle to survey the room.

"It's called Serene Sage," Emma said with a small laugh. "I'm hoping it's a self-fulfilling prophecy."

"Yeah. Listen, I'm sorry about my mom making that scene."

"No need to apologize." Emma picked up her roller and began to paint again. As much as she didn't want to hear what she expected Angi to tell her, it was easier while she was occupied. She ignored how tightly her fingers gripped the handle of the roller. "It's obvious your mom relies on you and how much it means to have you at the restaurant. I'm disappointed, but I understand and we'll find someone to handle the kitchen and the catering portion of the inn."

"What do you mean 'someone'?" Angi's voice was whip-sharp. "Are you cutting me out of the deal? I promise my mom isn't going to show up here and freak out or whatever you think might happen."

Emma turned. "I'm thinking that you walking away today was a precursor of you coming here tonight to tell me you can't leave the restaurant."

"I'm leaving." Angi bit down on her bottom lip, looking away. "No lectures from my mom or my brothers about how much I owe her are going to change my mind. I love my family, but that restaurant isn't my dream. I have to take a chance on the life I want."

"Yes," Emma breathed, nearly sagging with relief and then realizing she'd mess up the freshly painted wall that way. "You do."

The fine line of stress between Angi's brows relaxed slightly. "You better agree. After all, you're the person who convinced me."

"Did you tell your mom that?" Emma cringed. "My mother is already mad as a hornet with me. I'm not looking to add more moms to that particular party of one. What if they unite or something?"

"It's my decision," Angi said. "She knows it's me. But we have to make the inn work because I just quit my job."

"Wow." Emma sucked in a breath. This was getting real. It was one thing to put her future at risk, but Angi had a kid to support. There was no way she could survive without money coming in. "Then we're in this together," she said.

"Don't forget about your other partner." Angi lifted a

brow. "Although I still think we should cut her out of the picture."

Emma held up her free hand, ticking off reasons Mariella was important to the inn's potential success. "One, she has money, which I'm quickly running through despite the insurance claim. Two, she might've had a bit of a fall from grace, but she's extremely talented and has a great eye for design, and not just fashion." Emma put down the paint roller and picked up her phone. "She's texted a dozen inspiration photos today. This place is going to look better than I could have imagined, and we have Mariella to thank for it."

Angi sniffed. "We could have picked out paint colors without her help. You've heard of Pinterest, right?"

"Three," Emma said, pointing three fingers toward the other woman. "She needs the Wildflower Inn. Just like you and me."

"She's not like you and me," Angi countered. "She's spoiled and pampered and too sophisticated for her own good."

"Unfortunately, that describes who I was or at least who I was raised to be. Mariella found Magnolia and chose this town as a place to start over. That means something to me. Everyone deserves a chance at a fresh start. Even her."

"You've watched too much *Oprah*," Angi grumbled, but she eventually nodded. "Fine, I'll deal with Mariella for now."

Emma gave a fist pump. "By the way, I take any comparison to Oprah as the highest form of a compliment."

"Did you think I was going to quit?"

Emma wanted to deny it but instead nodded. "The look in your eyes when your mom came to the table…" She drew in a breath. "I recognized that look. It said you didn't want to disappoint her."

"I hope she'll eventually support my decision."

"Let me know how that goes."

"You got it, partner."

"Is this the part where we hug?" Emma asked, taking a step forward.

"I'm not much of a hugger," Angi admitted. "Physical affection isn't really my—"

She laughed when Emma hugged her. "Me neither, but we're all about taking risks and making changes, right?"

"If you get paint on my sweater, I'm going to hurt you."

"Even more risk taking." Emma hugged tighter. "I like it."

After a few seconds, Angi finally relaxed into the embrace. "Fine, but don't make a habit of it."

With a laugh, Emma released her and they walked back downstairs.

"I'll be here around lunchtime the day before to prep for dinner and appetizers. I'm not sure what problem this Carmichael woman has with Holly, but she damn sure won't have anything to say about the food."

A sense of relief rushed through Emma. She liked the feeling of not being alone.

"Oh, this is an interesting turn of events." Angi paused and glanced over her shoulder at Emma as she opened the front door to let herself out.

Looking around her, Emma's breath caught in her throat. Cam stood on the porch, wearing a faded T-shirt with his hands jammed in low-slung jeans as he glanced between her and Angi. "Wanted to see if you needed help painting."

"So that's what we're calling it now," Angi said, and then let out a satisfied cackle.

Emma reached out and jabbed her in the ribs. "Don't even go there."

Angi turned fully around to face Emma. "I'm not, girl-friend. But if you have half a brain in that type-A head, you'll go there all the way." She whispered the words loudly enough that Cam chuckled behind her. "We'll talk more tomorrow."

"Not about this," Emma insisted, but Angi just laughed again.

"Have a good night, you two," she said as she skipped down the porch steps.

Emma gave Cam a tight smile and tried to will away the heat rising to her cheeks. "It seems wrong that one of my new partners takes so much glee in making me un-comfortable."

"I really did come over to check on the painting." Cam scrubbed a hand over his jaw and between the rough sound and the way his arm muscles rippled—literally rippled—Emma felt heat pool low in her belly.

This was the first time she'd been this close to him since Sunday on the boat. He'd mainly kept busy on projects up on a ladder or with Phil at his side. Sunday had been the best she'd had in ages. After lunch they'd swum and fished and lounged. She'd been completely relaxed. For those hours with Cam, she'd been able to put aside all of the stress of opening the inn on time and making sure Holly's wedding was perfect. With the whirlwind of the past few months, the respite from the stress in her life had been a much needed one.

She hadn't realized what a toll all of the constant busy-ness had put on her and how much of it she'd created for herself as a distraction so she wouldn't have to think about everything she'd failed at in her life. Her marriage, her re-lationship with her mother, the career she was supposed to have with the family foundation.

Not that any of those things magically disappeared, but out on the water fishing and breathing in the fresh air, they hadn't seemed as important as they did in the dark hours when she was alone. Cam gave that gift to her.

"Come on in," she told him.

"If this is going to make things weird for you—"

"Weird is my new normal," she said with a laugh. "I just finished the final bedroom. You can tell me how great my painting skills are and that you'll never find another crew member like me."

"I'm sure you're right." He closed the front door and followed her up the stairs. "Did you happen to get as much paint on the walls as you did on yourself?"

Emma looked down at herself at the top of the stairs. She did indeed have splotches of pale yellow and sage-green paint streaked along her legs as well as her shirt. "It's all part of the process," she told him. "Nothing a hot shower won't fix."

As soon as the words left her mouth, the image of Cam under the spray of a steamy shower filled her brain. To her surprise, he hadn't done more on the boat than kiss her. The looks he'd given her, especially when she'd taken off her sundress, had practically lit her insides on fire, but he'd been every inch a gentleman. It had practically killed her when she'd barely been able to keep her hands off him and his perfectly chiseled body.

But she'd followed his lead and kept everything platonic on the boat. It was for the best, she'd told herself.

"It looks great in here." His gravelly voice rolled over her, and she did her best to keep her features neutral as she turned to him. "You should be proud, Emma. All of your hard work is paying off. Even Holly's future mother-in-law is bound to be impressed."

At this moment, Emma couldn't have given a fig about some uptight society matron's opinion. She basked in the glow of Cam's approval, which she knew he didn't give carelessly.

"Thanks." She bent to pick up the paint tray. "Someone taught me to clean up the brushes right away so they don't get all gunky."

"I can help." He placed the lid on a gallon of paint. "When does the furniture arrive?"

"Tomorrow at ten." She led the way to the mudroom off the kitchen and began to rinse the brushes, talking nonstop about the different pieces of furniture. Emma wasn't even sure what she was saying. Her rambling was simply an attempt to keep her mind off the quiet and Cam and the way her body buzzed with awareness when he was around.

He dried each of the brushes and the roller as she finished washing them. When they were done, she flipped off the water, but before she could grab a towel to dry her hands, he reached for her.

His touch was unbelievably tender as he patted her hands with a fluffy white towel. "You're covered in paint," he said, and lifted a finger to her cheek. "I think it's time for that shower."

Heck, yeah, her body urged. *Danger*, her brain warned. She happily ignored her brain.

Clearly misreading her inner struggle, he took a step away from her. "I'm sorry, I didn't mean to suggest..."

"What if I'm interested in the suggestion?"

He closed his eyes for a moment. When he opened them, his gaze was so filled with desire it practically took her breath away. No man had ever looked at her the way he did.

"I'd like that very much," he said, his voice hoarse.

She took his hand and led him through the kitchen and

down the hall to the small guest bedroom she'd made her own. She wanted to be on a different floor than her guests and had come to love the cozy room with the four-poster bed and cherry furniture. In the first round of renovations, the crew had knocked down an interior wall and remodeled a closet in order to give her an en-suite bathroom.

To stay true to the age and character of the house, she'd used a color palette of black-and-white subway tiles with polished chrome hardware and colorful flower prints on the walls.

The bathroom wasn't big, but she hadn't expected to share it with a man. Certainly not one like Cam with his height and wide shoulders and the way he seemed to take up more space than he should. Or maybe it was just her reaction to him that sucked all the air out of the room.

He didn't seem to mind the cozy quarters as he reached past her to turn on the water. Almost immediately, the mirror began to fog, mimicking Emma's desire and muzzy thoughts.

It would probably be better if she just stopped thinking.

She grabbed the hem of her shirt and pulled it off, deciding the quickest way to make that happen would be to focus on the physical. But Cam clearly wasn't going to be rushed. He moved in for a kiss, slow and luxurious. Emma's heart hammered in her chest as he traced his hands down along her collarbones. Her skin burned under his touch, and when he skimmed his thumbs over the silk of her bra she couldn't help but let out a moan.

The sound made her aware of the reality of the situation and for a few brief, agonizing seconds she was transported to the night she'd spent in the hotel with a man she'd just met and the humiliating fallout of what came after.

Her body had shut down in the wake of her ex-husband's

betrayal, and she'd been almost relieved to have no interest in dating or sex. It was easier that way, less messy and no chance of being hurt again.

Cam brought her back to life with frightening ease.

"What's wrong?" he asked, and she was so shocked by his ability to read her that she couldn't even manage a coherent answer.

"We don't have to do this," he said. "Nothing you don't want to do, Emma."

"I want you," she whispered, because that was the truth.

"I'm here." He bent down and looked into her eyes. "I can wait right outside if you want to shower on your own. No pressure, I promise. I want to be with you, too, but only when you're ready."

He meant it.

She could tell by the sincerity in his tone and the tenderness of his gaze.

The anxiety that held her chest in a viselike grip loosened. She felt truly present, mind and body, in a way she hadn't expected.

"I'm ready for you to lose your shirt," she told him.

He rewarded her with a sexy grin as he pulled off the shirt.

"Better?"

She nodded, her mouth going dry at the sight of him. "Much." Then she pushed down her shorts and panties, stepped out of them and into the steamy shower. "But you're still overdressed."

"Easily remedied," he said as he stripped down and followed her in. He was physically perfect as far as she could tell, with toned muscles and a smattering of dark hair across his chest. She ran her hands over his wet skin, then traced her tongue over a pec, eliciting a sharp hiss from him.

This might be a temporary detour on the path to the rest of her life, but she wasn't about to turn back now.

He kissed her again, threading his hands into her hair before moving lower. Steam rose up around them, and Emma wondered if she was creating it with her intense desire. Between the hot water on her back and Cam's hot mouth all over her body, Emma quickly lost herself to the sensation.

Need rushed through her as he explored her with his lips and tongue, murmuring sweet words against her skin even as he drove her to the edge of the cliff and then over. It felt as though she were spiraling through the air on a wave of unending pleasure.

Her knees threatened to give out, but Cam was there to hold her steady.

"Wow," she said as he slicked the hair back from her face.

"I'll take a *wow*." He looked like the cat who ate the canary and Emma couldn't have cared less about his self-satisfied smile, not when he'd given her so much satisfaction in the process of earning it. Grabbing the shower puff from its hook on the wall, he began to slough the dried paint off her body.

"You don't have to do that," she said, but in some strange way watching him concentrate on the task was even more intimate than what had come before. And although she should have been fully satisfied, desire bloomed once more as heat pooled low in her belly and between her legs.

"It's my great pleasure," he said, then sucked in a harsh breath when she reached between them to wrap her hand around his hard length.

"I want you," she said, because they felt like words that needed repeating. "Now, Cam."

He dropped the puff and claimed her mouth again, the

kiss wild and rough. "I've got a condom in my wallet," he told her, breaking the connection. His chest rose and fell in the same ragged breaths she recognized in her own body.

"I'm on the Pill," she told him. "After my divorce, I was tested and I... Are you good?"

"Yeah." He turned her and pressed his body against her back. "But I'll be so damn much better inside you."

She rocked into him and he filled her, deep and slow. She let out a guttural moan at the potential of what was coming next. Pressure built inside her with each stroke. She could no longer tell where she left off and he began. They were one as the release exploded through her, and he followed a moment later, grunting her name like it was a prayer. She came back to reality slowly, aware of the water turning cooler and Cam's strong arms still holding her steady.

Emma didn't know what this would mean or how their arrangement might change in the wake of this new level of connection, but she knew enough to enjoy it while she could.

CHAPTER FOURTEEN

LATE FRIDAY AFTERNOON, Cam was sanding a piece of trim in the cottage next door to the main house when he heard the knock on the front door. Strange, because the only person he'd expect to see would be Emma, and she certainly wouldn't feel the need to knock when she owned the place.

He sure as hell hoped they were beyond knocking, given what had happened between them. Feeling her come apart in his arms had been one of the most amazing experiences he could remember, although a nagging fragment of regret lingered at how he'd left things.

The confusion in her clear gaze when he hadn't joined her in bed had made his heart ache for things that just couldn't be. Not yet. Not with him.

No matter how much he wanted them.

Emma was all potential and light, determined to make a new start in her life. In addition to the intense attraction between them, he simply liked her. He respected her. She deserved the best life had to offer, much like Dana had.

Which was what convinced Cam that he couldn't be it for her.

He placed the sander on the sawhorses and opened the front door to reveal a wide-eyed Holly standing on the other side.

"Aren't you supposed to be entertaining guests at the

inn?" he asked, his gaze flicking past her to the cars parked in the circular driveway of the property next door.

He'd seen Holly's fiancé, the senator, arrive earlier. She'd greeted him with an exuberant hug, and the woman he considered a little sister had looked truly happy as she led Brett Carmichael into the front door of the inn. Cam knew he'd done the right thing by agreeing to help.

Not to mention it had brought him to Emma.

That wasn't right. He couldn't count Emma as something—someone—that was his. She didn't belong to him and never would.

"I can't go back over there," Holly whispered, letting herself into the cottage and shutting the door. She leaned against it and lifted her gaze to the ceiling as a single tear tracked down her cheek.

"What's going on, kid?" Cam took a step closer, hating to see the woman he'd known since she rode a bike with training wheels so visibly upset.

"I need to cancel the wedding," she said, then pressed her lips together like the words caused her physical pain.

Cam blinked, trying to make sense of what she was saying. He couldn't fathom how she'd changed so completely from the happy bride-to-be he'd witnessed a couple of hours earlier.

"Did Brett Carmichael say something? Did he do something?" Cam fisted his hands at his sides. "Because I'm not afraid to kick some senatorial a—"

"No." Holly dashed a hand across her face. "It's not like that." She bit down on her lower lip, then shook her head. "Brett is amazing, Cam. He's everything I could want in a life partner. He loves me the way you loved my sister."

Ah, hell, wasn't that just a sharp uppercut to the chin?

"Then what's going on, Holl? Why the talk about calling off the wedding?"

"I'm going to disappoint him." She met Cam's gaze, then looked away. "His mom is right. I don't know the first thing about being a political wife, let alone doing it on a national stage. Do you know that Brett has a list of ex-girlfriends that includes an Oscar-winning actress, a ballerina in the New York City Ballet and an astronaut?" She barked out a harsh laugh. "He literally dated a rocket scientist."

"So what?"

"I can't compare to that caliber of success. I know it. His mother knows it. I'm sure his friends know it, and it's only a matter of time before Brett realizes it. I'm a nail tech with a high-school education, for goodness' sake." She pushed away from the door and went to the front window to peek out. "It was easy to fool myself when I came back to Magnolia to plan the wedding. I'm comfortable here. Even after the debacle with the initial plans, it seemed like it was going to be okay. Emma has been amazing, and you've stepped in to save the day."

"I'm not a hero," Cam said tightly. "We both know that."

"You're one to me," Holly argued, glancing over her shoulder at him. "And Emma has been telling Brett how much progress you've made in such a short time. He has a house down on Tybee Island in Georgia, and he's already coming up with a plan to hire you to renovate it."

"I'm not going to Tybee Island."

Holly flashed a small smile. "That's what Emma said. She sounded quite possessive of you."

"She needs me to focus on her job." Cam did his best to ignore the feeling of pleasure that permeated his being at the thought of belonging to Emma. "She needs you to not freak out about the wedding."

"I can't do it." Her voice trembled.

"Do you think your sister made a mistake marrying me?" Cam forced himself to ask.

Holly turned to face him. "That's the stupidest thing I've ever heard. Dana loved you so much, Camden. You made her happy."

"But I was also the reason she—"

"If you say 'died' I'm going to punch you. Her accident was horrible and tragic but not your fault."

"I don't want to debate blame right now," Cam said, mainly because to his mind there was nothing to argue. He inclined his head toward Holly. "But I appreciate your conviction in threatening bodily harm to me."

She sighed. "You know I don't mean that."

"I also know that because of me, Dana didn't go away to college. She gave up her scholarship to the University of Chicago, Holly. It could have changed her life."

"She didn't want to move that far away."

"Was she wrong?"

Holly immediately shook her head. "I miss her every day, but she wouldn't have changed anything about the choices she made. She loved you and the life you built together. Nothing else mattered to her."

"Do you think Brett could feel the same way about you?"

"I see what you did there." Holly shook a finger in his direction. "That was sneaky, Camden, but it's not the same."

"I know," he agreed. "You are so much better of a person than I could ever be, Holly. Brett is damn lucky to have you. I think he knows that. I hope he does, otherwise I'll be the one threatening bodily harm. Trust yourself, kid."

She clasped her hands tightly together and faced the window again. "I do love him, and I want to make it work. So badly."

"You can do this. Besides, I don't care what kind of a snob his mother is. If you love him, you have to trust him and yourself. There's going to be no more beautiful wedding than yours. Emma and I will make sure of it."

"Thanks, Cam." Holly leaned forward and hugged him. "I wouldn't have guessed it, but you two make a pretty good team."

"I wouldn't have guessed it, either." Holly was right. He just couldn't admit it out loud. "You should get into the house before they really do think they've got a runaway bride on their hands."

"Will you come in with me?"

He laughed. "Me? You can't bring the hired help to a fancy party."

"You're my brother in all the ways that count," she said, and his throat clogged with untamed emotion. "I'm keeping Mom and Dad away until the weekend of the wedding. But I'd like to have someone from my family with me tonight."

It humbled him that after all this time and the way he'd cut himself off that Holly would still consider him important to her.

"Then I'll be at your side."

"Besides…" She released him and gave his arms a squeeze. "Maybe all your overt manliness will distract Mrs. Carmichael. Could you flex or rip off your shirt or something when you get in there?"

He chuckled and at the same time felt color rise to his cheeks. "Real funny, Holl."

"I remember how you used to come over and wash your car in our driveway just to entertain Dana."

He brushed a bit of sawdust from his jeans. "Not discussing that with you."

"At least put on your tool belt."

"Freaking me out."

She led the way toward the main house. "Has Emma seen your tool belt, Camden?"

"Is giving me grief helping your anxiety?"

"Immensely," she said with a wide grin. "Let's go in through the kitchen. Maybe no one will have noticed I went missing."

Cam didn't believe that for an instant but followed her toward the back of the house, anyway. Typical for this time of year, it was sticky and hot, although the inn's backyard still felt like a sanctuary from the heat.

Before they'd reached the edge of the patio, the back door flew open. "Holly, where have you been?" Angi gestured furiously from the doorway. "Emma is about to have a conniption fit."

"What exactly is a conniption fit? Would it distract Brett's mom?" Cam asked, leaning close to the redhead and earning a giggle.

Angi glared at him but he shook his head and gestured toward Holly. "The bride-to-be just needed a few minutes to collect herself."

"Fine," Angi said, understanding dawning in her dark gaze. "As long as you don't disappear on the actual wedding day." She backed into the kitchen and picked up a tray of tiny appetizers from the counter. "I was about to bring these out. Tell everyone you were helping me."

"Thank you," Holly whispered, then glanced at Cam. "Are you ready?"

At Angi's small squeak of protest, Cam lifted a brow. "Maybe I should stay in the kitchen to help."

"I want my brother-in-law with me. My family," Holly said definitively.

"Good idea." Angi shooed them toward the hallway that

led to the formal living room. "Maybe take off your shirt, Cam. Brett's mom seems like the kind of uptight old bat who has a secret dirty side."

Holly flashed a smile at Cam. "I told you it was a good idea."

"Is this some kind of perverted conspiracy?" Cam muttered.

"Desperate times," Holly said.

He squeezed her thin shoulder. "You've got this, kid. I've got your back."

With a deep breath she moved down the hall. He could almost feel the tension coming from her, and the higher strung she seemed, the more certain he felt. Confident that no matter what Brett Carmichael or his uptight mother threw at Holly, Cam would be there to deflect it.

He expected a tense scene with fancy people standing around tapping their watches and looking perturbed. Instead, Brett was the only one who seemed the least bit upset that Holly hadn't joined them.

Emma sat on the sofa with his mother and another man, who looked just as rich and high-class as the senator. They were looking at something on Emma's phone and all three of them wore matching smiles. Cam's gut clenched when the man, who was handsome in that quintessentially grown-up frat-boy way, leaned in and his leg pressed against Emma's.

"I brought snacks," Holly announced, and everyone looked toward them.

Brett's face visibly relaxed while his mother's gaze narrowed.

Emma popped up like she had a side hustle as a jack-in-the-box. She wore a fitted skirt with a silk shirt and looked completely at ease with her upscale guests. "Holly, you're here. With the canapés."

"I believe she called them snacks," Mrs. Carmichael said as if *snacks* were another word for *booger*.

Cam plucked the tray from Holly's hands and popped one of the little toasts with smoked salmon and cheese into his mouth. "They are excellent, I might add." He flicked a glance in Brett's direction and then focused on the prickly matron. "I don't think we've been introduced. I'm Camden Arlinghaus, Holly's brother-in-law."

Brett moved forward but paused when his mother spoke. "I thought her sister—"

"My wife was killed in a car accident five years ago," Cam confirmed. Nothing shut people up like a little over-share of personal tragedy. As he expected, Mitsy's eyes went wide but she said no more. "I've known Holly since she was a girl, and I insisted she introduce me to her fiancé. It will take a special man to deserve someone as wonderful as Holly."

Mitsy stood with a sniff. "I assure you my son is special. He's a US senator."

"Ah, but that tells me what he does." He moved closer to the sofa. "Not who he is or anything about his character. His heart."

"His heart is pure," Holly said from behind him.

"As the driven snow," Mitsy confirmed tightly.

"My two favorite women agree," Brett said with an awkward laugh.

Cam grinned at Mitsy. "That's a good start, eh?" He leaned in closer. "Although if Holly hadn't told me I was meeting her future mother-in-law, I would have assumed you were his sister."

He heard Emma's slight intake of breath but kept his gaze focused on Mitsy, adding a quick wink for good measure.

As he'd hoped, she blushed and gave him a coy smile.

"You'll have to excuse my appearance." He lifted the hem of his shirt to wipe a bit of invisible dirt off his chin, making sure he revealed his abs and watching Mitsy's eyes glaze over ever so slightly. Holly and Angi had the older woman pegged correctly. "I got the time of this appetizer shindig wrong so was still working. I didn't have time to change from all the heavy lifting I was doing in the cottage next door. Maybe I could give you a tour later."

"No tours," Emma said, a little too loudly. "Cam, let me introduce Alex Ralsten." She gestured to the man next to her. A smile played at one corner of his smug mouth. "He's Brett's best man."

"Nice to meet you." Cam reached out a hand. He still didn't like how close Alex stood to Emma, but otherwise he couldn't complain yet.

"And this is Brett," Holly said, and he turned to find her with an arm around her fiancé's waist. Brett had her tucked in against his side, and she looked over the moon, which was so much better than her mood in the cottage. Cam didn't care if he had to parade shirtless all night to distract Mitsy Carmichael. As long as it made things easier for Holly and Emma.

The senator shook his hand with sincere enthusiasm. "Holly has told me a lot about you," Brett said, nodding. "It's a pleasure to finally meet you."

"Likewise," Cam said, but couldn't help adding, "Take care of her, okay?"

"I will."

For the next thirty minutes, Cam did his best to keep Brett's mom entertained with stories of life in their small town.

He breathed out a sigh of relief when the woman excused herself to take a phone call, feeling like he needed a shower, a drink and a nap in equal measure.

"You're a consummate host," Emma said, coming to stand next to him in front of the window. "Although showing off your abs might have been taking things a bit too far."

"Mitsy didn't seem to mind," he said, earning a soft chuckle from Emma that sent awareness zinging along his nerve endings.

"I thought I might have to hold her back from jumping you," she said, giving him a gentle elbow to the ribs. "I didn't like it."

That made him smile. "Jealous of the mother of the groom?"

"I shouldn't be. I definitely shouldn't admit it."

"If it makes you feel better, I want to drive my fist into Alex Ralsten's perfect face every time he smiles at you."

"Alex isn't my type," Emma said and reached out to trail her finger across Cam's forearm.

She was lying. Alex or some successful, buttoned-up suit like him would be exactly her type.

"What do you think about the senator?" he asked, because he didn't want to think about Emma belonging with someone other than him.

"I think he's a good guy. He truly loves Holly. She's tougher than she gives herself credit for, so I think she'll be fine."

"How does it feel to have your first guests?" He took a step back to examine her. "You look absolutely in your element." With her fancy clothes and hair pulled back into a low bun, she looked beautiful and radiant and like hope for the future all wrapped up in one lovely package. It made Cam yearn for that same hope, any hope.

"I love it," she admitted, like she couldn't quite believe it herself. "It feels like where I'm supposed to be." She placed her hand on top of his. "Thank you for helping me make it happen."

"Me and my super abs." He made the joke because to answer her seriously might reveal too much.

"Look who was able to join us, after all."

Cam turned, along with everyone else, to see Mitsy standing in the doorway to the room with Karen Adams, Holly's mom, at her side. Karen held an aluminum tray covered with foil.

"I made brownies," she said as her nervous gaze snagged on Holly's. "It's not polite to show up empty-handed."

"Mom, hi." Holly rushed forward, and Cam had the sudden urge to dive out the window or behind the sofa or anywhere to keep him out of Karen's line of sight.

"You okay?" Emma shifted closer, like she knew what he was thinking.

"She can't see me," Cam answered, sweat pooling between his shoulder blades. He hadn't seen Karen since the day of Dana's funeral, when she'd told him outright she would always blame him for her daughter's death. He didn't care about the blame. Hell, a part of him welcomed it even still.

But he wasn't sure what reaction Karen would have to finding him with Holly and learning of his role in her wedding preparations.

As if on cue, she glanced past Mitsy's shoulder and her gaze snagged on his. He went stock-still, like an animal in the crosshairs of a hunter's rifle.

"Cam." The color drained from her face, and he watched in horrified slow motion as her fingers released their grip on the tray. It crashed to the wide plank floor with a clatter, pieces of fudgy brownie flying through the air like bits of shrapnel.

The look of horror in her eyes sliced through Cam's heart with the same intensity of a sharp blade.

Holly took her arm. "Mom, it's okay. Cam has been working on the repairs to the inn. I asked him to help so everything would be done on time. He's the reason we can have my wedding here."

"No." The word was spoken in a guttural whisper. "Not him." Her wild gaze darted around the room before settling on Holly. "Not after what he did to your sister."

"It was an accident." Holly shook her head. "Mom, you know it wasn't Cam's fault. It's been too long to keep this going. Dana wouldn't want it."

"You don't know," Karen shouted. "You can't know that because she isn't here to tell you."

"Mom, please."

"I'll go," Cam said, more to himself than anyone else. Again, he glanced toward the window. He'd almost rather hurl himself out that way than have to walk past Dana's mother and her palpable sorrow.

Emma stepped closer to him. "You don't have to."

He looked down at her, amazed that she could manage to utter those words with the chaos erupting around them. This scene could ruin everything she'd worked so hard to make right. Mitsy, Brett and Alex were watching Karen's breakdown with similar looks of horrified curiosity. It was like a literal train wreck happening in front of them.

As comforting as it would be to lose himself in Emma's confidence, Cam knew better. It wasn't an accident that he'd kept himself far away from most people for the past five years. He never should have allowed himself to believe it could be different.

Holding his breath like that would protect him from feeling anything more, he walked toward the front door, keeping his gaze forward so he wouldn't have to make eye contact with anyone.

"Cam, don't go," Holly said as he moved past her and Karen. "It's okay."

Dana's mother flinched away, curling in on herself like his presence was a physical blow.

"It's not, kid. But you'll be fine. You've got this."

The sooner he retreated, the sooner he hoped he'd be able to say the same for himself.

CHAPTER FIFTEEN

EMMA CHECKED THE clock on the stove as she walked through the darkened kitchen toward the back door the following night.

"Thank you for not letting Holly give up on me," a voice said from the shadows.

She startled and raised a hand to her chest. Flipping on the pendant light above the sink, she turned to the breakfast nook to see Brett at the table. He sat forward, his hands cupping a tumbler of dark liquid.

"I thought everyone was asleep. Probably need to get used to not being alone in the house since I hope to have a full inn most nights."

He gave a small laugh. "Believe it or not, I only sleep well when Holly's next to me. My personal security blanket. I tried to convince her to stay over, but with my mom across the hall, there was no way."

"That would be a lot for Holly to handle."

"Everything about my life is a lot to handle," he told her. "I'm wondering if any of it is worth the effort."

"Holly thinks so."

"You're the kind of woman my mom would have chosen for me."

"I'd make a terrible political wife." Emma didn't bother to deny that she'd be right for him on paper. The old version of her, anyway. "Although it would have made my mom happy, as well."

"And we'd be miserable."

"I already had an unhappy marriage," Emma admitted. "Been there, done that. I've stopped living for my mom's benefit."

Brett lifted his glass in her direction. "I don't know whether to be jealous or inspired."

"Neither. Life is complicated no matter what."

"Speaking of complications…" He gestured to the set of keys in her hand. "I'm guessing you're going to see Holly's brother-in-law."

"The infuriating man only has a landline so I can't even text to check in with him, and he's not answering his phone this weekend."

"Holly told me how much her sister's death had affected her mom, but I didn't realize the extent of it until that scene yesterday."

"Cam knew," Emma said quietly. "I think it's part of why he keeps such a low profile in town and definitely why he didn't want his involvement in repairing the inn widely broadcasted."

"Why wouldn't he move away?" The question sounded rhetorical, but Emma answered, anyway.

"This is his home. It's the place he was happiest and holds his memories with Dana. I don't think it's as simple as leaving. At least for him." She gripped her keys tighter. "Your mother handled it better than I would have expected."

"She's good in a crisis." Brett nodded. "As twisted as this sounds, I think understanding that facet of Holly's life made her attitude soften a bit. I'm not sure how long it will last, but she's been lovely and supportive to both of us this weekend."

"Lovely and supportive." Emma tried not to cringe. "All it took was Karen Adams practically having a breakdown in my living room."

Brett sighed. "Right. Now you understand why I'm here and not in bed. I need something to help calm myself."

"I understand that need, but I think counting sheep works almost as well."

"Will we be on our own for breakfast tomorrow?" Brett asked with a wink.

"You don't know me well enough to ask that question," Emma told him in her best schoolmarm voice.

"I'm sorry," he said immediately. "I was trying to lighten the mood. I didn't mean—"

"Joking," Emma told him, and moved toward the door. "I'll be here in the morning."

"Please thank Camden for how he helped smooth the waters with my mom yesterday. It was slightly disturbing to watch her drooling over a guy who's close to my age, but it helped Holly relax and that's what counts."

"He cares a lot about her."

"Maybe not just her," Brett observed.

"Good night, Senator."

Emma walked out into the night trying not to think about whether Cam cared about her. She wasn't even certain it was a great idea to head to his house this late, but like Brett, she hadn't been able to sleep.

She hated not hearing from Cam or knowing how he was doing after the scene yesterday, but she'd barely had a minute to herself with all of the wedding planning and entertaining over the past twenty-four hours. She'd called Mayor Mal earlier and asked him to check in on Cam since she knew he was friends with Cam's family.

He'd texted her just before dinner that Cam had been at home but refused to talk other than through the screen door.

She drove through the quiet streets of Magnolia and along the two-lane highway that led to Cam's house. The closer she got, the more her heartbeat seemed to pick up. Twice, she pulled over to the side of the road and talked herself out of turning around.

Finally she parked outside his house, relieved to see a light still on inside. They were friends, she told herself. At the very least, she needed to make sure Karen's outburst hadn't convinced him not to return to the inn on Monday.

Well, that wasn't exactly true. She could pretend all she wanted that her concern was his job at the inn, but finishing the work wasn't what kept her up most of last night. It was thinking about the pain in Cam's eyes when Holly's mom reacted the way she did.

Emma never wanted to see that kind of hurt or guilt in his dark gaze again.

As soon as she got out of the car, she heard Toby's bark from inside the house. At least her arrival wouldn't be a surprise.

The porch light flipped on and Cam appeared in the doorway. He opened the screen to let the dog run down the steps to greet her.

"Hi, sweet boy," she said as she bent to scratch the top of Toby's head."

"Hello to you, too," Cam called.

"You need a cell phone," she told him as she approached the house. "How am I supposed to know if you're okay when you don't answer your landline?"

His full mouth remained tipped down in a frown. "You are under no obligation to worry about me." He whistled for Toby, then added, "Neither is Malcolm."

"I worried, anyway."

He crossed his arms over his chest, and Emma realized he wasn't going to make this easy for her. Fine. She'd gotten used to dealing with hard in the past few months. No matter what he thought about himself, she believed Cam was worth the effort.

"Can I come in?" she asked.

"Why?"

"To talk to you."

"Mal did a lot of talking earlier today. I might be all talked out."

"What if I want to come in for a little hot, blow-off-some-steam sex?" she asked conversationally.

"Nothing little about that idea." He pushed open the screen with a smirk.

Okay, he'd called her bluff. But if he wanted to play the jerk, she'd go along with it. She'd already told herself that this night was about him. He'd been there for her when she needed a release. The least she could do was return the favor.

In truth, she wanted to be with him in whatever way he'd have her. They could blow off steam now and talk later, but she wouldn't let him wallow in his crushing sadness alone. She glanced around the living room, neat and tidy but devoid of any keepsakes that would make the house look like a home.

Turning to face him, she began to unbutton the sleeveless blouse she wore. Cam's nostrils flared and she could see desire flame in his dark eyes. Praise the Lord she'd at least had the foresight to wear a decent bra.

As she began to lower her blouse to the floor, he reached out and drew the two sides together. "Keep your clothes on," he said, his voice hoarse, then he let out a low string of curses. "Seriously, I have no idea how your mind works. You can't just show up here and strip down for me."

She shrugged. "If it will help you feel better, I can."

"You'd let me use you like that?"

"I wouldn't consider it being used."

"You need a better self-preservation instinct." He shook his head. "How's Holly?"

The concern in his voice tugged at Emma's heart. How could this man think he was such a monster when at every turn he was willing to sacrifice himself to take care of the people he loved? Again she wondered what would it be like to be on the receiving end of that sort of devotion? Her breath caught at the mere thought of it.

"She's doing well, thanks to you."

"You must be joking. Everyone saw how her mom reacted to me."

"Yes, but for some strange—and possibly twisted—reason, Brett's mom has been nicer to her ever since. It's like somehow Karen's freak-out caused some cosmic emotional shift inside Mitsy. She's now suddenly being maternal and decent and no one understands why."

"Do you think it's an act?"

"I want to believe Mitsy's had a change of heart because she sees the origin of some of Holly's self-confidence issues and insecurities. It doesn't seem like an act, and I'm watching them closely."

"I hate that I caused her to have self-confidence issues."

"You?"

"Of course me." He lifted and lowered one big shoulder. "Holly was a happy-go-lucky teenager before Dana's death. It's my fault if that changed."

"I've never met a happy-go-lucky teenager," Emma

countered. "Do you take the blame for climate change, as well?"

"Excuse me?"

"Cam, the world doesn't revolve around you and everything you touch. Every person you encounter won't suffer because of you." She leaned and said in a stage whisper, "You might need to work on the ego."

His eyes widened in shock, but before he had a chance to answer, there was a faint scratching at the front door. He turned to let Toby in, and Emma hid her smile. If nothing else, she was distracting him from self-pity.

"You're right," he said as he faced her again.

The dog trotted over, nudged her leg and then climbed on the couch.

"Toby, off," Cam said with no real heat behind the command.

Toby lifted his head and then began cleaning his manly bits.

Emma laughed and started to lower her arms before realizing her shirt was still undone. She buttoned it, but a moment later, Cam's hands covered hers.

"Why are you here?" he asked gently, so close that she could feel his warm breath on her cheeks.

"I wanted to make sure you're okay. That was rough yesterday."

"Yeah."

"Holly's mom has a lot of unresolved anger and grief."

"Understandably."

"That doesn't make your late wife's accident your fault."

"It's easier for everyone if it is."

She lifted a hand to his cheek and tipped up his chin until he met her gaze. "Not you. No matter what you tell me, I don't believe it's easier for you."

"I'd rather blame myself and stay holed away in my small world than to venture out if it means someone reacting the way Karen did. Dana had a lot of friends around Magnolia."

"I bet you did, too."

"Not really."

"You have a family."

"They're better off without me."

"Don't say that." Emma lifted onto her tiptoes and placed a kiss on the corner of his mouth. "Don't ever say that. People aren't better off without the ones they love. You lost your wife, which is a horrible tragedy, Cam. But now your parents have lost their son, and that wasn't necessary."

"I was broken." He pressed his forehead against hers. His breath came out in raspy puffs. "I still am. My pain was so big. It was like a black hole that sucked in everything around me."

"Bent is different than broken. We're all a little bent, but you're still standing. You have to remember that."

"Would it be wrong to say I wish I was horizontal with you instead of standing?"

She laughed. "If you remember, I tried seducing you a few minutes ago. You weren't interested."

"I'm interested." He leaned back and cupped her face in his big hands. "It scares me how much I'm interested."

His eyes were intense on hers, and there was no way to doubt the truth in his words. Still…

"We're in this together."

"Repairing the inn?" he asked, and she knew he was purposely misunderstanding her words.

"The horizontal part. I'm not…you can't just…" Heat rose to her cheeks. "I want to be with you, Cam. All the way with you."

He didn't smile, but his eyes crinkled at the corners. "I want to be all the way with you, Emma."

His lips met hers in a melding of wanting both a physical and emotional release. Just like that, her doubts about whether she was doing the right thing vanished. It could only be right to feel this kind of connection.

The need between them stoked higher, like a flame that had been doused with kerosene. Soon they were tugging at clothes and nipping at skin. Emma gave herself over to the feel of his hands on her and the sensation of his mouth exploring the most sensitive parts of her. As frenzied as she felt, Cam didn't rush the tempo. It was as if during their one time together he'd memorized everything she liked the best and now could use it to turn her into a puddle of lustful goo.

But Emma wasn't going there alone. She dragged her teeth along the base of his throat, wanting to elicit the same reaction in him as he had in her. And it worked because he let out a low groan and then lifted her into his arms, carrying her toward the back of the house and what she assumed was his bedroom.

Of course Toby thought this was a game he wanted to be involved in, and they almost went down when Cam tripped over the excited dog.

"On your bed," Cam commanded the animal as Emma choked back a laugh.

"I don't think laughter is supposed to be part of foreplay," Cam said, his voice still rough. "You're going to give me a complex."

"Laughter should be a part of everything," Emma corrected. "Trust me, I know you have skills."

"You have no idea of the skills I have," he said with an exaggerated leer.

She laughed again as he lowered her to his bed. He

hadn't turned on the lights in the room, but from the glow of the hallway light she could see dark wood furniture with simple lines, exactly what she would have expected from Cam. The room was neat with no clothes strewn about in piles, and the sheets smelled fresh like laundry detergent.

Since when had laundry detergent become an aphrodisiac?

Cam hooked his fingers in the waistband of her black yoga pants and tugged them over her hips. Her breath caught as his gaze went even more heated. If a man could worship her with a look, that's how Cam made her feel. She sat up and undid her bra clasp as Cam took off his shorts and boxers.

This was happening. It should terrify Emma that her heart was just as involved as her body.

She needed to keep her heart out of this mix.

As he lowered himself on top of her and claimed her mouth once more, the bond clicked into overdrive and the thrill of being with him tamped down any of her doubts like a heavy snowfall. There was no distraction, no noise, only the rustle of the sheets and the quiet of discovering even more ways they fit together perfectly.

She arched up to meet him. They drove each other to the edge of pleasure and then over again, demanding and responsive. Sensation roared through her, and she knew there was no way to keep her heart safe from this man.

CAM HAD STAYED awake for hours on Saturday night, holding Emma in his arms as she slept. It wasn't as if she was the first woman he'd been with since Dana's death, but no one else had meant anything.

Emma meant more to him than was prudent for either of them.

She'd come to Magnolia to start over and build a new life for herself, not to saddle herself with a man dealing with enough issues to keep a therapist busy for years.

Cam hated being the guy with issues.

He liked that he didn't feel that way with Emma. When they were together, he felt like he could be whole again, but he understood it wasn't fair to put that kind of responsibility on her.

He needed to deal with his own life, and despite how working at the inn made him happy, he still didn't feel as though he deserved it.

He'd eventually drifted off only to wake as the first rays of light began to curl across the sky in ribbons of orange and pink by the sound of Emma getting dressed.

"I need to get back before anyone wakes up." She spoke quietly even though it was just the two of them in the room.

Disappointment pinged through him, although he understood her rationale. "I'm going fishing with my brother later."

Her face lit with pleasure. "You are? Cam, that's fantastic."

It was also a lie, and he didn't even know why he'd made the claim. But after she left, and fueled by several cups of coffee, Cam dialed Ash's number. His brother picked up on the first ring. He sounded both shocked and genuinely pleased that Cam was inviting him for a day on the boat.

They fished for hours and talked about everything and nothing. Ash was a year older than Cam and growing up he'd cast a large shadow in his wake. Cam had wanted to follow in his big brother's footsteps but didn't have the brains or the focus to make that happen. It had been easier to go in the opposite direction—if he couldn't live up to his parents' expectations, why not lower the bar as much as possible?

His lack of direction might have frustrated the hell out of Mom and Dad, but Ash had taken it all in stride. It was as if his brother never lost faith that Cam would eventually find his way.

For a while, everyone thought he had, but the furniture making and the goals he set ended up being just a prelude to the biggest failure of his life. The failure to take care of his wife. To keep her safe and out of harm's way.

They didn't talk about Dana or that part of the past. Ash asked about Cam's work on the inn and whether he might continue to take on clients around town after he finished with Emma.

"She's pretty," Ash observed while discussing the Wildflower Inn. "I met her at a town meeting. I think Mal wanted to set me up with her."

Cam's heart skipped a beat. Of course it shouldn't surprise him. He'd seen the way Brett Carmichael's friend had been drawn to Emma. She wasn't flashy or overt but held an inherent beauty and level of class that was even more appealing. Ash would be a perfect match for her.

Perfect in a way Cam could never manage.

"She's focused on getting the inn up and running," Cam told his brother with a shrug. By the way Ash studied him, Cam wondered if his tone had given something away. But Ash didn't push the issue.

In the end, the day was easy in a way that made Cam wonder if Emma was right. Why had he cut himself off from the people who loved him for so long?

He and Ash had made a plan to go for a beer the following week. Then Cam returned home and forced himself not to call Emma to tell her about his day. Maybe he needed to revisit the whole cell phone deal, after all. Late-night texting with Emma might be fun.

Now it was Monday, and he refocused his attention on the list he'd made of supplies he needed to finish the bathroom at the cottage. He stood in the hardware store, just after they'd opened at seven on Monday morning. He wanted to get to Emma's before Phil arrived. He couldn't very well steal a few kisses from her with an audience watching.

As he turned down the far aisle, someone stepped into his path.

"Cam."

He sucked in a breath and forced himself not to turn and run. "Hi, Dad," he murmured, heart hammering in his chest.

"Hello, son." His father studied him for several long moments before releasing a sigh. "You look good. Ash told us you looked good, but I had to see it for myself."

Cam silently cursed his brother. He hadn't specifically told Ash not to go running to their parents about spending the day together, but Cam figured it was an unspoken understanding.

"You look good, too," he said, even as emotion clogged his throat.

"Your mom still limits the desserts, you know?"

Cam nodded. They'd had a heart scare with his dad several years back, and his mom had gone into high gear with the heart-healthy diet. He wondered if his dad still kept the secret stash of Oreos hidden in the drawer of his workbench in the garage. Beer and Oreos were his father's favorite combination.

"She'd make an exception if you came to dinner." Chester straightened an already straight row of boxes on one of the shelves.

"That's not a great idea."

"You spent the day with Ash and it was fine."

"I also saw Karen Adams a few days ago and the results were less than fine. She practically had a nervous breakdown in the middle of a cocktail party. I don't want to upset Mom."

"It would make your mother so happy to see you," Chester said quietly. "Karen has struggled since…"

"I know why she struggles." Cam glanced down at his list without seeing anything. "I'm the reason she struggles."

"Come to dinner," his dad urged. "It's been too long, Camden."

"Mal told me you're still dealing with damage from the storm."

"We'll get it fixed eventually. In fact, I need to pick up some replacement shingles for the garage."

"Dad, you shouldn't be on the roof. Let Ash take care of things."

"Ash has enough to worry about. Hell, he's got the whole town to worry about." Chester squared his shoulders. "You know I'm plenty capable of handling roof damage."

Cam thought about the steep pitch of his parents' roof. "I'll come for dinner tomorrow night," he said before he could think better of it. "We can figure out what needs to be done, and I'll make time for it."

"Okay, then." When his father didn't argue, Cam knew he'd been played. "I told Ash I had to pick up materials this morning. You knew I'd be here."

"It's been too long," his father repeated. "We should have never let you stay away."

"I don't think you could have stopped me, Dad." Cam

ran a hand through his hair. "I'm not sure this is smart for anyone. I don't want to get Mom's hopes up that things will get back to normal."

"She doesn't care about normal." His father lifted a hand like he wanted to reach for Cam, then lowered it again. For that, Cam was grateful. His emotions felt like spun glass. If his father touched him right now, he might shatter into a million pieces. "She cares about *you*."

"I might bring a friend tomorrow." Cam felt as shocked as his dad looked when the words tumbled out of his mouth. "The woman who's opening the inn. She's new to town and doesn't know a lot of people." Not that meeting his parents would do much for Emma's social life, but the thought of having her at his side made him feel slightly less nauseous.

"Sure," his dad agreed readily. "We'd love to meet any friend of yours."

He had no idea if Emma would even agree to go with him. He just knew he wanted her there.

CHAPTER SIXTEEN

"TELL ME AGAIN how you agreeing to dinner at your parents' house is my responsibility."

Emma glanced over at Cam, who gripped the steering wheel so tight she feared he might crack a bone. He'd shown up at the inn yesterday morning hot under the collar because of an invitation he'd accepted to have dinner with his mom and dad. He'd barged into the kitchen while she was cleaning up after trying a new peach muffin recipe, spewing out a convoluted story of fishing with his brother, who was a disloyal traitor, and how his father had ambushed him in the hardware store.

"Happy Monday to you, too," she'd said, and walked forward to kiss him.

"You kissed me."

"Yes."

He'd glanced around the kitchen like he expected to see a camera filming them. "You can't do that in public. What if someone sees?"

"No one is here but you and me."

She hadn't understood his worry, but at least it had seemed to defuse his agitation. He'd sunk into one of the kitchen chairs, and she'd managed to pull the story out of him while he inhaled almost a half dozen muffins.

How much Cam appreciated her baking skills made her inordinately proud. Of course, Brett and his friend Alex had enjoyed what she made just as enthusiastically, but they didn't matter to her the way Cam did.

Cam mattered a lot.

Which was why she'd agreed to accompany him to dinner with his family, even though she knew he was just using her as a buffer. But the fact he'd agreed to see his mom and dad was a huge step.

"I was happy keeping to myself," he muttered as he pulled onto a tree-lined street with rows of modest ranchers on either side.

"You weren't happy."

"I wasn't unhappy," he countered.

"You were miserable."

"Rude of you to point it out."

She grinned. "I like that I don't have to censor myself around you."

"I'd prefer a bit of censoring."

"I don't think so." She reached across the console and covered his hand on the steering wheel with hers. "I think you like me just the way I am."

"I like you better naked and in my bed." He loosened his grip and linked their fingers together. "Let's skip dinner and go to my place."

"She's waiting for you," Emma murmured as she caught sight of a woman sitting on the edge of a small porch about halfway down the block. There was no doubt in her mind the woman was Cam's mother.

"I said horrible things to push her away."

"She knows you were hurting."

"That doesn't make it okay."

"Then you can make it up to her now."

"I don't know how."

"Dinner is a start."

She saw his chest rise and fall as he slowed the truck. For a hot second, she thought he might spin the vehicle around and head in the other direction. But he pulled to a stop at the curb.

"You've got this."

"I keep picturing the reaction Holly's mother had to me. Like she was coming face-to-face with the devil himself."

"Your mom is waiting." Emma squeezed his hand before releasing it. "I have a feeling she's been waiting all this time."

He got out of the car, and Emma stayed where she was as he walked toward the house. She was here to support Cam, but this reunion belonged to him and his mother.

She swiped at her cheeks as his mom stood. Tears streamed down the older woman's face. Emma could see the resemblance. Although Cam's mom looked to be nearly a foot shorter than him, she had the same thick, dark hair—albeit streaked with gray—and similar olive-toned skin. As he got closer, his mother opened her arms and moved forward to embrace him.

Emma's chest constricted at how tight the other woman held on. For a ridiculous moment, Emma wondered what it would feel like to have that kind of welcome from her own mother. The love Cam's mom felt for him was palpable even from where she sat in the car.

But she pushed away thoughts of her situation. Tonight was about him, and she understood how much he needed it after the scene with Karen Adams.

Cam needed unconditional love and a chance to believe he was worthy of it more than anyone she'd ever met, and his mother gave it without reservation.

After a few minutes of quiet conversation, Cam turned and gestured to her. His face was flushed with unspoken emotion, but as she got out of the truck, Emma realized he seemed more at peace than he had been at any moment since she'd met him.

"Hi, Mrs. Arlinghaus," she said as she walked forward. "I'm Emma. It's nice to—"

"Thank you." The woman rushed forward and wrapped her arms around Emma's shoulders. "Cam said you encouraged him to come to dinner tonight. I can't thank you enough."

"Oh. Okay." Emma returned the hug and tried not to think of how much it meant to her.

"You have to call me Melinda," the woman told her. "And I want to hear all about your plans for the inn. It's such a lovely idea for the Reed house."

Emma handed Melinda the small hostess gift she'd brought, which resulted in another warm hug. Cam was grinning at the two of them, and she was amazed he'd been able to stay away from this kind of easy affection. Emma felt like a sponge soaking it up.

By the time they got to the cozy kitchen, she was practically drunk on the feeling of acceptance his mother offered. The back door opened and a tall, husky man just a few inches shorter than Cam walked in.

"Chester, come and meet Cam's new friend."

Emma's cheeks colored at the emphasis placed on the word *friend*, especially when she didn't know how to describe what she felt for him.

"I hope you like burgers," Chester said, then shook her hand and patted Cam on the shoulder.

"Yes, and I appreciate being here," Emma told him. "There's so much to do to get ready for the wedding and opening the inn. I tend to work around the clock. It's nice to have an excuse for a night off."

"Son, you need to make sure this hardworking young lady gets a break."

Something sharp flashed in Cam's gaze and a heavy cloud of remorse seemed to permeate the room. She could almost feel the weight of his lingering guilt begin to choke off the air Cam breathed.

"He works even more than I do," Emma said with a purposeful grin. She refused to let the past creep into this night and cast any sort of pall over Cam's first attempts at a reunion with his mom and dad. "I think he just likes to parade around in his tool belt."

Both Cam and his father choked back equally disbelieving guffaws of laughter. Cam's mom offered Emma a grateful smile.

"I do not parade around," Cam protested, but his eyes softened.

"I'd love to see the changes you've made to the house," Melinda told Emma as she took condiment bottles from the refrigerator. "The property definitely needed some tender loving care. What made you decide to open an inn?"

Emma didn't relish being the center of attention, but she realized Cam's mom was also working hard to keep the tone of the evening light. "I first came to Magnolia to visit my brother. He was staying out at the beach. I fell in love with the town and the house. It seemed like the perfect place for a boutique inn that would welcome guests and make them feel at home. I want whoever stays at the Wildflower to appreciate how special it is. And, of course, to give them a place to hang out at night after a perfect day of sightseeing or fishing or sunbathing at the beach."

"I hope you have a board game closet," Chester told her. "People love board games."

"That's such a great idea." Emma nodded. "I hadn't gotten that far, but I'm going to order some online tomorrow. What are your favorites?"

"Cam is a master Scrabble player," Melinda offered.

Emma turned to him, blinking. "Scrabble?"

"What can I say?" He shrugged. "I get lucky with the triple point words."

"It used to annoy the heck out of Ash," Chester said as he took a spatula from the drawer and picked up the serving plate Melinda had placed on the counter. "The boys were so competitive, but Cam always won."

"It irritated him because he was smarter," Cam clarified.

"You're both smart," Melinda said.

"I'm pretty good at Scrabble," Emma announced.

"We'll play after dinner," Chester said, winking at her. "It's about time someone knocked Cam off the Scrabble throne."

Cam and his father took some time after the meal to discuss the repairs needed from the storm damage, while Emma helped his mom clean up the kitchen. Emma appreciated Melinda's efforts to keep the conversation light, as if she wanted to tread carefully with her son's new and unexpected friend.

The rest of the evening passed in undulating waves of effortless camaraderie and awkward tension. One minute they'd all be laughing and joking. The next a casual comment would send Cam into long minutes of preoccupied silence. Emma appreciated that his mom and dad never gave up. It was obvious how much Cam's parents loved him and also how scared they were of pushing him away.

When she'd commented on a striking desk that had been given pride of place in the family room, Chester proudly explained that he and Cam had built it together. She'd turned to Cam, only to see a muscle twitch in his hard-set jaw, like having his gift with carpentry recognized was almost painful. His dad quickly changed the subject and got out the Scrabble game board while Melinda served a generous helping of strawberry trifle to each of them.

By the end of the second round—both of which Cam won—she could see tension pooling around the edges of his mouth despite his smile. He'd gone way out of his comfort zone tonight, far past what she would have expected from him when they'd first met.

It was clear how much he didn't want to hurt either of his parents and how worried he was that he might do just that.

Emma faked a yawn and pushed back from where she knelt next to the coffee table. "I'm sorry to cut the evening short, but I have an early day tomorrow."

Cam popped up from the sofa like a Mexican jumping bean. "Which means I do, too. She's a taskmaster."

"Of course," his mom agreed, and his father nodded. "We're so glad you both could be here tonight." She patted Cam's arm, clearly unable to resist touching him. She'd been doing it all night, finding tiny reasons to reach out. He seemed to understand, although Emma wondered if the physical closeness was part of what contributed to his strain.

They walked to the front door only to see Cam's brother striding across the grass toward the house. It was clear the two were related. Asher Arlinghaus was leaner than Cam with his dark hair close-cropped and his strong jaw clean-shaven.

He wore the tan uniform of the local sheriff's department and a gold badge glinted from above the chest pocket on his shirt.

"I just finished up at work," he called, waving as he

approached. "Thought I'd stop by and see if Cam left any food."

"We have a burger for you," their mom said. Emma could practically see her bursting with happiness at having her whole family together, if only for a few minutes.

"You missed a couple of rounds of Scrabble," Chester said, hitching a thumb in Cam's direction. "One guess who won."

Ash's easy smile widened and he turned to Emma. "He's annoying as hell with those triple points."

Emma giggled, then put a hand over her mouth. She imagined Ash had that effect on most women. He was handsome and obviously charming, but he didn't make her heart stutter the way his moody, often sullen brother did. "I'll get him next time," she promised.

"You two should get together and practice," Cam said tightly, then inclined his head toward his brother. "Plus, Emma likes nature. You could take her to your cabin in the mountains."

The words were like a fart going off in church. Emma, along with his parents and Ash, stared at Cam like he'd lost his mind.

"Well, we should go," Emma said, not sure how to respond to Cam's bizarre outburst.

They said goodbye, and Melinda promised to stop by the inn later that week. Cam's entire demeanor had changed with the arrival of his brother. Emma wanted a do-over on the past five minutes and she wanted to throttle Cam for ruining a perfect night with his folks. She couldn't decide which was higher on her wish list.

"DID YOU JUST try to pimp me out to your brother?"

Cam blinked at Emma's abrupt question and the temper

in her tone as she asked it. He was already feeling strung out from trying to stay happy and chipper with his parents. To be the son they deserved, if only for one night.

He could barely admit, even to himself, how much it meant to hug his mom again. It had been tempting to allow himself to sink into the swamp of regret at how much time he'd lost because he was too much of a coward to try to re-build the bridges he'd burned. He'd convinced himself that it was better for everyone if he stayed away, but he could no longer stomach the lie.

"I've already heard from Ash that the mayor wanted to set you two up. I know you both, so it seems natural I'd help things along."

"Natural?" The word came out on an angry squeak. "It seems natural to you to push me on another man when I'd bet money my scent is still on your sheets."

Ouch.

She sucked in a breath that was both ragged and sharp. "Is that why you let things go as far as they did with us? Was I a way to stick it to your brother? You resent him, so you turn me into some kind of sloppy-seconds showdown?"

"What? No." Cam shook his head, not sure how they'd gone down this miserable path so quickly. "Emma, no."

He'd just turned into the long driveway that led to the inn, and panic gripped his chest. This was why he remained a loner. No matter how hard he tried to be normal, he could muck it up like a pro.

"Pull over," she commanded.

"I can drive you to the door." Cam shook his head. In truth, he'd hoped to spend the night with her. He needed the comfort and distraction, a way to take the edge off his tumbling emotions after the evening at his mom and dad's.

Oh, hell. He was truly an ass.

"I'll walk to the door," she muttered, but he was already in front of the house.

"Emma, I'm sorry. Please don't go away angry. I screwed this up. Tonight. You. I'm sorry."

She placed a hand on the door handle and then paused. "Why?"

"It's what I do," he answered without hesitation.

"That's a cop-out." She glanced over her shoulder, and he could see the tears shimmering in her eyes. He hated those tears. Not quite as much as he hated himself right now.

"Ash is perfect. My parents are great." He thumped his open palm on the steering wheel. "They could give Ward and June Cleaver a run for their money."

She arched a brow. "Are you really going down the *Leave It to Beaver* path right now? We're a few generations past the golden age, Cam."

"What can I say? I watched television with my grandpa when he was in the nursing home. It was all old-time stuff. Black and white."

"No distracting me," she told him with a sniff.

Right. "You make me happy, and I don't think I deserve to be happy."

There, he'd said it. That was as honest as he could be, and it cut to the very heart of every issue in his life.

"You do."

"No." He shook his head. "Tonight was the perfect example of why. It was a great night in so many ways, and I have to find a way to ruin it. Will you look at me?"

Her fingers tightened on the handle and for a terrifying span of seconds, he thought he'd pushed her too far. That she was going to well and truly walk away.

Then she shifted to face him, and something inside him moved, as well. She hadn't given up or walked away, when both of those options would be much easier. He desperately wanted to prove he was worthy of her faith in him.

"I'd given up on having any sort of a fulfilling life until you. I'm not even sure I have the guts to keep trying after you don't need me anymore. Self-sabotage seems to be my specialty, but I'm sorry you're having to feel the repercussions of that."

"Do you really want me to date your brother?" she asked quietly.

"God, no," Cam breathed. "It would be like shoving a hot poker in my eye to think of seeing you with him. Honestly, I don't want to think about you dating anyone, although you should be with a fantastic guy, Emma." He reached out and tucked a long lock of hair behind her ear. "Your ex-husband is a dou—a doofus."

Her mouth quirked on one side. "I'd agree with that, but it doesn't mean the things he found fault with in me aren't true."

"You're perfect," Cam insisted.

"I'm not," she argued. "Neither is your brother. No one can be, and it's a standard I don't want to be held to anymore. I just want to be me. I like that I can do that with you."

"I'd like to be someone else but me," he admitted, leaning his head back on the headrest.

"Your parents seem to like you the way you are. Although I agree with Ash that your propensity to win at Scrabble would get annoying."

"Dana refused to play with me," he said, and then regretted the words. "I'm sorry. I shouldn't talk about her."

"Don't apologize for that. She was and still is a part of your life. Do you think she would have been glad to see you with your parents?"

He nodded. "Family was important to Dana. Loyalty. She wanted to take care of everyone, sometimes at the expense of caring for herself."

"She sounds like the one who was perfect."

Cam thought about that. A few weeks ago he would have agreed with the assessment. Maybe even a few minutes ago. But he realized that putting the people around him up on these pedestals was just another defense mechanism. He didn't have to try to be the best because how could he measure up to perfection when he had so many flaws?

In a lot of ways, the flaws were what made things interesting. He'd taken his happiness with Dana for granted. He'd been careless with their time together. Now he realized how precious of a gift it was to feel happiness instead of the never-ending deluge of sorrow.

"No," he said, and instead of feeling disloyal as he expected, the memories of his late wife were softer and sweeter for the truth. "She had plenty of imperfections. I guess everyone does. Even Ash, although the people around here would be hard-pressed to name one."

"It's probably because they're distracted by his butt in that uniform."

Cam snorted. "Were you ogling the sheriff's butt?" he demanded. "Ogling and now taunting me with that knowledge."

The teasing light had returned to Emma's eyes, and he was profoundly grateful for it. "You're the one who wanted to play matchmaker."

"I take it all back."

"Good." She leaned in closer. "Because you're the one that I want."

He nuzzled his nose into the crook of her neck, breathing in her sweet scent. "Is this the part where I tell you that my grandpa also had a thing for cheesy musicals, so now I've got chills that are multiplying?"

Her laughter bubbled up, making an answering effervescence shimmer in his chest.

"Do you want to come in?" she asked, pulling back enough to meet his gaze. "Because maybe you need some TLC for those chills."

"Yeah." He nodded solemnly. "They're actually electrifying."

She laughed again, then began to hum as she got out of the truck.

"Did we just have our first fight?" she asked as she linked her fingers with his. "Because if so that means we get to make up now."

"I don't want to fight, and I don't want to hurt you, Emma." He paused, digging in his heels when she would have tugged him forward. Every sensible fiber of his being told him to shut his mouth and enjoy the moment. The problem was he wanted so badly to cherish all the moments he got to spend with her. But he didn't want to give her false hope. Emma spoke very little about her life before coming to Magnolia.

Hell, she knew almost every dark shadow in his soul, and all he knew was that she had an ex-husband who'd done a number on her self-confidence.

"I can take care of myself." She placed a finger on his lips to quiet him when he would have argued. "I mean it, Cam. I understand what you can and can't give, and I'm not looking for something more."

"Okay," he agreed, shocked to find his heart screaming in protest. How could she know what he was able to give when he had no clue?

"But I expect you to be honest with me. I let someone

take advantage of my heart once before, and I won't do it again."

His chest constricted, but he forced a light smile because that's what she needed from him. She'd given him so much, it was the least he could do. "Then I better shape up," he sang in an off-key baritone and scooped her into his arms.

CHAPTER SEVENTEEN

"I HATE THAT Cam left when his mom is coming to visit."
Emma paced back and forth in the kitchen later that week,
glancing between Angi and Meredith. Her brother's fiancée had stopped by on a social outing with one of the puppies Emma'd met at the gallery because the dog's sister
had been adopted.

"I don't want her to get depressed," Meredith had explained when Emma bent to greet the puppy, and somehow the statement made complete sense coming from the
animal rescue authority. Meredith seemed impressed with
the progress they'd made, and Emma appreciated the approval of her changes to the house from another of Niall
Reed's daughters.

"Mom, can we get a dog?" Andrew poked his head in
the back door. He was playing with the labradoodle mix
in the backyard.

"When hell freezes over," Angi said without hesitation.

"You shouldn't swear," Andrew said with an eye roll
before disappearing into the yard again.

"Doodles are great with kids." Meredith sat perched on
the corner of the island's countertop. She wore overalls
with a tank top under them, her dark hair held back with
a striped scarf. Despite her casual appearance, Meredith
looked both gorgeous and like the kind of woman who'd

naturally take command of either a litter of frisky pups or maybe an entire army.

Angi shook her head, not giving an inch. "They don't allow dogs over thirty pounds in my apartment complex. And I don't—"

"Then I'll find you a small one," Meredith interrupted before Angi could finish her thought. "Or a cat. Cats are good apartment pets."

"Can we focus on the issue at hand for a moment?" Emma took a deep breath and tried without success to calm her fluttering nerves. "Melinda will be here any minute."

"Of course," Meredith agreed with a nod. "In just one second. What if you foster her for a couple of weeks, Em? One puppy is much easier than two, and Ethel is fairly laid-back on her own. She'd benefit from meeting new people, and you kind of need a mascot. Every good inn has one."

"Has anyone ever told you that you have a one-track mind?"

Meredith made a face. "Occasionally, but it's for a good cause. Ethel has come a long way. I'm positive her previous family thought they were getting the image of the perfect Christmas card dog. But animals are more work than that, even the fluffy ones. She just needs a chance."

Wow. It was as if Meredith could read the doubts and old hurts in Emma's mind and had found a way to make the dog the perfect living, breathing metaphor for what Emma had gone through in her own life.

"Why haven't you asked me to foster earlier? I figured you didn't think I merited one of your animals."

"You figured wrong," Meredith said, "but you were also dealing with too much already. You seem settled, if a little anxious right now. A dog can help with that. Plus, I'm a big believer in matching the right animal with the right person. You and Ethel will be good together."

"If I agree to foster the dog," Emma said, not quite believing she was willing to make the bargain, "temporarily, that is. If I agree, can we talk about my problem?"

"Absolutely." Meredith did some sort of complicated heart-crossing thing.

"Well played," Angi told her, leveling a spatula in Meredith's direction.

"Coming for you next," Meredith warned.

"Okay, the dog can stay for a week." Emma held up a hand when Meredith would have argued. "Final offer."

"Done." Meredith hopped off the counter. "Why is it such a problem that you'll be giving her a tour on your own?"

"He purposely left to avoid her. I'm sure it's going to make her sad."

"A guy who wants to avoid his mother?" Angi laughed. "Not exactly unique behavior for a guy. My brothers try to evade my mom every chance they get."

"Cam finally reconnected with his mom." Emma closed her eyes and thought about the look of happiness on his mother's face when she'd first seen him step out of the truck before their dinner. "What if she's upset with me because he isn't here?"

"From how you described her, she's super nice." Angi smiled gently. "She isn't going to blame you."

"It's my fault," Emma confessed. "Or it might be. I might be pushing him too hard and too fast. I'm still afraid he's going to revert to his old behavior after Holly's wedding. There are only two weeks left until her big day, and it's important that he keeps moving forward with his life."

"More important than the publicity for the wedding or

booking the inn or scheduling a media open house?" Angi sent her a questioning look across the room.

"Yes," Emma breathed. She shouldn't admit that. She needed to focus on her life, on her goals. Cam was an adult. He could handle himself. Heck, he'd probably appreciate it if she'd leave him alone.

But she couldn't. She wouldn't.

"Then it might be good that he isn't here," Meredith said, moving around the counter to pluck a stuffed mushroom off the tray Angi had just taken from the oven. "If his mom is desperate to reconnect with him, I'm sure he can feel that."

"It probably freaks him out," Angi added.

"So she can talk to you." Meredith gave a soft moan when she bit into the bite-size hors d'oeuvre. "These are so good," she told Angi before returning her attention to Emma. "You can help her understand that she needs to take it slow."

"I don't think that's my role."

All three of them turned to the front of the house when the doorbell rang. "It is now," Meredith said.

As Emma suspected, the light in Melinda's eyes dimmed when she realized her son wasn't going to be the one showing her around the inn.

"If you want to come back at another time when he's here, I understand," Emma told her. "We had a good time at dinner the other night. It was a last-minute errand today."

"Camden doesn't do things on accident," his mother said gently. "There's a reason he's not here, and I'm going to respect that. I'd still like to see the work he's done if that's okay with you?"

"Of course." Emma led her through the house. It was actually quite fun to see the changes through another person's eyes. She could see by Melinda's reaction how far they'd come.

She introduced the older woman to Meredith, Angi and Andrew. Meredith was taking Ethel back to the rescue to pick up supplies and bedding before dropping her off again, and Melinda seemed to think it was lovely that Emma would be fostering a puppy despite everything else going on in her life. Emma's mom definitely would have voiced a different opinion.

"Holly's wedding weekend will be the soft opening for the inn," Emma explained as they walked through the cottage next door. "We have a couple of rooms booked for the following week and I've talked with two other potential brides who might be interested in having their weddings here. I still find it hard to believe that I'm in the wedding business. If it wasn't for Holly, I never would have gone in that direction." She placed a hand on Melinda's arm. "If it wasn't for Cam, we never would have gotten this far so quickly."

"He seems happy," Melinda said, a note of wonder in her voice. "I wasn't sure he'd ever let himself be happy again."

The woman had just voiced Emma's greatest fear. "I don't know if he can sustain it. He's so determined to blame himself."

"You're helping him." Melinda took both of Emma's hands in her own and squeezed.

Something about Melinda's words rubbed her the wrong way. Emma had come to Magnolia to help herself. The whole point of walking away from the life she'd known was to leave behind the part of herself who felt the need to take care of people, to make sure everyone was perfect and happy because that was the image expected of her. She didn't want that. She didn't want to be responsible for any-one other than herself.

"He doesn't need me," she told Cam's mom, even though they both knew it wasn't true. "If anyone deserves credit for any type of transformation, it's Holly. His dedication to her is what started all of this."

"I don't want him anywhere near my daughter."

They both turned to see Karen Adams standing a few feet behind them on the grass. Another reason Emma could use a dog around the place—so that people couldn't sneak up on her. Despite the summer heat, Karen wore a drab gray sweatshirt and baggy jeans with her hair pulled back from her face in a severe bun. She looked fragile and like she might be pushing the edge of feral. Her gaze zeroed in on Melinda, whose features had gone slack.

"He's cost me too much," Karen said to Cam's mother.

Emma thought Melinda would retreat, turn and walk the same way Cam had when Karen first saw him. Then she gave a small shake of her head and stepped forward. "Dana's accident wasn't Camden's fault."

"She was driving to a job she wouldn't have needed if she didn't have to support him." Karen clutched at the purse she held so tightly Emma thought she might rip the leather bag in two.

"Your daughter was one of the strongest women I knew. We loved her like she was our own daughter."

"She wasn't yours," Karen said, her words sharp like spikes.

If Melinda felt the sting, she didn't show it. Emma thought she might be witnessing firsthand what people meant by the phrase *steel magnolia*.

"She loved my boy," Melinda continued as if Karen wasn't shooting daggers from her red-rimmed eyes. "They belonged to each other. He might not have been the man you would have chosen, but they were good together. He would have done anything for her. You know that, Karen."

"I know she's gone."

"Her death broke him in the same way it did you. He cut off his family and friends, shrank his life to something that could fit on the head of a pin. He's been punishing himself for the past five years."

"Good," Karen whispered.

"No." Melinda's voice was stronger now. "Dana wouldn't have wanted that. She wouldn't have wanted you to live with this much hate in your heart, either. It's hurting you and Dave. Holly most of all. She came to Cam for help, and he's giving it to her. In return, he's stepping out of his self-imposed prison. Don't take that from him. It won't bring back Dana or minimize your pain."

Karen's eyes closed and a shudder ran through her. "I don't want to be the only one who's hurting."

"You're not," Melinda assured her as tears ran down her cheeks. She didn't bother to wipe them away. "You don't have to be alone. You have a beautiful daughter who needs you."

"I can't be here." Karen opened her eyes and looked around wildly.

"Cam's not here," Emma said, wondering if that would make Holly's mom feel better. Her pain was like a physical force. Emma appreciated Holly even more knowing that she'd come back to plan her wedding in Magnolia as a way to help her mother, to draw her out of the blackness that clearly surrounded her.

Karen lifted a shaky hand and pointed to the arbor at the edge of the lawn. After Cam finished the construction, Emma and Mariella had planted clematis and honeysuckle around the perimeter and she could imagine the whole structure covered in beautiful vines and flowers, a tangle of scent and texture.

"I'm not sure I can watch my daughter get married under a structure he built. Every time I look at pictures or think about her wedding day, Cam is going to be a part of it."

Emma felt her mouth drop open. What was Karen saying? "It's too late to change the venue," she managed, heart hammering in her chest. "The invitations have gone out. RSVPs are streaming in. There are no other options."

Karen's feathery brows lowered as she chewed on her bottom lip.

"You can't possibly consider skipping the wedding," Melinda told her. "Holly has worked so hard and she needs you to be there for her. It will break her heart."

"I don't want to do that," the other woman answered. "I'm not sure I have a choice."

"Everyone has choices," Emma said with conviction. "If there's anything I can do to make you more comfortable with this, I will. Cam has done amazing things in such a short time. For Holly. For Dana's memory. This is positive if you let it be."

Karen didn't look convinced, and Emma thought that maybe she understood her own mother a little better looking at her through the lens of Karen Adams's sorrow. Gillian Sorensen couldn't admit that Emma might be right in moving on from their family's foundation or give up control because she didn't know how to be a mom in any other way.

"I have to go." Karen spoke the words on a rush of breath, then bolted toward the front of the house. As she rounded the corner, the back door slammed shut.

Emma looked toward the house and winced as she saw both Holly and Cam standing on the patio. Holly's hand was over her mouth and she looked devastated by what she'd obviously overheard from her mother.

She reached for the man standing next to her, the one Emma knew she still considered her big brother in every way that counted. But after meeting his mother's teary gaze, Cam walked back into the house without another word.

How quickly Emma's intention to help had instead caused more pain for all of them.

CAM WOKE UP the next morning with a mouth full of cotton and a head that felt like someone had taken a baseball bat to it.

Honestly, if he had to choose between the bat and remembering the scene from the backyard at the inn, he'd gladly choose a beating every time.

He'd decided to return during his mom's visit because he didn't want to be a coward. Yes, he was scared to death of the way the protective shell around his heart was starting to crack and crumble.

The evening at his parents' house had brought up so many memories and emotions; feelings bombarded him like the recent hundred-year storm that had battered the town. Most of all, he remembered how much he'd caused them pain by lashing out after Dana's death.

It hurt his heart in an entirely different way to see the looks of shared sorrow that his mom, Dana's mom and Holly had each displayed. He couldn't believe he'd actually been excited at the thought of his mom's reaction to the work he'd done for Emma. Like he was a scrawny kid back in third-grade show-and-tell.

Instead, he'd overheard Karen's threat about not coming to the wedding because of his involvement. Not that she'd consciously meant it as a threat. She'd been hurting.

He was responsible for her pain. No matter what he did or how he tried to make up for it, he was responsible.

The words his mom said about Dana had gutted him, mainly because they were true. He knew his late wife would want him to move on, but it felt too disloyal.

His feelings for Emma felt disloyal, now more than ever.

He sat up with a groan, and Toby trotted over, tail wagging as effusively as ever. Sometimes it amazed Cam that the dog could tolerate his mercurial moods. Sometimes he wondered if Toby's devotion saved him.

This morning was a perfect example. He hadn't been drunk since the morning he'd started work for Emma. But last night he'd finished nearly a half of a bottle of whiskey on his own, and he was paying the price.

The dog didn't care in the least about his monumental hangover, so Cam downed a couple ibuprofen with a big glass of water, forced himself to eat a bowl of cereal and then headed out for a run.

From his experience, the best way to overcome a night of overindulging was to sweat it out. He set a punishing pace for himself, and although it was early morning he was drenched in sweat by the time he hit the second mile.

Normally, Cam followed a consistent route, running along the road parallel to the beach. The briny scent of the ocean relaxed him in the same way fishing always had, although Emma had seemed to change that, as well. Although she'd only been on his boat one time, he still caught whiffs of her citrusy scent on occasion. And when he reeled in a big one, he would remember her delight at that first catch of the day.

But now he'd hurt her, as well. She'd looked stricken by the back-and-forth between the two mothers. Emma had worked so damn hard to ensure the inn would be a success, and now he'd tainted her big kickoff event.

He was so caught up in thoughts of the current situation that he was shocked to realize he'd ended up at the gates of the cemetery where his late wife was buried.

His heart pounded like crazy and not from the exertion of the run. This was the first time since the burial he'd been this close to Dana's gravesite.

He started to turn away when a particularly giant squirrel ran past and Toby took off after the small animal. The dog was normally so well behaved that Cam didn't bother with a leash. Toby was content to keep pace at his side. Now some instinct had kicked in, and no matter how fervently Cam yelled, Toby didn't give up his quarry.

Cam jogged after him, glad the cemetery seemed empty of visitors who might be upset to see a dog tearing across the neat lawn with its rows of grave markers.

When Cam finally caught up to the dog, standing on hind legs whining at the squirrel that had taken refuge in a high branch of an overgrown oak tree, Cam realized he was in the section of the cemetery where Dana was buried.

Sensing the change in his mood, Toby slunk over to him, tail between his legs, clearly offering an apology for his lapse in canine judgment. Squeezing his hands into fists, Cam slowly made his way over the grass to the headstone inscribed with his wife's name.

Someone had put fresh flowers in the small metal vase that sat in front of it. Another obvious way for Cam to realize he'd failed. He hadn't even brought her flowers.

Toby gave a sudden bark, and Cam looked over his shoulder to see Karen Adams approaching from a nearby bench.

"I change them out at least once a month," she said, then

smiled as Toby shoved his snout between her legs. "Your dog has an interesting way of greeting strangers."

"I'm sorry. Toby, off." Cam felt his face flood with color. As if he needed one more way to offend Dana's mother, now his dog was accosting her.

To his surprise, she crouched down and accepted a few sloppy licks from the animal, her smile widening. "You're a sweet boy," she cooed, then straightened. "You and Dana talked about getting a dog." Her smile faded.

"We'd planned to adopt one at Christmas."

"I remember." Karen darted a quick glance at the head-stone. "Do you visit her often?"

Shame churning in his gut, Cam shook his head, then felt compelled to add, "She's always with me."

Something shifted in Karen's gaze, and she nodded. "I get that. I used to come every week, right after the acci-dent. I felt closer to her here. But..." She shrugged. "Well, a therapist told me it wasn't healthy to spend hours at her gravesite."

Cam wanted to sink into the ground. "Again, I'm sorry, Karen. If I could change what happened or take Dana's place in that car, I would in a second."

"I know."

"You have every reason to blame me and hate me," he continued, somehow relieved to get the words out. Words he'd never been able to say to her before. "I wish she would have broken up with me after high school when she had the chance. Before the wedding. Her life would have been so different—"

"But not as happy."

Shock reverberated through Cam, and he had trouble pulling in a full breath.

"My daughter was happy with you." She crossed her

arms over her chest. "I'd allowed myself to forget that part until your mom reminded me."

"I should have kept her safe." He shook his head. "It was my job."

"Maybe," she agreed. "I wish you could have. I wish *I* could have kept her safe. But you loved her well, Camden. As much as I've hated you and blamed you, I know that much is true."

"It wasn't enough."

"It was for Dana." She breathed out a sigh. "It is for Holly."

"She needs you at her wedding," he said. If nothing else, he had to convince Karen of that. "I'll take down the pergola tomorrow morning first thing. Or you can burn it to the ground if that's what you need to do to purge the thought of me from the inn. Please don't let me ruin Holly's wedding. She needs you there."

"She came to you. That means something. She trusts you. She thinks of you as her brother. Dana's death didn't change that for her."

"Maybe it should have."

Karen shook her head. "Holly has a good heart." She looked like she wanted to say more, like maybe she was going to tell Cam he had a good heart. Words he shouldn't need but desperately wanted to hear. Instead, she murmured, "I'll be at my daughter's wedding and no pergola bonfires necessary."

"Okay," he answered, almost afraid to say more and set her off again. "If there's anything else…"

"I'm not ready for more, Camden." She met his gaze, but instead of anger or blame, he saw compassion in their depths. "Not yet."

"Okay," he repeated, then whistled for Toby. "Again, I'm

sorry for the pain I've caused you and any I continue to be responsible for. If I could change everything, I would."

Karen looked away but nodded, and he moved past her.

"She'd want you to be happy," Dana's mother said when he was almost out of earshot.

Cam glanced over his shoulder and met her gaze. "She'd want the same for you."

CHAPTER EIGHTEEN

"You brought donuts!"

Emma stood in the mudroom loading paper products into a supply box as she heard Cam's deep voice respond to Holly's enthusiastic proclamation the following morning.

Angi and Emma were working on preparations for the booth at that afternoon's farmers market on the town square with Holly helping before she went into the nail salon for her shift. Meredith had suggested the Wildflower Inn have its own setup, where locals could meet Emma and sample both her baked goods and some of Angi's best finger foods.

At this point, Angi was even more nervous than Emma at the thought of putting herself out there in front of the town, as well as her mother.

Ethel gave a happy bark of greeting and she could imagine the dog circling Cam with her fluffy tail wagging. Emma had to admit that fostering the dog was a great distraction from the continued complications that seemed to plague her life.

After a round of tears from the bride-to-be and hours of uncertainty as to the future of the wedding, Holly had called Emma last night to tell her Karen had made peace with Cam's involvement in the repairs. Emma wasn't sure if she should trust the older woman or if the heartbroken mom might have another breakdown that could turn all of their careful planning and preparations sideways.

Emma didn't have a lot of experience going on faith, but she was getting better at it each day.

Especially because she was quickly running through her remaining savings and didn't relish the thought of applying for one more zero-interest credit card in order to pay both the bills and the salary she and Angi had agreed to. She had reservations booked for several weekends into early autumn, but she needed to get the word out even more.

Tonight would be the start of her new phase of shameless self-promotion.

"We're making scones," Holly told Cam as Emma walked into the kitchen with the plastic tub of paper products.

His gaze met hers across the room and it was like being slammed in the chest with a thousand volts of electrical current.

Did she really think a box would act as some kind of shield against the energy that pulsed between them?

Oh, how she wished she could deny her feelings for him. How much easier that would be for all of them.

Instead, she searched his face for signs of distress. He'd seemed gutted yesterday at the conversation he'd overheard and his former mother-in-law's continued insistence on his guilt. Emma could relate to self-blame. She had a laundry list of failures, but she'd folded the whole stack and put them away neatly in a dark cabinet. Moving forward was the only thing she could control, and she wanted to believe that soon enough all this momentum would help her leave behind the scars of past hurts and betrayals.

"I got you a jelly," he announced, pushing the brown cardboard box a few inches forward on the counter. "Mary Ellen at Sunnyside said that was your favorite. I like your new dog." He bent down to love on Ethel, who immediately sank to the ground and exposed her soft underside for more petting. So much for the animal's loyalty.

"Oh, yeah." Holly opened the box and pulled out a donut with pink icing and rainbow sprinkles. "Mary Ellen has an amazing memory for orders."

Angi picked up a glazed donut. "I stick with the classics," she said before taking a big bite. She used a napkin to grab the iced jelly donut and held it out to Emma. "I'll make another pot of coffee to counteract the sugar coma we're all about to experience."

"I need to load this box into the car." Emma didn't reach for the donut. She didn't want to admit that her feelings had been hurt when Cam didn't call or check in after the scene in the backyard. And she sure hadn't gone over to his house again, even though she'd wanted to.

Angi placed the donut back in the box with a shrug. "You can save it for later. At least until Andrew is done with soccer camp. That boy can take down some donuts."

"He's welcome to mine," she told Angi, then turned to Cam. "How long until you're finished with the walls in the cottage? Mariella wants to start moving in some pieces she found at a consignment store up in Raleigh."

He frowned slightly. "I should have everything primed by the weekend. If you need help painting—"

"I don't."

Both Angi and Holly were munching on their donuts as their gazes darted between Emma and Cam like they were watching prime-time television. Emma felt her face color at the scrutiny.

"Phil texted and said he'd be here to help after his doctor's appointment this morning."

Holly pointed a finger at Cam. "Even Phil has a cell phone. Get with the program, Camden."

He didn't answer but continued to stare at Emma like she was a puzzle he wanted desperately to solve.

"I'm going to grab a tablecloth from the upstairs linen closet," she announced to no one in particular, and then turned and headed up the back staircase. She didn't trust herself to walk past Cam without reaching for him, and there was no way she was going to show that kind of lack of self-restraint right now.

She'd barely reached the top of the steps when she heard heavy footsteps behind her. Maybe she increased the pace—just a touch—but it didn't take him long to catch up.

"What's going on?" he asked as his hand brushed the back of her shoulder. Although the touch was soft, it ricocheted through her like a bullet, tearing flesh and muscle and leaving an aching burn in its wake.

"I'm getting whiplash from your moods," she said, probably with more intensity than was warranted. She didn't turn but opened the hall closet to look for the tablecloth she wanted to use at the farmers market. The task soothed her raw nerves.

"I'm sorry," he said automatically. "It was tough to see both my mom and Dana's mother in tears yesterday. I stopped by my parents' last night and talked to my mom if that makes you feel better. She knew I was okay."

She closed the closet door and whirled to face him, frustration drowning out her typical awareness of him. "I'm glad for your mother, really I am. She's a lovely woman, and she loves you very much." Her voice broke off on the last word, and she was afraid she'd revealed too much just with her tone. Cam's gaze remained steady, if a little bewildered, like he couldn't figure out what was happening with their conversation.

Join the club, Emma thought.

"*I* didn't know you were okay," she said tightly.

"Oh." He seemed flummoxed by her response. Seriously, could a man be that clueless?

"It doesn't matter," she continued. "Your emotional health is none of my business." She couldn't help a quick poke to the chest. "Although if you had a cell phone, one simple text could have done the trick."

She went to step around him, but he shifted so that he remained in her way. He lifted an arm and his hand pressed against the door next to her head. Suddenly she felt surrounded by Cam—his heat and the scent of soap and toothpaste. Far too appealing of a combination.

"I'm sorry," he said, leaning in closer. "Although I know it makes me a jerk, I like you to worry about me."

"You *are* a jerk," she mumbled.

"I'll try to be less of one," he told her, his mouth curving up at one end. "I'll also try to make it up to you."

Emma drew in a breath when his mouth hovered inches from hers. There was something different about Cam today, a sense of lightness he'd never shown before. Another facet of this excruciatingly complex man and one that tempted her even when she knew it wasn't smart for either of them.

"If you'll let me?" he asked in a whisper.

She nodded, but he still didn't kiss her. Her body yearned for him. Stupid, stupid body—not to mention her heart. Forward, she reminded herself. She was moving forward.

So she closed the small space between them and claimed the kiss she wanted.

Cam responded at once, a low moan of satisfaction rumbling up from his throat. He kept one hand levered on the wall above her while the other sifted through her hair, his thumb massaging the tense tendons along the back of her neck.

The pressure was exquisite and she knew she was in deep when a kiss had this much of an effect on her.

"I'm going to do better," he promised as he nibbled a trail of openmouthed kisses along her jaw. "You should be with someone better, but until you realize that, I'll try like hell to convince you otherwise."

The words were spoken with so much sincerity they warmed Emma's heart and made her knees go weak. As if sensing that, Cam wrapped both arms around her waist and pulled her against him. The kiss deepened, both of them demanding and giving in equal measure. Emma lost all track of time. It could have been seconds or minutes or hours that they kissed. Cam seemed content to savor the time, although her body went into overdrive, wishing for and wanting more.

Always more.

Despite the lessons she'd learned about expectations, she couldn't stop herself from craving the intimacy and belonging she felt with Cam. She might accuse him of being a jerk or get her feelings hurt, but he'd never been anything but honest about how much he was willing to give. Physical pleasure, he was all in. Emotional intimacy, Emma was on her own.

She broke the kiss and rested her forehead on the soft fabric of his shirt. His heart beat like the flutter of hummingbird wings in his chest, and she could feel the evidence of his desire pressing low against her.

She told herself what he was able to offer her would be enough for now, but she knew it to be a lie.

Just like she knew she'd have no one but herself to blame for the broken heart that was sure to come.

CAM WAS HOVERING on the edge of the farmers market crowd later that afternoon when he saw Emma's brother approach.

He'd met Ryan Sorensen on only one other occasion, when the tall and somewhat aloof physician had stopped by the inn to bring his sister a scented candle as a good luck gift before her first round of guests.

She'd been delighted by the small present, although Ryan had seemed genuinely surprised by her enthusiastic response.

Emma had told Cam that she and her brother hadn't been particularly close growing up. Cam got the impression Ryan didn't grasp how often Emma had settled for scraps of affection from the people she cared about.

Including Cam, he realized with a start, which was why he ended up glaring at the good doctor.

"Is there a problem?" Ryan asked casually, holding up his hands to reveal two plastic cups with the logo of a local bar printed on them. "One that a beer can't fix?"

To his credit, Ryan appeared more curious than defensive at being on the receiving end of what Cam knew was a menacing stare. He seriously needed to work on his resting jerk face.

"All good here," he answered, fixing a smile on his face. "Just thinking about a problem with work."

"At the inn?" Ryan handed him the beer. Normally, there were laws against open containers in Magnolia, but during the summer at the farmers market, local restaurants and bars were allowed to sell tasting-size cups to attendees.

"Nothing I can't work out," Cam said instead of answering directly.

"Emma says you're the best carpenter she's ever met."

Cam quirked a brow. "I have a feeling your sister hasn't met a lot of carpenters in her life before coming to Magnolia."

"True. She's done a lot of new things recently." With his

mahogany-colored hair ruffling in the breeze and a speculative gleam in his dark eyes with their enviable lashes, Ryan looked across the square, which was lined with booths selling everything from goat cheese and produce to local honey and handmade soaps.

Emma stood next to Angi in the Wildflower Inn's booth. She'd hung twinkle lights between the posts on either side of the table with a hand-painted sign, one that he'd helped design. The sign had taken him less than an hour to craft from leftover lumber, although Emma had made him feel like he'd given her the keys to the kingdom when he was finished. He'd stained the boards with a light honey finish, and she'd stenciled on the inn's logo, which Mariella Jacob had designed, in faded chalk paint.

She'd had a photo album printed with before and after photos of the house's interior as well as the cottage, and created flyers with a coupon for a discounted locals' weekend at the end of September.

Cam appreciated her creativity and ingenuity. She'd already won most of the business community over by offering cross-promotions and free publicity on the inn's website.

The rest he figured would be swayed by her energy and Angi's amazing food.

"I bet your mother is sorry to lose her at the foundation," Cam murmured before he thought better of it. He quickly held up his free hand. "Scratch that. Your family business is none of mine."

"It's fine," Ryan said with a humorless laugh. "You know, I honestly believed Emma was just like our mother before she moved here."

"I don't know your mother," Cam felt the need to point out. "But Emma isn't like anyone I've ever known."

Ryan inclined his head. "She was always preternaturally

mature and responsible. You could call it an 'old soul,' but it was more than that. Emma never got into trouble. She was never late with homework or forgot to make her bed. She could be paraded out at a dinner party with a hundred stuffy guests and she'd find a way to charm every one of them. I thought that life was a perfect fit for her." He took a long drink of beer. "Turns out she was just a consummate actress."

"You don't think she's acting any longer, right?" A sense of unease trickled down Cam's spine like condensation on the rim of his cup.

"I hope she doesn't have to pretend anymore," Ryan said after a long pause. "But my mom did a number on her with all of her expectations of perfection. Emma's husband wasn't much better."

"She doesn't talk about him."

"World-class ass. I wish I'd been closer to her or seen that she was struggling. Unfortunately, I was too consumed with my own struggle. Emma is not only a top-notch actress, she's also got the caring-for-others thing down pat. After my accident, I was a mess." He placed a hand on his thigh. Cam had heard from Emma that her brother had been shot during an outbreak of violence at the hospital where he worked in DC. "Em pretty much picked me up and dragged me back into the land of the living."

"Sounds familiar," Cam murmured, and he didn't like what that said about himself.

Ryan sighed. "I figured. She cares deeply. In that way, the inn is a perfect fit for her. New guests to fuss over all the time, but she doesn't exactly take to being the one cared for. I hope she finds someone who can break down those walls." He shifted slightly so that he was staring at Meredith and the Furever Friends booth, which was surrounded by people and four-legged creatures alike. There was an immediate softening of Ryan's tense posture. The serious doctor and the spirited animal rescuer had seemed like an odd match, but it was clear Ryan was crazy for Meredith.

Cam wanted to bang his head against a nearby tree. He'd been so consumed with his heartache and wallowing in guilt that he'd all but ignored the fact that Emma had her own issues. Yes, she'd told him she didn't want something serious, but that didn't make his ineptitude at supporting her any less callous.

His instinct, honed in a long season of avoiding emotional entanglements, was to walk the other way. As if she could read his thoughts, Emma looked over. She wore a yellow sundress with tiny clumps of red flowers printed across the fabric. Her hair curled around her shoulders and her cheeks were flushed, like her body couldn't contain its excitement at the attention she and the inn were receiving.

She gave him a smile filled with so much pure joy that even Ryan let out a soft "Whoa," turning fully to face Cam. "I guess this is the part where I tell you I'll kick your butt if you hurt her."

"I'll kick my own butt, thank you very much," Cam countered.

"That works, too."

Somehow the soft-spoken threat allowed Cam to relax. Emma had someone looking out for her, and he had no doubt Ryan would make good on his promise. He'd have to get in line behind Angi, Mariella, Holly and probably Cam's own mother.

They stood in companionable silence for a few minutes until Meredith gestured to Ryan with a wave of her hand.

"Good talk," Ryan told Cam with a smirk. "Thank you

for helping my sister, and I'm glad we're on the same page as far as her happiness."

"Yeah. Thanks for the beer." As Ryan walked away, Cam turned his attention to Emma and considered her happiness.

She looked happy now. Radiant as she laughed with Angi and then hugged Carrie Reed as she approached the booth. The things that made her happy seemed so inconsequential in the grand scheme of things. A tiny flower blooming in the garden. Enthusiastic greetings from Toby. A perfectly baked muffin.

Maybe he couldn't give her what she needed long-term or become the man worthy of a place at her side, but what if those things didn't matter? Well, they mattered, but not as much as the simple act of bringing her joy. Making her smile the way she did with her never-ending enthusiasm and attention to the quirkiest of details.

What if he gave himself the freedom to try?

He'd been alone, trapped in a cage of self-imposed isolation, for so long that he barely remembered how to make an effort. A couple walked by, the woman holding a homemade scented candle to her nose and then offering it to her companion to sniff.

Cam tossed his empty cup into a nearby recycling bin and, for the first time in five years, purposely headed toward a crowd of people. As the market wound down, he approached Emma, who smiled like a kid on Christmas morning.

"Everyone has been so supportive," she said, pressing her hands to her flushed cheeks. "I thought the town might feel weird about me repurposing Niall's old house, since he was such a famous figure, but they seem to love it. Or at least they're keeping an open mind." She gestured to the empty platter on the checked-cloth-covered table. "Angi's samples were gone in a snap. Even her oldest brother, who's in town for a visit, stopped by to try one." She leaned in like she was telling him a secret. "Did you know Angi's brother is movie-star handsome?"

Cam felt his jaw drop and quickly snapped it shut. Clearly, Emma didn't need him to worry about her happiness. She was plenty capable of handling her life on her own.

"Nowhere near as handsome as you, of course," she said with a wink, the teasing lilt in her voice garnering an answering pulse in his chest. She reached out and traced a finger over the bone in his wrist, like she couldn't resist touching him even though they were in public. "You don't know how much I appreciate you being here, Cam."

"I didn't do anything," he muttered as his heart pounded even harder. His mind went in a thousand directions, a sensation he should be used to when Emma was involved. He'd made this big plan to contribute to her joy, and once again he was on the receiving end of her sweetness and light.

She pointed a finger upward. "Not true because the sign is amazing. I got a lot of compliments on it. And even more than that…" She leaned forward and without actually touching him somehow still made him feel as though he were being embraced. "You came even though I know crowds aren't your favorite thing. It means a lot to me."

Ah, hell. He truly didn't deserve her. All the times he'd been short or turned away or let his sorrow and rudeness mess up a moment, and still she wanted to give him credit where he didn't warrant it.

He shoved the brown bag he held toward her. "I got this stuff for you. I didn't know what you'd like so it's kind of random."

A look of wonder crept over her features as she peered into the bag.

"I just thought…" He massaged a hand over the back of his neck. "Maybe some of it would—"

"This makes me so happy," she told him, and Cam released a breath it felt like he'd been holding for ages.

Emma set the bag on the table and began pulling out the small trinkets he'd purchased. A bar of handmade soap, a candle, some beeswax lip balm and a few other fancy-looking bath products. He hadn't quite bought one of everything from the row of booths selling frilly gifts, but it was close.

"You did all this shopping for me?" Emma was grinning but she looked disbelieving at the same time.

He felt heat flood his face. "The shop people kept making eye contact with me. I couldn't say no."

She threw back her head and laughed. "I love it," she told him, and damn if a dark, secret part of him didn't wish she would replace the "it" with a "you."

Emma picked up a bag filled with giant-looking gumballs.

"I don't even know what you're supposed to do with gum that big," he told her.

"They're bath bombs," she explained. "Which means I'm going to relax with a bath tonight." She swayed closer. "But I've got this spot on my back I can never quite reach. Maybe you could help me?"

Her eyes had gone dark with desire. If this was a side benefit of making her happy, Cam would be bringing his A-game from now on. Before he thought better of it, he leaned in and kissed her, cupping her cheeks between his hands. Once again loving how soft her skin felt under his calloused palms.

"I can definitely reach that for you," he said against her lips. "I can reach all the places you need."

"Cam? Emma?"

Cam whirled to see Holly standing behind him with eyes as wide as saucers. "Were you just kissing her?" she asked, her voice shaking.

"I…um…" Cam glanced around wildly. No one else had seemed to notice, but then Holly was the only one who counted.

"We can explain." Emma stepped around Cam, her features tight.

To Cam's utter shock, Holly wrapped her arms around Emma and pulled her in for a huge hug. "This is so great." His former sister-in-law gave him an enthusiastic thumbs-up behind Emma's back. "Two of my favorite people are now a couple. Happy endings all around."

Cam didn't know how to respond, but he could just about guarantee that this wasn't going to end well.

CHAPTER NINETEEN

EMMA WAS ON the back patio later that night, a cup of tea cradled between her hands despite the balmy air, when Cam walked across the lawn from the cottage.

"I'm impressed," he said, his gaze on the ceramic mug that said Nothing Messes Up a Friday More Than Realizing It's Wednesday. "I was tempted to go deep on the whiskey after that little scene with Holly."

"Tea is medicinal," Emma told him.

"So is alcohol."

She'd turned on the strands of lights they'd strung around the perimeter of the flagstone patio, and she searched Cam's face as he came into the warm glow they cast.

"I didn't mean for Holly to find out that way," she felt compelled to say.

"I'm the one who kissed you in the middle of the farmers market."

Her mind returned to their kiss and the way her heart had filled when he'd given her the bag of gifts. The fact he'd purchased so many things because he couldn't say no to the local artisans made it even sweeter.

No matter how gruff he acted, Cam was a big softie at heart.

Especially with Holly. It had clearly upset him to be caught kissing Emma. Holly's reaction had surprised them both. Emma would have assumed the bride-to-be wouldn't want another woman getting close to her late sister's husband, but Holly had been genuinely overjoyed.

Which had seemed to leave Cam anything but. He'd offered a flimsy excuse about tracking down his brother and fled the town square almost immediately after Holly discovered them.

"I know we're not a real couple." She made sure her voice remained steady as she said the words. "This is temporary while we're working together. You don't want people to get the wrong impression."

"What impression are we talking about?" he asked conversationally, lowering himself into the rocking chair next to the outdoor sofa where she sat.

"That you kissing me means anything."

"It means I like you."

"You like having sex with me," she countered.

He pressed two fingers to his forehead. "I'm confused. Is that a bad thing?"

She blew out a laugh just as the breeze kicked up and carried it away into the darkness quickly overtaking the yard. The scent of flowers and freshly cut grass permeated the air. In the distance she could hear the hiss of a sprinkler watering a neighbor's lawn. As she drew in a shaky breath, Emma tried to let the calm of evening soak into her veins.

Cam had probably meant the question as a joke, a way to ease the uncertainty between them, but given her recent experience, intimacy could not be that simple.

"My ex-husband blackmailed me during our divorce," she said, keeping her gaze trained on the backyard where fireflies were just beginning their evening dance. Truly, this place must be magical because it gave her the courage to voice her greatest humiliation once again. It had been difficult enough sharing it with women, but she couldn't force herself to make eye contact with Cam as she revealed her shame to him.

"Blackmailed?" Cam repeated as if the word made no sense.

Emma remembered feeling that way, as well, when Martin had first shown her the video. He'd been so damn smug, and the memory still made her skin crawl.

"I suspected him of cheating, although I had no proof. He told me he wanted a divorce and we quietly separated. I left for a philanthropic conference in Chicago. While I was there..." She rubbed her hands over her bare arms when goose bumps erupted along her skin. "I met a man in the bar. He was sweet and kind and knew exactly what my bruised ego and broken heart needed to hear." Her fingernails dug into the crook of her elbow. "Martin had hired him to seduce me."

"That doesn't make any sense." Cam sat forward, and Emma could feel the weight of his gaze. "If you were separated—"

"The guy filmed the two of us together," she said quietly. "I didn't know, of course. It seems like not a big deal in the age of reality television, but our family's foundation was built on a specific set of standards. My grandfather wanted to leave a legacy of community support and philanthropic responsibility. Martin threatened to release the tape. It would have embarrassed my mother to see it and tainted the foundation's reputation."

"His endgame was a better divorce settlement?" Cam asked, sounding shocked.

"His endgame was taking everything I had," she admitted quietly. "I went along with it because I was so humiliated. Maybe I should have fought him, but I couldn't at that point. I felt broken and used and violated. So dirty."

"Emma, no." He shifted closer and placed a gentle hand on her knee.

Part of her wanted to flinch away. How could he not hear that about her without envisioning the crudeness of that video? But she forced herself to meet his gaze, surprised and profoundly grateful to not find censure in it. She knew he was a master at hiding feelings but somehow didn't think he was doing that in this instance. She hoped he wasn't.

"If I had to go back, maybe I would have handled it differently." She shook her head. "I doubt it, though. Even coming to Magnolia, I don't want to be known as the sex tape innkeeper. It's disgusting."

"Your ex is a disgusting pervert."

She flashed as much of a smile as she could manage. "So being with you is a good thing, but I'm a little messed up in my head around…" She swallowed when her voice cracked. "I'm more than a little messed up." It was easier to look at his hand on her knee than directly into his dark eyes. "You're the first man I've been with since that weekend."

"I would never betray you." Cam moved onto the sofa next to her and the heat of his body soothed her. "Emma, I mean it." He tipped up her chin with one finger. "Your ex is the lowest of the low. I'd like to give him a lesson on how to treat a woman."

"Look at you and the chivalry." Emma made her tone light even if his words meant more than they should to her. Other than her brother, she never felt like she had anyone in her corner. "Be careful, or I may find you a set of chain mail for your knight costume."

His smile turned smoldering. "You'd like to see me in a suit of armor and nothing else, right?"

Emma surprised herself by laughing for real. "Thank

you for not making this horrible, weird thing I have to share as horrible and weird as it could be."

"Was the blackmail the reason you quit your job with the foundation?"

She started to shake her head, then stopped. "I'm not exactly sure. I definitely didn't want my mother or the foundation to be exposed to that kind of scandal."

"It might have blown over."

"You haven't met my mom. But the blackmail wasn't the only reason I wanted a change. When I came to Magnolia to visit Meredith's rescue, Ryan had changed so much. The last time I'd seen him had been after the incident when he was shot. He was like a totally different person. He had hope. I wanted that for myself, and then the house called to me. Maybe it was a perfect storm, but it worked."

"Like the storm that brought Holly to you." He traced a thumb over her cheek.

"That same storm brought you to me," she said, suddenly feeling breathless.

"I don't think you're a mess."

"Maybe that's because you're an even bigger one."

"Could be," he agreed with a smirk.

"Not as much of a mess as Holly thinking we're a real couple."

His smile faded. "That's not the worst thing I can think of." He leaned in and brushed his mouth across hers. "Want to get messy with me, Emma?"

The question was spoken lightly, but this moment had changed what was between them, and she knew it meant something big. He'd sought her out tonight when she would have thought Holly's reaction would have sent him into another retreat.

She'd told him her deepest secret and he hadn't seemed

fazed by it. The reaction left her breathless with a fragile hope for the future.

"Yes." She wrapped her arms around his neck. "I do."

EMMA AND MARIELLA rearranged furniture in the inn's front room the following morning, still trying to decide on a piece to use as a focal point of the room, when Holly burst through the front door.

"It's a disaster," she announced, a frantic look in her eyes.

Emma felt her heart just about thump out of her chest as Mariella darted an I-told-you-so glance her way. The first thing the prickly designer had said when she walked in that morning was "Why the hell have you been snogging Cam Arlinghaus on the sly?"

Emma had apologized for not sharing, although in truth her relationship with Cam was no one's business. Apparently, that fact didn't make a difference in a small town. Mariella had heard accounts ranging from Emma and Cam making out to the two of them practically doing the horizontal bop on the table at the inn's booth.

"Slow news day," she'd said when Emma had been affronted.

She'd explained the situation and also that Holly had seen them and appeared more than fine with the situation. Not that she could precisely label their relationship as such quite yet. Last night was a big step in that direction, but she didn't want to push it.

"I thought you were okay with Cam and me," she said, taking a step toward the distraught bride-to-be. "If not—"

"The florist went out of business."

Emma blinked. "What are you talking about? We just met with her last week."

"I know," Holly said, sounding more hysterical by the moment. "I guess she found out her husband was cheating on her. He'd been having her make these beautiful flower arrangements and telling her they were for displays at his office." She drew in a deep breath. "He's an insurance agent. But they were really for his girlfriend. Luna found out "

"Luna is the florist?" Mariella asked.

Holly nodded. "She destroyed everything in the shop and then tried to set it on fire. It's all in his name, and she didn't want him to get any insurance money. She called on her way out of town. She's driving to her mom's condo in Tallahassee. She's gone. Just gone."

"What about your deposit?" Emma nearly groaned aloud when Holly's face crumpled and tears spilled down her cheeks.

"Why is my wedding cursed?" she asked.

"Who's cursed?" Angi asked, coming to stand behind her. "Someone left the front door open." She took one look at Holly and drew her into a hug. "Don't worry, sweetheart. We'll take care of it."

Emma pressed two fingers to the throbbing vein in her temple as Holly blinked at Angi. "I just wish I knew how." She dashed a hand over her face to wipe away the tears. "I just want my wedding to be beautiful." She sniffed. "Bonus if some part of the planning was easy."

"Your dress is going to be amazing," Mariella promised with more conviction than Emma would have expected. The dress designer hadn't said much about the gown, and Emma was worried that stepping back into her former role as a wedding dress designer was taking a toll on Mariella, despite how tough she appeared on the outside.

It wasn't easy to walk away from a former life, especially when that life had been so much easier than the current one.

"Thank you." Holly sounded grateful for the vote of confidence.

"And your senator loves you," Angi reminded Holly. "That man looked at you like the sun rose and set by your smile. He wouldn't care if you walked down the aisle clutching a handful of dandelions."

A wistful flutter of longing stole through Emma's heart at that description, which was absolutely true. She wondered what it would be like to inspire that sort of adoration in someone. Her ex had never looked at her that way.

Holly sniffed and gave a watery nod. "Sometimes I feel like I'm doing all of this just to impress his mom, which might never actually happen. The only thing she seems to like about me so far is that my mom made a terrible scene." She looked at Emma. "The flowers are important for the photos. I can't have a wedding without flowers."

"We'll think of something," Emma promised. "There has to be another florist who can help."

Angi made a face. "There's not enough time. The wedding is right around the corner," she reminded all of them, as if anyone could forget. "Any decent florist will be booked or charge an astronomical amount for whatever they have on hand."

"Can we DIY the flowers?" Emma asked, turning to Mariella. "You must know something about floral arranging. You seem to know everything."

"I appreciate the vote of confidence," Mariella answered. "But no. I do have an idea of someone local who might be just the person we need."

"No." Angi took a step away from Holly and shook her

finger at Mariella. "I know what you're thinking, and it's the worst idea ever."

"We're desperate," Mariella insisted.

"Not Gabriel Carlyle desperate," Angi argued.

"Who is Gabriel Carlyle?" Emma glanced up from her phone. She'd immediately started searching the internet for florists in the area. "Wait. In Bloom is the local shop Carrie mentioned to me. We went with Luna because she had such a great website, but I saw some of Gabe's work in the art gallery. He's quite talented although not the friendliest based on my conversation with him."

"Yes," Mariella said at the same time Angi muttered, "No way."

Holly looked as confused as Emma felt. "I thought that shop was going out of business because the woman who owned it got sick."

"Her grandson took over," Mariella explained. "He moved to Magnolia when Iris went into the hospital, and he's stayed on now that she's in assisted living. He's not the most outgoing store owner, not like his grandmother. But I bet he'd help us."

"He's a jerk," Angi said forcefully. "Not someone we want to work with on any level."

"I like Gabe," Mariella argued. "He's kind of an acquired taste, but he's good with plants and flowers. I'm not sure the floral shop is exactly his favorite, but he keeps it open to honor his grandmother."

"Jerk-wad of the highest order," Angi insisted.

"We can deal with a jerk if he can help," Emma said.

"I need the flowers to be beautiful," Holly added. She straightened her button-down shirt like she was preparing for battle. "Will you go with me to talk to him this morning?" she asked Mariella. "Since you've met him."

Mariella glanced at her watch. "I have a meeting at the store in thirty minutes, otherwise I would. Angi knows him. She can go."

Emma answered a text from Malcolm, then nodded. "If I'm able to reschedule the meeting at the mayor's office, the three of us can go together."

"No, thanks." Angi crossed her arms over her chest.

Holly let out a small sigh. "It's fine." She patted Angi's arm. "I'll handle it on my own. Emma's got inn business to deal with and you're busy, too. You three have saved me enough."

"We're all saving each other," Emma assured her. "I'm going to text Mal and reschedule my meeting, but Angi needs to be there, too." She met the tall brunette's steely gaze. "If Gabriel Carlyle owns the only floral shop in Magnolia that can work with us on short notice, you're going to have to find a way to make peace with him."

"Fine," Angi agreed. "But I won't change my mind about him being a jerk."

"Uh-oh. Pretty sure my ears should be burning," Cam said as he walked into the room.

"You're not a jerk," Holly assured him. "You're a hero."

He choked out a laugh. "Hardly."

Emma had a tendency to agree with Holly, but she was trying not to make eye contact with Cam. She didn't need to add fuel to the fire of people thinking they were a real couple.

"Some florist guy is a jerk according to Angi," Holly explained.

"Gabe?" Cam lifted and lowered one broad shoulder. "He's decent, and he's devoted to his grandma."

"You know him?" Emma asked.

"He booked me for a fishing trip when he first got to

town, and we've been out on the water a few more times since then."

"It figures," Angi told him with a snort. "The guy you'd pick as a friend is Gabriel Carlyle. The second least sociable person in Magnolia."

"Is that supposed to offend me?" Cam asked with uncharacteristic humor.

In the past couple of weeks, he and Angi had developed an odd brother-sister vibe of trading good-natured insults that seemed laced with more affection than animosity. Emma had only met Angi's one brother briefly at the farmers market, but there had been an invisible thread of contention between the two of them. The same subtle distance she'd felt in her relationship with Ryan before coming to Magnolia.

She stepped forward before Angi could answer. "That's great. Cam can come with us and help convince Gabe to take on Holly's wedding."

Cam narrowed his eyes slightly, and she guessed the last thing he wanted to do was go hunting for a wedding florist. She also knew he wouldn't say no to anything that involved Holly. His sense of loyalty was beyond reproach.

"Let's pick some flowers or at least a florist," he said, resulting in a whoop of delight from Holly and a groan from Angi.

Emma smiled, and as they all moved toward the front door, she slipped her hand into his. "I'll make it worth your while later," she promised.

CHAPTER TWENTY

As Emma and Holly climbed out of his truck ten minutes later, Cam wasn't sure whether he needed a drink or a handful of ibuprofen or maybe a full-on mental health exam. Angi parked in the diagonal spot next to him and joined them on the sidewalk.

How had he gone from years of living a solitary life to being designated the person to convince a man nearly as cantankerous as him to step into the whirling hurricane of last-minute wedding preparations for an event sure to bring national publicity to any business involved?

Holly tucked her arm into Emma's as they approached the flower shop, and both of them laughed at some private joke. In an instant, Cam's heart melted, and he knew exactly his reasons for the complete one-eighty his life had taken.

"No way is Gabe going to agree to this," Angi muttered at Cam's side.

"He's seriously a good guy." Cam glanced over when she gave a snort of disbelief. "Did he do something to you?"

"No," she said immediately. "I barely know him now. He's come into the restaurant a few times, but I won't wait on him."

"Now?" Cam scratched his jaw. "Was there a before when you did know him?"

She shrugged. "He spent a few summers in Magnolia when we were kids. Didn't he mention that?"

"We talked fish and a little about where he'd traveled during his time in the army. Not much recounting of childhood adventures."

"More like a nightmare," Angi said. "He was a weird kid, and he didn't fit in around here at all. His grandma wanted him to have friends badly, but it never took."

"Kids can be jerks," Cam said quietly.

"He wasn't exactly a jerk back then," Angi admitted, almost reluctantly. "Just different."

Cam elbowed her. "I wasn't talking about him."

"I was never a jerk," she said on a hiss of breath, but he could hear the guilt in her tone.

"No judgment here." He held up his hands. "Been there, done that. Something I've been learning is you can't change the past but you can move forward."

"Thanks, Dr. Phil," she mumbled as they caught up with Emma and Holly.

The windows of the flower shop were covered with heavy drapes, not exactly boarded up but certainly not welcoming, either.

"It feels like we're the Scooby-Doo gang about to walk into some new, creepy mystery. Or a little shop of horrors." Angi put a hand on Emma's arm. "I think we'd have more luck in the grocery store's floral department."

"Coward," Cam said against her ear, then pushed forward. He turned the knob and walked in calling out a greeting, "Gabe, are you around?"

The three women followed, and Holly practically ran into his back as he stopped moving and took in the interior of the shop. He remembered seeing Gabe's grandma around town when he was a kid. She was a petite woman with pale silver hair always held back in a giant scarf or colorful clip. He'd never set foot in her flower shop so had no idea if the space had always looked the way it did now.

Like some sort of lush, tropical retreat with an abundance of plants, cut flowers and a coordinated ribbon wall.

The whole place smelled earthy, an aromatic mix of various flowers as well as decaying blooms that was unique and intoxicating. There were incandescent lamps and natural light shone in from a row of skylights in the high ceiling. It was absolutely more than he'd expected.

Based on Holly's gasp, Emma's whispered "Wow" and the muttered curse Angi let out, he wasn't alone in his assessment.

"Cam?" He turned as Gabriel Carlyle entered the room from a back work area. "Hey, man." The lean, muscled former Army Ranger offered a confused smile, appearing even more bewildered as Holly and Emma peeked out from behind Cam's back.

Cam knew the minute Gabe's gaze landed on Angi because his posture stiffened and his mouth thinned into a grim line. "What can I do for you?" he asked, suddenly all business.

"This place is fantastic," Cam said, stepping forward. "How come you never mentioned that in addition to tying a hell of a fly, you can also work magic with plants and flowers?"

Gabe lifted a big hand to massage the back of his neck, looking somewhat embarrassed at being called out for his talent. "It's not a big deal," he said. "I'm just doing what my grandma taught me back in the day. Uh, is there something I can help you with?"

"That's exactly why we're here," Emma said, moving around Cam and holding out her hand. "I'm Emma Cantrell, owner of the Wildflower Inn here in town."

Gabe shook her hand but showed no recognition. To Emma's credit she only turned up the wattage on her charm. "It's Niall Reed's old house."

"Right." Gabe nodded. "I heard some Yankee bought the place."

Emma sniffed. "I was born and raised in Virginia, hardly a Yankee, as if that's even a bad thing."

"You don't sound like you were raised in the South."

Cam felt Angi bristle behind him but he held up a hand. He had no doubt Emma could handle Gabe Carlyle.

"I can bless your heart with the best of them," she told the man, her smile never wavering. "And the reason we're here is because I have a woman in distress who needs your help." She leaned forward ever so slightly. "Assuming you're a real Southern gentleman."

Gabe blinked and his gaze darted to Cam as if to ask, *Is she for real?*

"This is Holly Adams," Emma continued without giving Gabe a chance to respond. She tugged Holly forward. "She's getting married to an amazing man next weekend— a US senator for what it's worth."

"I don't follow politics," Gabe interjected.

"That's probably the best thing for your blood pressure," Emma said, and for the first time since he'd met her, Cam heard the trace of a Southern lilt in her tone.

This woman was truly something special.

"Holly's wedding is taking place at the inn," Emma explained. "It's our grand opening and the first of what we hope will be many successful events."

Holly nodded. "Emma saved my bacon when the place I planned to have it was ruined in that massive storm." She hitched a thumb at Cam. "Cam is my brother-in-law. He's made all the repairs on the inn and built the most beautiful pergola and redid the carriage house. Everything is perfect." She frowned. "Almost everything. I love Brett so much, but his mom doesn't approve of me. She thinks I'm not good enough and that he could find someone better. Someone classier or fancier or... I don't know, but I'm going to prove her wrong. The wedding is important, which is why we need your help. You *have* to help."

Gabe took an automatic step back, and Cam almost felt sorry for him. He recognized the flummoxed look on the other man's face, like he wasn't quite sure what had just happened or how he'd been sucked into the vortex of these women and their whirling energy.

"The florist Holly was using had a family emergency and needed to leave town."

That elicited a small laugh from Gabe. "By emergency do you mean setting fire to her own shop?"

"She didn't even return my deposit," Holly said, her voice quavering slightly.

Gabe winced in response.

Holly truly had faced a string of bad luck with her wedding planning. Cam was happy to let her and Emma work a deal with Gabe, but Cam was also ready to step in with whatever collateral the apparent flower whisperer needed to be convinced to help.

"I'm not in the business of supplying flowers for weddings," he said apologetically. "Even if I was, I'm not sure there's enough time to get you what you want and need. I'd guess the arrangements Luna had planned were traditional in style. She and I have different sensibilities."

"Sensibilities," Angi muttered with a snicker. "Like we're in some kind of Jane Austen florist novel or something. Mr. Darcy does flowers."

Gabe's gaze flicked to Angi. "What are you doing here?"

"Trying to convince my friends that it's a waste of time to ask you for help," she said, ignoring the quelling look from Emma. "I knew you wouldn't be willing to step in."

Cam wasn't sure what to make of the tension between Gabe and Angi, but there was a definite flash in the other man's eyes at her words. "I'll handle your flowers," Gabe said to Holly, although his gaze remained trained on Angi.

"Unbelievable." Angi threw up her hands and then turned and stalked out of the flower shop, the door banging shut behind her.

Holly and Emma both stared after her with twin looks of confusion. "Do you have a problem with Angi?" Emma asked, her tone wary. "Because we need help, but she's my partner. If you're going to upset her…"

"I promise not to glance in her direction," Gabe said with a wry smile. "It would be better for everyone involved."

Holly clasped her hands in front of her chest, clearly unsure whether to be excited at the possibility of her perfect wedding being saved or distressed by the potential of bringing another difficult guy into the mix.

"You and Holly sit down and talk about ideas," Emma said slowly. "The first step is to decide on a plan that's executable in a week. I'll find Angi and make sure she's okay."

"You have to make her okay," Holly insisted, gesturing to the abundance of color filling the shelves around them. "I know Gabe can help. Just like I knew Cam could."

Emma sighed. "You have an amazing ability to remain optimistic."

"Dana taught me that," Holly said, then looked toward Cam. "Remember how she used to say that attitude is the difference between an adventure and an ordeal?"

"I remember." He pressed a hand to his chest, expecting to feel the sharp ache that always accompanied thoughts of his late wife. Instead, he only found only a sweet sorrow that had him offering Holly a genuine smile. He didn't feel guilty that regret wasn't assailing him from all sides. Finding peace in her memory was still new, but he thought it would have made Dana happy. Holly was right. Her sister had always looked on the bright side, and it would have broken her heart that he'd shut himself off from happiness.

He wondered if he could truly find the courage to claim the new life he'd discovered.

EMMA FOUND ANGI on a bench in the middle of the town square, twirling an oversize oak leaf between her fingers.

"You're holding out on me," she said as she sat down next to her friend.

"Am not."

"What happened between you and Gabriel Carlyle?"

Angi rolled her eyes so hard Emma was surprised they didn't pop out of the sockets. "Not a damn thing. I've barely spoken two words to him since we were fifteen. I hardly remember the guy."

"Then you have no problem that Holly and I will be working with him on flowers for the wedding?"

"Sounds great," Angi said with the same amount of enthusiasm she might offer a potential root canal.

"If he does a good job, he could be our go-to florist."

"Does he look like a typical florist?"

"No, but if the shop is any indication, he's gifted."

"Gifted," Angi repeated with a sniff. "At being a judgmental, resentful jerk." She held up a hand when Emma would have spoken. "Forget I said anything. I have no real problem with him. I'm just in a bad mood."

"Care to share?" Emma nudged her with a gentle elbow. "You've dealt with plenty of my issues over the past few weeks. Are you having second thoughts about partnering with me?"

"I haven't felt this happy working since I left New York," Angi said quietly. "Sometimes I don't understand how I can feel so sad at the same time. My mom won't talk to me, and my brothers mainly want to lecture me about how I've hurt her feelings by going out on my own. Why is it that by doing what I want I'm upsetting the people I love?"

"A question for the ages." Emma ran a finger along the edge of her skirt. Even though she finally felt like success at the inn was within her grasp, it was bittersweet knowing she'd cut off her relationship with her mom in the process.

"It would be easiest to blame men," Angi murmured.

Emma laughed softly. "Yes, but also not true."

"Ignore my reaction to Gabe." Angi stood and then grabbed Emma's hand and pulled her to her feet. "If he makes Holly's wedding look beautiful with his magic flower power, then I'm all for it. As long as I don't have to talk to him."

"We'll keep him away from the kitchen," Emma promised.

"Good." Angi nodded. "Because I'm fairly certain I have a frying pan with his name on it." She checked the time on her cell phone. "I'm heading over to pick up Drew from camp. He's the only man I really need, anyway. I'm going to do my potential future daughter-in-law a favor and raise him to be a good guy."

"He's lucky to have you."

"I'm glad someone thinks so," Angi said cryptically, then waved and headed out of the park before Emma could question her further.

She stood gazing at the bustling streets of downtown. The air was heavy, but with the shade of the big oak tree above her, she felt strangely refreshed. This was her home. She'd left behind the constructs and confines of her formal life in order to create something substantial, a foundation and a refuge from the world. She couldn't wait for the inn to open so she could offer that same thing to her guests.

After a few minutes, she turned and headed in the direction of home, assuming she'd be walking back since she'd left Holly and Cam in the floral shop together.

To her surprise, she saw Cam's truck at the curb when she emerged from the path that led across the square. He was leaning against the side, lost in thought. Her heart did the little kick she'd become used to when she saw him, like he was a shot of adrenaline to her system.

"Tell me that's an asiago cheese bagel," she said, eyeing the brown bag he held.

His mouth spread into a slow grin, and she realized that he now smiled on a regular basis. So different than when they'd first met. Did she have something to do with that? "The finest the Bagel Buggy has to offer," he told her, inclining his head toward the food truck parked around the corner. "With tarragon cream cheese, of course."

She'd mentioned to him her deep devotion to the staple of the Magnolia food scene, and the flavored cream cheese. The fact that he remembered gave her a genuine thrill.

"Where's Holly?" she asked as she stepped closer.

"I dropped her off at the salon for her shift—she had a client. She's over-the-moon excited at the initial ideas Gabe had for the arrangements—a little more rustic than her original plan, but as long as she's happy, that's what counts."

"Thank you for the bagel," she said as he handed her the bag. Without bothering to glance around to see if anyone was watching them, she lifted onto her tiptoes and kissed him. "Bagels make me happy."

"You might think about raising your standards."

She pulled back enough to glance up at him. "My standards are just fine. I also appreciate you coming with us to visit Gabe. I know you were there to twist his arm if he wasn't willing to help."

"Luckily, no arm twisting needed. Is Angi going to be able to deal with him?"

"She's okay with it, although I'm going to keep the two of them far apart."

"Good idea." He wrapped his arms around her waist.

"People will talk," she warned him.

He rested his forehead against hers. "Let them."

Okay, this was a change. One Emma liked.

"Assuming there are no other emergencies, the wedding is going to be amazing."

"It will be amazing even with unforeseen emergencies. I have every faith in your ability to handle whatever comes your way."

His faith meant the world to her.

"I couldn't have done it without you. Wait until you see Holly's dress and taste the cake Mary Ellen at Sunnyside is creating for her."

His smile faded. "You'll have to save me a slice. I won't be there."

"Of course you will." She shook her head. "Did you not get the invitation? I know Holly had you on the list."

He released her and shifted away. Despite the summer heat, a shiver rippled along her skin. "I got the invitation. Did you notice I failed to RSVP?"

Emma shrugged. "Well, yes. But we just assumed you were coming. I thought…" She broke off because the words about to tumble from her lips seemed so dumb given his bristly stance. She'd thought he would be her date. They'd get through the ceremony and the official parts of the reception, and then Cam would lead her onto the dance floor and put his arms around her as they swayed to the music.

Shouldn't life have beat the sentimental streak out of Emma already?

"I agreed to help get the inn ready for the wedding. Once that's taken care of, my job is done."

"Your job with me," she felt the need to clarify. "Phil told me there's already a line of other customers wanting to meet with you for their projects."

"I'm not taking on other projects." He looked past her shoulder. "I have my fishing operation to keep me busy."

"But you want more than keeping you busy, right?" Emma couldn't understand how she'd gotten that so wrong. He might like being a fishing guide, but it wasn't his calling and wasted his talent. Had she misread Cam and his intentions for the future? "I thought you were going to get back into construction and the furniture making. Your dad said—"

"My dad doesn't understand what those old dreams cost me." He moved away from her like he was propelled by some invisible force. She watched as he began to pace the sidewalk. Three steps away, pivot, three steps back. But even though his footsteps brought him closer, she couldn't deny the distance that had materialized between them.

"I think he does," she said quietly. "And what they meant to you. Please come to the wedding, Cam."

"Holly will be fine without me."

"Not for Holly." She didn't bother to keep the emotion from her voice. "For me." She inclined her head. "For us."

For a brief, terrifying moment she expected him to deny that there was an "us" between them. A frown line appeared between his heavy brows, and she could almost feel the struggle inside him.

"I'll try to make it," he said finally, and she felt like she'd won a huge battle. One step forward that actually meant something.

Everything.

"Thank you." She pulled a bagel from the bag, tore off a piece and held it out to Cam like she might try to feed a feral animal. At this point, she wanted him to trust her. To trust the connection between them. To trust her love for him, even if he wasn't ready to hear her say the words.

He stared at her outstretched hand as if he understood exactly what that bite represented. Then he took it, popped it into his mouth and chewed. "It's my favorite, too."

CHAPTER TWENTY-ONE

CAM GLANCED UP as Malcolm Grimes lowered himself into the seat next to him. The inn's backyard had been transformed into a charming mix of down-home country and elevated sophistication with neat rows of chairs covered in linen slipcovers and rose petals leading the way up the aisle. In the late-afternoon sunlight of a perfect Saturday afternoon, the whole landscape seemed to glow with a light that gave the impression of an ethereal wonderland.

Gabe had created flower arrangements using a mix of pale roses and peonies, the soft colors complementing the classic motif of the day. Vines and organza spilled over the pergola Cam had built while vintage tables and chairs in neutral tones were lined up, ready for guests to dine on Angi's creative menu made with locally sourced ingredients.

He knew from Holly that several well-known bridal magazines and websites had interviewed her about the details of the day, and Cam could imagine this event putting Emma and the Wildflower Inn on the map, just like she'd planned.

"You clean up nice," Mal said with a wry grin, wiggling his eyebrows as he took in Cam's dark pants, crisp white button-down and pale blue tie.

"Back at you, Mayor."

Mal scoffed and touched a finger to the brim of his hat. "I always look good. Got a rep to protect and all that."

"Where's your better half?"

The mayor's grin grew wider. "Our youngest went into labor last night, so Gwen drove down to Wilmington to be with her. Expecting news on my third grandbaby today."

"Congratulations in advance," Cam said, and patted the older man on the arm.

"Where's your lovely date for this blessed event?"

Cam shook his head. "I came alone." But he couldn't resist the urge to glance around, his gaze searching until it came to rest on Emma. He could see both pride and pleasure radiating from her as the final guests took their seats.

"I'm guessing you won't leave alone," Malcolm said with a chuckle. "She's a good fit for you."

"You mean for the town," Cam clarified.

Mal laughed again. "I said what I mean."

Cam knew he should have protested, but his heart wasn't in it. He and Emma did fit in all the ways that counted. She softened his rough edges and he hoped he helped her recognize her own strength.

"I've never seen so many fancy people in one place." Mal's dark gaze roamed over the faces of the guests. "It's like a who's who of political power. I'm surprised we don't have CNN parked at the curb."

"Did you ever aspire to politics on the national stage?" Cam asked, curious about the older man who'd been a part of his life for so long.

He'd never really thought of Mal—or his parents for that matter—as people in their own right. People with struggles and hardships. The blessing of being young was the blissful narcissism that came with it, when he'd believed that the iceberg tip of his mom and dad's life he saw as a child was the whole of the glacier. Now he understood there was much more to them; it had just been submerged.

"Nah." Mal made a face. "Magnolia has always been home to me. I'm just glad I get to see the town come back to her former glory. That started with this house and Niall's girls. Emma is part of it now, of course. Lots going on around here." Cam felt the weight of his assessing gaze. "I hear your skills are in high demand after your work at the inn. Gwen and I have dinner every night on the table you made for us."

"We both know you only commissioned that table as a favor to my dad," Cam said, remembering how excited he'd been to cash Mal's check when he'd been struggling to get his furniture business off the ground. It had been the most money he'd made from a single customer, and he remained grateful.

"That table is a work of art." Mal turned to look fully at him. "I can't count the number of visitors we've had over the years who've commented on its unique beauty and asked about the artist who created it. That was before the recent popularity of sustainably crafted pieces. Camden, there's a market for your talent if you put yourself out there again."

Cam felt a flicker of promise along his skin. Just like being with Emma had reopened a part of his heart that had been locked away, working on the inn had made him remember his love of creating and working with his hands.

The string quartet situated to the right of the pergola began to play Pachelbel's *Canon in D*, saving him from having to answer. Recognition skittered across the back of his neck as he watched Holly begin her walk down the aisle on the arm of her father. She'd chosen the same song Dana had for her wedding processional.

Memories crept up like weeds out of new dirt and took hold of him with a strength he couldn't combat. Dana in her white dress, so young and hopeful. Their vows to love and cherish. All the ways he'd failed to protect her.

He fisted his hands tightly to distract himself from the grief that still plagued him and focused his attention on Holly. His gaze caught on the flutter of wings behind her, and he heard a collective gasp whisper through the guests as a gorgeous yellow butterfly landed on her bouquet.

Holly's mouth curved up at one end, and he knew exactly what she was thinking. That the delicate creature was a sign from her sister, a blessing of sorts. Cam wanted to believe it. He wanted to rush from his seat and capture that butterfly between his palms, holding it close like he could no longer do with his first love.

Then the butterfly alighted from the rose petal where it had landed. It hovered in the air between Holly and Brett for a few seconds before flitting over the wildflowers that still dotted the edge of the lawn, then disappearing up and out of sight into a copse of trees.

That was the sign, Cam realized. Dana was with them in her own way—she always would be. But she was also free now and maybe Cam could be, as well.

After dabbing at her cheeks, Holly turned and handed the bouquet to her maid of honor. She had one friend standing up for her, and Brett had the guy who Cam had met during that traumatic cocktail party. The one who'd seemed a little too friendly with Emma.

He shifted in his seat and found Emma again. Now she stood near one of the long banquet tables, along with Angi and Mariella. She looked both radiant and exhausted, somehow able to pull off both ends of the spectrum. They hadn't spent time alone together since he'd bought her the bagel. The last-minute wedding preparations had taken all of her time, and the first overnight guests to the inn had arrived the previous day.

Other than finishing up the punch list, Cam had made himself scarce. Maybe he and his former mother-in-law had come to a sort of fragile understanding that day at the cemetery, but he wouldn't take the chance of spoiling Holly's wedding in any way.

He wondered if her mother recognized the song or if it meant the same thing to her as it did to him.

Just as sorrow tried to get the better of him, the butterfly that had landed on Holly's bouquet reappeared, flitting above Emma and her friends, so high over their heads they didn't even notice.

"Thank you," Cam whispered, taking it as a sign.

"For what?" Mal whispered back as the minister gave the couple a blessing and they shared a tender kiss.

"Never mind." Cam's heart felt the tenuous promise of new possibilities swell to something more.

Holly and her new husband turned to the crowd, and he knew all the emotional turmoil he'd dealt with had been worth it.

"You did right by that child," Mal told him, patting his leg.

"She helped me more than I helped her," Cam answered.

Holly's smile was radiant as she walked back down the aisle with her new husband, and even the senator's mother looked pleased as the families followed. Cam hunched down slightly when Karen and Dave Adams moved past.

"You gonna dance the night away?" Mal asked while more guests filed by.

"I don't know," Cam admitted. "I'm not much for crowds."

"My nephew's the lead singer in the band playing at the

reception. They're worth dealing with a crowd just for the rendition of 'Unchained Melody.'"

Cam chuckled. "Righteous."

"Exactly," the mayor agreed.

Maybe he would stay. Emma had asked him to, and he wanted to make her happy. He made his way toward the bar that had been set up near the edge of the patio and ordered a club soda with lime.

"Cam Arlinghaus?"

He turned and swallowed back a groan as Lance Rieber joined him at the bar. "Hey, Lance. Haven't seen you for a while."

"Since Dana's funeral," Lance said, and asked the bartender for a gin and tonic, rolling his eyes when he was told liquor wasn't being served.

"I didn't realize you were friends with Holly," Cam said, trying to keep his tone neutral. Lance and Dana had gone to the same high school and dated for a year before she and Cam met. The stocky former high school linebacker hadn't been thrilled to lose her to Cam, a guy from the wrong side of the tracks as far as Lance was concerned. Even after they'd married, Lance never stopped flirting with Dana when they ran into him in town. It used to drive Cam crazy, and he found his feelings hadn't changed much over the years.

"My girlfriend works with her at the salon," Lance offered. He picked up his Sprite and glanced around at the other guests. "Although I'm thinking of an upgrade after checking out some of the new options in town."

Cam followed his gaze to Emma, who was talking to Alex and Holly's maid of honor.

"She's not available," Cam said tightly.

"You're joking, right?" Lance drained his glass in one

long swallow. "From what I hear, you haven't gone beyond the fishing dock for years. Now suddenly you're going to make a play for the hot chick in town." Before Cam could answer, Lance added, "Granted, she seems a little uptight, but I can work with that. Might be fun to loosen her up."

"Shut it, Lance." In case he'd been unclear, all the reasons why Cam couldn't stand this guy were coming back to him.

"I'm serious." Lance straightened and turned to face Cam. "And not because I want to compete with you again, Arlinghaus. Even if the smokin' innkeeper and I don't make a run at it, she seems like a nice enough girl. Do her a favor and stay away."

Cam wasn't sure how to react to this change in tack, especially when Lance was giving voice to Cam's secret fear. "I'm just helping with repairs on the inn," Cam said, hating the defensiveness in his tone.

"Sure you are. You ruined Dana's life. Don't take another woman down."

Heat poured through Cam as Lance walked away. His gaze tracked to Emma again, and he watched as Meredith pulled her to the center of the dance floor, along with Carrie Reed and another blonde, who Cam guessed was the third of Niall's daughters. The band sang the perennial reception favorite "We Are Family," and Emma laughed as she shimmied along to the music.

Her joy only made his breathing thunder harder. Would he bring her low the way Lance suggested? The same way he had with Dana?

His skin burned under his suit, and he stalked toward the shadows along the edge of the line where the forest met the manicured lawn. Always toward the shadows.

The noise from the reception became muted as he moved

through the trees. There was still enough light that he could see without stumbling, and the woods offered some respite from the emotions that seemed to taunt him. He placed an open palm against the rough bark of a nearby tree to ground himself as he drew in rough gulps of air.

He shifted closer to the tree when he heard an unfamiliar noise to his left, one that sounded like someone crying. A man.

Impossible, Cam thought, and almost immediately realized it was not only possible but it was Holly's dad, who stood ten yards away, his head tipped forward as he quietly sobbed.

Cam felt like he was trespassing on some too-private moment. Dave must not have heard him approach. Cam took a step back in retreat.

He would have liked to escape without speaking to the other man, but a fallen twig snapped under his shoe and Dave turned.

"No one was supposed to see me like this." He rubbed his jacket sleeve across his face.

"Consider me no one." Cam started to move toward the house, but Dave's hollow voice stopped him.

"It's just so hard," his former father-in-law murmured.

Cam drew in a shuddering breath. "I know."

"I couldn't be happier for Holly," Dave continued, and Cam forced himself to turn around. The least he could do for this man was to listen if he needed to talk, even if it just about killed Cam to witness him so broken and know his role in causing it. "I didn't exactly support her when she called and told us she was marrying into the Carmichael family. But just like her older sister, she knew her mind and her heart, and there wasn't a damn thing I could do to stop her."

If only he'd been able to stop Dana. Maybe she'd still be alive. A hundred times over Cam would choose a world where he didn't end up with Dana but she got to live a full life over one without her in it.

"You're a good dad, Dave. I think Brett might surprise you. He seems like a decent guy. He loves your daughter."

"It surprised me that she went to you for help."

"That makes two of us. I'd do anything for her. And if I could change what happened to Dana, I'd do it in a second."

"That also makes two of us," Dave said, and used two fingers to loosen the tie around his neck. "I feel guilty for being happy. It's why I'm out here instead of celebrating with the daughter I can still hug. Are we partners on that, as well?"

Cam started to say no. He hadn't let himself be happy since Dana's death. But that wasn't exactly true. True at all, if he were being completely honest. Emma made him happy.

"I live with guilt every day," he said instead of answering directly. He couldn't even admit he felt happy. There was too much guilt in that.

"It's a heavy burden."

"Nah," Cam denied, even as self-disgust nearly swept him under. "It's not bad."

"I don't want to carry it anymore. Dana wouldn't want that." Dave dusted off his trousers and started toward the house. After a few steps he looked over his shoulder. "Are you coming?"

Cam wanted with every fiber of his being to rejoin the reception, to walk into the warm light, happy voices and buoyant music, but if he did, what would that say about him as a husband? What about his devotion to Dana?

"I'm going to head out," he told Dave, and the words almost felled him.

"You sure?"

"Yeah, this isn't my scene. Enjoy the reception."

He moved in the opposite direction, keeping to the edge of the yard as he walked toward where his truck was parked. Always on the fringes, stupid to think he'd ever belonged anywhere else.

He'd almost made it to the truck when he heard Emma call his name. Although he didn't turn around, she caught up to him in a few strides. "Holly's dad told me you were leaving." She sounded joyous and bubbly, and his heart ached. "But you promised me a dance."

He rounded on her then, letting his voice snap. "I didn't promise. I don't owe you anything."

She took a step back like he'd slapped her, and he wanted to punch himself for using his anger to wipe the sweet smile from her face. "I don't think you owe me. I thought—"

"Don't." He cut the air with a jackknife motion of his hand. "If this night showed me anything, it's that I'm not moving forward. I can't be the man you want, Emma."

"What if I want the man you are?"

Oh, hell. What a siren song that question was. As much as he would have liked to believe she could, he knew that wasn't true. How could anyone love the man he was when he was so filled with self-hatred?

"It doesn't matter," he forced himself to say. "I don't want you."

Her eyes widened and then narrowed. "Because you're still devoted to Dana?"

He looked past her, unable to confirm her question. Refusing to deny it.

She took his silence as assent, even though he hadn't meant it that way.

"She wouldn't want this," she said, but her voice was

cold. A repeat of what others had told him, but it was harder to hear it from Emma. "Nothing I've heard about her from Holly or her parents makes me think she'd want you to punish yourself like you do."

"Yet she's not here to tell you that in person. Because of me."

"No." Emma shrugged, like his guilt meant nothing to her. "Because a tragic accident took her life. I get it, Cam. I understand why you have to go."

She did?

"You're afraid, although it took me more time than it should have to see it. Maybe even a coward, if we're being totally honest." She leaned in, ignoring the shock that must show on his face. "We can be honest, right?"

"I'm not afraid," he insisted, even as something that felt a lot like fear curled through his gut. "I'm just done."

"Honesty," she reminded him, like a mother might tell a child to wash their hands before dinner. He wasn't sure how he'd expected Emma to react to him walking away again, but this wasn't it. "I get the fear because I lived most of my life with it. Trying to be perfect so I wouldn't disappoint my mother. Trying to be fun and funny and overtly sexy so I'd make my husband happy."

"You don't have to try to be sexy," he muttered, like it was some sort of accusation. "Or fun. You're tons of fun."

Her mouth gentled for an instant, and he thought he might coax a smile out of her. Then her gaze sharpened once more. "The point is I lived with fear every day. It was so imprinted on my soul that I didn't even realize it."

She laughed, but there was no humor in it. "In the spirit of honesty, I'm still afraid almost every day, but now the fear is different. Now I breathe into it and step through it.

I use it as a catalyst to move forward, not a chain to hold me back."

She lifted a hand as if to reach for him, then lowered it again. "You're rolling around in your own emotional dirty diaper, Cam, and I'm not going to be a part of that. I don't mind your broken parts or your shattered heart, but it breaks mine that you won't even try." Her eyes drifted closed. "You won't even try," she repeated.

He stood there, stunned by her bravery in revealing so much. Embarrassed he had nothing to offer in return.

"Thank you for your help with the inn," she said after clearing her throat. "It turned out better than I could have imagined. I'll have the final check to you within the week."

She turned and walked back toward the house.

Denial roared through him. No, she couldn't walk away from him. Not when he'd walked away first. Unsure of why it mattered, he opened his mouth to call to her, but no sound came out. He was well and truly gutted.

Didn't she understand the courage it took to deny himself the happiness he craved? Couldn't she see that he was doing this for her? He'd done everything for her.

In the end, it didn't matter. She climbed the front porch steps and disappeared. Cam knew that eventually some lucky man would claim her. It just wouldn't be him.

CHAPTER TWENTY-TWO

As EXPECTED, THE WEDDING of Brett Carmichael, US senator and heir to a venerable political dynasty, made the national news. Brett's mother had even given a quote to the *Town & Country* magazine website, welcoming her new daughter-in-law to the family and offering a few words of praise to the proprietress of Magnolia's Wildflower Inn for making the blessed event a picture-perfect celebration.

The inn, which was already at capacity for several weekends during the late-summer tourist season, was now booked well into the fall with several weddings that would bring in a much-needed infusion of cash.

Emma was beyond elated by the feedback she'd received from the first crop of guests and by the flurry of positive write-ups from local and regional press outlets. Although she knew Angi still struggled with her mother's disapproval, the talented chef was also busy creating menus that would put the Wildflower on the map as a culinary standout in the regional hospitality industry.

Emma wondered how long her talented friend would be satisfied working at a boutique inn if Angi's star continued to rise, and Emma had no doubt it would. But for now, Angi seemed thrilled to have a channel for her creativity in the kitchen, and Emma was determined to make the most of their partnership.

Even Mariella seemed excited to move forward, although

she still wasn't willing to take a named role in the event side of the business. Holly's dress had received a lot of attention, although no one had questioned her in more detail about the "vintage designer" she'd employed to create it. Both Emma and Holly had tried to convince Mariella to reveal her involvement, but she refused.

"I'm not that person anymore," Mariella had said simply. "I don't want to go back to her."

Emma understood the desire to move forward, although she'd spent way too much time over the past few weeks nursing her broken heart. Losing Cam felt like cutting out a piece of her heart, but Emma had to admit she might not have actually had him in the first place. That hurt even more.

She'd gotten used to seeing him every day, even when they each went about their own business around the property. He was part of her world, her new life, and she'd let herself fall totally in love with him despite knowing it might end with her in a crumpled heap on the floor.

But she'd only spent one night wallowing, remaining true to her determination not to be a person who floundered about in her sorrow. Mainly there was plenty to keep her busy. She'd already learned a lesson about continuing to move forward even when things didn't go according to her plan. It was difficult to let go of the dream she'd allowed herself to imagine, a world with the inn and friends and, most importantly, Cam at her side. But even with her heart splintered in a thousand pieces, Emma knew she had the strength to keep going.

Ethel barked once when the inn's doorbell rang. "Good girl," Emma said automatically. The dog had been a huge comfort during the lonely days and nights since the breakup with Cam. Could it be considered a breakup when they hadn't even been an official couple?

By the standards of Emma's shattered heart, then definitely yes. She glanced at her watch as she walked to the front door. The guests booked for tonight weren't scheduled to arrive until later that afternoon. However, she'd already put clean sheets on the bed and placed a fresh bouquet on the dresser in their room, so she could handle it if they were early.

She felt as though she could handle anything at this point.

Until she opened the door to reveal her mother standing on the other side.

"Hello, Emma." Gillian lifted a brow when Emma simply stared. "May I come in?"

"Sure." Emma tried to hide her shock as she stepped back to allow her mom to enter. "I didn't know you were in the area. Did you come to see Ryan?"

"I came to see you." Gillian frowned at Ethel, whose tail wagged in enthusiastic greeting. Then her gaze lifted to Carrie's wildflower painting, which dominated the inn's foyer. "Things have changed quite a bit since my last visit."

"Yes, they have," Emma agreed as she led her mother toward the kitchen. Ethel scampered past, nails clicking on the hardwood floor, and Emma smiled just a touch. She'd signed the adoption papers the Monday after the wedding, another on Meredith's long list of foster fails. The doodle had quickly captured her heart, and she made a perfect guest greeter. No matter what came of the visit from her mother, Emma knew some snuggle time with Ethel would make it better.

"Next time call or text to let me know you're driving down. It will be easier to give you time that way. As it is, I only have a few minutes to spare." It wasn't exactly a lie. She did have a long list of to-dos for the day. More importantly, she needed some boundaries. She was done making other people a priority while she muddled through with scraps.

"I'll do that," Gillian said, and Emma could almost see her mother's teeth clench. Gillian did not like to be told what to do. But this was Emma's life, and her mother would need to honor that if she wanted to be part of it.

Why was she there? Did she want to be part of it again?

"Would you like something to drink?"

"Do you have Earl Grey?"

"Of course."

As the dog settled onto her bed in the corner of the kitchen, Emma set about making a pot of tea and waited for her mother to get to the point. There was always an agenda with Gillian.

"Several of my friends read about the Carmichael wedding in society pages."

Pride washed through Emma like cool rain on a hot summer day as she turned on a burner under the ceramic kettle. "Yes, we received some great publicity from the event."

"They still don't understand why you'd want to give up your role at the foundation to act as a glorified housekeeper."

"Innkeeper," Emma clarified.

Her mother didn't answer, and Emma kept focused on the task at hand and tried not to let the tacit condemnation affect her. One cup of tea, a few minutes of awkward small talk, and she could send her mother on her way.

It had been silly to think this visit meant something had changed.

"I explained that you want to make your way in the world

on your own, just like your brother did." Gillian cleared her throat. "I told them I'm proud of you for that choice."

Emma paused in the act of taking two mugs from an upper cabinet and turned. "You did? You are? Since when?"

"Don't be sassy."

"Mom, you disowned me like we were part of some prime-time soap opera. Cue the sad violins and all of that. This is a bit more than a simple pivot or change of heart." There were times in her life when Emma had wondered if her mother actually had a heart.

"I'd still rather have you working for the family business." Gillian set her purse on the counter with a sniff. "But you set your mind to something different, and you've done well so far."

"You know most of my guests and events won't receive national press coverage. If this is because of the *Town & Country* mention, you're going to have dine out on that one for a while."

"Can you let me apologize?" Gillian demanded with more emotion in her voice than Emma had ever heard.

The kettle whistled, and both women were quiet while Emma poured the tea. She placed a steaming mug on the counter in front of her mother. "Is that what you're doing?"

"Yes. Perhaps badly, but yes nevertheless. Don't expect me to come here and wait on strangers like the hired help—"

"I don't expect nor did I ask that of you," Emma said with more calm than she felt.

"Of course," her mother agreed, waving her hand toward Emma. "You never needed any help."

"I learned from the master."

Gillian laughed softly and picked up her mug. "I imagine you did. I was angry when you left the foundation. It felt like a repudiation of me and everything I'd built. Your father resented my family's wealth. Your brother wants very little to do with me. You were my person, Emma. I was losing my person."

"No." Emma shook her head. "I was trying to find myself, not lose you or our family's history." She gestured to the kitchen. "I saw something in this place, a home that had been ill-used, and I wanted to make something better."

"You have."

"Thank you." Simple words, but they meant something. Emma could tell her mother knew it, as well.

"I also came here today to tell you in person that you no longer have to worry about the tape."

"What tape?" Emma asked, then sucked in a breath as she realized what her mother was referring to. "Wait. How did you know? How did you—"

"Martin came to me." Gillian's lip curled as if the words left a bad taste in her mouth.

"No. He promised—"

"Do you honestly believe a man who would set you up that way and then blackmail you for money is the sort who can be trusted to keep a promise?"

Emma dropped her gaze and placed her mug back on the counter with a trembling hand. Hot tea sloshed over the side onto her skin. She barely registered the burn. "I never wanted you to find out about that."

"I understand, but you should have come to me, Emma. Money doesn't solve everything, but in these types of situations—"

"Mom, no. Tell me you didn't pay him. I'll never forgive myself if you had to pay for my stupidity."

"I didn't pay him."

Gillian shrugged when Emma stared at her in confusion.

"I threatened him. I hired a private investigator to dig up every nasty skeleton in Martin's closet. Your ex-husband might know a lot about Eastern European history, but he has the common sense of a brick. He paid the man from Chicago with a personal check."

"He...really?"

"Yes, so it was simple enough to make him understand that the dean and other administrators would find out about his behavior if he didn't turn over the video to our lawyers. Martin won't be coming after you again. If he ever tries to make contact with you, there will be consequences."

"Thank you, again." Emma could barely fathom the idea of not having that mistake held over her head for the rest of her life. "I'm sorry, Mom. I can imagine how disappointed you were that—"

"Let's not focus on the negative," Gillian said in a clipped tone. "We've both done things we would like to change, but those are in the past."

"Right." Emma nodded. "How's Patricia settling in at the foundation?"

"She wasn't the right fit. I think you knew that before I did. For now, the role has been filled by Ann Baltman."

Emma sucked in a breath. Ann was the program director she'd hired and her favorite employee at the foundation, but she was also young and didn't have the pedigree Gillian seemed to expect from her staff. Emma was both stunned and elated to hear her mother was giving Ann a chance. "She'll do an amazing job."

"I hope so. She was hired and trained by the best." Gillian made a show of checking her watch. "I've taken up more than my allotted time. You're busy, and I've said my piece."

Emma grabbed a towel hanging from the oven door and

wiped the spilled tea from the counter. "I have a couple of extra minutes. If you'd like an official tour of the inn, I could make that happen. We have leftover pasta salad for lunch, as well."

"That would be lovely," her mother said. They were both cautious, but that was okay. Sometimes it took time to get things right, and Emma had found a newfound appreciation for patience.

Emma started the tour at the far end of the hall, Ethel trailing alongside her, and explained to her mom how they'd chosen the decor for each of the guest rooms.

"You're happy here," Gillian observed as they walked up the stairs, "but something is off."

Emma shook her head. "It's been busy since the wedding, and I don't want to miss any opportunity. I'm a little tired. That's all."

"Is it Martin and the reminder of how he betrayed you? I know you have a big heart, and I can't say I was happy you gave it to him."

"Martin doesn't have my heart. He hasn't for a while."

"But someone does," her mom said quietly. Emma would never deny that her mother was observant.

"Not anymore." Emma pasted a serene smile on her face. Ethel nudged her legs, like the dog knew she needed a bit of extra moral support. "My only focus now is the inn."

"There was a man on your patio the day that we argued in the backyard. The way he watched you…"

"I don't want to talk about men, Mom. Please. Can we just focus on the tour? It's all a little much for me now."

"Okay." Gillian reached out and placed a hand on Emma's arm. "Just know I'm here if you need me."

The ache in Emma's heart eased a little. It was difficult to imagine ever leaning on her mom, but Emma was done fighting. She'd created a new life and she welcomed anyone who wanted to support her in it. She only wished Cam was among those who did.

"Is THIS THE boat we're taking? Are you the captain?"

Cam looked up from where he was inspecting the aerator and the live well on the boat, ready to make the boy who'd spoken feel welcome. Instead, he bit back a groan and shook his head.

"I've got clients today, Andrew," he told Angi's darkhaired son with his serious eyes and small frame. Cam had seen the kid around the inn during his time working there. Usually he was exploring near the edge of the woods or kicking a soccer ball around the yard with way more enthusiasm than skill. Andrew was an odd little duck, but Cam liked the boy. Not enough to deal with his mother on the boat.

"He's got us," Angi said with false cheer. "I booked Captain Cam for a half-day tour."

"I don't think so." The last thing he needed was a reminder of his time with Emma that her friend was sure to offer. Cam checked the notebook where he kept his reservation log. "I don't go by 'captain,' and I have a Maria Andrew on the schedule."

"Mom, this is the wrong one," the boy said, sounding heartbroken.

Angi ruffled his thick mop of hair. "No, sweetie. I'm not sure what happened but there must have been a mix-up with the name on the reservation. Maria is my middle name, and obviously Cam wrote your first name where the last name should be."

"I didn't mess up with the reservation," Cam said tightly. "I don't mess things up."

"Sure you do, Captain." Angi flashed a knowing smirk. "I bet by now you realize how much."

He couldn't deny it. In the three weeks since Holly's wedding, Cam had tried his best to slip back into the routine of his former, solitary existence. But life without Emma and the light she brought into his world was nothing more than a sad pit of loneliness. After Dana's death it hurt to be alive. Now Cam was ready to live, but he'd managed to lose his heart for a second time. He had no doubt Emma would be better off without him, but that didn't stop him from wanting her.

He'd bought a bottle of whiskey from the liquor store on his way home that first night, but just one sip had made his stomach turn. There seemed to be no way to numb his feelings or anesthetize himself against the emotions that wouldn't be kept at bay. He stayed busy on the water and with punishing runs in the early morning and sometimes late at night. He couldn't run from his regret.

Only now it was different. He'd finally come to understand that Dana's death had been a tragedy but not his fault. So many people had told him she would want him to move forward, but he hadn't allowed himself to believe them. He hadn't wanted to accept that as truth, because if he moved on he would open himself up to being hurt again.

Turned out, he'd moved on despite himself and damn did his heart ache from messing it up beyond repair.

"Mom's really busy," Andrew said, stepping forward and looking him straight in the eye. "She's always working and sometimes she forgets things. The other day she forgot to pick me up at soccer camp, and Taylor, the coach, had to wait with me. Coach was supposed to go on a date with her boyfriend so she was really mad."

"I didn't forget," Angi said, crossing her arms over her chest. "I was late."

"It's okay because Mom gave Taylor some extra money to use on her date. She could give you some extra money, maybe? Would you take us out if she did?"

Cam blinked. He hadn't even realized the quiet boy could string so many words together. He darted a glance at Angi, who lifted a brow as if in challenge.

"Today was going to make up for how much she's been working." Andrew pointed at his mom. "If we go back home she'll just start working again. I want to do something fun. Can you please take us fishing? I don't think anyone else is coming."

Cam pulled a twenty-dollar bill from his wallet and handed it to Andrew. "Go up to the bait shack and buy some sandwiches and drinks. Your mom and I will work something out."

The boy plucked the money out of Cam's hand and ran for the shop.

"Are you paying him to lay it on that thick?" Cam asked Angi.

"Trust me, no. The last thing I want is my kid sharing with you all the ways I'm failing as a mom."

"Why are you here, Angi?"

She shrugged. "Andrew wanted to go fishing. He wasn't exaggerating about how much I'm working lately. I thought a few hours on the water would be fun."

"With me?"

"I trust you."

He started to offer a sarcastic reply, but what the hell could he say to that? "I don't want to talk about Emma," he told her through clenched teeth.

"She's amazing, by the way," Angi said as if he hadn't

just laid down a moratorium about mentioning Emma. "The inn is already gaining a fantastic reputation as a perfect getaway destination. She's going to be busy with all the success coming her way."

"Good for her," Cam offered, and tried to ignore the tightness in his chest. He wanted to celebrate with Emma. He wanted to tell her how proud he was and rub her shoulders at the end of the day and wake up with her every morning.

Andrew came running back down the hill with two bags in hand. "I've got lunch, and I got shrimp for bait."

"That was fast." A rusty laugh escaped Cam at the boy's enthusiasm. "Did you bring my change?"

Andrew came to a stop next to his mom. "I wanted to get back quick so I just handed him the money." He glanced up at Angi. "I told him to keep the change the way people do at the restaurant."

"It's important to be a good tipper," she confirmed with a gentle smile.

It was strange to see this side of Angi. In some ways, she reminded Cam of himself, closed off and outwardly hardened, but she was vulnerable with her son.

He took the bag of food from Andrew but shook his head when the boy tried to hand him the bait. "Before I agree to take you out, I need to understand your goal for this excursion. Do you want my usual tourist tour or do you want to become a real fisherman?"

"Real," Andrew said solemnly.

"Then this is going to be a working trip. Are you ready to work?"

"Yes, Captain."

Cam's heart clenched. He'd always thought in some vague way that he'd be a father one day. Those dreams had died along with Dana, but now he could imagine having a son of his own, one with a mop of caramel-colored hair and a wide, bright smile just like Emma's.

If only he hadn't pushed her away.

He cleared his throat and gave Andrew a few simple instructions for how to be a good first mate. The boy handed the container of bait to his mom and hurried to do Cam's bidding. Angi stepped onto the boat and, as if she could read Cam's mind, she leaned in close.

"It's not too late," she told him.

"She's your friend," he countered. "You should encourage her to find a better man than me."

"Probably," she said with a laugh. "But you're the man she wants, even if you are an idiot."

That pretty well summed it up. Cam busied himself with checking the instruments on the dash, and they motored into open water. He set up the downrigger, and Andrew dutifully took watch.

"What do I have to offer her?" Cam asked Angi when he couldn't stand it any longer. He kept his gaze focused on the open water in front of them. "She's got so much going on, and there are moments when I hurt just being alive."

"You can love her for starters," the lanky brunette told him. "It's obvious you do."

"Sometimes love isn't enough for a happy ending."

"Sometimes it is," she argued. "But if you feel the need to prove it with something tangible, there's still an empty place inside the Wildflower's front entry."

"What does that mean?"

"You're a talented craftsman, Cam." She lifted her sunglasses onto the top of her head and stared at him. "I understand why you've turned away from that part of you, but it might be time to reclaim it. It might be the step you need."

"I destroyed my woodshop after Dana's accident. I couldn't spend my time making things when that's what destroyed her."

"Things can be rebuilt," Angi told him. "With time and patience. No one should feel alone when there's a person in the world to love you the way you need to be loved. You have a second chance. Don't be a fool. Take it."

"I'm freaked out that you're being nice."

"Don't get used to it." She chucked him on the shoulder. "Emma deserves to be happy, and you do, too. Think of this as my one good deed for the year, and you'll owe me big-time after."

Cam drew in a deep breath of the salty ocean air. The idea of creating a new life terrified him, but not as much as the thought of trying to live without Emma. For the first time in forever, Cam felt hopeful for the future. Starting over wouldn't be easy, but if Emma gave him even the sliver of a chance to make things right, it would be worth it.

"I will definitely owe you," he told Angi. He smiled for the first time in weeks as he took in the sweep of shore and sea that had been his refuge for so long. It was time to find a new harbor.

CHAPTER TWENTY-THREE

Hi.

THE TEXT CAME through midmorning, exactly one month after Holly's wedding. She didn't recognize the number, although it was local, so ignored the text. Probably some kid messing around with his mom's phone.

Hello. Are you there? Emma?

Okay, not a mis-text.

Who is this?

Me.

She'd come into town to meet with Mariella and pick up a few odds and ends for the guest rooms. Now she paused on the sidewalk in front of the bookstore, staring at her phone.

Can you be more specific?

Me Camera.

My Camera.

Her heart fluttered as the three little dots flashed.

Why does this stupid thing keep changing my worlds around?

Words. Changing words.

She thumbed in a response.

It's called autocorrect. Best and worst part of texting.

Worst. This is Cam.

Yes, I know. When did you get a phone?

Twenty minutes ago. I wanted to text you.

Her thumbs hovered over the screen.

I missile you.

She frowned. Her phone dinged again almost immediately.

Missed

Miss

I. Miss. You.

I'm sorry for being an ask.

Assistant

Ass

I hate this thing.

She quickly sent a response, her mind and heart racing at warp speed.

I get your point. How are you?

Scared.

Her breath caught, and although she expected another text to come through in short order, her phone remained silent.

Was that autocorrect?

"No."

She glanced up to see Cam standing a few feet away, just outside the entrance to the hardware store. A few people moved past, and she tried to ignore the speculative glances the two of them received.

"You're afraid of texting?" she asked softly, drinking in the sight of him even though her brain warned her body not to react. He wore a navy T-shirt and twill pants. His hair was even longer than she remembered, and a few days of stubble darkened his jaw.

"I'm afraid of a lot of things," he said with a small laugh. "But I'm not letting that stop me. Someone taught me to breathe through the fear."

"Oh." Funny, because at the moment Emma couldn't draw a steady breath to save her life. "No fishing trips today?"

"I've cut back to only guiding on the weekends."

She nodded, disappointment spiking in her gut. Was he withdrawing into his own private hell again?

"I was heading to the inn next, but then you appeared. Maybe it's a sign. I hope so. I'd like to show you something," he said. "Are you busy?"

"With a to-do list that will take me weeks to complete," she said, then added, "Right now I'm supposed to be meeting my brother for lunch. We've started hanging out a bit more. It's nice."

Cam nodded as if she'd told him she was going to invent the cure for cancer. "I was coming over to ask if you'd stop by my house later tonight. Or tomorrow. Or whenever you have time." He shrugged. "But now you're here. We've determined I'm garbage at texting, so I was thinking…"

"It's probably not a good idea," she said, because how could she open herself up to him again?

"That I think?" His mouth curved into the hint of a smile, and her body immediately reacted. Stupid body.

"That we see each other." Emma gripped her phone more tightly. "I wish you nothing but the best, Cam. Honesty policy, this is hard for me."

"Me, too," he agreed, and a flare of vulnerability flashed in his gaze that both terrified and elated her. "Just once," he said. "I…there's just something I need to say and I don't want to do it on the sidewalk with half the hardware store staff staring at us."

Her gaze flicked to the store's large front window. Lily Wainright gave her a thumbs-up.

"Small-town life," she murmured, attempting to laugh around the ball of emotion lodged in her throat. She missed laughing with Cam. She missed a lot of things about him but laughing most of all. Or maybe the way he held her. Or the way he listened when she spoke like there was nothing more important than whatever she was telling him.

No, going to visit him would be a huge mistake.

Her phone vibrated, and she read the text that had just come through from Ryan.

"Emergency at the hospital," she said, glancing up at Cam from under her lashes. "Raincheck on lunch."

He pointed across the street. "There's no line at the Bagel Buggy. Please, Emma."

"Okay," she said, telling herself she was not caving. That it was a small town and she was going to be mature and handle this like it was no big deal. As he'd pointed out the night of Holly's wedding, Cam had promised her nothing. The fact she'd read more into their connection...well, that was on her.

They ordered bagels, and she insisted on paying separately, like that somehow showed her independence. Cam didn't argue, and he didn't seem bothered when she insisted on driving her car to his house instead of riding with him. Emma would be mature but no way could she handle being so close in the confined space of his truck cab for an extended period of time.

The radio in her car was tuned to an oldies station, and she hummed along, telling herself she wasn't nervous or affected by the fact that Cam texted he missed her.

She parked behind his truck and smiled when Toby trotted down the front porch steps to greet her. "Do you smell Ethel on me?" she asked the dog when he sniffed her up and down. "She misses you."

At Cam's sharp intake of breath, Emma glanced up. She probably shouldn't have admitted that her dog missed his. Silly but true. Sometimes Ethel would climb up next to Emma on the couch, place her furry snout in Emma's lap and look up with eyes that questioned where her best friend had gone. Emma had never related more to a dog than at those moments.

"What's up, Cam?" she asked, suddenly regretting she'd said yes to this little venture. He'd walked away from her, and she could barely admit—even to herself—how much her heart had broken. Not that she was hiding it from anyone. Her friends knew. Meredith and Ryan could tell—her brother offering to throw hands with Cam if Emma needed him to defend her honor.

She didn't. She just needed to get over him.

"It's in there," he said, gesturing to the barn behind the main house. "How are you doing?" he asked as she fell in step next to him.

"Great," she answered, which was true and not. She decided to focus on the true. "The inn got a lot of positive press from the wedding, so things are picking up just like I'd hoped."

"I saw some of the articles. Holly brought them out when she came to say goodbye."

"I hope all my brides are as easy to work with as Holly. We already have three weddings booked for the fall."

"Congratulations," he murmured. The word felt like a caress, and Emma had to force herself not to lean into it. Into *him*.

They'd gotten to the barn, and he met her gaze as he pushed open the door. "No one except me has been in here for five years. Until recently, even I haven't had the guts to enter."

Her heart did a funny skip in her chest. "Okay," she answered because she didn't know what else to say.

He flipped on the light as she followed him into the large, open interior. It smelled like furniture polish and sawdust, and she blinked as she realized what the space was used for. "Your workshop."

"I've started making furniture again," he said, leading her forward. "Because of you. *For* you."

"For me?" She gave a shaky laugh, her heart thudding dully. "What does that mean?"

Then her gaze caught on the gorgeous walnut sideboard and hutch that held center stage in the middle of the workshop. The craftsmanship was as good as anything she'd ever seen, with clean lines and details that included five drawers, shelves that looked to be adjustable and the silhouette of an oak tree carved into either side. The beauty of the piece took her breath away.

"I still have some work to do and it needs another coat of poly. I thought if you don't find something for the entry, maybe this would work. I was going to drop it off to you, but that seemed presumptuous. Maybe it's not even your style. Maybe it won't fit or you've found something but—"

"Stop." She held up a hand as her thoughts coalesced. She stared at the one-of-a-kind creation for a few more seconds before switching her gaze to Cam. "It's amazing. You have to know it is."

"I'm rusty with the details," he said and ran a hand through his hair. "It's not always easy being back in here, both from a skill and an emotional standpoint. I'm working through it. Breathing and all that."

"Breathing," she repeated, reminding herself to do the same. She spun in a circle, taking in exactly what was going on in the barn. Not a barn in the traditional sense. A workshop with a variety of tools that looked to be state of the art, although some of them were a bit dusty. "This is who you are." She turned to face him more fully. "The renovation business, the fishing guide shtick. Those were just masks you hid behind. This is what you were meant to do."

The smile he gave her was filled with sorrow. "It's who I wanted to be and what I was trying so hard to do while Dana supported us. I'd sold a few pieces and was in negotiations to partner with a prominent furniture company near Asheville as one of their lead craftsmen. I was in here when Dana left for her shift that night. I didn't even say goodbye."

"You couldn't have known what would happen."

"There are moments when it's still difficult to accept it wasn't my fault, but I'm focusing on forgiveness. I'm focusing on what matters. You're right, Emma. She wouldn't want this sad, lonely life for me. Hell, I hate who I've become."

She took a step closer. "You can't hate the man I fell in love with. I refuse to let you. Even though things didn't work out with us, I still care about you, Cam. I'd be honored to have this piece in the inn."

His eyes drifted shut for a moment, and his jaw tightened. "I'm sorry," he said finally. "I'm sorry I was callous with your heart. I didn't realize or care how much I'd let fear take over my life until you pushed me out of my comfort zone." He shrugged. "I'm not saying I've got it all figured out or there won't still be struggles, but I'm going to try. Try to live in a way that makes me worthy of the life I want."

"I'm glad to hear it," she said, only sharing a sliver of the truth. She was grateful she'd been a part of bringing him back to the land of the living, but that didn't change how much she'd miss being a part of his world.

He placed a hand on the smooth top of the sideboard, gripping the edge like he was holding on to one of the *Titanic*'s life rafts. "I want you in my life. I want you. Full stop."

Her mouth went dry. "You don't have to say that. I know

you feel beholden to me because I strong-armed you into becoming human again, but you don't owe me anything."

"You're wrong, Emma." Cam took a step closer to her until they stood toe to toe. Those golden-color flecks in his brown eyes drew her in. "I owe you everything. It wasn't simply that you bullied me into breaking out of my self-imposed exile. You made me feel human again. You helped heal my heart."

She shook her head. "I didn't do those things."

"Yes." He reached out a finger and tipped up her chin. "I want to be worthy of you. It might take me years or a lifetime to get there, but I'll do anything for that chance. I love you, Emma. My heart might be battered and bruised, but it's yours for as long as you'll have it."

"I want to believe you." Wild hope spiraled through her, refusing to be contained.

"You can trust me."

Trust. The million-dollar word for Emma. She'd spent so long not trusting herself or her decisions. She wasn't even sure if she knew how to start now. No, that wasn't true. It was an excuse. She'd trusted herself enough to pursue her dream in Magnolia. She'd trusted Cam enough to give him her heart. Even when she wanted to deny her feelings, he had her heart.

He must have taken her silence as a rejection because his mouth pulled down and pain filled his dark gaze. "I understand you have no reason to trust me at this point. If there's any hope, I won't give up. You are worth fighting for, Emma."

"Cam, I…" She tried to catch her breath as her heart hammered inside her chest. This was everything she'd wanted to hear from him. Everything she'd wanted.

"You're worth risking it all."

Without thinking about it another second, she threw her arms around him and buried her face in the crook of his neck. "I love you," she said against his skin. "The battered and bruised parts especially."

Cam held her tight, like he'd never let go. Then he pulled away far enough to cup her face between his hands and kiss her. It was deep and intense and felt like coming home.

She'd done it, Emma realized, her heart singing with joy. She'd found her home. Not a place on the map but a place in her heart. A place filled with love for this complicated, wonderful man, her friends and the life she was building in Magnolia.

She'd finally come home.

* * * * *

A CAROLINA PROMISE

CHAPTER ONE

HOLLY ADAMS WAS literally walking out the back door when her boss called her name from the front of the salon.

She paused with a sigh. Chances were Everlee wasn't using that commanding—and oddly desperate—tone because she wanted to tell Holly to have a fun weekend.

Everlee didn't do small talk, at least not with the employees of her high-end beauty salon and day spa in the quaint Virginia town about a half hour from Washington, DC. She saved her kindness for the political wives and society matrons who frequented Fusion Salon.

Not that Holly was complaining. Most of her coworkers were nice, and she wasn't doing nails to make friends, although she did like talking to clients. But she also liked the steady salary and the generous tips that paid the rent on her adorable studio apartment and kept her pair of tuxedo cats in gourmet food.

Twenty-four and she was already a cat-lady cliché. There were worse problems to have. She knew that for a fact.

"I need you up front," Everlee said, her voice still laced with tension. "We have a VIP."

The sixtysomething Hungarian immigrant had opened her business when she'd arrived on the shores of the Chesapeake Bay three decades earlier, and a good portion of her success had come from her exemplary customer service.

She made sure her clients were happy, and her staff was expected to do the same.

Holly had been working there for six months and felt grateful for the job, but she also had a date. A first date with a guy she'd met a few weeks earlier in the produce section of the local grocery.

They'd exchanged a few flirty texts and were meeting tonight for a drink and then dinner at a local brewery.

"Brenda is almost finished with her current client," Holly offered as her boss appeared in the doorway of the break room. "She's got—"

"It has to be you," Everlee interrupted, shaking her head. "You're the best, Hol. Right now I need the best."

Holly nodded, because what else could she do?

"I'll be there in a few seconds," she promised and hung her jacket on the peg next to the door that led to the alley behind the salon. It was a perfect early June evening, not too hot but pleasant enough that she didn't need more than a light coat. She pulled her phone from her purse and sent a quick text to Michael, telling him she'd be a bit late for their dinner reservation.

He'd responded with a frown-face emoji and then a thumbs-up, and she bit back the trace of doubt she had about a man who was such a fan of emojis. Michael sent emojis with every text. But he was cute in an unassuming sort of way and, more important, the first man who'd asked her out in over a year.

She headed to her station then stopped in her tracks when she caught sight of the man sitting on the other side of her table.

Everlee stood by the reception desk talking to a very buttoned-up older woman, one she recognized as a regular customer. Her boss shot Holly a meaningful glance and hitched her chin at the man with a slight nod.

Okay, not a joke.

That didn't change the fact that the man looked nothing like the type of person who'd be making time for a manicure on a Friday night.

His attention was trained on his phone, so she had time to study him as she approached. Probably a bad idea, because her pulse quickened and she felt a tremble snake along her spine. He had thick, dark hair and the kind of chiseled jaw that Holly had only seen on the movie screen. He wore a dark suit with a crisp white button-down and a red tie. His shoulders were broad and his skin golden like he spent more time outdoors than in some stuffy office.

But she could tell his clothes were expensive. Heck, there were tiny initials stitched on the cuff of the shirt that peeked out from his suit coat. She couldn't make out the letters, but Holly had never met a man who actually wore monogrammed shirts.

"Hello," she said as she drew closer, embarrassed that the word came out on a husky breath.

The man glanced up, then did a double take, and heat bloomed in Holly's cheeks as his gaze caught on her hair. Her mom used to call the color titian, as if Holly were some Nancy Drew type, but the kids at school had a more appropriate name for her...carrot top.

"I'm Holly," she said, busying herself with setting up her supplies, which she'd carefully put away only fifteen minutes earlier. "What would you like tonight?"

Her chin jerked up at the disbelieving snort that came from the man. He'd risen from the chair, and it didn't surprise her to discover that he was well over six feet tall and even more handsome close up with those golden flecks in his light brown eyes practically winking at her. It just made him look like more of a movie star.

The suit screamed politician, however, so she didn't bother trying to figure out if she'd actually seen the man on the silver screen. There was no denying he seemed familiar to her, but she couldn't quite say from where.

"I'm Brett." He held out a hand, and she stared at it for several long moments before allowing hers to be swallowed by his larger one. "It's nice to meet you, Holly."

The way he said her name made her smile for no discernible reason. Butterflies stormed her middle like a gang of delicate warriors. "I'm going to recommend a paraffin treatment for sure," she told him, needing to stay focused. "It'll help with the calluses."

"I don't mind the calluses," he answered, amusement clear in his tone.

She turned his hand over, studying his scraped knuckles and ragged cuticles. "You don't look like the type of guy to have work-roughened hands."

He chuckled and drew his hand away from hers, lowering himself into his seat. "What type of guy do I look like?"

"The kind who can afford to pay people to do your dirty work." She cringed when something that looked like distress flashed in his eyes. Everlee would be angry as a hornet if Holly chased away a VIP. "It doesn't matter, though. We'll get your hands cleaned up in a jiffy." She gestured to his suit jacket. "You might want to take that off and roll up your sleeves."

"Sure," he agreed. "For the record, my assistant agrees with you." He tilted his head toward the woman still talking with Everlee. "There's an event tonight, and she says I can't shake the hands of foreign dignitaries with mine in this kind of shape."

He shrugged out of his jacket, and the scent of cedarwood drifted toward Holly, making her feel light-headed. "What kind of dignitaries?" she asked, needing to remind herself that she had nothing in common with this man. He was a onetime client, and not Holly's type even on a good day.

Right. Because gorgeous, rich and chiseled were definitely not of interest to her. Yeah, right.

"A few heads of state, one crown prince and a couple of random European ministers." He rattled off the list like he was talking about a few buddies stopping by to watch the game.

Holly dipped his hand in a bowl of soapy water, ignoring her growing awareness. "Who are you?" she demanded, keeping her eyes trained on her work.

"Just a guy with calloused hands."

"Nice try. What's your last name?"

The pause lasted only a few seconds, but the air between them suddenly felt charged, like the moments before a massive lightning storm.

"Carmichael. My name is Brett Carmichael."

Holly sucked in a breath and tried not to let her reaction show on her face. "So you're more than just your calluses," she said, proud of how steady the words sounded given the fact that she was currently filing the nails of a man who was most likely going to be president one day. His grandfather had held the Oval Office several decades earlier, and his own father had been vice president for two terms back in the late '90s. As it was, Brett Carmichael was currently a US senator, the youngest to have been elected to that office.

"Well, I know you can afford not to have calluses," she blurted, then wanted to kick herself. Holly was popular with her clients because she was naturally upbeat and positive.

She never made conversations awkward, but now she had this handsome, successful, wealthy man in her chair and she couldn't seem to stop throwing shade.

To her surprise, Brett only grinned. A real smile, not the patently fake kind she'd seen from politicians on television or at local events when they made an appearance. He leaned in closer. "Do you want to know how I got them?"

"If you want to tell me," she said casually, like it didn't matter. Like her heart wasn't stuttering inside her chest at the idea that he might share some part of himself with her that other people didn't know.

"I'm building a cabin." His grin broadened, and a light shone in his eye that made her think of a boy talking about his first paper route or a clubhouse he'd crafted in the backyard all by himself.

"In the woods?" she asked, then wanted to slap herself for how stupid that sounded. Like she didn't know where cabins were built in the area.

Brett nodded, seeming not to notice that she was having trouble putting two words together in his presence. "I know I can afford to buy one—"

"And doesn't your family own some sort of Kennedy-esque compound-type thing?"

"Something like that," he admitted, his smile turning wry. "But I wanted to do it myself. It's about an hour west of the city, but it feels farther than that. I like to get away."

She dried the hand that had been soaking and replaced it in the bowl with the other one. "You know they sell these things called work gloves to protect your hands?"

"Sometimes I forget to wear them. The feel of an ax or a saw in my bare hands is…"

"Manly?" Holly suggested with a wink then practically

swallowed her tongue. What was she doing, flirting with a US senator?

"Satisfying," Brett said, then grinned again.

He had an amazing smile, complete with dimples on both cheeks. And she could just imagine him swinging an ax in the hot sun, maybe without a shirt on. Satisfying indeed.

"What do you do for fun, Holly?"

Seriously, he had to stop saying her name like that. She was going to melt into a puddle at those two syllables spoken in his deep voice.

"I read," she said.

He didn't look shocked, which was how many of her clients reacted. As if a nail technician couldn't also be literate. "What sort of books?" He asked the question like he really cared about the answer, so she told him the truth.

"Anything with a happy ending." She thought about the last novel she'd devoured, a romantic suspense that had kept her up into the wee hours of the night. "Some romance and some inspirational fiction. I like personal development books, too. At least the ones with an uplifting message."

Taking his hand in hers to massage his palm, she looked at him from beneath her lashes. "You probably think that's stupid."

"I don't."

She shrugged. "It's okay if you do. Lots of people don't see the value in believing in happy endings, but I know they're important. The real world can break a heart. I want to surround myself with things that make me feel good."

"You read for the same reason I destroy my hands," he told her, flexing his fingers.

"Well, no crown prince will be complaining about your

hands when I'm finished," Holly promised, wondering at this chance encounter, which was making her smile more than she had in months.

CHAPTER TWO

THREE MONTHS LATER, Brett Carmichael pushed back from the high-top table at the local bar in his Georgetown neighborhood where he'd met a friend for Friday night happy hour. "One round of darts before you go," he told Simon Marshall, whom he'd first met when they were both at Yale Law School.

Simon was now on the partner track at a prominent firm, while Brett had quickly rocketed up the political track, thanks in large part to his last name and family connections. He wasn't fool enough to deny or ignore the doors the Carmichael legacy opened for him, but he was also determined to earn the respect of his constituents and colleagues. To prove he was worthy of his position. To be his own man.

"Look at your shiny nails," Simon said with an eye roll. "You and those manicures. Every time Beth goes to the salon now, she tries to talk me into joining her."

"You weren't complaining when these hands pitched a no-hitter at last week's bar association softball game."

"I'm not saying you aren't wicked good on the field." Simon grabbed a set of darts from the shelf at the bar's far wall. "Also at darts. Hell, you're annoyingly perfect at almost everything. But seriously, man. Weekly manicures?"

"Not every week," Brett clarified. "Just when I beat up my mitts working on the cabin. My staff is thrilled they don't have to worry about dirt or sap stuck under my nails in photos."

"Right," Simon said with a wink. "It's all for the image."

Brett drained his beer then took the darts Simon handed him. He faced the board hanging on the wall, aimed and then let the dart go sailing through the air. It stuck to the edge of the bull's-eye ring with a satisfying pop.

"These soft hands will kick your butt at darts, buddy. Don't forget it."

Simon lifted a brow as Brett lined up again. "Have you asked her out yet?" His friend posed the question just as Brett released the dart. It made a wide arc in the air then bounced off the board and clattered to the scuffed wood floor.

"That was uncalled for," he said, frowning at Simon. "Especially when you know the answer."

"But I don't understand the reason," Simon countered. "I know you like this girl."

"Holly and I are friends." Brett twirled his remaining dart between two fingers. "At least I think she considers me a friend. Or a client she's friendly with. I hope it's more than that."

"You want it to be way more," Simon reminded him. "What's stopping you?"

Brett's stomach tightened as he thought about how to answer the question. "I like her," he repeated as if that explained it.

"Exactly my point."

"Maybe too much to invite her into my world. She's sweet and kind—"

"And pretty," Simon added.

"Beautiful," Brett corrected. The thought of Holly's bright smile made his heart stutter. "Just being near her, even at the salon, makes my day better. She's like no one I've ever met. Holly likes me, not the senator or the Carmichael family heir."

"Not to burst your bubble," Simon said with a wry smile, "but those things are part of you, too."

"The parts that might scare her away." Without warning, Brett threw the final dart. It hit the target a few inches to the right of center, but at least it stuck this time. "Plus, she's dating that loser Michael."

"You're afraid." Simon signaled the waitress for two more beers. "I can't believe it. I've never seen the unflappable Brett Carmichael nervous. A cute little redhead from some no-name small town in North Carolina has you all twitterpated. I need to buy this Holly a drink."

"*Twitterpated* is a stupid word," Brett muttered, although he didn't deny it. He was completely smitten with Holly, even though he'd never spent time with her outside the salon. She was a breath of fresh air in his stodgy, staid world. He loved everything about their conversations— hearing reviews of whatever books she was reading and sharing his progress on the cabin. He could talk about anything with her, even his worries involving his career or reelection or living up to his mother's expectations. "But I'm not going to ruin a friendship over something as superficial as physical attraction."

"What you feel for her isn't superficial," Simon said. "I've never seen you like this, Carm. You've got to tell her how you feel."

The thought both thrilled and terrified Brett. It was getting more difficult to keep his feelings to himself, but what if his feelings weren't reciprocated? She didn't seem happy with loser Michael, whom she'd been dating on and off since Brett had first met her. What did Brett really know about love? His parents' marriage had been more of a business transaction, and his mom wouldn't stop throwing appropriate, well-bred women toward him, like he was supposed to choose a partner for his life based on her pedigree instead of his heart.

He wished he could discuss Holly with his dad. Bart Carmichael had been a career politician, but he'd had the heart of a teddy bear. He'd been gone for five years now, killed in a private plane crash that had made national headlines and, in some ways, catapulted Brett into the public eye even sooner than expected.

He couldn't talk to his dad, but he had a feeling he knew the advice Bart would have given. *Follow your heart.* That's what he'd told Brett at every critical juncture in his life, even as Mitsy Carmichael had scoffed at the sentiment.

Brett wondered if he took that advice now where it would lead. Either to an amazing future with Holly at his side or to potential heartbreak. He wished he knew the outcome.

His phone vibrated in his pocket as the waitress brought another round. He pulled it out and sucked in a breath at the name on the screen. He'd given Holly his number after she'd told him a story of her car breaking down on the interstate. The thought of her stranded or in trouble was intolerable to Brett.

She'd never called until now.

Swiping the home screen to answer, he held the phone up to his ear. "Holly?"

"Hi," she said so quietly he could barely hear her with the noise of the popular bar in the background. "You said I could call if I ever needed anything."

"Yes." He swallowed. "What's going on, Holly? How can I help?"

His blood turned cold as he listened, and he was already heading toward the bar's front door. Simon called to him, and Brett waved a hand but didn't break stride. Holly needed him, and he wasn't wasting any time.

CHAPTER THREE

HOLLY LIFTED A hand to the thin bandage the ER doctor had placed over the seven stitches above her eye and tried not to wince.

Her head hurt, although they'd ruled out a concussion. Mainly she felt embarrassed and alone. So alone.

The door to the exam room opened, and she made her features neutral, not wanting to make more of a spectacle of herself than she already had.

Instead of the kind nurse who'd given a sympathetic smile when Holly explained how she'd been injured, Brett appeared in the doorway. Her heart leaped at the sight of him, and she wanted to rush across the room and into his arms.

She stayed where she was perched on the edge of the exam table and gave a little wave. "Thank you for coming," she said, trying not to sound as pathetic as she felt. "I'm sorry for interrupting your Friday night. I can probably—"

"There's no place I'd rather be," he said with such sincerity she couldn't doubt him.

Except that he was a politician—and an undeniably charming man—so maybe he was just being nice?

He approached the bed, and Holly tried not to notice how handsome he looked in his casual navy T-shirt and cargo shorts. She ignored the flutters in her stomach, which she knew weren't a result of the extra-strength ibuprofen the nurse had given her.

They were in response to Brett.

"You called the hospital," she told him as if he didn't realize that fact. "To make sure I was seen right away."

"You said the bleeding wouldn't stop." He was in front of her now, and she caught the scent of his cologne, adding an extra ripple to her nerves. Her hyperawareness of this man had reached the level of epic infatuation. Maybe that accounted for why she hadn't been the least bit heartbroken to end her relationship with her boyfriend of the past three months in the middle of a laser tag course.

Holly hated playing laser tag, one of Michael's favorite weekend activities.

"Tell me again how this happened." Brett reached out and smoothed her hair away from her forehead, his clear dark gaze darkening as he examined the cut.

"My own clumsiness." She shrugged. "We were in the middle of a game, and I'd run behind a pile of old barrels to hide. I kind of tripped over my own feet when Michael came up behind me. Hit my head on a corner as I went down." She went to touch the bandage again, but Brett took her hand, smoothing a thumb over her knuckles.

"And your jackass boyfriend wouldn't leave to drive you to the hospital?"

The anger in his tone shocked her.

"Ex-boyfriend," she clarified. "He wanted me to wait until after the session. He'd paid for a VIP experience."

"VIP?" Brett scoffed. "As in a very idiotic piece of..." Brett rolled his lips together. "Sorry. That's none of my business."

"I won't disagree with you about Michael being a jerk.

It took a knock on the head and some stitches to get me to end it, something I should have done long before now."

"Why didn't you?" Brett studied her like she was some kind of riddle he wanted to decipher.

A silly thought, because Holly was ordinary and boring and uncomplicated. Not at all the kind of accomplished, well-educated and sophisticated woman who'd be a match for a handsome US senator.

"It was easier that way," she said, which was only a tiny glimmer of the truth. Easier because being single allowed her fantasies about a romance with Brett to take flight, and those sort of fanciful thoughts would only lead to disappointment.

Except he was here now. He'd come when she called without hesitation.

"Michael is even more of a loser than I suspected for letting you go." Brett's voice had grown rough with an emotion Holly couldn't name. "If you were mine, I'd never let you go."

"Oh."

Well, wasn't that just enough to make her want to swoon?

She was saved from the temptation to throw herself at him when a nurse bustled into the room. "You're free to go," she announced, then glanced between Holly and Brett, recognition sharpening her gaze. Holly was used to that. Clients at the salon did their best to find excuses to walk past her station when Brett was in, although he never seemed to notice or care.

Unlike those women, the nurse grinned at Holly. "This is the friend picking you up?"

"Yep."

"Then I don't even need to tell you to take care of yourself. Honey, you've got that part covered."

With a chuckle, the woman disappeared out of the room. Holly's cheeks flamed with embarrassment. "I guess you're used to that."

"Do you need a wheelchair?" Brett asked like the nurse's teasing hadn't registered with him. "Shouldn't they give you a wheelchair to leave?"

"I got stitches." Holly reached out and placed a hand on his arm, confused but also charmed by his concern. "It wasn't major surgery."

"Right." He nodded then frowned as he looked at the front of her shirt. "You weren't exaggerating the blood."

She grimaced at the dried bloodstains that covered the soft cotton. "There are a lot of blood vessels close to the surface on your head, and the cut was deep. Luckily, this top isn't my favorite."

"The yellow flowy one is your favorite," Brett said absently as he picked up her purse from the nearby chair.

Holly stared at him as she climbed off the exam table. "How do you know that?"

"You wear it when you're upset about something—like a conversation with your mom—and you want to cheer yourself up."

Her stomach pitched like it was on the first big dip of a mammoth roller coaster, and her heart beat a crazy rhythm, knocking against her ribs so hard she thought they might crack. The yellow peasant blouse was indeed her favorite. It had been a gift from her mother for Holly's birthday two years earlier and reminded her of a happy visit to her hometown of Magnolia.

Since the car accident that killed her older sister four years ago, Holly's mom had struggled with grief and depression. The fact that they'd had an amazing time that weekend seemed to imbue the top with positive vibes, and Holly's mood always improved when she wore it.

The fact that Brett had noticed something she barely registered on a conscious level blew her away. Was it any wonder she had an all-consuming crush on the man even though he was way out of her league?

"Luckily, I wasn't wearing that one," she said, trying to make her voice light. "This one is heading to the trash as soon as I get home."

"My car's out front," he told her as he held open the door.

"Okay." She swallowed hard. "Thank you again for coming. I could have called one of the girls from work, but—"

"I'm glad you called me, Holly."

She bit down on her lower lip but didn't respond.

They walked out of the hospital in silence. She should think of something more to say but was so nervous about the idea of being with Brett outside the salon.

She'd imagined it a thousand times, although not quite like this. But what if she said something stupid and he stopped coming in to see her? It might not make sense, but his visits to the salon had become important to her. He'd become important.

"Are you sure you're okay?" he asked, placing a hand on her lower back and sending a cascade of shivers along her spine.

"Yes," she managed.

"What about your car?" They'd made it into the parking lot. Shadows fell across the asphalt as darkness slowly descended on the summer night.

"I'll have someone drive me over to get it tomorrow."

"I can drive you."

"You don't want to come out here from the city," she said as she followed him through rows of cars.

"I'm actually heading up to the cabin tomorrow morning for the day."

"Even more of a reason."

He stopped in front of a black Jeep, just the sort of car she'd expect him to drive. Cool but understated. Holly drove a basic two-door hatchback. Efficient and ordinary.

"Would you like to come with me?" he asked as he opened the passenger door.

Her breath caught in her throat. She knew how much the cabin meant to him. Heck, it was the reason his hands and nails were always in need of her help. Brett had such a high-profile, impactful career, but he seemed most proud of the work he'd done to build his dream getaway. The idea that he'd share that with her...

"You probably want to rest," he added when she didn't immediately answer.

"I don't," she said at the same time.

"Want to go with me?"

"To rest. I'd like to go with you."

The smile he flashed took her breath away. "Then it's a date."

She climbed into the Jeep, and the butterflies in her stomach took flight once more. A date with Brett Carmichael. Was this the chance she'd secretly dreamed of these past few months?

CHAPTER FOUR

THE FOLLOWING MORNING was perfect for a drive into the Blue Ridge Mountains. Although the leaves had yet to begin their colorful change, the September sun hovering in the cloudless sky overhead bathed the forest in a warm glow.

Or maybe it was the woman sitting next to Brett that made the day seem nearly too good to be true. Anticipation made his heart clutch and his palms sweaty.

Would Holly like the simple cabin he'd built, or would she be disappointed that it was so rustic? Brett knew his family and most of his friends thought he was wasting his time on the project. Why spend so much effort on four walls and a roof when his family owned several well-appointed homes situated on an enviable piece of property overlooking a white-sand stretch of the Atlantic Ocean?

"We used to drive over to Asheville when I was a kid and camp for the weekend," Holly said, her gaze taking in their surroundings. She wore a white V-neck shirt and a pair of faded jeans, her bright hair loose around her shoulders. The small gold hoops in her ears matched the delicate chain around her neck, and she'd never been more beautiful to him.

Because taking her to the cabin meant something. She was special, and he wanted her to realize it. "This reminds me of those mountains. I used to love to roast marshmallows over the fire."

He grinned. "I'm building a firepit in the backyard. Or what will be the backyard. Right now it's just a staging area for most of the construction."

"Maybe I'll get you a bag of marshmallows as a house-warming gift."

"The fact that you agreed to drive up here with me is plenty." He drummed his fingers on the steering wheel, then added, "You'll be my first visitor."

She turned to him. "Really?"

"The cabin is personal to me," he explained. "I don't want to share it with just anyone."

"I'm flattered," she said quietly and reached out to squeeze his hand.

Hers were small and dainty, her nails painted with a soft peach polish. It felt like he'd spent hours watching her hands as she worked on his at the salon. He didn't hesitate in turning over his palm and linking their fingers.

Holly stiffened, and Brett wondered if he'd gone too far, too fast. At this point, he wanted so much more than to simply hold her hand, but it was a start.

If she'd let him.

After a moment she relaxed, her thumb tracing a circle on the center of his palm. They didn't speak, but to Brett her touch was enough. It was everything.

"THIS HAS BEEN the best day." The words slipped from Holly's mouth before she could stop them. The thought had been percolating since they'd arrived at the cozy log cabin Brett had built in the middle of a picturesque meadow surrounded by towering trees and thick undergrowth.

Before she'd even gotten out of the car, Holly had known that the time spent with her handsome senator would be everything she'd hoped and more. Despite their different backgrounds and lifestyles, she felt comfortable with Brett. He was easy to talk to and even easier on the eyes, although she'd almost gotten so used to his movie-star looks that they didn't affect her.

Almost.

He'd taken her on a tour of the two-bedroom cabin with its rough-hewn pine walls and maple floors. There was still a lot to be done, he'd explained, since he wanted to handle every aspect of construction on his own and his time was limited. He had a small refrigerator plugged into a bare wall in what would become the kitchen, although he'd almost finished the bathroom with its slate tile and walk-in shower.

"I'm hoping to have the certificate of occupancy by Christmas," he'd told her with a proud smile. "Although that will depend on how busy things get at work."

At work. He said the words like he was an accountant or insurance salesman who might have a taxing week at the office instead of a United States senator with demands on his time coming from a myriad of places.

"It's really a perfect space."

"I'm glad you think so." They sat on a picnic blanket overlooking the valley below. "The cabin means a lot to me." He lifted his hand to tuck an errant strand of hair behind her ear. "You do, too, Holly."

Cue the butterflies. She tried not to read more into his words than she imagined he meant, but when she finally met his gaze, there was so much emotion in his eyes. The kind she'd only dreamed of.

"I'm glad we're friends." She managed to keep her voice steady as she said the words, although she wanted to tell him more of what he meant to her. But how could she do that and not sound like a lovesick schoolgirl?

"I don't want to be just your friend." His rumbly tone

seemed to scramble her brain cells until she couldn't put a coherent thought together.

"What do you want?" she whispered, every cell in her body on high alert.

Instead of answering, he leaned in and brushed his lips across hers. It was gentle and insistent at the same time. She opened for him, light exploding behind her eyes when his tongue met hers. Their joining was all-consuming in a way she couldn't explain but felt like she'd been waiting on for ages.

When he finally pulled away, Holly could tell that his breathing was just as ragged as hers. "I've wanted to do that for so long," he told her, searching her face like he wanted to make sure she'd wanted it, too.

"How long?"

"Since the first time I saw you."

"Not possible." She shook her head.

"True nonetheless." His gaze was so open and honest, she knew he wasn't making it up. This handsome, success-ful, arguably out-of-her-league man was looking at her like he wanted her more than a drowning man wants a life raft.

Like she might be his life raft.

She cupped his gorgeous face in her hands, thrilled to be touching him. Wanting to touch him all over and suddenly realizing that was a distinct possibility. He could be hers.

"What took you so long?" she asked, genuinely curious.

"Well, loser Michael for one," he said with an eye roll. "More important, I wasn't sure you'd want to deal with every-thing that comes with dating me. My life is…complicated."

"You and I don't have to be." And she knew that was what they both needed to hear when he pulled her into his arms.

CHAPTER FIVE

"WHAT IF SHE hates me?"

Brett reached across the console and took Holly's hand in his. He couldn't get enough of touching her. She grounded him in a way he couldn't explain. Over the past couple of months, she'd become as essential to him as the air he breathed.

Sometimes he thought back to her question after he'd kissed her the first time of what had taken him so long. All of his reasons for not wanting to push to be more than her friend had made sense at the time, but now he couldn't imagine her not being the center of his world.

"No one could hate you," he said as he pulled into the country club parking lot where his family had been members for four generations. He meant every word but kept his gaze facing forward so Holly wouldn't see the glimmer of doubt he couldn't completely tamp down.

Tonight was an event honoring his late father. A level-one trauma hospital in Northern Virginia was dedicating a pediatric wing to Bart Carmichael after a generous donation from Brett's mother. Mitsy Carmichael played the role of matriarch like she'd been born for it, which in many ways she had. The daughter of a former US ambassador, she had an impeccable pedigree that had made her a perfect political wife.

Brett had grown up believing his parents' marriage was

a happy one, but he'd come to see that it was based more on mutual respect and shared goals than true love.

It was the expectation his mom had for his choice of a life partner, but Brett didn't share that view. He was dedicated to his career and public service, but he also wanted a private life that would be a safe harbor from the demands of the outside world. He had that with Holly more than any other woman he'd dated, and he knew enough to appreciate all the wonderful things about her.

He just wasn't sure his mother would see Holly in the same light. Although they'd spent nearly every night they could together since that day at his cabin, he hadn't introduced her to his mom. She'd met some of his work colleagues on the Hill and several of his college and law school friends. Everyone loved her.

Just like he did, although he hadn't said the words out loud yet. He was still worried about going too fast or scaring her away. His life was big and didn't always feel like his own. But Holly felt right, and damn, he wanted his mom to like her.

The valet took the keys, and Brett hurried around the front of the Jeep to take Holly's hand again as they walked into the building. She wore a sheath dress in a deep emerald-green color that highlighted her coppery hair and creamy skin. He almost couldn't wait to finish the evening so they could head back to his place, where he'd take great pleasure in helping her out of it.

"Are you sure this is the right place for me to meet your mom for the first time?" Holly asked, her hand cold as ice in his. "Maybe a casual Sunday brunch would work better?" She stopped just inside the front door. "I could grab your car and pick you up later."

"I want you here," he told her. It was true. He would

have introduced her to his mom long before this, except he wanted more time with just the two of them. But the longer they dated, the surer Brett became that Holly was the one for him.

He'd even started ring shopping and planned to ask her to marry him on Christmas Eve. They'd made plans to visit her parents in Magnolia after Thanksgiving Day, and he wanted to ask her mom and dad for their blessing. She'd told him how fractured her family had become since her older sister's death, and he hoped that a wedding would give all of them something positive to focus on.

"Then this is where I belong," she answered and shifted closer to him.

Exactly. They belonged together.

"Where have you been?" His mother's crisp voice called from the other side of the massive foyer decorated in yards of greenery and holiday lights. Turkey day was still a week away, but the club had gone straight to the winter wonderland holiday theme. The whole place was festive and bright, but his mom looked positively scroogey as she waited for him to approach. She wore a brocade jacket and flowing tulle skirt with subtle—but flawless—diamond earrings and a matching necklace winking in the soft glow of the crystal chandelier overhead.

"Hello, Mother." Brett released Holly long enough to lean in and kiss Mitsy's unlined cheek. He had no idea his mom's beauty secret, but she seemed to remain ageless, and Brett tried not to conjure up an image of Dorian Gray in his mind. "This is Holly."

"I'm so excited to meet you, Mrs. Carmichael." Holly's enthusiasm was real, although he could hear the nervousness in her voice.

His mother smiled, but it looked more like a grimace. "Of course. The nail technician."

"My girlfriend," he clarified.

"Yes, well." She glanced between the two of them, and Brett looped an arm around Holly's waist. His mom could intimidate the most hardened career politician, but not Brett. Not about Holly. As if realizing she wasn't going to win in that way, Mitsy finally gave a subtle nod. "We're happy to have you with us tonight. My son speaks highly of you."

"I think the world of him," Holly answered without hesitation, and there was a slight downgrade in the icy vibes coming from Mitsy.

He wanted to believe his mom would give Holly a real chance.

They started toward the club's grand ballroom at the end of the hall. "Do you like wine, Holly? We have several lovely varieties being served."

"Yes, ma'am."

Holly's Southern accent was more pronounced tonight, a sure sign of her anxiety. Brett gave her hip a gentle squeeze.

"I don't drink a lot," she said, obviously trying to connect with his mother on any level. "But I always keep a box in the fridge for those nights when I want a glass after work."

Brett inwardly cringed as his mother stopped short. Mitsy was a total wine snob, and he knew what her opinion of Holly mentioning a box versus a bottle would be. She turned to face the two of them. "Do you serve this boxed wine in a red plastic cup?"

"No, ma'am," Holly answered. "My mom gave me the cutest set of glasses last year at Christmas. My favorite one says, 'sip happens.'"

"I can see why that would appeal to you," Mitsy said. To Brett, it felt like the temperature had dropped about twenty degrees in the last few seconds.

He could tell Holly noticed the change, as well. It was as if she shrank several inches in an instant.

"I'm partial to 'love the wine you're with,'" he announced with more vehemence than the statement warranted. But he wouldn't let anyone, even his mother, make Holly feel less than. Not if he could protect her.

They continued into the ballroom, and the rest of the evening passed in a flurry of back slaps, hand shaking, and small talk with people who'd been friends of his father. Brett and his mother both said a few words about his dad's dedication to affordable health care and accepted thanks from the president of the hospital board.

He did his best to keep Holly at his side, but they were separated several times as he got pulled into various conversations with old family friends. By the end of the night, Brett was exhausted and his cheeks hurt from smiling. All he wanted was to take Holly home and climb into bed with her.

She was subdued as they said goodbye to his mother and the gaggle of friends who surrounded her. Once in the Jeep, he reached for her hand, but she crossed her arms over her chest.

"Can you take me home, please?"

"Is everything okay?"

"I want to go home."

He pulled out onto the dark road, his heart suddenly beating like mad in his chest. "Thank you for coming with me tonight. You did great."

She snorted in response.

He racked his brain, trying to figure out what had put

her in this mood. The event had been a bit of a trial by fire but based on the comments he'd heard, Holly had charmed everyone she'd met.

"I know it was a lot," he said, keeping his tone carefully neutral. "But you and I—"

"This isn't going to work," she interrupted quietly.

Brett felt like he'd been sucker-punched. "What are you talking about, Holly? Everything about the two of us works."

"I drink wine from a box."

He ran one hand through his hair, trying to tamp down the panic clawing at his insides. He'd never heard her sound so resolute. "Who cares?"

"Your mother." She turned to him. "Your mom mentioned it to almost every person she introduced me to in that ballroom. And they all gave her the same sympathetic glance before they turned their judgy, high-class gazes to me. Like I was some kind of lowbrow country bumpkin."

"You're not—"

"I am, Brett. I'm a girl from a small town with a high-school education. I don't belong in your world."

"Of course you do." He took the ramp onto the highway, nearly stomping on the accelerator in his frustration. This could not be happening. "Holly, I love you."

She let out a sound of distress that nearly broke his heart in two but didn't respond. He wanted her to say the words back to him. He needed to hear it, to know that she wasn't going to end this.

Not when it meant so much to him.

"You should be with someone who comes from the same background as you."

"I want you," he insisted. "I love you." He'd never told anyone that, and now he couldn't stop saying it.

"I might not have an Ivy League education," she answered, "but I'm not stupid. I understand that someone in your position needs a partner who can help him with—"

"You. Help. Me." He gripped the steering wheel as he willed her to understand. "You're the woman I want at my side, Hol."

"I can't," she whispered miserably. "I'm sorry, Brett. I just can't."

He clamped his jaw shut and kept his eyes on the road in front of them. His gut told him to pull over onto the shoulder and get down on one knee and beg her not to do this, but a bigger part of him knew she might be right. Not about being her not being good enough or whatever line of garbage his mother had fed her. But in some ways he couldn't blame her for not wanting to help carry the burden of his public life. It sometimes felt like too much weight, even for him.

So he didn't stop the car. He couldn't. If she chose not to fight for their relationship, he would love her enough to respect that choice.

Even if it gutted him to his core.

CHAPTER SIX

THE KNOCKING WOULDN'T STOP.

Brett held the pillow more firmly over his head and prayed for quiet.

His silent plea went aggressively unanswered as the knocking turned into full-fledged pounding.

With a curse, he threw back the covers and headed for the front door of his condo.

"This better be a damn emergency," he said as he threw open the door, muttering a few more colorful curse words as he gaped at his mother standing on the other side.

In the three years he'd had his place, Mitsy had only visited once. To her mind, children were responsible for coming to see their parents at the family home. Brett made regular trips for Sunday dinners and holiday get-togethers, although he'd spent yesterday's Thanksgiving holiday with the curtains pulled at his place, in front of the television on a Middle Earth marathon. He figured the orcs of Mordor were a better choice than facing his mom and explaining that Holly had broken up with him.

"You aren't too old for me to wash your mouth out with soap," she said as she glided past him into the condo.

"As I remember, you had the nanny do it," he shot back.

Her thin shoulders went rigid, but she didn't respond.

"We missed you yesterday," she told him instead.

"I wasn't feeling well."

She inclined her head toward the half-empty scotch bottle on his coffee table. "Shocking."

"Was there something you needed, Mother?"

It was then he noticed the brown paper shopping bag she carried. "I brought you leftovers. Two slices of pecan pie, because it's your favorite."

"Thank you," he said and took the bag from her, duly chastised for his rudeness without her having to scold him outright.

"The nail girl isn't here?" She made a point of glancing around. "I assumed she was the reason you missed dinner."

"She has a name."

"I know that." When he didn't say anything more, Mitsy sighed. "Where is Holly?"

"North Carolina, I assume." He used the sleeve of his sweatshirt to wipe his mouth, which felt like a breeding ground for cotton at the moment. "You'll be pleased to hear she broke up with me."

"That doesn't please me," she countered, "if only because it obviously makes you miserable."

He narrowed his eyes. "Did you make fun of her wine-in-a-box comment with your friends?"

"It was sweet and entertaining." Mitsy shrugged. "She actually drinks wine from a—"

"It was mean," he interrupted, pacing to the far end of the room and yanking open the curtains before turning back to her. "She was already nervous about her background compared to my family and friends, and you made her feel stupid. Badly done, Mom."

"I don't appreciate being scolded," Mitsy told him with a sniff. "As your mother, it's important that I look after your best interests and the future of this family. Someone like Holly Adams—"

"Makes me happy." Brett shook his head. "I love her. I want to spend the rest of my life with her if I can convince her to take me back."

"You don't mean that. It's a fling. She's too young, too naive, too provincial to make an appropriate political wife."

"I'm not choosing a wife based on whether she knows what fork to use during the salad course."

"It's important."

"Not as important as my happiness."

His mother's expertly lined lips pursed. "Of course not. I want you to be happy, but I don't think one twenty-something nail technician is imperative for that."

"You're wrong."

"I'm never wrong."

Brett moved to stand in front of his mother and bent his knees so they were at eye level. "You're wrong about Holly. She's incredible, and she would be an undeniable asset for my career. Do you know why?"

Mitsy gave a sharp shake of her head.

"Because I love her and she loves me. I know she does. Or at least I think she does. I hope she does."

"Which is it?" his mother asked softly.

"I'm not sure at the moment, but I am sure that she and I were meant to be together. She likes me for me, Mom."

"You're extremely likable."

He massaged a hand across the back of his neck. "You don't understand. She doesn't care about my career or our family or the money, and that's rare. I can be myself with her, and I like her just the way she is. I understand what's expected of me. The career path you and my staff and the party want."

"I thought you wanted it, too?"

"I do." He turned away then, looked at the small tree in

the corner that Holly had insisted they put up so he'd have a bit of Christmas in his otherwise stuffy condo. She was like that tree, a guaranteed smile in the midst of the chaos of his life. "But I want it on my terms. I want it with Holly at my side."

He waited for his mother to argue. To list all the reasons she knew better than him what he should want. It wouldn't matter. He was going to fight for Holly despite his mom's objections. She'd just have to come around.

"Then you'll need this." He glanced back at her, shocked as she pulled a black velvet box from her purse. Mitsy flipped it open to reveal his grandmother's emerald engagement ring. The stone was the same rich color as the dress Holly had worn to the hospital event.

It would be perfect for her, but...

"You said you didn't approve of her. You just spent the past few minutes subtly dissing her."

One perfectly sculpted eyebrow lifted. "I said I didn't think she was the right choice for you. I also realize that you're a grown man capable of choosing for yourself. You're my son, Brett. More than anything else, I want your happiness. If this nail—"

"Her name, Mother."

"If Holly makes you happy," she amended with a nod, "then I'll respect your decision. It's the reason I'm here."

"And you'll be kind to her? Make her feel welcome?"

"I'll do my best. I've brought the ring, after all. I wouldn't offer this for you to give to just anyone. It was obvious how you felt about her at the event. And you're right, it was badly done to make her feel that she didn't belong."

He took the ring box and gave his mother a grateful hug. "I have to admit I'm shocked. I never thought you'd accept this."

Mitsy gave him a quick squeeze around the shoulders then pulled back. She'd never been much for physical affection. "Actually, I just finished the latest season of that series about the royal family. The last thing I want is you pining away for a lost love and shirking your duties."

"No shirking. I promise." Brett bit back a smile. Classic Mitsy Carmichael, but he couldn't even bring himself to be offended. He had his mother's blessing, and now he just needed to convince Holly that he was worth the trouble.

CHAPTER SEVEN

HOLLY SAT ON the cold sand and looked out to the dark ocean waves pulsing toward shore. She'd come to this stretch of beach outside her hometown of Magnolia, North Carolina, probably a hundred times or more over the course of her lifetime.

As a girl, she and her sister had splashed in the waves and built sandcastles for hours during endless summer days. Dana had been six years older than Holly, but she'd never complained about her little sister tagging along or all the time she missed with her friends because she had to baby-sit Holly while their parents worked.

Dana had been the best big sister, and while Holly missed her every day, the ache was particularly acute at the moment. She wanted to talk to someone she trusted about Brett and her broken heart and whether she'd been a complete fool to let him go.

Definite yes on the fool. She knew Dana would have agreed, although her kind sister would have said it in a nicer way. Dana had married her first love, and although she'd given up a lot of her dreams for Cam Arlinghaus, they'd been happy together.

Holly could be happy with Brett.

Or she would have if she'd had the courage to fight for him. Instead, she'd let a few rude and snobby women chase her away like she was dirt on the bottom of their red-soled shoes. Everlee and the other girls at the salon had tried to convince her to call him and work things out, but she was scared of failing. Of not being good enough and disappointing him.

Although Holly didn't suffer from the same disabling depression as her mom, she'd been afraid to take risks since Dana's accident. Her parents had been through too much already, and Holly felt the burden of responsibility to live a simple life with no added drama.

Politics was all about drama in too many ways.

Not that it dimmed her feelings for Brett or assuaged her heartbreak.

She missed him like she'd left behind her heart but understood she probably wouldn't see him again, even at the salon. He'd want a clean break from her and to find a woman who wasn't such a coward.

A seagull swooped in the sky above her, flapping its wings as it flew into the oncoming wind. Holly felt a strange kinship to the struggling bird, clearly working hard but with little progress to show for it. Then something changed. The seagull dipped a few feet and angled its body until a strong gust lifted it higher and the bird accelerated forward. Instead of fighting, the bird morphed the shape of its wings to use the force of the wind as an advantage.

Holly huffed out a laugh. Even the bird was smarter than her.

But she could learn. She could try again. If she explained to Brett her fear, they could work together to get through it. She had to believe they could get through anything together.

With a new sense of resolve, she stood and brushed off the back of her jeans, then turned to head back to the path she'd taken to this spot.

Only to see Brett walking toward her.

The breeze blew his thick hair away from his face, but he didn't struggle or slow his progress, even when a torrent of sand billowed around him.

"You're here," she said, unable to do anything but state the obvious as he drew closer.

"I came to see you," he said, his eyes as clear as a mountain stream.

"Hi," she whispered.

One side of his mouth curved. "Hi."

"How did you know where to find me?"

"I went to your parents' house. Your dad gave me directions to this spot. Your mom had no doubt you'd be here."

"Did she seem upset about it?" Holly couldn't help but ask the question. She purposely hadn't mentioned where she was going to her parents, because she didn't want to remind her mom of happier times with Dana.

Brett shook his head. "She was worried about you being sad and alone. I explained that was my fault."

"You can't take the blame," Holly said, then glanced up when the seagull circled again, squawking as it soared. "I'm the one who walked away."

"I should have never left you alone that night."

"I'm a big girl, Brett. Old enough not to let a joke at my expense rattle me that way."

"I know how my mom can be." He closed his eyes for a moment, as if steeling himself for something. "I want to tell you she means well, although sometimes I'm not sure."

"She wants what's best for you," Holly said, even though the words made her throat ache with unshed tears.

"She wants me to be happy."

Before Holly realized what was happening, he leaned in and kissed her. The heat of him and his spicy scent felt like a homecoming. She'd missed him so badly.

"You make me happy," he said against her lips, and she let her eyes drift closed, reveling in the words. Maybe it wasn't too late for them after all.

She'd hardly processed the thought when he suddenly dropped to one knee in front of her. Holly's heart plunged right along with him.

"What are you doing?" she demanded, taking a step back.

He pulled a small black box from the pocket of his jacket. "I love you, Holly. From the first moment we met, it was like my heart had come home. I know that I come with a lot of complications, but loving you is the easiest thing I've ever done. Please give me a chance to earn your love in return."

She shook her head, and his face fell. Oh no. She needed to get a grip so she didn't mess up this chance. She lowered herself to the sand along with him and took his free hand in both of hers. "You don't need to earn anything," she told him. "I love you, Brett. With every fiber of my being, I love you."

His relieved sigh was so endearing and sweet, it made happy tears spring to her eyes. He opened the box to reveal the most gorgeous ring she'd ever seen, a gold band with an oval emerald stone—her favorite color in the entire world. "This belonged to my grandmother," he said, plucking the ring from its velvet case. "My mom gave it to me so I could give it to you."

"Your mom approves of this?" Holly had a hard time believing that.

"Yes," he answered without hesitation. "She came to see me, Holly. We have her blessing and your parents'."

She sniffed and swiped at her cheeks, joyful emotion overwhelming her. "You talked to my parents?"

He nodded. "The only person remaining is you. The choice is yours, Holly. It always has been. Will you marry me?"

"Yes," she whispered.

"Even with everything that comes along—"

She wrapped her arms around him, pushing him down to the sand and straddling his hips. "Everything and anything, Brett Carmichael. As long as we're together. I love you now, and I'll love you forever. I would be honored to become your wife."

He pulled her close, his lips crashing against hers in a kiss that was both a plea and a promise. "I'm going to spend the rest of my life making you happy. Making any dream you have come true."

"All I need is you," she answered, knowing that her dearest dream had already come true.

* * * * *

SPECIAL EXCERPT FROM

HHARLEQUIN
SPECIAL EDITION

*Marcus King and Violet Cortez-Hill had been united in their
youthful dreams of a future together. But after so many years
apart, they're now on opposite sides—even as they're reunited by
his father's funeral. The attraction might still be there, but they've
both changed —a lot. And if they want to build a new life together,
they'll need more than sparks to do it...*

Read on for a sneak peek at
Not Their First Rodeo
*by Christy Jeffries,
the new book in her Twin Kings Ranch series!*

"What do you think your mom is going to do when she finds out
you're still here with me?"

Violet rolled her eyes. "Marcus, I'm a grown woman. I pay
my own bills and make my own decisions. Nobody makes me do
anything I don't want to do. Including my mother."

He made a scoffing sound. "I don't know why you're getting so
defensive. You have no problem telling me how I should feel about
my family. Hell, you're being paid to interfere in my relationship
with my mom and my brother."

Violet shook her head. "I'm not being paid. I agreed to represent
MJ pro bono."

He paused a beat. "So what's in it for you? The chance to get me
back for something I never even did?"

"That's cute how you think my being here has anything to do
with you," she replied. "You're giving yourself too much credit if
you think my career choice had anything to do with you. Unlike

you, I hadn't been creeping around on the internet trying to figure out what you did for a living."

"I wasn't creeping." Marcus's expression was so insistent, he looked like his sons when they asked for seconds of dessert. "But speaking of what you do, whatever happened to your dream of becoming a prosecutor?"

"That dream crashed around the same time my dream of becoming a mom was shot down."

"You mean when we lost the babies?" His correction caused the air to suddenly whoosh from her lungs.

She quickly recovered, though. "You say *we*, as though both of us went through that traumatic experience together."

"Physically, no. Obviously, you had it way worse than me, and now I have to live with the fact that I wasn't there for you when you needed me most. But just because I didn't know all the circumstances at the time doesn't mean I didn't suffer a loss." Marcus's eyes seemed to glisten, and his voice grew wobbly but more passionate as he stopped dancing altogether. "Vi, I wanted our babies as much as I wanted you."

Don't miss
Not Their First Rodeo *by Christy Jeffries,*
available July 2021 wherever
Harlequin Special Edition books and ebooks are sold.

Harlequin.com

Don't miss the first book in
The Magnolia Sisters series by

MICHELLE MAJOR

*An inheritance brought her to Magnolia,
but love just might keep her there...*

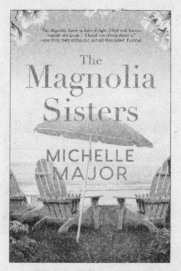

"Michelle Major crafts these complex, engaging, and likable
characters and fits them into an intriguing storyline."
—*Lightning City Books*

Order your copy today!

HQNBooks.com

PHMMBPA0420Max

Get 4 FREE REWARDS!

We'll send you 2 FREE Books plus 2 FREE Mystery Gifts.

FREE
Value Over
$20

Both the **Romance** and **Suspense** collections feature compelling novels written by many of today's bestselling authors.